# The Narrative

## 2nd Edition

No part of this book was written using
Artificial Intelligence (AI) in part or full

# A note from the Author

Whilst Artificial Intelligence (AI) is an important development for the furthering the human race in so many ways, such as potential cures for serious illness, the ability to engineer what was thought impossible, getting us to the stars and so much more, there is always something missing from machine generated output.

Whilst efficient, it, in my humble opinion, will always be without soul.

The act of creativity requires the individual's input, the experiences, history, likes, fears, loves, loses. It involves effort, often hard effort, conflict, happiness, tiredness, passion and a deep-down desire to create something to the best of their ability, for others to enjoy.

AI cannot begin to match the humanity of what it takes to create art, whether written, drawn, painted, sung, played, or indeed in any of its forms.

I can promise that no part of this book was researched, nor written in part or full, using any form of AI.

It is simply born of thought, ideas, heart, passion and everything else that makes art, well art.

I will also admit to the dreadful tiredness at times that comes with holding down a busy full-time job and pursuing a deep desire to create stories that transport people into a new world with new characters to meet and adventures to follow.

I will also admit to being a little tipsy at times during the writing of this book, partly to counter the former, but also to 'grease the wheels' of creativity!

AI absolutely has its place in society and it will accelerate it forward at unprecedented speeds, but art, that has to contain humanity, that has to contain soul.

There is a little of me in this book, I hope you enjoy it.

# Dedication

This book is dedicated to all of those who have suffered at the hands of tyranny. Either at the societal level or at the individual level.

Those who have endured suffering of the most-evil kind, evil of man demonstrating how existence can be driven by hate and a lack of moral guidance, whatever that source may be, for nothing more than an evil narcissist's needs.

My research and previous visits to haunting places in Europe truly humbled and shocked me to my very core, my very soul in how anyone could possibly let it happen, let alone actively create it. How the powerful use the poor and the weak as pawns in their deadly games.

I thank you, those who have suffered, for keeping that evil in the public domain in an unaltered state, despite the pain it causes. You have every right to bury it for evermore but instead, with bravery, you choose to use it to teach others.

Softening the evil to save the emotional wellbeing demands of the new generations is the first step on the slippery slope to allowing those who state, in ignorance, that it cannot have been that bad due to their inability to comprehend its evil, given how they have lived lives largely free of its existence, or even deny its existence entirely.

Through your strong, proud voices, others have avoided that suffering. That history has not been buried even though so many try to do exactly that. History must never be forgotten but used as a warning and a tool for teaching, and you are the bravest teachers this world could ever wish for.

Even in these modern years, these places still exist in the world and we must come together as a global people to destroy not only the physical buildings but the ideological structures that allow them to exist in the first place.

We must never allow it to happen again anywhere by anyone, we must never forget any of those who suffered so terribly.

Science and history must remain the truth and be saved from the poison of politics. Truth is freedom; freedom must not be what it is perceived to be but what it is.

May you be blessed with peace for the rest of your lives and may we be blessed with freedom—so easy to give away, so very hard to win back.

# Contents

# Preface

You have been warned; those little bits of freedom you give away under the pretence of a disaster, a need for greater protection, from your enemies, from the evil 'out there', both real and perceived, including those threats that you knew nothing about before those in power told you about them; they are precious and not ours to give away, for we do not own them, our children do, who then have a duty to pass it to their children in the same protected manner.

Does it not raise an eyebrow that 'temporary measures' become permanent, oh so quietly, and how those in power claim to be looking out for you and your wellbeing, your safety, by taking away your freedoms?

Those freedoms are not removed for your protection; they are removed for the centralisation of absolute power. Little by little, drip by drip we allow our right to freedom be taken, for fear of being seen as someone who is on the wrong side of history. We keep our heads down for fear of losing what we have but inadvertently give away the one thing that we cannot afford to lose.

Freedom; worse still, our children's freedom.

A life of the apathetic only grants more power and control for those who seek it. Those are the very people who must not be allowed have it.

As Edmund Burke said, *"The only thing necessary for the triumph of evil, is for good men to do nothing."*

Have no fear of death; instead, fight for freedom, always. Even when the fight is scary and dangerous, for the powerful prey on the fearful like a bully in the playground. They want you cowed, scared and beaten so they can do the very things they are willing to put you in prison for doing.

Power and Evil are bedfellows and should be held in check by the masses who should always have the ultimate power over those who claim to govern them.

Freedom is everything and it should never be traded, amended or adjusted for any reason whatsoever. Never even temporarily suspended to allow those in power to 'help' resolve a situation the people may be facing.

Remember how we were imprisoned in our own homes during Covid?

Freedoms torn from us and ruthlessly policed by not only authority but in many cases, excitedly, by our very own neighbours.

The weak of mind and character always rush to the false protection of power.

Those in power always have another agenda to the one they speak of. Look for what they are not talking about or are doing in the shadows for that is where their true aim lies.

YOU stand between them and the absolute power they seek.
YOU own freedom, NOT those in power; fight for it till the last breath.

**To Those Who Seek Absolute Power:**
Freedom is not yours to give away.
We know the game.
We see you.

First they came for the Communists
And I did not speak out
Because I was not a Communist

Then they came for the Socialists
And I did not speak out
Because I was not a Socialist

Then they came for the trade unionists
And I did not speak out
Because I was not a trade unionist

Then they came for the Jews
And I did not speak out
Because I was not a Jew

Then they came for me
And there was no one left
To speak out for me

**The Holocaust Memorial Trust**

# Chapter 1:
# Xe

"It's chaos, Sir, they are all dead."

"How many?"

"We don't know, there is no one left to count but we know it is at least 23 million dead already, the Medicare system has completely collapsed. Violence is endemic, the rule of law non-existent, it is every person for themselves. The remaining Presidential Guard are still protecting this bunker, but it is in here too."

"What?"

"Yes Sir, it is here too, we are all as good as dead. I suggest we release everyone to fend for themselves; it is over, the whole country is over."

"How?"

"The biological weapon of some sort we had been discussing. We do not know the details because all the labs are down, there is no one left to examine them."

"But it has only been a matter of weeks since we started this, it cannot be that effective? We war-gamed for this possibility!"

"We underestimated them, Sir. It is devastating, they have won and there is nothing left to try to protect or save but ourselves. We played by the rules on these weapons; they did not. As you know, representations were lodged with the Global Unity Organisation but we all know it is corrupt and toothless. They have just declared that they will not get involved in domestic matters. I guess his bribes to them were greater than ours."

"More like they have seen what he is capable of! Go, go see to your family."
"They are all dead, Sir, no one is left, not even the kids."

"I am sorry. I am so sorry for starting this war, DAMMIT! I trusted the Generals and advisors when they said it would be short and we could not lose!

They told us that his military was weak and all we had to do was expose him and his New Government to the people and the country would fall. We would be seen as their saviours!

"How could he do this? How could he do this? There are rules even in war!"

"Not in his eyes, he is insane. We never thought he would go this far."

"Launch the nukes, fuck it; if we are going down then so are they!"

"We cannot, Sir."

"Why?"

"Everything is down, everything, all command and control is lost. Sir, it's over, there is nothing left, there is no one left."

*\*\**

Xe 805491997 was just an ordinary human, of no outwardly descriptive sex, religion, orientation or in fact anything in this brave new world of neutrality, a world slowly created whinge by whinge, perceived victim by perceived victim, cancellation by cancellation.

Xe, everyone just referred to each other as such to avoid long numerical introductions, stood staring out of the window of his apartment, seeing nothing with his eyes but instead deep into his dark place where he could hide from himself and the world. How he needed this inner sanctum, this hiding place more and more as he grew older.

The rain was incessant and had been for three straight days, pounding on the glass like fists hitting a punch bag. It was continuous, rhythmic and symptomatic of the social control, regular, like a heartbeat. He loved the sound though, it helped him achieve his sanctum of nothingness, his trance like state where he could go to hide from everything but the damn dream!

This deep depression had gripped him in a vice like grip with no escape, one minute thinking that he may as well go and end this miserable existence, the next a tiny spark, driven by the dream, would fill his heart with hope for the future, that he may one day be able to change things and give purpose back to himself, perhaps others, but then life would beat the hope back out of him and the cycle would start again.

Never-ending darkness deep in his soul which gave him nowhere to hide in this obsessively introverted nation. He just stood there staring, head half-cocked to one side, lost in the darkness of his mind, pondering, like he often did, how it had come to this? His head occasionally moving to the other side without conscious effort as a new thought traversed through the dark, deep recesses.

So many questions remained unanswered, so much desire remained unfulfilled, so much purpose remained without direction.

This was life to Xe, nothing more than existence and waiting to die.

A sharp pang of discomfort in his stomach snapped him out of his trance. He looked at the cup in his right hand and taking a sip of cold coffee, he realised that he must have been standing there for some time. It was light when he first looked out, the clock on the TV stated it was now 1:14 am.

Putting the cup down, he turned to look at his apartment. Apartment number 1-317-884-777-87-4-22-8 was of the standard modular layout in a block of identical dwellings, such demanded equity of outcome, all must have the same no matter what anyone did.

The ferocious and seemingly endless pursuit of neutrality, equality and equity reduced everything possible to numbers, deemed neutral enough to be accepted. 1 for the Region, 317 the City, 884 the district, 777 the sub district, 87 the road, 4 the Building, 22 the floor and 8 the apartment.

There was no longer any desire for names or anything that would indicate a gender to a building or a location. Historical figures had long been removed from buildings and streets, someone, somewhere had always managed to find a reason why they should be considered historically evil for some reason, often made up; sometimes just a hysterical attempt to be 'relevant' in their time.

Only statues of those with a numerical reference and of those who furthered the word of the narrative remained. Only those deemed 'pure' enough could be considered for adulation and they were few are far apart.

Neutrality and avoiding offence was the narrative and the narrative was everything.

The apartments comprised of three rooms, a living/kitchen area, a bedroom and a bathroom. The outer hallway door opened directly into the living/kitchen area which comprised of a standard sofa and chair. They were made of leather and were actually quite comfortable. Next to them was a small round foot stool that doubled up as a table, which was made of the same material as the sofa and chair, upon which was a copy of 'Good Citizen' magazine.

At the back of the room was the kitchen area, where he stood. This had the standard appliances used to store and heat food and drink from a pre-determined menu of choice published the week before in Good Citizen and was ordered through the touch screen TV, along with other basics required to maintain the standard of living and personal hygiene demanded of all citizens. Forgot to order? Well, you will be a little hungry and perhaps a little smelly this week then, won't you?

Everything was packaged up in single service packaging that required a certain amount of time in the heating vortex, as it was called, and hey presto! There was your meal or coffee or whatever tasteless gruel you were subjecting your body to. Even the deadest of pallets, such as Xe's, struggled with it at times.

The food itself was delivered to your apartment delivery box on the ground floor every Friday with just enough nutrition to keep you alive, but not enough to do anything overly strenuous unless you were registered on the New Government fitness programme when your allowed food intake was linked to your attendance at the provided gyms around the city you lived in.

There was never enough, only just enough based on your circumstance. Hunger was always kept at bay, just, and deliberately so to serve as a reminder that if you stepped out of line, you would be in deep trouble very quickly.

You could always buy more food, even alcohol from a shop if you had enough money and a high enough citizen status. As with everything, this was linked to the New Government database and sanctions applied immediately. Found drunk somewhere? Your ability to purchase alcohol was removed. Some did make their own alcohol to avoid this issue but it usually ended up with people going blind or apartments randomly exploding, sometimes both.

These two areas comprised of half of the apartment. On the other side was the bedroom and bathroom.

The only bedroom comprised of a single bed and a wardrobe and that was it. If you were in a coupling, then the bed would be replaced by a double. There was a carpet and the walls could be painted any of the agreed neutral colours, there was certainly no option for any colour that would denote a gender type resided in the room.

If you had a child, then an additional bunk would be added for your maximum of one child. After the birth of the child, both parents would be immediately sterilised. The country had too many people and there was no requirement to increase it. Hiding the birth of a child was an offence punishable by life imprisonment for both parents, unknown for the 'illegal' child. In the event of multiple births, then you just had to squeeze in more, no allowance was made berthing wise.

Along the opposite wall was the wardrobe and storage space for the apartment. Each apartment was supplied with a dirt and dust cleaning items. Clothes washing and pressing was managed on the ground floor of the apartment block in a communal laundry. It was a requirement, by law, to always have clean and pressed clothing when out in public, so was often filled with other people from the block. Xe, whilst introverted, did enjoy the limited discussions with his fellow apartment block residents. Polite, informal but above all, always neutral in nature.

Upon the wall in the bedroom was an image he had created himself of a stream running through a small, wooded brook, with a small wooden shack next to it. It was crude but he knew what it meant and it meant so much to him he did not care.

The bathroom was again basic and functional in nature. A toilet, sink and bath were present. All of the tiling was white as was the bathroom suite. The only mirror in the apartment was a large mirror above the wall with the sink, which was showing signs of age with the corners starting to turn silver in colour, but he still got to see his face in it every day, staring as he often did into his own eyes for several minutes before shaving.

After dealing with his immediate problem in his bladder, another coffee went into the heating vortex. He wasn't tired, he was too lost in his mind to sleep. He needed a distraction.

Taking out his coffee he moved over to the sofa and picked up the copy of Good Citizen which was a New Government produced publication delivered to every apartment, free of charge, which detailed how every citizen was expected to live their life.

A monthly publication, it regularly had articles about how great the New Government was doing, including what new initiatives were being brought in to improve everyone's lives. It was all bullshit and everyone knew it, but the New Government propaganda machine had to put out something to pretend that purgatory was in fact paradise and that they really were working for the betterment of the people they so mercilessly controlled, yet so often seemingly happy to be controlled, naïve to how life could be, naïve to the concept of true freedom. He often wondered why it was still produced as a glossy paper copy rather than electronic like everything else, which was the most attention he usually paid on it.

Flicking through to the 'celebrity' section, he read interviews with the people seen on the TV, how they lived the same lives as everyone else and were dedicated to the cause of the narrative. He did not believe a single word uttered. The drivel of perfection was so on point it was simply impossible to believe. The fact that they lived in an area of the capital that could not be seen from any vantage point around, along with the senior politicians, officials and Brutus champions, that was completely off limits to the rest of the population, guarded as it was by roadblocks and armed guards, said it all to him.

So to say that they lived in the same one-bed apartment as him was an insult to his intelligence, but that is exactly what it said and you were expected to believe it.

Moving onto the car section, showing all of the new beautiful machines that were carbon negative and perfect, he let out an audible sigh. Outside they were pure white and covered in lights, inside there was so much gadgetry, he could hardly understand how it was even drivable, even with auto-driver capability, but of course he did not need to worry about such things as vehicles were completely unaffordable and only belonged to those at the top of society, living in the same apartment as this, 'yeah whatever' he scoffed.

With a yawn, he flicked to the TV section. Programming was so controlled by the New Government that it may as well have been broadcast from 1-1-1-1-1-1-1-1 itself, for this was the building that contained the office of Premier Xe, leader of the New Government and glorious leader of the nation. Never a bad thing happened anymore such was the perfection shown. A perfection that was in total contrast to the reality around the general population, shown by a media that claimed that they were free and fair and absolutely not under the control of the New Government. They claimed to always report on the events of the day with facts and absolutely not with political leaning at all; after all, they stated "The truth of today, direct to you, direct to your home" in the opening credits, so it must be true.

His favourite show of choice to stare at when seriously drunk and in a dreadful mood, being the only time he actually watched TV, was 'Show Me Showtime!' Aired at 10 pm on a Saturday night. It was quite frankly, awful. The show was now projected in holographic 3D, so as to make the home audience feel like they were sat in the studio, which did not make it any more bearable to him.

JJ was the host. As he was part of the 'others' that lived in the restricted part of town, he was allowed to dress differently and to refer to himself as JJ, unlike every other average person. Xe noted the hypocrisy of it, but there was nothing that could be done to change it so who cares, such was the apathy of life and of actually trying to highlight the inconsistencies of the narrative and the projection of how everyone was supposed to be living the same equitable life, irrelevant of their role in society.

He had no time for JJ and thought he was a desperately unfunny dickhead. A pathetic crown styled hair, with a large spike in the middle that was designed to make him look 'funny' but actually made him look like someone who speared fish from a lake with their hair for a living. He spouted the usual platitudes and neutral jokes that were utterly unfunny, saved by the canned laughter played by the TV production team. The programme format was always the same and with a choice of only three channels it was not like you could go anywhere else for your entertainment. Opening with the inane 'jokes' canned laughter and a smile so white in colour, he thought that it could act as a searchlight for lost souls at sea.

After this came the funny video clips, usually of people seriously hurting themselves, again supported by the canned laughter, before JJ would finally move onto the family challenge part of the show.

This usually consisted of families, who did not want to be there but were offered twenty citizen credits to do so and were expected to show that they were very happy about doing it, or else. Taking part in various, stupid challenges that always resulted in them getting drenched in various unknown liquids, eating various unimaginable 'foods' or just plain being humiliated. Poor shits, he thought, but for twenty credits he would do it as well.

The humiliated family, still smiling badly, sometimes injured were then congratulated by JJ, for being such fun and were escorted off the stage. Once off screen they were given their twenty credits and ejected outside to make their own way home or to the nearest medical facility. The child was always crying at this point but they had served their purpose and were of no use to the programme anymore.

Then the finale! A musical act playing the current official drivel. Dracona Doob it was called and it was the only type of music allowed. Boring repetitive beat, boring repetitive music on top, it seemed to fit perfectly with the boring repetitive life that everyone endured.

Why he watched this drivel he did not know, but it seemed to make him smile sometimes and smiling was a rarity in his life so with a drink in hand and raising a glass to JJ he would sit, watch and drink himself into oblivion.

Reading Good Citizen had done the job and he drifted off to sleep on the sofa, coffee still in his hand, magazine on his chest, snoring that made even the bugs scuttle for cover.

He woke late morning the following day, wearing his coffee over the chest of his shirt. Getting up with a groan of a person who was significantly older than him, he decided to get out of the place. The continuous rain, though good to help him find his hiding place, had kept him indoors for three days straight.

He needed to get out.

"The park is where I am going today, my little friends," he said out loud to the spiders and bugs in the apartment that he refused to kill by sweeping them up. They gave him something to talk to and he had grown to like them being around.

Looking in the wardrobe, he looked amongst the New Government approved clothing to wear. The control on what clothing could be worn was another law raised in the past to manage a societal complaint that differing clothes for the genders was not neutral and that colours could be defined to genders so had to go, all because some idiot had nothing better to do than run around finding offence in something.

Each item of upper clothing, neutral in design and colour of course, pastel beige and green being the only accepted colours in these modern times of equality and design. For the lower half, there were only black trousers or shorts. Socks and shoes completed the outfit, both black with no markings on them.

Two sets of exercise clothing were allowed, all black with no shape to them at all. These were provided by the New Government if you registered to visit the gym. Most did it to get more food and then exercised as little as possible, for not turning up for the gym at least three times a week meant a warning. More than one warning and you had to return the clothing and lose the food privileges that went with it.

He opened the bedroom window and felt outside to see if it looked cold; not too bad, he thought as he turned back to the wardrobe. He had a choice of a thin black jumper, a thick black jumper or a coat—again black in colour. Putting on the thin jumper before the coat and taking one last look in the mirror, he headed to the door picking up his mobile comms device and his Personal Citizen Device from the table along the way.

The Personal Citizen Device was a small silver metallic device oblong in shape, portrait in layout, with a small wave-like shape down one side to add some sort of styling. On the front it had ten small lights that each indicated 10% worth of battery level of the device. Despite there being recharging points all over the city, if a citizen allowed the battery to run out, all access to places that required Personal Citizen Device contact, such as transport or entry into buildings would be revoked, there would be no access to the person's money and if stopped by the police would result in a lot of unwanted, and probably painful, attention.

Too lose it completely was not bearable to think about.

There was further styling of three narrower, inlaid black sections interspersed by the silver metallic of the main device. It did not seem to add any actual function, which seemed odd to Xe. At the bottom was etched the number of the Xe it related to which was issued at birth, along with the Personal Citizen Device itself and stayed with you until your death.

The Personal Citizen Device itself had every detail about the individual. Where they lived, their designated citizen identification number, their police 'interest' level, their medical status, including inoculations against the various pandemics that had plagued the nation in the past and most importantly of all, their good citizen status, for no one in these modern times were allowed any rights for anything unless their 'citizen status' was at sufficient level.

It was also used to manage the person's money as all payments were made electronically. This was of course very convenient for the user, but more convenient for the New Government who frequently used the system to either revoke all access to a person's ability to travel and/or buy anything but also used the system to systematically steal small amounts of funds from people's accounts to shore up the country's finances. It was known and widespread but who could prove it? And even if you did it would only result in you losing all of your money, perhaps more, if you made too much noise about it.

He laughed to himself at the thought of citizen status. Do a good thing like get your jab you would get a point or two, drop litter would mean ten points off, it was so disproportionate it was laughable.

It was not that way to start with of course. Good citizenship was easy to achieve, so no one objected to this new idea, after all it would prevent antisocial behaviour and make everybody feel safe and keep them safe, but of course the credits for good behaviour were quietly reduced and the debits for bad quietly increased, without warning, such was the drip, drip, drip nature of the way the authorities changed things so as to not alert anyone of the changes until it was too late.

To be without your Personal Citizen Device would mean arrest, to have a citizen status lower than 0 would mean a trip to Detention Centre One, which was widely regarded as a one-way trip, but deserved. The main issue was that a citizen could never see what their status was, you only knew when you could not take a magtrain or you heard the knock on the apartment door; therefore, you took extra care to do the 'right' things and avoid doing that which was likely to knock off a point or ten.

Still, no one at the time complained because life was getting quieter and there was virtually no anti-social behaviour anymore, the population saw what was happening but were willing to give away their freedom for some peace and quiet.

Device attached and leaving the apartment, allowing the door to slide shut and lock itself which it automatically did, Xe walked off down the hallway. Beige in colour with a beige hardwearing flooring. At the end of the hallway were the stairs. Climbing down all twenty-two flights, he came out through the small entranceway that looked the same as all the other tower blocks lined up in rows next to each other in the Northeast part of the city. This was the housing quarter where the vast majority of the population of the capital lived.

Between the rows of housing blocks was a grid pattern of roads. The only vehicles that used these in the housing quarter were the police and military vehicles. Nobody owned a car around here. The magtrain station and the busses were the only way to get around, those and of course your own two legs.

There was still a cold chill in the air, but it was brightening up nicely and the rain and cloud had finally receded being replaced by bright sunshine, warming the air just enough to warrant taking off his coat. As he walked along more people started to come out and to wander around as he was, most without any purpose, however those with a child were on their way to the park to get them to burn off some energy and stop driving their parents insane indoors after so many days of being cooped up.

Between the housing quarter and the park was a small shopping complex. Shops were not that plentiful. The food and living basics were delivered to the apartments, so the only food shops were those designed for lunchtime coffee or snacks if you were lucky enough to have enough money or a job, the quality was no better and it was all New Government controlled but it did offer some sort of tasteless alternative as an occasional treat.

The main shops were those that were outlets for the New Government called 'Gov. Centres'. If you needed new clothing you could take your old and exchange it there; if you needed additional materials required to keep apartments clean and in the best possible condition such was the demand of tenancy, you went there, pens or other stationary, in fact anything at all you went there. Everything you needed would be manufactured by, and purchased from, the New Government, for a profit to them, of course.

Aside from shops, there were an abundance of gyms, being fit and strong was encouraged by the New Government. Xe sometimes wondered why, perhaps as a distraction from life, perhaps a healthy population was better prepared for war with some unknown enemy of the country perhaps.

Seeing the gym reminded him he needed to go again this week, but maybe tomorrow, such was his mantra which is why he usually ended up there three days in a row to ensure he had attended enough for the extra food portions.

Eventually, the housing quarter was left behind and in sight was the park. It was absolutely monumental with every possible climbing frame, roundabout, slide or other item that a child could let their imagination run riot on. It was actually very well maintained, but health and safety was not so high on the priority list and often a fall from height would result in a trip to the hospital to be patched up.

It would have been amazing to play in here as a child he thought, he did not know why he never did, or perhaps he did do, his memory of those days were robbed of him, but none the less he found it relaxing listening to the kids playing, arguing and basically being feral. It gave him a small window into life without his pressures.

Sitting down, he slowly ate the cheese and onion sandwich he picked up at the food shop on the way. It tasted a little better than the food that got delivered to the apartments but cost a fortune and he was worried he was starting to run low on available funds, still he was determined to enjoy this treat for the week.

Watching as they played and wishing that one day they would see freedom, he felt he was too old now to fight to machine, but those kids in all their innocence, if only they could be set free with their uncomplicated approach to life, perhaps they could change the world one day. 'Why do I always have this pipe dream of freedom when everyone else seems so happy to be completely controlled?' he said to himself as he finished off the sandwich.

Putting the packaging in the bin, dropping litter would wipe out his remaining money in a fine and do who knows what damage to his citizen rating, if he was seen, he looked for something else to do. Looking behind him, he realised that he had never climbed the steep hill behind the park and with absolutely nothing else to do with his life right now, decided that this would be today's challenge.

After a few stumbles that he thought would see him in a heap at the bottom with children pointing and laughing at him, he got to the top completely out of breath. It reminded him of just how unfit he was, even within his muscly but slender frame. I need to go to the gym more often he promised to himself in his usual 'no intention of doing it' way, every time he was out of breath or not strong enough to do something.

At the top of the hill there was flat unmown grass area for about 50 yards then a high wire fence with signs all along stating 'Nature Reserve No Trespassing!' Behind the fence and following it around for as far as he could see was a dense wooded area that you could not see nor hear anything behind.

'OK, that was boring!', he said to himself as he turned and stood looking out over the city, its magtrain rail lines and a grid system of roads, again largely clear of vehicles. The city centre itself could be seen from the hill. At its heart was the New Government complex of buildings that took up the vast majority of the space within the capital. The only other buildings were those that supported the running on the country such as the TV station, various security buildings, the hospital and some smaller buildings that he had no idea what they were for nor had no access to, nor did he really care.

Closest to him were some smaller buildings of various purposes with a network of alleyways crisscrossing behind and between them. These were mostly buildings for specific manufacturing tasks such as the food production for the weekly delivery and clothing manufacturing along with other items needed for the Gov. Stores.

Dominating the city was the Brutus stadium, home to the national sport and a game of extreme violence. It was huge, easily the biggest building in the capital, and could hold 120,000 people with ease.

In the games themselves, the competitors would use various weapons to inflict as much, supposed, non-lethal damage to each other until one could no longer defend themselves. It was brutal and it was massively popular with all citizens, including Xe, who reminded himself he would take a trip there soon to get his fill of complete and unadulterated violence.

Between the sports stadium and the park was one of three churches, whose steeples you could see for miles. Whilst religion as such was no longer permitted in this neutral world due to the complete lack of neutrality, not to mention wars and civil unrest it caused, there were the Sages whom you could go to speak to in times of personal need.

The Sages of the Stoics were always there should you need them and it was a free service that he partook in often. Besides attending a sage's service got you citizen credit points.

Xe just stood and looked and pondered like he always did, staring into the distance, across the city but not actually seeing anything other than the inside of his mind. A scream broke his daydreaming as another child had plummeted to the floor from a climbing frame of some description and was being scooped up by its parents to be carted off to the hospital.

With the clouds starting to roll in again and the day waning, he decided he should get down the hill before it became slippery and he ended up in a heap at the bottom. Neither hills, nor running were his strong point, unless he absolutely had to and even then, were still not his strong point; besides most of the kids that were not hurt in some way had started to drift away due to the weather closing in and weary parents rounding them up for another evening indoors. He decided if he did end up in a heap at the bottom it would only be mildly embarrassing. Besides it was Saturday and he had a hot date with a bottle of Vodinaski. Soon JJ would be on TV ready to blind him with his teeth.

Getting to the bottom of the hill with only two small slips and feeling proud of himself for doing so, he noted that the best way to get down a hill without breaking your neck, was to go along it rather than straight down. I will note that should I ever need to run down a hill he said sarcastically but glad he had actually achieved something today, no matter how small. Putting his coat back on, he headed straight off home, with his incessant feeling that he was being followed or watched. This feeling often came across him as he kept thinking he saw movements in the shadows.

Increasing his speed due the uneasy feeling, he caught the attention of a police patrol vehicle which stopped and demanded to know what he was doing and where he was going.

"Just going home," Xe said.

"Personal Citizen Device NOW!" demanded the officer.

Xe started to get nervous, why was he being stopped? "I am just going home, officer."

"Did I fucking ask you to talk?" the officer replied without looking up.

Xe noticed the second officer was looking around and appeared nervous, this was not a good sign and Xe was starting to prepare for a beating.

Out of the corner of his eye, he definitely saw something pull back into the shadows behind a wall. 'This is not good, not good at all. That was not in my imagination, not this time, someone is watching either me or the police'.

The officer scanned the device, before stating, "Go home now. If I see you out again, I will be looking at you in more detail. Now fuck off."

Xe did exactly as he was told and headed straight back to the apartment. The police did not say these things without meaning them and if he was caught outside again that night, it would only end very painfully for him. He had history with the police and did not want to repeat it, no matter how much he despised them.

Finally getting home and opening his door with his device and walking in, he breathed a huge sigh of relief as he dumped his coat on the chair and grabbed a bottle of Vodinaski with a glass and slouched on the sofa.

Who was the person in the shadows? "This is not in my imagination, my friends!" He said to the various bugs scuttling around. "Or maybe it is, maybe I am going mad," he told them.

'Fuck it!', he thought, 'this is where I plan to be for the next ninety minutes, after all, I have sod all to get up for in the morning so who cares, may as well get hammered'.

Pouring a Vodinaski into his glass and then necking it immediately, he started to watch as JJ came on blinding everyone with his teeth and threatening to take out the lighting with his hair. He chuckled, poured another and necked it again.

And so his Saturday night ended, as per normal, drunk, unconscious and snoring on the sofa. At midnight, the TV switched off as he snored loudly, cuddling the bottle as if it was a child's teddy.

# Chapter 2:

# Absolute Control Achieved

Xe 1, as the Premier Xe was officially titled, stormed into the Premier Planning Office with a face of absolute thunder. Everyone in the room shifted nervously in the luxurious leather chairs that surrounded a huge, polished oak table.

The gathered group were known as the 'Primary Function' and it was their job to control everything in society past, present and future. It was broken down into three further sub areas, known as the 'Trifecta of Control'.

The first arm of the trifecta was known as 'Strength'. It has two sub-branches and its sole job was to control the population by any means required, usually by force.

At the end of the table was Xe 2, Commander General Military, who was the head of all branches of the military. Dressed in his finest uniform, used for official matters, he looked professional, impeccably smart and capable. This outward appearance betrayed a soul so dark that the killing of a child would be a mere annoyance of having to manage the paperwork involved. He had no time for anyone, was short in response and did not suffer fools gladly. That said he knew he has reached the top of the pile and was a sensible enough politically to not push it with Xe 1. Premier Xe got what he wanted so that the Commander General Military got to be kept in luxury and full command, although outwardly this would never be admitted. Not much was known about the military to wider society, nor the group in the room due to its absolute secrecy, however it was widely considered that should someone go against their wishes, it would not end via a 'friendly' discussion.

They did their job very well and without argument or fuss so Premier Xe let them do whatever they wanted behind closed doors as long as it did not cause him any political issues.

To his left was Xe 3, the Commander General Police, who was the head of all branches of the police. Dressed in an equally smart but all black uniform, there was real tension between the police and the military. Their leaders hated each other as the military were considered superior in rank to the police, but the police carried out all of the 'dirty' work on the front line of the streets.

That being said, in many ways the Commander General Police preferred to be out there brutalising the population, it was just sport for her and she would often be found in the ranks of the front-line officers dealing out punishment as she saw fit, which made her very popular amongst the rank and file.

Again, as per the Commander General Military, she did as she was commanded by Premier Xe to maintain the lifestyle she had attained.

The second of the trifecta was known as 'Administration' with four sub-branches. Its job was to keep things ticking over and keep the public relations message positive and upbeat so that the population believed that they were being looked after.

Sat opposite the Commander General Police was the most senior member of the administration arm, Xe 4 the Communications Chief. Dressed in a smart black suit with a black shirt and tie, he was without doubt the most irritating person to talk to, having an ability to twist whatever was said to fit the narrative; gas lighting was his specialist subject. You could give every citizen a million credits each and he could make you look evil for it. Kill 500 citizens? He would make it look like it was for the better of the country and the majority would lap it up. There was no point in trying to talk to him about anything, he would be able to slither his way out of anything like an oiled-up snake in a pond of grease and leave you wondering what on Earth you were actually talking to him about in the first place. The permanent smug grin on his face did him no favours either.

His immediate reports, who were waiting in his briefing room further down the corridor of New Government House, were the heads of Global Life, Television and Publishing, who between them 'owned' every part of communication in modern day life. The latter two were under total control of the New Government, however Global Life was a private company that owned all social media content.

It took a number of years for Global Life to come together slowly taking over its competitors one by one until it became a black hole and sucked in everything. The bigger it got, the more dominant it became and the more power it had until it became big enough to take on the Government of the time in a public spat. The Government quickly became heavily damaged so backed down and created the symbiotic and very lucrative relationship of control it enjoyed today.

At the right of the Communications Chief was Xe 5, the Chief Treasurer. A short man with round glasses and gelled swept back hair, he was wearing one of the finest suits available to anyone but a citizen, pinstripe three piece, with his Personal Citizen Status device pinned to the front pocket, which displayed a white handkerchief within. His main function was to control the money for the country, or at least that was his official position. Basically, he spent most of his time cooking the books and stealing from the people to make it look like the country was not the completely insolvent wreck it actually was.

A ruthless politician his ultimate desire was to be Premier Xe, and thus he plotted very carefully in the shadows. It was a very dangerous game, but his life was politics and Government. With no partner nor children he could not care less. Even his immediate family were dispensable and they knew it keeping themselves distant from him so as not to allow themselves to become a dead pawn in his political gamesmanship.

He was widely reviled by everyone in the room, even Premier Xe, but had access to the computer and the right people that made the money, to keep the New Government running, so they needed him, for now.

Opposite him was Xe 6, the Chief Scientist. Always dressed in her white clothing with white lab coat, she looked every part her station. It was her job to 'discover' new pathogens in her secret labs and to 'perfect' the immunisation jabs against them. Should a new pandemic be needed, she was ready with a freezer full of the most hideous diseases known to the nation, to be used without remorse either internally or against foreign threats.

It only took one such event during an 'altercation' with a small foreign power who made the mistake of threatening to expose the New Government to its people. They saw it as an introverted nation and thought it would not be able to defend itself, especially as its military was proven to be effective against its own people but had never been tested against a foe that could actually fight back for decades. It was easy pickings, or so they thought.

Less than four weeks after the 'disagreement' started, it found itself with 85% of its population dead or horribly afflicted. No one knew what really happened, but no foreign nation had dared challenge the New Government since the world's attention had been focussed clearly on how good they were at inventing and silently delivering these killers and without any admonishment from the Global Unity Organisation, they had gotten clean away with it.

It was also her role to oversee every aspect of science and sustenance in the country, so it was in her remit to design the 'meals' for the population to order, aimed for keeping everyone just about fed. Not starving, but also not massively far from it. She also managed the country's healthcare system.

To her left was Xe 7, the Chief Manufacturer. Dressed in a drab, functional suit it was his job to manage the output of anything that was required from pathogens to TVs to missiles to food. All manufacturing was centralised under his direct control as was transportation and infrastructure.

Lastly was the only member of the third arm of the trifecta known as 'Soul'. Xe 8 was also known as the Supreme Sage of the Stoics. Dressed in a heavy but luxurious crimson velvet red robe with a black cord belt, the Supreme Sage ran the only allowed 'religion'—Stoicism.

Completely divorced from the Sages that actually spoke to the people, the Supreme Sage had no idea what was happening on the ground and neither did he care as long as they did as they were told and he held this position; the position which came with a huge level of money, power and luxury. Most of all it came with absolute protection, such as he needed due to his love of all things food, alcohol and carnal in nature, things that he would preach were not becoming of a Sage, let alone the Supreme Sage.

Everybody in the room had something on everybody else that could take the other down. They all hated each other with a passion but had to work together to maintain their own particular lifestyles, so they met as infrequently as possible and only as necessity demanded. It was a perfect stalemate for Premier Xe to exploit and take advantage of, which he did so ruthlessly, such was his skill at all things political.

This particular gathering was demanded by Premier Xe, the head of the New Government, the third in the generational leadership that had ruled over the country for so long that no one actually knew if they had ever not been in charge.

Premier Xe was an absolute bastard and everyone hated him, but his brilliance as a politician and use of his comms division had made him almost God like in the eyes of a very large proportion of the population. Although a while ago now, the war and subsequent victory four weeks later had basically ended anyone trying to take him out. Anyone doing so would be seen as a traitor to the population and in turn would be sent to Detention Centre One, so there was nothing, currently, to gain. Besides with Premier Xe taking all the pressure of running the country it allowed the others of the Primary Function to further indulge themselves in their personal fantasies which suited them just fine.

He also had a certain penchant to ranting and shouting and otherwise abusing everyone around him, after all he was Premier Xe, voted in overwhelmingly time and time again and the incumbent of the longest political dynasty in history.

His grandfather was Prime Minister Hendricks and the father of the dynasty. He was a consummate liar who simply did not care and waffled his way out of any sticky situation using his daddy next door, bumbling idiot but lovable public persona, along with the use of a friendly media of the time. The people knew it, but their lives were so busy that as a long as it did not affect them, so be it.

Hendricks, being a politician saw his opportunity in the apathy and initially solidified his power through a series of minor emergency legislations.

It all started with small steps. There was an increasing voice being heard in society of individuals and their opinion on something. Perfectly fine at first but eventually started to turn nasty if you did not agree with their opinion. First it was through words, then threats, finally forcing people's silence due to physical intimidation.

The minority that was prepared to be vocal and violent, had started to silence the majority who really just wanted a peaceful life and so simply kept quiet and stayed out of the debate, at least publicly.

This only encouraged more to come out and seek offence in something so that they could jump on the bandwagon and attempt be famous to earn their living rather than actually being good at anything. The seeking and finding offence in everything became a full time job for some, so much so that a cereal packet character could be considered offensive for the most ridiculous of reasons by a single person and the pathetically weak company leadership, desperate to keep their ridiculous and unjustifiable salaries, simply folded at the perceived threat of retribution and the real violence at their factory or headquarters.

The first divisive wedge had been driven into the heart of society and the strategy was underway.

The majority continued to stay silent and hoped it would pass over. It didn't. Hendricks passed some small minor laws that nobody really noticed as the mob started to take control.

Sometimes it was a noble cause on the face of it, so as to make any dissenter an easy target under the statement, 'Well, you must be for xyz then!' If you complained or offered any sort of opposition or disagreement with the mob's approach, even if you agreed with what they were trying to achieve, you just became another target for them, such was their emboldened hysteria. As the demands of the mob became ever more ridiculous, public support waned away, sick of being on their side but somehow suffering for it.

It continued whinge by whinge, perceived offence taken by perceived offence taken, and protest after protest.

For Hendricks, this was political and power grabbing gold dust. Let the mob run riot, pass a few smaller seemingly inconsequential laws and let them build into bigger control. The mob would be dealt with later in the strategy.

The mob became emboldened by the lack of any form of control or retribution and so like a small child that is never told "no" it just got wilder and wilder in its demands and actions. Hendricks was simply allowing it to happen, each drama leading to more and more quiet control attained.

The majority continued to put up with it and largely ignored it as they went about their day as it was still not knocking at their door if they just kept their heads down, hoping that eventually the tide would turn and normality and common sense would return. But it didn't, wedge after wedge continued to be driven through every single minor and inconsequential crack in society that could be found. The majority could no longer avoid it, it was everywhere, pervasive in every aspect of life and some decided to fight back and stand up. They failed, painfully.

The unforgiving and extreme violence that was unleashed against anyone who went against the new 'neutrality' was either destroyed professionally or simply harassed so much that they had to move home, often multiple times if the mob felt like making it happen. On more than one occasion they were beaten, sometimes to death. The sight of people trying to protect others and property from the mob, being arrested and imprisoned, such was the perverseness of the 'justice system', just added another layer of confidence to the mob, which grew as more and more as people left logic behind at the hope that they would be heard, seen as the next leader, the next person to be in power, in control.

Most of the mob had no idea what they were actually doing there, they just went along as part of a pack, they had company, a reason for doing something, anything in a world where hard work no longer paid off, a world where you could spent thirty years building a professional profile, only to have it ripped away in a matter of days by someone you never knew existed, who had spent no more than six months in the mob and who would receive adulation for doing so.

It had become a self-feeding, self-serving, self-justifying monster that had no ability to flex or change but instead simply steam roll through anything or anyone who got in the way of its self-perceived justified reason for being.

The politicians, the social media and the mainstream media all stayed silent as the petulant child ran amok and became more feral by the day, always finding an excuse for their outrageous behaviour, always using the power of the narrative to destroy any fact or truth put up against its disgusting actions.

Eventually, no one argued, no one said enough was enough, because to do so could literally end your life. No one spoke up anymore, instead they looked for escape, but there was none because this fever had gripped the entire nation.

Eventually, road names were replaced with numbers as were addresses, locations…in fact, anything that could have a numerical reference instead of a name was actioned.

Neutrality or death became an acceptable statement to be made by the mob, then this was adjusted to the more politically acceptable 'neutrality for peace' by the Government as they passed more minor laws to allow expressions to be made 'to allow even the smallest in society to have a voice.'

If you disagreed, you were a bully and wanted to hold down the small; those with no voice and oppress them, you were evil. It seeped like foul water from a broken pipe, relentless, into every aspect of society.

The politicians simply went where they thought the votes and thus power lay, blind to what they were creating as no one thought too far ahead tactically, it was all about now, this day, this chance, this payday, this power grab, this days' offensive item, this day's news. Each day using the current vibes to drive the overall strategy of achieving unlimited power.

The rich and famous were on the bandwagon from the start, so addicted to likes and followers on the pre-cursor platforms for Global life, they succoured up to the mob, fawning and telling anyone stupid enough to believe them that they were 'sooooo on their team'. The Narrative was taking control and they were going to take advantage of it. "Gotta have those likes," said one celebrity when challenged in a non-establishment media outlet. "The more likes and followers I got, the more money comes sitting in my wallet, bitch."

When the news outlet published the interview, their offices were burnt down. Their printers were threatened and refused to work with them. The CEO was found dead and their staff were physically threatened with their lives. It took less than four months for the publication to cease trading. The mob had won again, only now they were being fed by the fact that they could take down the big beasts and their corporations, such was the weakness of the CEOs. They had become the hyena with jaws bloodied by their victim's blood and flesh. Their victim cowering underneath waiting for the final blow that dealt them death before it remorselessly finished them off and with its prey desperate, beaten then silenced they move onto the next target.

Ironically, the celebrities soon started falling foul of the mob and its narrative. With a decreasing target list due to complete subservience, the mob turned in on itself more and more as it sought new victims. It had to have a continuous flow of victims to fuel it and to justify its existence. Its supporters knew that it had to find new targets to feed its insatiable appetite for power, control and money.

When the mob came for the celebrities and the famous, for not following their increasing insane demands, they hid in their high-walled, gated communities. They tried to resist it and change the narrative. It failed and they started to suffer their worst possible fate—cancellation! Becoming a nobody, a 'normal' person overnight was simply not allowed. Some simply could not cope and ended up taking their own lives.

No one really knows when the narrative took over from reality, but at some point it became almost a religion. Despite the vast majority of society either being against it from the start or were now waking up to what they had created, it no longer mattered. The only thing that mattered was the narrative, and that narrative was 'neutrality for all'.

Hendricks continued to use it, quietly, to his political and power grabbing advantage.

The rich soon realised that their private security of armed guards were no match for an armed mob in their hundreds. Security contracts were ended as their guards simply refused to guard any celebrity that was deemed a target for fear of their lives, the rich and famous were now vulnerable.

Calling the police was their next desperate step. The police that they had spent so much time vilifying, denigrating and downright insulting simply replied with a response of "we are too busy dealing with a riot unfortunately", karma can be a real bitch if it wants to and it was in full swing. In desperation they turned to bribing the mob. At first this worked and managed to keep them at bay, but the mob soon turned greedy and the money they were demanding was unsustainable.

In total desperation they turned to Hendricks, demanding that the Government stop the mob. Hendricks realised he had reached the limit of what he could get away with politically, though being the consummate politician, he still saw the political potential and so passed the first of the major pieces of legislation in his premiership.

He passed the 'Temporary restriction of the right to protest' law that of course was going to be anything but temporary. It was passed unanimously by the Government and supported by just about the whole population, so desperate were everyone to end the madness. They did not however look at the small print which also 'temporarily' removed the right to free speech and the removal of any legal liability of the police force in enacting any emergency legislation.

The mob were, as expected, completely apoplectic by this and immediately hit the streets rioting. Hendricks simply turned to the police who had been on the receiving end of them and stated "I tried to stop them through peaceful means, I tried my best to include them in the decision making, but they will no longer listen and I can no longer allow this violence to happen. They are all yours, bring peace back to the streets using any means necessary."

Another minor law passed, this time it spread like wildfire. The police, who had been decimated in numbers due to the lack of support from the Government were recruiting and entry was basically authorised off the promise of allegiance to the Government.

Police recruitment rocketed as those cancelled or impacted by the mob's narrative saw their chance at revenge and with Hendricks use of the phrase 'by any means necessary', they knew what necessary could mean.

Carnage ensued; the mob demands to meet with the previously supportive Hendricks were rejected outright. They realised that they had been totally played by the master politician and now they were the target. The narrative was to remain but they were to be removed, they had served their purpose.

In desperation they attempted to negotiate with the Government but were completely stonewalled and ignored. The targets had been painted on their backs and they knew it. There was no hiding place as when they were in control they made no attempt to hide who they were on the social media platforms of the time and why would they? At the time they were in complete control with the apparent, if unsaid, support of the Government.

They could and would be hunted like prey, so they had no choice but to stand and fight a battle they knew they had no chance of surviving.

After several weeks of 'control being restored' as the Government described it, peace was eventually returned to the streets and towns of the country. Rumours stated that hundreds of thousands died (Nobody was taken prisoner, not in this revenge opportunity that had no consequence) but nobody knew the real final body count, any victims were quickly removed and their existence destroyed by newly created clean-up crews.

As there was no right to free speech anymore, the details were banned by the Government under the order that it would only encourage more to rise up and for the violence to continue. The media, more accurately the media CEOs desperately protecting their pay packets, obeyed and continued to fawn over the Prime Minster and his actions.

By the end of the chaos, Hendricks had scored three major victories. The first was the ending of free speech. The ability to silence any person or publication for anything he deemed as not in the interests of the country which gave him control of the narrative that the mob had done such a good job of creating for him without him having to say a word or make a single instruction. He now had control of it and with it came control of the people.

Secondly, he now had a brutal police force that had no issue whatsoever with using extreme violence to achieve what they wanted and a police force that felt this was appropriate and required. It was used on several occasions with brutal effect. The people now had no voice and no strength.

Thirdly, his series of minor law changes would be used to keep power centralised with him, rather than the Government in general. He was extremely clever at wording the laws as such and thus Parliament became more irrelevant as the years passed by. As long as he was Prime Minister, his word was law.

The first step in his strategy was complete.

Some years passed and as peace, albeit with previously held qualifications of what freedom actually meant, was restored, people settled into the new routine. Soon Hendricks was up for re-election again. Whilst he had not passed any major legislation in recent years due to needing to cool things down for a while, he was not idle. The quiet phase had been used to build a network, hidden behind the ban of free speech to rig every subsequent election in his favour in return for large amounts of money.

It worked and he was re-elected by a large majority. Many thought this dubious in the extreme and calls for investigations were made, but with his new powers attained during the riots, they were immediately dealt with and never gained traction.

Now was the time for him to kick off his second part of his strategy. He needed to find a way of gaining absolute power. There were still chances that an election might go against him, he needed one last major power grab to settle the future once and for all.

For that he needed something dramatic to happen though, to give him the cover needed to implement laws under cover again, after all it worked so well before, why not do it again? The mob had been completely defeated and so could not go there again. Wars were not an option at the moment, no one had an appetite for it and they are very unpredictable in their outcome politically, even if you won.

He needed something, preferably invisible and deadly that could happen, so that he could be seen to be handling with perfection. He needed a ghost, a killer, something to scare people again.

Whilst thinking up his options, one of his chief of staff attended a meeting with him in an extremely animated state. His scientists had created a jab that could prevent almost all known diseases in one jab. Cancer, heart disease, diabetes and all the other mass killers could be eradicated. The jab itself was uncomfortable but could be made effective against all diseases and viruses that were known to the world at the time. Hendricks listened and smiled; he had found his ghost.

Spending the following months explaining to the country that the fight with disease was almost over and how he had led the team to find it, he used this to formulate his next power grab. During this time Hendricks had also been spending a lot of time in meetings with his military scientists, talking about how a virus could spread across the country, if it could be targeted at certain demographics and what its efficacy could be, under the banner of national defence.

Boyed with the answers he wanted being given, in absolute secrecy he called for it to be released sometime in the following year. The ten most populous cities, including the capital, were chosen and the manufacture was complete.

It was time for release but it needed an antidote first and the military scientists were struggling so Hendricks called in a select few that were involved in the new 'the jab' as it was marketed. They were forced to sign strict secrecy paperwork that had retribution on family members as part of the 'fine' for breaking it but did so gladly such was the opportunity presented to them. They did however think it unusual that such a high-level Government meeting was being held in a hotel, under such secrecy, but still went along hoping for some sort of honours recognition, or better still, increased research funding was coming their way.

He revealed that the military had a virus, a deadly one, but were struggling, much to his openly displayed disgust, that they could not seem to make it work with 'the jab' and needed them to 'sort it out'.

Of the eight scientists, four immediately started asking difficult questions why they were being asked to do his and what were the consequences.

"They were not to ever know before the event," was the response given and at that point four refused to take part and walked out. Within two hours three were dead through tragic accidents. One was held back physically and when the time was right, was thrown off the 14th floor balcony.

The very visible threat worked and the other four agreed to work with the military. They were escorted out through the kitchens of the hotel and spent the rest of their lives developing 'the jab' protection against his new pathogen, all tested on prisoners. After successful completion was confirmed, they all died in a 'lab explosion' that was not reported.

The 'friendly' coroner confirmed this and then promptly purchased his new and rather large house. Two weeks later, he was found by his wife in an apparent suicide, who also 'apparently' committed suicide by gunshot at the thought of living the rest of her life without her husband, such was her grief.

Everything was now in place. Operation 'mist' was enacted, and ten million people died. The virus was engineered to be perfect, it would kill only those with poor or compromised immune systems such as the infirm, the elderly, those with multiple medical complaints, those not deemed useful to society anymore. Sure a few hundred thousand healthy people, including children died, but that was acceptable collateral damage.

To manage the spread of the virus, Hendricks enacted further 'temporary' emergency legislation to 'save lives and protect the healthcare system', after all he was just 'following the science'.

With each passing law, the country became more and more introverted and backed off from the rest of the world. Communication would be on a need basis only and the needs became fewer and fewer as it became inward looking and insular. Travelling abroad was eventually banned for 'security reasons' without Governmental permission, which was never forthcoming.

It worked; the strategy was complete and absolute power was now his. He had unquestionable power, whatever he said happened, whatever he did not want said was not. He had a military and police force completely under his personal control and had completely duped the nation into thinking it was the right thing to do. Bit by bit he had managed to take away a piece of freedom after a piece of freedom and not only did no one notice, but they actually voted for it! An entire population had been hoodwinked.

Ultimately, the Government declared they had found a vaccine and had managed to incorporate it into 'the jab' and once again Hendricks had saved the country and was seen as a saviour and spent the rest of his life grooming his eldest to follow in his footsteps.

After his death, Hendricks was given a state funeral with all its pomp and pageantry, going down in history as a great man and leader of impeccable integrity.

With a nation in mourning, there were fresh elections.

Hendricks II was promptly voted in by a huge majority thanks to the voting law amendments that were introduced by his father to ensure free and fair elections. The political legacy was firmly in place.

Upon his father's death, the new Premier Hendricks assumed total control, but was not the skilled politician his father was, due to being raised for one purpose and one purpose only, that he did not care for and with such wealth and privilege from birth had absolutely no concept of the real world nor how to manipulate it for his own personal gain.

He slowly started to lose control, giving it up under pressure to those who sought his power for themselves. In order to maintain the luxury lifestyle, he had for as minimal effort he could employ, so that he could indulge in his fantasies of debauchery.

Hendricks II's son could see what his father was and hated him. Over the years, he became increasingly impatient for his father's death. He had a deeply disgusting desire for wealth and power and viewed his father with utter contempt and his grandfather as a hero and role model. As the years passed, he saw control and his opportunity at absolute power slowly ebbing away.

Technology was improving along with robotics and it was not long before first AI-controlled robots started to replace the less skilled jobs. People started to lose their income and the unemployment numbers rose dramatically year on year as companies started to replace people with 'intelligent' machines.

The population was becoming restive. People whilst not starving were unemployed and had nothing to do. Thousands upon thousands would apply for every job and as such pay was hit by huge deflation, exasperating an already bad situation.

Hendricks II floundered and allowed all of his advisors to effectively run the country, he simply could not be bothered or was completely out of his mind on drugs and telling the prostitutes they could own the country if they wanted.

Hendricks II son, known at the time as Hendricks III or Cornelius by his proper name, was basically left to raise himself. His mother had died of alcohol poisoning due to her lack of any desire for the man she was married to, nor her station in life, so replaced the emptiness with gin. It was called mother's ruin for a reason and her wild drunken rages would often result in a beating for Cornelius with a belt that would leave him with severe bruising and sometimes broken bones, usually for the smallest of indiscretions. The remorse was always there when she occasionally sobered up and realised what a monster she had become, but the damage was done. He hated her, so when she died he rejoiced, even taking to dancing on her grave at her funeral.

Her death made no difference to Hendricks II who continued to live in a parallel universe to everyone else. He had money, power in fact anything he could ever desire but still had no direction or reason for being. Cornelius could not allow his future to be thrown away by such a pathetic individual as his father, so he convinced him that those taking his power were working against him and would take everything from him, including his women and drugs. The only way he could keep his lifestyle was to allow Cornelius to take control back.

Terrified at the thought, Hendricks II made Cornelius more and more important and required in the decision making of the Government. Initially challenged by those reclaiming power in the name of the people, with his father's absolute authority still written in law and demands, written by his son, Cornelius took back all the control he could from the civil servants, being as he was positioned as chief advisor to the Government by his father. This allowed him to direct policy and reclaim the powers that were being eroded but it did not have the ultimate control of being Prime Minister, the final say. It did not make him the man in charge that he so desperately had been waiting for all his life.

Eventually and with patience finally running out, Cornelius called a meeting with his father in their official Government mansion. They ate the finest meal, drank the finest whisky and smoked the finest cigars, whilst discussing Government policy and strategy for the upcoming decade. Cornelius was unimpressed as always by his father's lack of knowledge nor grip on what was required to keep the populous under full control. This confirmed his fears and made his final decision for him.

At the end of the evening Hendricks II was completely comatose on fine living and collapsed on his bed. At one in the morning, Cornelius walked in with full confidence and a syringe he had sourced from the scientists now under government control. Stating out loud to his comatose father that he was a total fucking loser, he injected him with the content of the syringe between the toes on his right foot. Hendricks II did not even move as his heart stopped beating. "Step one complete you pathetic prick, you and my 'mother' are welcome to each other in hell" he said as he left, returning to his bedroom to fall into a deep and self-satisfying sleep.

Over the next week, Hendricks II's death was announced. As chief advisor to the Government and as his son, Cornelius stated that he would run the interim Government until new elections could be called. Most of the population could not care less. They rarely saw Hendricks II or knew of anything he had actually done for the country and were perplexed about how he had managed to get voted in at every election. This was something that Cornelius noted and would use to his advantage for his reign. Control the media, control the narrative and you will always be seen to be the leader in control and on the side of the people.

The coroner's report dutifully reported that Hendricks II had died peacefully of a heart attack in his sleep. The coroner himself was dutifully removed from the living population three months later without notice to the wider population.

Hendricks II received no state funeral like his father and was buried in an unmarked grave, to be forgotten by time.

Now, all that was left for Cornelius was to get elected as the new Prime Minister. He led a campaign in the elections under the strapline that the country needed a 'New Government', one that would actively step up for the people again.

His election was already a forgone conclusion of course with one of the only two challengers in the election died in a car accident, even though they did not drive, nor own a car and always stood on the platform of being one of the people and taking public transport. The other challenger unsurprisingly became less 'enthusiastic' in their campaigning and withdrew.

Election Day came and the perfectly executed plan came into force, after all he was the only candidate, so he could only lose to himself! Cornelius had become the new Prime Minister. He immediately declared the position of Prime Minister to be defunct and a throwback to the old ways that let the people down. He would become Premier Cornelius Hendricks III leader of the New Government.

As he enforced his new powers, he pushed the one thing that was not in his promises and manifesto. He pushed through the final stage of the neutrality strategy started so many years ago by his grandfather, he took away the final piece of the puzzle, he took away people's names.

Xe was the new name, to be suffixed with a number. He would lead the way and declare he was now to be known as Premier Xe.

All dissent was crushed, the people agreed, after all they had voted for him. The dynasty was continued, Premier Xe was in total control and he had all of the power in the country, personally.

The strategy was complete. Absolute control was finally achieved and it was wholly in the hands of Premier Xe.

# Chapter 3:

# Sage Advice

Premier Xe slammed a pile of papers on the desk in the Premier Planning Office ranting, "NEVER IN THE ENTIRETY OF HISTORY HAVE I BEEN SO INCENSED BY YOUR PATHETIC INABILITY TO DO ANYTHING FUCKING RIGHT! WHY DO YOU ALL JUST SIT THERE WAITING FOR ME TO TELL YOU WHAT TO DO? YOU ARE ALL USELESS FUCKING MORONS!" He did not see the irony in the rant, seeing as no one was allowed to blink, let alone mutter an idea without his explicit permission, yet were expected to take the dressing down for doing exactly that.

He walked around the room staring at the walls that were adorned with the finest wallpaper available, the carpet deep pile so soft you could spend the night on it quite comfortably.

As he walked behind the seated Supreme Sage, the Chief Treasurer and the Communications Chief he looked at his portrait and those of his two forebears. Pointing to them he stated, this time in a fuming but more controlled voice, "Do you think they would put up with this? Huh? Do you think they would accept this sort of incompetence?"

Walking behind Commander General Military and next to the end wall that had the biggest TV you could imagine with all sorts of smaller screens surrounding it, he silently stood in front of the room's long window, looking out over the capital.

His rage slowly subsiding, he started in a calm yet still maniacal way, "The Speech Sanctuaries are still operating, there are rumours that they are still out there despite MY DIRECT ORDER TO DESTROY THEM ALL! THEY SPREAD EVERYTHING WE STAND AGAINST; THEY ARE A BREEDING GROUND OF DISSENT AND WILL BE THE BIRTHING GROUND OF OUR DOWNFALL!" ending in full rant mode whilst still looking out of the window waving his arms around.

Spinning around to face the room, red in face and bulging veins in his neck, he screamed and pointed down to the table with each point being made: "FIND THEM, BURN THEM TO THE GROUND AND KILL EVERYONE WHO IS IN THEM OR ASSOCIATED WITH THEM! I WILL NOT SAY THIS AGAIN AND ANYONE THAT LETS THE TEAM DOWN, THAT TAKES OUR LIFESTYLES AWAY FROM ALL OF US IN THIS ROOM, WILL FIND THEIR BODY PARTS DECORATING THIS FUCKING ROOM! IF ONE PART OF THIS ROOM DOES NOT DO ITS JOB, WE ALL LOSE! NOW GET OUT THERE AND SORT THIS OUT ONCE AND FOR ALL!" Pointing to the door, he ended his rant by stating, "GET THE FUCK OUT OF MY OFFICE!"

The gathered audience left the room, thinking, 'we came all this way for that?' Once outside and out of earshot, the Communications Chief said to the Chief Scientist, "The Speech Sanctuaries really seemed to be getting to Premier Xe lately; what isn't he telling us?"

"Don't know," said the Chief Scientist. "Don't care really, you know he is a dickhead, I know he is a dickhead, we all know he is a dickhead, we just have to either get them all or find out who is telling him about them and silence them, so we can get on with what we want to do."

The Communications Chief nodded as they went their separate ways.

Premier Xe had slammed the doors shut, as he did so his phone rang. Taking it out of his pocket he looked uncomfortable as he read who was calling on the screen. Walking over to the window, he looked out at the capital and answered "Yes."

"If you do not sort out the problem, Premier Xe, we will finance someone who will," came the voice on the phone, which promptly went dead.

Premier Xe just stood looking, staring, 'why can I not end these damn places once and for all?' he thought to himself. 'I WILL end these places, even if I have to kill every fucking person in this country. I am Premier Xe, born to rule and no one is going to take that from me!'

\*\*\*

With a snort and an intake of breath, Xe opened his eyes, slowly realising where he was, he sighed and buried his head back into the pillow on the sofa, his head was pounding, as it always after listening to JJ and his 'entertainment', not to mention the ocular damage caused by those teeth.

It was Sunday April 1st but this life was no April fool, it was purgatory. Relentlessly empty of any promise, any future, any hope nor desire. Just filled with drudgery, an inane existence even if you were lucky enough to have a job. Ah yes jobs, something else from the old days. Work, something to do, something to take pride in, something to pass time however even that was taken away from most people when artificial intelligence combined with machines replaced over half of the workforce. It was then that the human existence largely became pointless. The world was now full of people wandering around aimlessly, nothing to do but pass time until sleep.

He sighed as he wondered what life was like before all this happened, when people had things to do, when the day was not filled with a desperate attempt to find something, anything to do, in order to clear the utter boredom from people's minds.

With a loud exclamation of someone who's swollen brain had just been beaten on the inside of their skull, like a boxer on the ropes, for a full 6 hours straight, he sat up and decided it was time to get out of the apartment, too much time in these modular boxes could drive anyone insane, but first was the crawl to the bathroom for two pills and a glass of water to contain the road drill currently being used in his head.

His mind was racing; he felt insanity touching him ever more every day and this pounding headache was getting worse by the minute. He decided he would head for church, he had no interest the only allowed 'religion', called Stoicism, but the place was cool and peaceful and allowed him an uninterrupted delve into the darkness, he seemed to need it more and more these days, like something was building but had no idea what, the voices, the thoughts, it often became too much and he would crumble in paranoia, sobbing his heart out and calling for his mother.

The Church and the Stoics seemed to be home, for no reason other than inner feeling.

Putting on his primary clothing, such was required for formal occasions, demerits of your citizen status if not adhered to of course, he placed his Personal Citizen Device on his chest and left apartment 8 heading for C-1-317-884-758.

Getting onto the magtrain at TSA-1-317-884-777 he stared out of the window looking at the buildings and the city pass by, lost in a daydream within a daydream. He sat thinking about the dream, the recurring dream that would just not leave him alone. He did not know whether it was cause or effect in that his thinking about the dream was causing its recurrence or whether it was the other way round, either way it would not leave him alone. Even the darkness struggled to keep it out such was its intensity.

For his life clashed like the waves of a storm lashing at the sea defences, becoming angrier and angrier that it cannot penetrate the wall in front of it, throwing everything it has, just wanting to be heard, respected, yet getting nowhere, until exhaustion forces it to wane and die off until the next time the fury builds from a place unknown, raging at the world around it, demanding to be known, yet ultimately knowing it's efforts are pointless.

A life without ambition, without wonder, without desire, without purpose, without love. What is this thing called love? He knew the word as it kept coming into his mind, a light penetrating the darkness, yet knew nothing of it. How did he know of it?

He had a lot buried in his mind, in the darkness, including his desire to openly refer to his presence as 'he'. If he dared to say that out loud the police, notified by the neutrality spies that were everywhere, would have him arrested in an instant, such was the lethality of neutrality in these times and he could only imagine what happened in Detention Centre One. All he knew was that people went into it but never seemed to come back out.

These thoughts continuously tumbled around in his mind like clothes in the apartment block laundrette. As much as there was an attempt to supress these dangerous thoughts, they kept coming back. Day after day, dream after dream, he dreamt about a life that had some purpose, in them he even had a name but he would always come shuddering back into reality and realise, the purpose of life is neutrality. It is how it was told on the news, by the politicians, by the 'leadership'. It had to be that way else we would end up in the brutal violence of the past, whatever that was, the authorities kept saying it would happen but never tell you what actually happened. It was the threat of it that drove the fear, a fear of something completely unknown to the masses.

"Station TSA-1-317-884-758 is the next stop," came over the sound system. It snapped him back into life, it was his stop. The magtrain stopped and he got off and headed for the exit, not even noticing those he left on it, namely a woman with her child and a Sage.

As he left the magtrain station, he hesitated, there was trouble here and he could feel it and hear it. There was an incident happening but did not know what. Trouble was a relatively rare event in life such were the levels of punishment given out, in the name of 'keeping everyone safe'.

He walked over the bridge leading to the exit and as he approached the station entrance took small, silent steps forward until he reached a corner wall. Peering round the corner, very carefully so as not to be seen he saw a group of about ten young people, who seemed to be beating someone up. Was it a mugging or just a random act of violence by bored kids? He was unsure but whatever it was he wanted to be no part of it. Squinting and looking closer, he suddenly darted back into the shadows. FUCK! SHIT, SHIT, SHIT, SHIT, SHIT, SHIT! he thought as he realised they were beating two police officers. He looked around in complete panic, hoping no one saw him there just as a full troop of police officers pulled up. The youths scattered.

Less than five minutes later, a number were brought back and held against the wall at gunpoint. Xe just stood statue still, unmoving. Any attempt to get back to the magtrain platform would be heard or seen and he would become another person stood against that wall.

All of the officers were dressed in a similar fashion. Their boots were thick leather had metal plating and armour all around, flameproof trousers and shirt with a solid field belt around the waist. All wore a balaclava, none wore a Personal Citizen Device and everything was black.

On top of the standard uniform most would wear the riot protection comprising of shin and thigh armour, made out of very light composite materials but which had the strength of steel. Further armour would be found around the groin with large but surprisingly flexible thoracic, shoulder and arm protection. On the head would be a full helmet with tinted visor and necks flaps that would surround the officer's neck and sit on their shoulders.

Some in the support roles would opt for the lighter armour options, none went without any at all.

Originally, each Troop officer had a location tracker in their Personal Citizen Device, however after some officers were abducted, tortured, mutilated and their body parts put on display some years ago, the trackers were implanted.

This became known to the wider population as 'the tracker incident' when two officers were abducted and taken to a rural barn for their fate. As the gathered crowd started to prepare for their revenge, three troops of officers stormed the barn. No one escaped, no one's family escaped and no one's friends escaped. Rumour had it hundreds were killed in the end, some simply through association. From this incident onwards, any retribution against the police was always delivered immediately.

One of the officers called on their comms devices and a Centurion appeared.

The Centurion led a unit of fifty-seven other officers called a Troop. They were identifiable by the three red stripes that went from one side of the helmet to the other. Under their command were three cohorts, each comprising of a Primus, identified in a similar fashion to the Centurion, with the exception that they were only two stripes and were blue. They in turn had three corporals, designated by one blue stripe on their helmets, reporting to them. The corporals in turn had five officers reporting into each of them who did not have any stripes or other identifiable markings on their uniforms.

The first cohort was called Peditata and was tasked with 'going in first'. They were, quite frankly evil. Their sole role was to eradicate any opposition that stood before it, by any means necessary, or so desired by the officer, to achieve the task at hand. This was usually achieved by causing as much damage as possible to anything or anyone that was unfortunate enough to be located in their path, delicacy was not an art they were familiar with.

Although all carried a firearm of some description, they could be armed with any weapon they desired. Most Peditata officers tended to prefer the so called 'trench apparel' which comprised of clubs (often homemade), knuckle dusters, knives and any other hand to hand items that would allow the user to inflict critical levels of damage whilst looking into the eyes of those on the receiving end. These were favoured weapons in the Brutus games if the officer were to partake and often seen as a proving ground for their development and effectiveness.

They were usually huge, fierce, unrelenting, unemotional and brutal although the size was often not a good indicator for the level of brutality, as some smaller officers could be the most violent. Uninterested in the reason for their deployment, they had no care nor sympathy for anything or anyone who stood before them and were known for their desire to make death as painful and as long as possible. They were knowns as 'The Premier's Butchers' for a very good reason.

The second cohort was called Secundarium or Sec for short. With the same structure as the Peditata cohort, they were tasked as a reserve. Other duties were to act as a liaison between the Peditata and Auxilium cohort. Should a Peditata officer fall a Sec corporal would immediately fill the position in the rank, always with great delight. It would be a position they would maintain until retirement or death.

The last cohort was called Auxilium and usually comprised of officers that were new to the force and needed to be 'bloodied'. Their role was threefold, with a corporal and five officers leading each responsibility.

Firstly, was the role of medic. Should an officer fall or become injured the medics were tasked to retrieve the officer and deal with the injury or return the body to whatever vehicle had brought to the scene. Due to the potential danger of the role they were usually wearing full body armour and carried medipacks rather than weapons. When retrieving injured officers, further officers would support them from the Sec cohort. A well drilled Troop would practice this routine to precision for ultimate speed and effectiveness back in the training grounds of their headquarters.

A medic under no circumstance, would offer aid or assistance to any person other than those in the Troop. Medical support to those whom the Peditata cohort had 'had a quiet conversation with' was strictly forbidden and would result in immediate dismissal from the Police. If anyone managed to survive the clean-up crew would take them to the hospital. This was an extremely rare event.

The second Auxilium role, again with a corporal and five officers was one of re-supply, of both ammunition, but any other supply needed. They had the nickname of 'runners' as they were often seen running around all over the scene of the incident, carrying just about anything that could be imagined. There is lore in the runners that once an officer was seen running with a large pair of knickers to a Peditata officer, whom then used it to choke a protestor to death. Runners always had these tall tales of what they had witnessed. Nobody knew how many true and how many were made up, but there was always the desire amongst them for a runner to be asked to find something unusual for another officer, so they could brag about it for the next few months.

Lastly were the Communication team or Commies for short. They had the same structure and a twofold task. The first was to keep open and secure communications with headquarters open and available at all costs. If a Troop was in the thick of it and needed back up it was vital the message got through.

Unsurprisingly, should a troop become overwhelmed, retribution would be carried out in the same fashion as what was given out. No comms combined with losing a fight meant a fast death for every member of the troop if they were lucky.

Their second task was to block all electronic devices for a significant radius. The command vehicles had very effective jamming devices that rendered every electronic device inoperative. Should someone be inside and this happen, they knew what was going on and were wise to stay inside the building they were in and not try to observe what was happening. To be seen to be looking, would mean the person would be equally guilty of whatever illegal activity was in progress under the 'guilty through association' laws, that nobody noticed being written into the books.

Global Life also always blocked anything negative to do with the New Government as this went against their 'community standards' and thus deserved to remain hidden from the population at large. Anyone distributing images that were considered anti-establishment, simply disappeared.

As such, any incident with a Troop was never recorded or distributed, other than through folk law and of those who witnessed an event but managed to remain hidden. Society in this respect, had regressed back to tales spoken in groups and handed down through generations.

The Centurion walked up to the officers on the floor and looked at the medic. The medic shook his head to indicate that they were dead. Nodding in acceptance, the Centurion turned to the Peditata Primus currently holding the youths.

The Centurion simply walked away. What Xe witnessed next, made him sick to his stomach, a reminder of past days. The Peditata cohort had been given permission to deal with the youths by whatever means they desired. This would unleash the most despicable evil contained within each officer, often using techniques and weapons usually handed down to them from their parents. A police officer almost always came from police officer stock, with a police officer attitude to their role in society.

One by one, in turn for each one of the victims to see what was coming to them, each youth was held down and savagely beaten. They were ultimately tortured and killed by an officer of the Peditata cohort, whom cheered in a wild, animalistic euphoria at the kill before them, before walking away to let the next officer take their turn on a victim, calling each one out by preference, by who they felt the urge to murder. Two of theirs had fallen and all those involved would pay.

Such was the grotesque display before them, the three new members of the Auxilium cohort were violently sick, however others would watch with such excitement that they would reach a euphoria at what they witnessed and the thought that one day they would be in a Peditata cohort.

Butchers by nickname, butchers in real life.

Some of those held tried desperately to escape, none did. One stood firm and spat in the face of the officer that had chosen them and suffered a longer, slower and more painful end than the others. At the end of the slaughter, a new member of the support cohort was 'bloodied' by the Peditata Primus, an initiation into the force to which he had joined. He had their face drenched in the blood of an offender, using an organ of choice hacked from the victim's body. Today's organ of choice was the liver, which was removed and used on the Auxilium officer whilst its original owner, who thought to spit in their face was a wise act of defiance, was still very much alive, twitching on the floor.

After twenty-five minutes of unadulterated violence and brutality, the police simply left, leaving behind the bodies mutilated, destroyed and unrecognisable, for the waiting clean-up crews to come and deal with. No bodies were ever returned to their families and no one really knew what happened to those who became 'involved' with the police and 'their duties'.

The clean-up crews themselves had evolved over the decades into an efficient evidence removal team and were affiliated with the police and under the control of the Commander General Police. Whilst the comms truck continued to jam all signals, they would move in with two trucks. One would remove what was left of the bodies with the other containing enough water and equipment to make the site look like nothing had happened there at all. So efficient were they that not even any DNA would be left behind, just a perfectly clean and sterile patch of ground.

When it was over, a trembling Xe immediately ran back to the station platform and took the next magtrain. Getting off at station TSA-1-317-884-769 and walking back towards the church. Despite best efforts he was visibly shaken by what had just happened. Those kids, they were kids, they could not have been more that in their late teens. Why, why did they do that? They knew the consequences of their actions, why? Why did they do it? He quizzed himself privately.

Tripping twice, he stumbled up the steps of the church, he needed to get into his dark place, he needed sanctuary and he needed it now!

Stumbling into the church he sat down on the first pew he came across. The service was in full swing and the Sage in full, unrestricted flow, cloak hood back with staff in hand, was installing the ways of Stoicism to the gathered audience, who had all ensured they checked in with their Personal Citizen Device to gain their credits of course.

The church itself was a magnificent structure. Built of old-world design, not the new modular designed crap, it was huge. Made entirely out of stone, vast arches rose into the sky, creating cavernous spaces, 100 times greater than they needed to be for the number of people inside the building. The space did not make for a warm environment, especially at this time of year, so Xe wrapped himself a little tighter in his clothing whilst watching his breath in front of him.

At one end there were equally vast windows made of coloured glass. The colours depicted scenes, long past and now without current meaning, but were strangely beautiful, almost hypnotic in nature, maybe they were to do with the old religion's teachings, some old characters of long forgotten tales of good and evil, of birth, life and retribution all in the name of a greater power or being, sarcastically wondering why Premier Xe had not insisted his image was in that glass, seeing as he considered himself the only power in leadership these days.

Religion itself had long been a source of violence and division, not to mention completely non-neutral so of course it had to go as part of the narrative. There were always those that complained, those that try to fight back, but as with all things in those days, to complain or try to argue back was met with gaslighting and the accusation that you actually wanted hatred and violence, that you wanted the world to be forever fighting itself. The defence was mainly led by the older people, but as they died off and any outward support was met with the usual mob viciousness and kangaroo courts of public and social media opinion, so people drifted away and the old ways lost their finance. With that, they lost their buildings into disrepair and could not be used.

The Authorities did nothing to support them financially as their removal was in the interest of the New Government, so it just died out. There were rumours of underground meetings and ceremonies, but those rumours were impossible to verify and he had never heard of any, let alone attended one. In the current world everything was carried out in secret, so it was more than possible that it continued as so often these things do, under the noses of the oppressor but secret and hidden.

As the old religions were slowly and deliberately being asphyxiated out of existence, so the Government at the time started to play in the new way of life (They were careful not to call it a religion) this way would be the Stoic way, a way of not wanting vast wealth, a sensible approach of self-control, a way of life that looked after the environment and the soul at the same time, whilst wanting the minimum for the individual. The key was the last part as it fitted the narrative perfectly "We will all have nothing and we will all be happy" was their strapline.

The Stoic Sage was describing to the gathered the principle of Pathos or passion. Passion was bad, passion led to thoughts that went against the great narrative and thus had to be suppressed. To have passion was to seek more than others, to have wants and desires, these can only lead to turmoil and worse, to non-neutrality. Passion was evil and it was every person's duty to prevent it in themselves as well as ensure that others too rejected the idea.

The Sage went on to describe how, in the old days, people would fight and steal so that they may own a bigger car or a bigger house. They would allow their passions to overcome them and sleep with others who were already combined in partnership, causing further anger and violence. They would not rest until they had what they wanted, whether gained through fair means or foul. But even that was not enough!

He said, "Imagine that you had unlimited access to money and had purchased every single item that was known to all of kind. This wealth would be more than any individual would need and in gathering it would remove the opportunity for prosperity and happiness from others, both human and that of creatures as you gained what they once had until you had it all. What comes next? Do you think that this wealth would bring you happiness as all those around you are unhappy when you parade around showing off?

How can you be happy without the happiness of those around you? This is not Ubuntu! Greed and desire leads to sadness not happiness.

When you have everything, what comes next? Owning everything has not dealt with the desire for more, so what next? Own the planet itself? Perhaps all of the planets and stars, then what? The Universe? Then what? Own all of existence? Then What? You see unless you remove the desire for more and more you can never be happy, you can only bring unhappiness to those around you, your thirst will never be quenched no matter how much water you drink! You should only seek just enough, just enough food, water, shelter that is required to live a life in comfort but not extravagance"

There was much muttering from the gathered audience, whom all agreed with the wise words spoken by the Sage, agreeing that desire and a want for more always leads to pain, anger and violence and thus must be avoided and all should be happy to live in the apartments without opulence but just enough comfort for the greater good.

The Sage finished, as always, with a reminder of the core principles of the new way of life.

In this message, the Sage stated the four traps that had to be avoided at all costs. Raising his hands and stating, "We must avoid the four traps, which bring us ill health and angst." He continued, "They are fear, strong desire, mental pain and mental pleasure. You do not need to feel fear as the New Government and its officers were there to protect you against all evil."

Xe said to himself that he had just witnessed this 'protection' first-hand and it certainly did not remove any fear from his mind.

The Sage continued, "We should avoid strong desire as this leads to wants that are beyond your ability to achieve and this will only bring further frustration and sadness. Do you not feel that it would be better to accept who you are and your position in life?

"Overreaching one's abilities will only cause you mental pain and we must try to avoid this at all costs. The best way to do this is to not seek the thing you seek in the first place, be content with what you have and not that which you cannot have," The Sage challenged.

The Sage summed up the speech by saying, "Mental pleasure leads to strong desire and strong desire is evil! All pleasure is to be avoided as much as possible. Every citizen was expected to control their pleasure. Pleasure equals evil and evil only results in the destruction of the individual. Everything, even sex is to be conducted without pleasure but as a function of the ongoing requirement of the nation.

"Now go, good citizens, refreshed in the ways of the Stoic and stay prepared for life. Until next Sunday whence we will remind ourselves of our societal obligations, be well."

The gathered crowd stood and thanked the Sage for the reminders of the way of life to be observed and dutifully filtered their way out of the church.

Xe just sat without listening, staring at the enormous, colourful designs in the window. Not realising the discussion had ended and having hardly listened to a single word, or a single sound of what had just been said, he remained in his safe space, eyes open, mind closed; how he needed this sanctuary right now after what he had just witnessed.

"Are you OK, Xe?" came a muffled voice. "Are you OK, Xe?" There it was again.

"Xe, Xe, XE!"

Suddenly, Xe snapped out of his trance. He was alone in the church with the exception of the Sage. Stuttering, he said, "Yes, yes, sorry I was miles away, wonderful speech, my Sage, it is truly helpful to listen to the ways of life, to help me…help me…yes, help me."

The Sage said, "You look troubled, my child, you appear as one of the occupati not one of the desired apatheia, how can I help?"

The occupati were those who were preoccupied with matters. They were focussed on things that were not to be desired or sought after. An occupati soul was a troubled soul engrossed in pointless pursuits.

All citizens were expected to be of the apatheia. Citizens that had achieved equanimity and psychological stability. To pursue passion was to invite an imbalance and was to be avoided.

Xe burst into tears, suddenly losing all control. "I know not of my purpose! I have no idea, perhaps to exist, perhaps to end this in glorious freedom, either way I know I will end up dead," he blurted out like a lost child crying for its guardian.

The Sage sat and let the worst of the outburst and emotion leave him, before stating, "Do not worry, Xe; after all, this world breaks everyone eventually." The Sage continued, "A wise man sees his turmoil but overcomes it."

"I know!" he snapped. "Sorry my Sage, but I have this inner storm going on that I find harder and harder to contain. It starts the moment I wake and is with me till I collapse at the end of the day. Often it is in my dream, but yet there is beauty in the scene I am seeing in my dream, there is sunshine and laughter, but eventually it vanishes before me and I awaken sweating and troubled."

"Do you fear death?" asked the Sage.

"Yes, no, yes, oh I don't know, I don't know anything anymore."

The Sage tried to placate the troubled soul before him, "If you wake in the morning feel humbled that you have escaped death for another day, be thankful for it. Death is just a destination, an end point, it is the journey that matters, what is the point of getting to 100 years old and achieved nothing in your life, just to say look I am one hundred years old! When you do die you will be immediately forgotten by the world. You need to decide what you want to do with your life Xe that is the first stepping stone."

"But how do I achieve anything with this wretched existence, an existence of emptiness, of nothingness, of total neutrality?" he replied without noticing the clear contradiction of life advice of accepting who you are, which the congregation had just been told.

"Trust your dreams, they are windows into your soul. Listen to them and they will guide you to your purpose of this Earth. You just have to trust them and trust yourself, even in the darkest of hours."

He looked up at the Sage. The Sage looked back with apparently genuine concern, which made him nervous. No one shows this kind of concern, this kind of compassion anymore.

"I have said too much," he stated, fearing that the Sage would report this conversation to the authorities. "I have to go now I need to have my injection."

Standing, he hurried out of the church. As he did so the Sage shouted out, "Remember Xe, not everyone is just a citizen. Come back and we shall explore your dreams further. I CAN HELP YOU; I CAN INTERPRET YOUR DREAMS!"

He paused at the words in the latter statement then rushed off again. It all sounded bizarre to him as he stumbled down the steps on his way to the magtrain station, not everyone is just a citizen, what did that mean? It did not make any sense at all, everyone was a citizen, equal and neutral, that is the way, that is the law, the Sage knew that, so why those words? And how on Earth can he interpret my dreams? None of that made sense he muttered to himself.

He wandered into the station. It only occurred to him when he was standing on the platform that he had completely forgotten to claim the credits for attending the church. DAMMIT! He thought, spending more attention at the loss of a credit than realising he had just walked straight over the point of the massacre not two hours before. The clean-up crews were good at their job, very good.

As he sat on the magtrain, in his mind he knew that the injection he was about to receive was nothing to do with risk, he had no choice. Those that controlled the truth, controlled the narrative and the narrative was that after the years of hedonism and recklessness of the early 21$^{st}$ Century, there was a pandemic, zoonotic in nature, or so the narrative said, and the citizens had to be protected against them, after all it was for their own good and the good of society.

So, like sheep, people started to get 'the jab'. The 'the jab' became 'the jabs' as the threat of more and more "deadly viruses" were apparently possible to be transmitted from animals to humans, before it became the 'one jab'. It was a sign of how humans were raping the planet and therefore was our own fault and thus we must pull back from the brink and relinquish all rights and ownership of everything. The narrative told us this.

It clearly explained how we must no longer own anything; we must give total control to those who know best and are following the science. The 'experts' were telling us so. Always those bloody experts he thought, experts in what exactly? Probably experts in hearing their own voices. Yes they had fancy titles, not just 'Xe' but 'Chief Scientist', but despite the fancy names these experts always seem to be advising on a hope or a chance and if it went their way they would exclaim how great they were, if it did not, no one knew and the truth was brushed under the carpet by a flurry of other more deadly things to worry about whilst the narrative was quietly adjusted in the background of the New Government Public Relations department.

Ha! PR department he thought as he got off the magtrain, more like propaganda department!

As he walked into the hospital, he reminded himself to get himself in check before one of these internal outbursts became so very public. Today he feared death and death would be the result of stating that the experts did not know what the hell they were talking about, however obvious that might be!

He walked into the reception area of hospital H1-1-317 on the Northeast side of the capital as he had done for as long as he could remember, every month, month in and month out to get his 'treatment'.
All medical facilities were managed in one location, the location you were registered in, the one you were born in. Social mobility was virtually non-

existent and simply travelling to other areas of the country was rare due to the grilling you got from the police should you be stopped and your Personal Citizen Device be scanned to reveal your current home location.

He checked in by scanning his Personal Citizen Device next to the receptionist and after a polite smile proceeded to find a seat. The reception area itself being the usual drab mass produced affair. Totally functional, no element of flair or design, just what was needed, cheap and functional and above all neutral. Looking at the receptionist he kept his thoughts private for the receptionist could be a neutrality spy, so could Xe seated opposite or in fact Xe sat by the door. Anything but neutral speak was to be avoided at all costs, such was the cost of an opinion, an idea or a thought that did not comply with the narrative.

# Chapter 4:
# The Awakening

Sat in the reception area of hospital H1-1-317 Xe waited to be called for the monthly jab that everyone had to endure. It was law to have the 'one jab'. Failure to turn up for your appointment would result in the relationship between your front door, its hinges and its vicinity with the frame being violently rearranged. No one escaped, no excuse was allowed and every citizen had to have it from the age of five, every month without fail.

Citizens are told it is to protect them from the viruses and disease and that it was "100% safe as certified by the National Medical Safety Board." No one really knew what was in it and to be honest it was hell, after each jab would come two days of fever and sickness that only the healthy would survive, despite its safety and efficacy 'guarantee'. Everyone involved with its manufacture and delivery had been indemnified by law.

Just another lie from the New Government that could not be questioned, nor was it, by the subservient media channels.

So often the elderly, the infirm, the 'undesirables' would succumb to this 'treatment'.

"It was because they had co-morbidity and not due to the jab" all were told, Xe often thought it was a convenient way to avoid pension payments for the over eighty fives and avoidance of supporting those that were deemed, non-productive to society. It certainly was efficient, legalised, population control that made eugenics seem like child's play and gave everyone a scare for their life every month.

He sat quietly flicking through 'Culture Now' magazine. It was a sister publication to Good Citizen and was eighty odd pages of banal 'celebrities' of limited talent, informing the world of their personal views on everything and how they were so well qualified to do so, always following New Government guidelines of course, one had to be careful, even when crawling up the arses of those on the ladder above them. They had it less bad than the majority of people and they knew it, so would say and do anything for anyone for a few likes and hits on Global Life which were far more important than silly things like morality or backbone. Likes and hits equalled cash and more importantly, status. Morality did not.

Page forty-five; an interview with Xe 762863548, film star, commentator and all round idiot. This month Xe is going to let us all know how wonderful life is because he is on the side of righteousness and if you disagree with his opinion you are not worthy of existence, he chuckled to himself as he made up the more realistic headline in his head. What an utter dick this prat was, along with all the 'celebrity set'.

Page forty-eight, the all new Mingo 865 car, reviewed by Xe 826735298. Beautiful inside and outside, efficient, perfect for the climate and obscenely expensive. Yep, my Statutory Monetary Allowance is really going to get me one of those, he thought, dreaming of even owning a 33rd hand me down. Cars were for the rich and powerful, not the peasant class, they had old shank's pony to get them around.

Page sixty-eight, the quiz pages. Two pages full of challenges and questions that a child could complete in under ten minutes. This month you could enter with a chance of winning the Mingo 865. He always thought it funny how last month's winner of the prize always looked nervous in the photo and never seemed to actually drive the car or in fact talk about any prize they won. Looking and seeing that half of the questions had been filled in incorrectly anyway, he dropped back onto the table and looked around the room, desperate to relieve the boredom.

Looking around he noted the Xe sat by the door staring straight at him wiping his nose with his sleeve, as well as the Sage that had just checked in, whose cursory glance over to him was less obvious than the apparent maniac by the door but still noted.

He was thankful when the call came, "Xe 805491997 to medical bay four immediately!" Standing and making his way to the designated bay, watched every step of the way by Nutjob Xe, as he was now labelled, he did not notice the Sage watching the interaction from the far corner of the waiting area. Entering medical bay four and closing the door behind him he was greeted with "Good morning Xe" by the average looking man stood by a bench full of vials of liquids and other medical necessities for the monthly jabs. The medical assistant stated, "Please wait over there whilst I prepare your jab" in an almost robotic voice and without even looking at him, probably as a result of having to say it for the fiftieth time today.

Xe did not like needles so stared out of the window at the rain that had started to fall again, ending up almost trance like, the thousand yard stare described in old times as someone who has given up hope of life, as it had become too much to bear and instead has replaced it with the hope that it will end swiftly and without pain. Maybe this one would be his last and finish him off. Chance would be a fine thing he thought to himself, got too many years left in this purgatory to be that lucky, when a voice appeared in his head stating, "I love you, change the world, be a…"

"OK," the medical assistant stated, breaking his daydream after standing and watching Xe in his trance like state. The hopelessness, the beaten, lost soul that sat behind those eyes, it was a common sight to him.

He said in the well scripted verbiage, "You will feel a little scratch and may feel unwell for a couple of days but thereafter you will be protected against all the known viruses and illnesses. The National Medical Safety Board has stated that it is 100% safe and effective."

It was like a script, heard with every injection, every visit, every time.

"That will be fine," Xe said the required response from memory whilst still staring out of the window.

"I accept all risks associated with the New Government's attempts to keep me safe and acknowledge it is in my best interests to have this protection given to me. I accept that it is my responsibility to ensure that I have been vaccinated so that I may also keep others safe. I therefore grant all immunity to both the New Government and those who produce the medication should I suffer any adverse reaction."

It seemed odd to him that in modern times that personal acceptance of something was even required, but it was stated as such and as per every visit, every month, he would not break that requirement and take the risk that the medical assistant was a neutrality spy.

After delivering the injection the medical assistant Xe stated, "There you go, all done. I hope you are well and fair wind to you", thus was the accepted leaving salutation.

"Thank you," said Xe. "My neighbour died after their last injection, I hope I fare better. He was only 37 as well."

Silence and immediate tension filled the room; this was a major mistake. To utter the word 'he' was an indication that you belonged to the old world, the impure world, the offensive world before neutrality. If medical assistant Xe was a member of the neutrality spy circuit, his days were now numbered.

He looked at the medical assistant with scared eyes, terrified that this error would result in cancellation, possibly being set to Detention Centre One, yet in a strange way he didn't care, he was beaten down, fed up and could no longer cope with constantly being neutral in every aspect of every part of his life. 'Fuck it' the internal voice said, as long as they kill me swiftly, then who fucking cares anymore, I cannot go on living like this. This isn't life, this is purgatory wrapped up in a PR exercise of utopia of society, perpetuated by those who pretend to care in order to enhance their status in this vacuous existence.

For a full twenty seconds they both stood looking at each other, staring into each other's eyes, trying to ascertain whether either was a neutrality spy and thus would be reported by the other, resulting in their lives and the lives of everyone who associated themselves with them being forfeit. Thus was the impact for such a mistake. Even with fervent disassociation with someone who make this type of mistake, rarely did anyone survive the rabid cancellation fervour and thus the end of any form of meaningful existence in this lifetime.

Finally, the medical assistant said, "I did not hear that if you did not say it." This was a massive risk but fortunately there was a door to this room and not a curtain so no one other than those in the room heard the statement. Still of course there was the threat of cameras and microphone bugs being everywhere, but this was not a concern at this moment.

"Of course," said Xe, "I apologise if I have put you in a difficult position. I must leave." The medical assistant suddenly moved in front of the door, blocking the exit. He was now terrified and confused.

"Do you want to speak freely?" he stated. "Do you want to know of the past, when free speak was not illegal?" The medical assistant was trembling as the words stumbled over his tongue and out of his mouth, looking around as if to see if there were spies hiding in the cupboards and under the bench.

He did not know how to respond initially, the statement was so alien to day-to-day conversation. If the response was no, it would be a betrayal of all that he looked for in his mind, if the answer was yes, then the danger that this would invite was untold. A conundrum, access to this 'free speak' or potential death. It was no choice in his mind, death was preferable than this mindless, pathetic existence.

"Yes, yes I do," he said with the nervousness of a child admitting to their parents that they drew on the wall and were expecting physical punishment as a result. The nervousness made him feel sick to his core, sicker than the aftereffects of the jab, he felt vulnerable, very vulnerable and was sweating a nervous sweat.

"Have you heard of the Speech Sanctuaries?" said the medical assistant.

"Yes," replied Xe, "but I thought they were nothing but rumours, people talking about raids on them and people being taken away. I have never seen anything on the news about them."

"No, they are very real. I visit one on the corner of 3$^{rd}$ and 45$^{th}$ street. You won't see them on the news as the New Government wants them eradicated. They fear them as they do not control them, nor what happens inside them."

Imagining the building, Xe replied, "That is a manufacturing centre isn't it? How can you have something like that under a New Government building?"

"Yes it is and we can talk more about it later. There is a service door on 3$^{rd}$ street down some steps. It has 'Staff only' written above in red, the y being missing. Go there Thursday, 20:00 hours, this week when the effects of the injection have worn off. You need to knock three times with one second between each knock, then a subsequent knock of five continuous knocks.

When challenged ask for Xe 872568972, that is my designation number and I will confirm your entry. He wrote the number down so as not to forget these ridiculously long personal tags, a dangerous associational link that had to be kept hidden away from search, so was folded into as small a piece of paper as possible and secreted between the buttocks, as close to the anus as possible, to avoid the causal and sometimes more than casual stop and searches sometimes carried out by the police.

"Needless to say, any betrayal will result in the instant cancellation of everyone within, their families, friends and associates. We heard that Speech Sanctuary Oscar went that way only last week, one wrong word, one lapse of judgement by a member and hundreds were gone within days, simply no longer existed. We do not know how or who, just lots of new neighbours as people for forcibly relocated to now empty apartments like sheep waiting to be sheared or cattle waiting to be milked." Said the medical assistant.

"Not a word," replied Xe, "Even if the bastards torture me." The medical assistant smiled. "Good, now go, you have been in here too long already and people will get suspicious."

They both nodded at each other before Xe left for home preparing for two days of painful recovery from whatever poison had just been put inside him. Before the door was closed behind him, he saw the medical assistant updating his information on the computer in the corner of the room. Sure enough five seconds later his Personal Citizen Device dinged to say it had been updated with the latest vaccination details and his 'Freedom Pass' was duly updated. Freedom Pass, huh he scoffed, freedom? What freedom? Since when did humans have to be 'allowed' to 'have' freedom, when did this world turn into this nightmare of nothingness? It just did not feel right to him, surely the point of freedom is that you are free, free from authority, free from needing permission to exist, free from a machine allowing you to exist!

Walking out of the hospital under the watchful gaze of Nutjob Xe, still wiping his nose with his sleeve and looking at Xe with a strange manic curl of his top lip, he made his way to the magtrain station.

Nodding at a Sage already seated, he sat on the magtrain on the way home looking at the same device, lost in thought.

Three days passed, two of them in a painful sweat and fever when finally, Thursday arrived. He put on his smartest shirt, pinned Personal Citizen Device upon it and set out for the corner of $3^{rd}$ and $45^{th}$ street. He walked all of the way, several miles so as not to flag his presence on public transportation or create a new regular route for the databases.

When he arrived, he shuffled and hung around so as to look inconspicuous but actually managing to look very conspicuous as if there was a neon sign above alerting every camera and authoritarian set of eyes in the process, he eventually built up enough encouragement and went down the steps, knocking as instructed. A voice sounded on the intercom, "The store is closed, come back tomorrow."

"I am here to see Xe 872568972 for an interview." He was not sure why that embellishment was added to the end, but nerves had taken over. Standing there sweating and shaking like the day after the monthly injection. Breathing had become heavy and noticeable and all of the bullish attitude of 'who cares, whatever' had vanished at the prospect of being identified and cancelled. For all the bravado he still wanted to live.

After waiting for what seemed like an eternity, there was a delicate and quiet 'CLUNK' sound of very heavy metal moving against equally heavy metal, in a strong yet quietly smooth manner. The door opened without a sound.

Behind it stood the most enormous person he had ever seen, at least seven feet tall and set with a bodybuilders frame. At five feet ten inches tall he just looked up with puppy dog eyes begging not to be beaten to within an inch of his life.

With a flick of the head, he was invited in. Quickly shuffling past the beast, who looked outside to check he was not followed, he was immediately met by another mountain of beef, this one with their hand outstretched.

"Personal Citizen Device!" it demanded.

"Sorry?" said Xe.

"Personal Citizen Device now!" came back the demand. He instantly handed it over which was passed through a hatch and disappeared. He gulped, was this a trap? Being without it would mean BIG trouble if caught, but he was in a Speech Sanctuary, not having it would be the last of his worries right now if the police walked in.

He felt sick again, no longer wearing the symbol of oppression yet strangely feeling naked and lost without it, such has the Stockholm Syndrome got into everyone's psyche regarding these devices, he was starting to sweat and hyperventilate a little. Taking two or three deep breaths he gathered himself before noticing that one of the door guards was standing, staring at him, giving him time to calm down before another flick of the head saw him through another door where he was faced with the medical assistant wearing the biggest smile and the most outrageous clothing he had ever seen in his life!

"Welcome!" said the medical assistant.

"Hello again Xe," was the cautious and downcast response.

"No, no, no, not in here my friend, in here I am John." WHAT! He immediately looked around nervously on the verge of panic in case anyone else heard. John laughed a hearty laugh, "Ha ha my friend, relax! Here there are no cameras, no spies that we know of (said with a wink and a laugh), here we all know each other by NAME, yes NAME!"

John led him through another door with another almost non-human beast guarding it, where do these mountains come from? He visibly twitched as he walked past, eye level with the man's nipples. "What's up?" said John inquisitively.

"Nothing," he replied sternly. Composing himself again, I must keep control, he thought, it is too dangerous to lose control now, CONTROL YOURSELF!

As they walked down several flights of stairs and through a thick, red velvet curtain into the main area he sucked in an audible amount of air, John smiled as with a swish of his hand said, "Welcome to Speech Sanctuary 22! Or home as we like to call it."

Before him was the most lavish, luxuriant place that could have even been imagined. Red velvet everywhere, deep pile red carpeting, lavish wallpaper, and lighting that he imagined only the richest of society could have, in their one-bedroom apartments of course.

He thought to himself that it must have cost millions to put this place together. How on Earth can they afford this? More importantly how did they even manage it? Especially with a New Government manufacturing building directly above them!

Continuing to look around with his eyes and mouth wide open, he looked at the seating all around, oh that red velvet he thought, pure and soft. Mixed with deep brown leather.

Most of the seating was arranged into booths that could seat eight people comfortable, ten at a push. There were about twenty booths, and in between, surrounding the internal pillars was shelving with tall stools to sit on.

The lighting could have come from a New Government office; low chandeliers made of the most beautiful glass with low soft white light. Small lamps in each booth and each table, lamps on the walls, both of which are red in colour and again soft in nature. The light made the room dim and difficult to see the other side of but did invite privacy and an almost demonic feeling of relaxation to the purveyor.

The wallpaper, oh the wallpaper, deep embossed golden velvet, so luscious that it required everyone who saw it to touch it, to feel just how magnificent it felt to the gentle touch of a fingertip. The pattern was a very old design, one that he had never seen but again invited total relaxation to those who were familiar with the Speech Sanctuary, with 'home'.

Looking down he looked at the carpet, which was the deepest pile he had ever experienced, so utterly soft he thought he would sink into it. He even wondered if he should take off his shoes out of respect for the quality, but as everyone else was wearing such elegant footwear, the decision was made to keep the shoes on.

Finally looking up, even the ceiling had deep designs running throughout, plaster moulding and painted to perfection. Scenes of the old world were all around. People free, people just living lives without a Personal Citizen Device in sight. The sun, stars, clouds, light, love, even a streak of strange lightening, all were depicted in the ornate finish.

Each of the seating areas had a bar assistant which were a drink delivery service, whereby a simple selection of a drink from the on-screen menu mixed with fifteen seconds or so of time delivered exactly what you wanted. No need to get up, no need to call a waiter, instant gratification. No one seems to be paying for them in here he thought. Maybe they have a tab system of some sort or just take it directly off your Personal Citizen Device that I no longer have, yes that must be the way they do it.

John continued to stand next to him with his huge smile as he stood watching him try to take in everything he was seeing. Xe was lost in his own mind and adulation for this place and John was going to allow him to enjoy this first view of freedom.

Continuing to look around in his own little world, Xe thought that this place has been designed, built, no crafted to absolute perfection. That is what this place is all about, freedom and gratification he thought and he loved it.

In the corner was a sign to the toilets. Next to that was a curtain that led to who knows what he thought, for now, he was in a place the mind could hardly comprehend.

All around were fabulous people, all dressed in magnificent outfits, not the official clothing allowed by the New Government, men and women, yes he thought men and women, proud to be such, celebrating their differences with no one telling them how to think or behave, just being themselves. 'Oh my', he said to himself in an overly excitable voice, this is oh so refreshing, so perfect, so…dangerous.

The dresses that the women wore were of the most luxuriant colours, many had tassels and they wore small material headwear of some type that he had never seen before. Their footwear had heels that were very high and slender rather than the flat New Government allowed shoes for all.

He noticed one woman in particular that had long dead straight black hair with a full length black shiny dress. He noticed a white flower in her hair and had seen nothing like it in his life. He must have been staring as she raised her eyebrows and smiled at him, which brought him back down to Earth and back in the room. He smiled back, nodded nervously and looked around sheepishly.

The Men were mostly wearing shirts made of similar shiny and colourful material. Their trousers were light in colour with a belt. Shoes so bright that you could have a shave in them.

Everyone had a beaming smile on their faces. This was the most magical place on Earth, no, the most magical in the universe and he just stood, mouth open in total disbelief!

He started to say, "I…I…I."

"I know," said John interrupting, "something to behold is it not! Good to have you back in the land of the living again! Come." He guided Xe over to a cubicle, giggling out loud.

"So," he stated matter-of-factly, "first things first, a drink. What is your poison, Sir!"

"Sorry, poison?"

"What would you like to drink? The drinks are displayed on the front of the bar assistant," John stated in a more slow and clear manner.

"Erm, a Rhapsody Blue please, actually a double." He had seen a Rhapsody Blue advertised on TV but had never had the justification to spend that sort of money on a drink, Vodinaski was more within his budget range, so thought sod it why not! "I think I am going to need it!" he said out loud as he sat down feeling the supremely smooth material on the seat. As he sat, thousands of small mechanical and hydraulic arms, moved and adjusted shaping itself around him, constant small adjustments being made as he lowered his weight in order to create the ultimate comfort for the user.

This place was pure elegance. John selected the drink from the screen at the side of the booth. Fifteen seconds later the front cover rolled up and there was a perfectly poured Rhapsody Blue. A rare drink, very expensive, but was supreme in its smoothness, ability to get the drinker completely hammered but in a slowly progressive way and yet allowed for a morning without a hangover.

"So, second order of the evening is to sort you out a name," said John. "Wait! What?" said Xe, still nervous at the thought. John laughed out loud, creating some attention from those around him.
"RELAX MAN! what is it with you? Even I was not this nervous my first time! So, what will it be then? Ever thought of yourself having a name?"

"No, never," said Xe, wilfully lying.

"Not even in one of your dreams?" said John. He immediately froze, how did he know about his dreams, no one knew about his dreams, how could they?

Was this John some sort of a witch doctor? "How do you know about my dreams!" he demanded starting to get nervous and thinking he had made the biggest mistake of his life. He was now supremely scared, this must be a trap, was there an implant in his head that alerted the authorities, just HOW?

"Whoa there tiger! I know nothing of your dreams but some people think they hear names in theirs and that becomes their home name!" said John

At this point a woman came over and introduced herself as Cassia. Cassia was tall, slim with long ginger curly hair. Her elegance matched Speech Sanctuary 22 to perfection. Her clothing was long, flowing, with a sparkle that matched that which was in her eye. "Hey new guy, time to chill before you implode my friend." Her voice was like silk, mesmerising, totally encapsulating him into a different world of emotions and thought.

He stood in politeness and remained listening and staring whilst his mind was in a full-scale fight with itself. People were dressed in colourful clothing openly talking without fear of using banned pronouns and names in a room that was so luxuriant it beggared belief and his 'one jab' medical assistant that he had previously barely shared twenty words with every month was laughing and joking whilst a gorgeous woman was talking to him and the lights were low and it was all going dark and the felt dizzy and with Cassia taking the glass from his hand, he promptly fainted.

Coming around with the use of some smelling salts, he sat bolt upright. He was now in a side room on a long sofa made of the same material as in the main hall. Next to him was John and Cassia. "Welcome back to the living... again!" said Cassia, "We have not had someone released like you for quite some time. You are the talk of the place at the moment!"

He started to get up, demanding his Personal Citizen Device and wanting to leave. "We cannot let you do that right now," said John. "In your state you are likely to go blubbering to anyone who will listen, you need to calm down first." John passed him his Rhapsody Blue, "here you started this, now get it in you to calm you down."

"Has this got some sort of drug to knock you out? Are you holding me here against my will? What do you want from me?" he blubbered

Cassia looked at John before turning to him. She had seen this before, some people take the transition from a life sentence of neutral existence to ways of the old world in their stride, like it was just a destination they knew was somewhere, which they had now found. Others, like Xe, have a complete meltdown, seemingly unable to escape the programming and narrative constantly pummelled into their mind by the New Government that anything but neutrality is evil, an 'ism' of every kind and a sign of your disdain for those around you, which will be punished to the fullest extent. Worst still was the public humiliation of being 'outed' and having society around you hate you for the crime of accidentally using a banned pronoun.

"No my friend, we are not drugging you or holding you against your will. Well, the second part is technically true, but that is for your welfare and for our survival at the moment," Cassia said with an understanding smile on her face.

Xe, hand shaking, finished the drink in one go and was immediately handed another by John, which was dispatched in the same manner, followed by a third. "Good," said John, "Now we are getting somewhere."

"He looks like a Tiberius to me," said Cassia, "Yes definitely a Tiberius, the square jaw does it for me, got to love a square jaw on a man."

"Hmmm," said John. "Yes, I see what you mean, yes, an unusual name, one I have never heard of before, but it fits, Tiberius it shall be!"

"Tiberius, good to meet you!" said John. "If of course that is the name you would like to be known by."

Again Xe just stared. This was too close for comfort, of all of the names that they could have chosen, they came up with the one from his dreams. It was still too much really for him to take in as John reached out to shake his hand. Tiberius, as he was now to be called, returned the greeting, slightly bemused as well as slightly drunk. "Is this how all people get their names in here?" said Tiberius to Cassia.

"Oh no, only the ones who I have to wake up!" she said with a smirk and a wink.

Tiberius looked down slightly embarrassed and accepted another Rhapsody

Blue from John, this one he drank a little slower, to ensure he was still conscious enough to get home, but home was not somewhere he would be going tonight.

"This is all too weird," Tiberius said slightly swaying and blinking furiously, "This morning the world was this grey, drab, boring neutral utopia, now I feel like I have died and gone to heaven. Have I died? Did that injection you gave me kill me off Xe…I mean John?"

John laughed again, "I like you Tiberius, you make me laugh. No, the injection is the same crap I put into people hour after hour, day after day. I do not know what is even in it, I get told to give someone a specific injection to a specific person, so I do. Sometimes they differ, sometimes they are the same. We are told that they are designed to fit with each individual's medical records. It does not bother me as I know I can come here and forget the hell above ground that is known as 'life'." He said the last word with such thick sarcasm you could cut it with a blunt knife.

"How did you find out about this place then?" said Tiberius.

"Same as you Tiberius," said John, "Someone saw something, I do not know what, but something and they took the life ending risk of telling me about this place. Sure, I was absolutely shitting myself when I first walked through that door, who wouldn't, the Keepers could crush you into non-existence just by flexing their eyelids! But somehow I had found the place that was in my dreams, a place where people were free to say what they wanted. Sure, it sometimes offends but people apologise and everyone gets on again. There is no need to ban everything that could possibly offend everyone like in the world above."

"We believe that if someone wants to find offence, they will and can do in every single thing they look at or hear. That baby is wearing pink and it is a girl and I think that babies should be allowed to make their own mind up to wear whatever colour they want and be free to suckle from either the mother or the father's breast because we are all equal and you should listen to me because I have a voice and I am sooo important in my world and in my opinion that I absolutely must project my opinion on to you and you must accept my opinion and that I am right and you are wrong if you don't agree with me and in fact are against me and thus must hate me for not agreeing with me kind of bullshit that happened in the old days." John took a long breath to recover from the diatribe of the old-world neutrality warrior.

As John recovered from his short-term lack of oxygen, Cassia giggled and said, "Offence is something that is always taken, whether given or not. You just need to extract your head from your arse and realise that no, you are not the most important person on the planet, no one is and just because you don't like something it doesn't mean that it has to be removed from existence. You know sometimes you can just say, 'I don't like that' and move on with your life."

"Here, here," John added suitably back in breath.

'The old days' it was something that Tiberius (damn he still could not get used to having a name, less one that he dreamed he had in his dreams) had heard rumours about. Tales handed down through verbal storytelling, never written down of course.

"So what do you know of the old days?" Tiberius asked. John merely looked at him and smiled, "You need to spend time here talking, learning, and living my friend. In time you will see, but it will take time and time is something you have I believe."

"What do you mean by that?" Tiberius asked abruptly.

"On your medical documents it stated Lay worker." Tiberius hated that description. A Lay worker was someone who was deemed not good enough for employment and thus received a basic living income, called a Statutory Monthly Allowance, from the state for doing nothing. It was just enough to keep someone from pursuing crime, but not enough to actually have any sort of life. He hated it, he was worth so much more, could do so much more, but some bureaucrat had labelled him as such and that was it, no way out, destined to spend his life dossing around, doing nothing, achieving nothing.
Noticing Tiberius's discomfort John stated, "Look we do not judge people down here, we judge people by the content of their character, by their deeds, their words, their actions and not by any label which they have been given. We are all individuals, we accept the responsibility that goes with that and behave accordingly, we do not need endless rules dictated to us by an authority, when in here, we live free, and you will too, when you have learnt to adjust. You are lucky to have time to be able to explore this new experience without something as banal as work getting in the way!"

Tiberius just wanted to sleep now. Whether it was the emotional rollercoaster, the several Rhapsody Blues or a combination of both, he was shattered. "I need to go home," he said.

"Nope," said Cassia as she pushed him into a reclining position on the booth seat. Tiberius was too drunk, too tired and with his brain feeling like it had completely melted, he offered no resistance.

"Sleep, the guys here will sort you out in the morning. Take it easy Tiberius and welcome to Speech Sanctuary 22, to home and to most of all welcome to a new life."

With those words, he closed his eyes and passed out.

Tiberius awoke the next morning to the sound of a hoover. Rubbing his eyes he looked around. "Morning!" the cleaner said merrily, it was one of the monsters on the door earlier, this time wearing a cleaning pinnie and a smile rather than the all black outfit and a frown that could kill you at ten paces.

"Morning," stated Tiberius slightly confused about what the hell had happened to him.

"I was told you would be in need of a full English when you woke up!" he said laughing. "Don't worry, John said it was on him!"

"Erm thank you," Tiberius replied. "Yes, that would be perfect."

"Stay put, I'll get it for you," he said as he chuckled to himself, strangely human now compared to the animal he appeared not a few hours ago.

It was exactly what he needed right at this point. John was so ahead of the game Tiberius thought, he must have been here a hundred times.

Ten minutes later a full English was placed in front of him and it was a full English. Tiberius demolished it and the coffee, the croissants, the juice, the toast and every last baked bean on the plate. "They always lick the plate clean after the awakening," said the monster come cleaner, "Must be some sort of emotional hunger I guess."

"Thanks, I was starving and this definitely beats the crap we have delivered to our apartments. I mean the eggs, sausages, bacon, toast, everything looked and tasted real," Tiberius said.

"That is because it was!" The monster chuckled

Real food, not the manufactured crap, just what is this place he thought? The authorities must know about it, otherwise how did they furnish it and run it like they do? He continued the conversation in his own head oblivious of the person stood there looking at him. Maybe it was a test and actually life is not that dull, maybe they need to go through this to be allowed to be free for some reason he thought.

Shaking his head at the ridiculous notion he looked up.

"Probably you best get yourself home now, looks like you need a dose of reality to bring you back down to Earth," the cleaner said. His voice snapped Tiberius out of his trance. "Yes, sorry was miles away there. Thank you. See you soon."

The monster come cleaner giggled as he walked off shaking his head. He did enjoy watching how these newbies reacted to home.

Tiberius collected his Personal Citizen Device by the front door, gave an obligatory nod to the huge creature stood there, apparently up here they were to be feared, downstairs they seemed more fun, then promptly went straight home taking the reverse route on foot that he had taken the night before.

He had millions of thoughts cascading through his mind, like the universal big bang in his head. Control, just fucking keep control till you get home he thought as he looked up and tried to pretend that he was just out for a stroll and that there was nothing to see here!

Closing his front door, he went straight to the bathroom and splashed cold water over his face and through his hair several times, before looking up and staring in the mirror at himself. "What the FUCK just happened?" He said out loud, before the biggest smile of his life spread across his face.

# Chapter 5:

# Secrets

"Your Statutory Monthly Allowance is costing too much. Do something to get it down or we will withdraw funding." The phone went dead. Premier Xe was not a happy person even when in his best mood, this call almost had him hyperventilating with rage.

The Chief Treasurer could make money to a certain level but even his cooking of the books could not produce endless cash.

Calming himself down before calling his Chief Scientist, he realised that he was cornered and had no option. The only way he was going to get the cost of having people sitting around doing nothing, was to reduce the number of people. The idea of killing off millions did not bother him, but it was risky and would require everyone to do their part and to keep their mouths shut.

The Chief Scientist answered her phone. Forgoing any introductions he simply stated, "Has syndrome XVS213-B been stabilised?"

"Yes, Premier Xe, I have spoken to the Chief Manufacturer and he said he can have enough for deployment and for the method of deployment in under a week, but I must insist it has not been fully tested yet and remains unpredictable. We do not understand how it will impact children predominantly and so we need more…"

"Release it," Premier Xe said then put down the phone.

Shaking her head in disbelief at Premier Xe, the Chief Scientist slowly put down her phone with a trembling hand. She may be heartless to most members of society, but she had a child and not knowing what this would do to them filled her with self-loathing and a burning hatred for the situation she was in. She knew the pain and suffering she was about to unleash on the country and she knew she had no choice but to do it.

With tears rolling down her face, she made the relevant calls. She had just become complicit in the mass murder of an estimated two million random people. "What the fuck have I just become," she said to herself as she slumped to her knees at home, sobbing. "I am not a monster!"

***

Tiberius woke eight hours later and immediately his mind started rushing with thoughts. Was the Speech Sanctuary a dream or was it real? Shaking his head he got up and walked into the bathroom, stepping into the shower, his mind buzzing again, he thought I have to go back and go back tonight, I need to know what this place is and what I can learn.

Tiberius was hooked on Speech Sanctuary 22 immediately, like a junkie after their first shot of Amaxocytin, the killer drug that so many took and that the authorities made no effort to prevent the sale of. It was a killer, but only of those stupid enough to take it, and the New Government were more than happy to lose a few more thousand people a year, saves money after all.

In fact, Tiberius pondered, the New Government did not seem to be that bothered about any drug anymore, but I guess the people need something to lift them out of the depression most felt and even the New Government did not begrudge them this small thing.

He shook his head and got out of the shower after the hot water had run out…again. Hot water in the showers was hit and miss lately. Still, it stopped him from daydreaming in there all day he thought and there is sod all I can do to change it so may as well get out and head off. Drying himself and putting on his clothing he stepped out into the fresh evening air and headed back out, this time, taking a differing route and method to be extra careful, he headed straight to 'home'.

Getting on the magtrain, he tried to not look suspicious. Looking around and seeing everyone else looking at him, he told himself to get a grip, he may as well be walking around announcing to everyone what he was going and what he was doing with all the fidgeting and scratching he was doing. He looked suspicious and he knew it by the way that parents were moving their children away from him.

Looking down, he got off at the next station and walked off the end of the platform, looking behind him to see if he was being followed. With a big sigh he gathered his breath as he saw he was the only one to get off. Turning back towards the way he was originally going he promptly walked straight into a pillar. 'FOR FUCKS SAKE!' He ranted at himself in his head, 'YOU ARE A FUCKING MORON, NOW GET A FUCKING GRIP MAN!' Waving his arms around whilst his brain argued with itself.

This did not go unnoticed, but the observer that saw it did, standing in the shadows with their hood up. He quickly walked up the streets, deciding to take a more convoluted route now after his display on the train and argument with a pillar, to be sure he had not blown everything already.

Eventually he arrived at the Speech Sanctuary and quietly knocked on the door in the correct manner. This time it simply opened. I guess the monsters, as he now decided he would continue to call the venue security, recognised him from the disaster of his first visit and probably felt real pity for him.

The Monster nodded his head to indicate that from now on he can hand in his own Personal Citizen Device, which he dutifully did, before making his way down the stairs, looking forward to his first Rhapsody Blue of the session.

Pushing through the curtain, he immediately stopped. It was Friday night and the venue was heaving with the free. There were people everywhere, laughing, joking and being well…happy.

In one booth there was a very heated debate going on that looked like it was about to get out of control before a monster slowly walked past. With his mere presence around they settled down, if a little grumpy. I guess there must be some rules of this place he thought, maybe I will get a guidebook one day he sniggered to himself, admiring the quality of his sarcasm that seemed to come from nowhere.

Again, mesmerised by the display of such fine clothes, he wondered how they got them, after all you did not simply pick them up in a New Government shop. The extravagant outfits were being worn by everyone, so silky and shiny, with beautiful cuts and designs, fitting so perfectly and well, not what he was wearing. Feeling slightly uncomfortable and standing out in the crowd he wanted to know how to get his own clothes.

"Tiberius!" shouted a familiar voice, snapping him out of the open-mouthed trance like state of an idiot he was obviously presenting to everyone, still standing by the velvet curtain. It was Cassia. "How are you feeling now?" she asked in that almost unreal tone of voice. She had a choice of words and a way of talking that would stop a riot dead in its tracks and succoured everyone into thinking she was the only person worth listening to at that moment in time, irrelevant of what she was saying.

"Hi Cassia," Tiberius said, "I could not get this place out of my mind, so I had to come back to make sure it was not a dream."

Cassia laughed a smooth and controlled laugh and said, "Come on in, I have a booth over here where we can have a chat." As they sat down and those decadent seats fitted around Tiberius's buttocks, Cassia ordered a Rhapsody Blue.

"You remembered," Tiberius said.

"How could I forget, you made quite an impression last night, you were the talk of the evening!"

Tiberius feeling rather embarrassed looked down at the table. "Oh come now Tiberius, don't worry, I could tell you how most of the people in here were on their first night. There is a reason we have smelling salts in this place. You were not the first and I very much doubt you will be the last, to faint!"

The bar assistant promptly served the Rhapsody Blue and Cassia passed it over to Tiberius. "How do I pay for these?" asked Tiberius.

"You don't," said Cassia. "There are rules of course, but just out of courtesy you do not get completely hammered and leave in that state. If you try then the Keepers will prevent you from leaving and you will spend the night in a booth. You may have noticed that they are rather large and more than capable of managing this task!"

Tiberius still preferred his name of the monsters for them, seemed more fitting.

"So what are these rules then?" Tiberius asked.

"I had better get to know them if I am to be frequenting this establishment!"

Cassia looked serious all of a sudden, which threw Tiberius out of his casual happiness.

"There are 6 rules. You do not, under any circumstance, break any rule or you will be silenced, by us. The Speech Sanctuaries are just that, sanctuaries and the New Government hold no mercy to them or to the people in them, if discovered. Premier Xe," Cassia almost went into a fit when she mentioned his name, "makes it his life's work to destroy them all. He knows that we are the biggest risk to his rule and he will do anything to shut them all. Speech Sanctuary Oscar was recently discovered by loose talk. The bastards waited and watched it for months before striking. Every person within was dealt with in the manner that the Peditata so relish. Those not in it at the time, were hunted down that night. Not one was seen again and no one has any idea of where they were taken, but we all suspect it was Detention Centre One."

"Yeah John told me about that when he invited me to come here. How many of these are there then?" asked Tiberius.

"No one knows," replied Cassia. "They are all independent of each other and you only stick to your own Speech Sanctuary out of respect and to limit the risk of one person being able to betray more than one home. This also limits the impact a New Government spy can have should they get into one. If this happens then only one will be destroyed."

"That is your first rule," Cassia continued, "Never visit another Speech Sanctuary, even if you know of another, you only ever go to your own, period!"

"OK, seems sensible." Tiberius replied a little sheepishly and took a mouthful of drink to hide his nerves.

"The second rule," Cassia said staring straight into Tiberius's eyes, "is that you never give away Speech Sanctuary 22, to anyone, no matter what! If you are casually asked, you know nothing of this place. If you are being beaten, you know nothing of this place, if you are drunk or off your skull on drugs, you know nothing of this place. Dammit even if you are being tortured and are at the point of death, you know NOTHING of this place! You die, it survives, clear?"

"Yes, crystal," Tiberius said taking another drink, visibly shaking the glass whilst doing so.

"Relax," said Cassia noticing, "These rules have to be hammered home for obvious reasons."

"Of course, I understand," replied Tiberius.

"Rule 3, never speak of who you see here to anyone. We have a lot of members and this place, this sacred place, is a haven for all. You may see some people you may know. In here we are all equal, irrelevant of status up there," Cassia stated as fact as she pointed up to the ceiling.

Tiberius nodded in acceptance as he finished off the first drink and ordered another.

"Rule 4, as I said, in here we are all equal. We never talk down to anyone nor offer any form of subservience to anyone, both are equally derided. We are one level, one people, behave like it."

"Rule 5, never start a fight. We encourage free speak, free debate, even if robust debate. It is the essence of life, of freedom, but we also encourage, in a somewhat firmer manner, respect for each other and for each other's opinion. If after a robust debate you still disagree with someone, then you agree to differ, shake hands and move onto a different conversation, perhaps with a different person. You never hold a grudge. Grudges lead to a desire for revenge and revenge destroys lives and Speech Sanctuaries. No one wins and people die."

"Now that you know of us and know these rules, we expect you to obey them."

Tiberius nodded as he started his next drink, boy he could drink a Rhapsody Blue all night. "You did say there were six rules though?"

"Good, you listen, that is a good trait to have." Cassia said, starting to smile again, "Rule 6…Be…FUCKING…FREE!" she shouted at the top of her voice raising her arms as she did so. A huge roar went up in the place as she did so. Tiberius looked around nervously with a half-smile on his face.

Cassia smiled in an attempt to calm Tiberius down a little stating, "Do not worry yourself, no one can hear anything in here, from out there. This was an old bomb shelter from times past apparently, completely soundproof to the outside world." This calmed Tiberius and he started to smile. "There," she said, "Your face looks so much prettier with a smile on it, even if it is only a half arsed one. What's up?"

"Why was I chosen? I mean why did John tell me about this place? If rule 2 is to not to tell anyone of this place, how come John broke that rule?"

"Now that is a good question! Good to see you are remembering the rules and engaging that soft, squidgy pink thing in there!" Replied Cassia pointing to Tiberius' head. "Some of us are allowed to invite new members, but only a few. John had been watching you for over a year and was moved by the way you looked out of the window how you appeared to be lost in your own mind even in a waking moment, thinking, and feeling about more than just getting a jab. It showed a deeper mind, one that could handle being free," Cassia laughed. "Well managed to handle being free after some Rhapsody Blues and smelling salts."

Recovering herself she continued, "He felt that you were deeper than most he saw in the hospital and we discussed you many, many times. You did not notice it but John continued to mention things, very subtly, to gauge your response. Remember the time you discussed with him about keeping secrets? That was a deliberate question to probe and understand you."

"Actually I do not remember that conversation," Tiberius replied.

"I am not surprised," Cassia responded, "John is very good at what he does."

"We had a good vibe about you so made the decision to invite you. I think it was a good decision."

"It is like my life has gone from A to Z in the space of less than a week," Tiberius said.

"I know it is a lot to take in," Cassia replied, "But you will in time."

At this point John came over. "Hey, how is my favourite John in the world tonight," said Cassia.

"Bloody marvellous," replied John, "I had a feeling you would be back, so thought I would pop down." John selected an Electric Ecstatic from the bar assistant.

"Oooh feeling naughty tonight are we," said Cassia.

"Yep. I have a good vibe about me at the moment so thought bollocks to it, get sexy!" said John laughing as he swept his hand down to show off his new shiny red shirt.

Cassia passed John his drink, it was also red in colour and seemed to have electricity arcing all over its surface. Tiberius went to touch it before John slapped his hand. "Ah! Ah! You will give yourself a nasty shock!" With a black plate like cover served at the same time, John extinguished the electricity and took a sip. "Oh boy, now that is a drink!"

Tiberius just looked and said, "Unbelievable! I don't think I am ever going to get used to this place, not even in two lifetimes!" Cassia and John laughed.

"So what's on your mind fella?" John said.

"I...I," stuttered Tiberius and sighed.

"Remember rule six my friend, you are free and rule four means you will be taken seriously," said Cassia.

"Ah good you have run him through the rules, that is one less job for me," John stated as he raised his glass at Cassia.

"It is a stupid question, but, well, how do you give people names? I mean you said I look like a Tiberius."

"We err, just come up with them. It just um, popped into my head," Cassia said.

"Yeah Cassia came up with that one, thought she was spot on as well," said John.

Tiberius said, "Well the reason I ask is that I have dreams, really vivid dreams about being free and out of the city, where there are no police, no Personal Citizen Devices just freedom. A bit like this place but for everyone. I have them all the time and in them people talk to me and they always call me… well, they call me Tiberius.

It just felt like you knew that I had these dreams and what was in them and it was all part of a conspiracy to catch me out and take me to Detention Centre One."

"Well that has never happened before, well that anyone has said to us! It was pure coincidence. We normally just name people by what we think they look like. John smelt like a toilet when I first met him, needed some serious freshening up, so his name came easily!" Cassia laughed

"Oi! Bitch! Yeah well I suppose it could be true," John replied chuckling. "There are all sorts of people of all different types in here, we try to use a different name for everyone, to further stick two fingers up to the New Government. We are not all the same to be herded like sheep, we are free and we all have our own identity and name."

"You all have stunning clothes as well!" said Tiberius pointing to them.

"Oh yes, yes!" Said Cassia tapping Tiberius' hand with hers. "You must come and see Flo. She makes the most exquisite clothing. Come on, drink up!"

John stood up to let Cassia out. "See you in a bit, I will be here trying not to electrocute myself!"

Cassia led Tiberius through a gap in the booths along one wall and through another thick red velvet curtain, which led to a room full of racks of clothes. At one end you could hear the whirring of some sort of machine. Tiberius just stood in total amazement and started to look through the clothes on the racks.

There were suits of every colour and material you could think of. Some had just a jacket and trousers, some had some other little mini jacket under the main jacket. Next to each suit was a shirt, sometimes the same colour, sometimes a different one but one that still went with the suit and was pleasing on the eye. Most of the shirts were made of the shiny material.

On another rack were ladies' dresses of just about every imaginable colour, style, and shape. The only thing they had in common was the fact that they were all beautiful beyond words.

Next to the dresses were the accessories. Watches, hats, strange stick like things along with necklaces and bracelets, as Tiberius was later to find out what they were called.

Next to the accessories was something that Tiberius had never seen first-hand before, but all of the women seemed to have on them in the sanctuary and on TV. "What is this stuff?" Tiberius asked.

"It's called make up, people use it to make themselves feel prettier and better in themselves." Fair enough Tiberius thought.

Just as this was said a man walked in and took one of the dresses off the racks, selected some jewellery and disappeared into a small booth. Tiberius looked back at the makeup, so many types and colours. What is this for?" he asked

Cassia said it was mascara used to make your eyelashes look darker and thicker.

"And this?"

"Lipstick, you put it on your lips like I have," she said as she leant forward and pouted her lips to him, displaying ample cleavage at the same time.

Diverting his eyes, Tiberius stated, "I often wondered how the people on TV and in those crap magazines look like they have painted their faces."

"Now you know!" Cassia smiled

After another couple of minutes of discussion over make up and accessories the man now wearing the dress, some jewellery and make up came out of the changing room and said hello to Cassia. They seemed to have a short conversation where Cassia appeared to be examining the man's face, now with makeup upon it.

With a few deft touches with her right little finger she smiled and said, "Perfect and beautiful!"

"Thank you," replied the man and placed the standard male clothing on the appropriate rack and walked back into the main room.

Cassia walked over and saw Tiberius looking confused. "Like I said, we are not judged in here and we are all free. Free to be who or what we want to be. Remember rule four?" Cassia said questioningly.

"We are all equal," replied Tiberius. "and rule six. Be...Fucking...Free!" He was liking this place more with every second he spent in it. Cassia nodded with a smile.

There was a chuckle coming from where the whirring sound was. Tiberius walked around the end of the rack of clothing that seemed half made to find an old lady hunched over a clothing making machine of some kind. "This... is the one and only Flo!" Cassia said using her arm to guide his line of sight to the only person stood in front of them, "The greatest seamstress our home could ever have dreamed of having."

"Hello Tiberius," Said Flo.

"Bloody hell, does everyone know who I am in here?" Tiberius replied.

Flo chuckled again, "Yep, well most anyway, you hit the deck with quite a thud when you fainted. Hee hee. I was in the booth across the way and saw it happen. I thought to myself I bet he is going to be trouble, never seen someone who's brain was in a complete meltdown quite as much as that before, I could almost see the sparks firing out of your ears! I thought this one is going to save us all or bring us crashing down. I sincerely hope it is the former of course."

Immediately changing the subject she said, "My immediate thought was blue, with a waistcoat perhaps. You look a dapper kind of man, just needs a little tidying up, like you all do when you first come in. You should have smelt John, oof had to tell him to get clean before I was going to go anywhere near him."

"Toilet," Cassia and Tiberius said at the same time looking at each other and laughing

"Yes, blue for the sky of freedom with a green shirt for the fields and trees," Tiberius started to feel nervous again, how do these people seem to know so much about his dreams?
"So, if you would be so kind as to strip naked and stand there for me, I will get you measured up for it if you are happy with my idea."

"Erm ok," Tiberius blushed at this point. He had never been naked in front of a woman before. Sex was apparently something that was required to keep the species running, not an act of love and he never felt the need to apply for a relationship permission licence that all couples needed. He certainly did not want to bring a child into this awful existence, for it would be better that a soul was born a bee than a human, at least it would be free.

"Oh for goodness sake, I have seen hundreds of naked men, I am sure your pendulum is no different to theirs!"

Cassia burst out in fits of hysterics, which did nothing to calm Tiberius down, nor make him feel less nervous. Cassia was still crying with laughter as Tiberius took off his underpants. "Well it is a little smaller than most I suppose!" Flo said in a dismissive and judging manner. It was too much and Cassia doubled up in the floor, barely being able to breathe.

Tiberius stood there as he was measured up, staring ahead and thinking *just put up with it, it is just part of being part of SS22. Well, I hope it is* he thought.

Cassia carried on looking over and a new round of laughter would hit her every time she did.

After about five minutes Flo stated, "There all sorted, your suit will be ready for you in three days' time. Just come in here and I will show you where it is, thereafter, you can just take it and change in the booths and hang your normal clothes on that rack over there. Make sure you put a tag on it so you know to get yours when you leave, this affront to fashion looks horrible no matter what body it is hung off of!"

"You can get dressed now and go back in."

"Thank you erm Flo, I er look forward to putting the suit on for the first time," Tiberius said in a nervous, stuttering voice, having to clear his throat a couple of times. Cassia was wiping the tears from her eyes indicating that she could not speak.
"Yes, yes, now go and have a drink, by the look on your face you need one!"

Tiberius picked up his underpants and looked up. A shadowy figure walked past, dressed totally in black, hood up, face hidden. There was no way of knowing who was under the clothing. They looked Tiberius up and down as they walked by, towards the opposite end of the room.

Tiberius just stood there with his pants in his hand completely naked. Cassia, standing next to Flo, both staring at his groin said, "I see your point Flo, it is indeed a little smaller than others you have seen I reckon," at which point Flo told her to go easy on the poor soul as Cassia fell about laughing again. When she regained her composure she looked up to Tiberius standing naked with all his clothes in his hands and said, "Come on let's go back in, I suggest you put those on first!"

Getting dressed Tiberius just looked at the two of them giggling and laughing to themselves now, in some sort of private conversation. Eventually dressed he said, "Come on then, seeing as you have had your fun for the day!" and walked back to the booth with Cassia.

John was still there and apparently had avoided causing himself any harm with his choice of beverage. John looked up smiling, "Did she get him to…"

"Absolutely," replied Cassia and the both of them fell about laughing. Tiberius was now starting to get a little annoyed. "What!" he demanded, "What is so frigging funny?"

"You do not need to take off your pants to be measured for a suit! It is Flo's little joke and she gets them every time! She calls it the 'Seamstress Privilege' and who are we to argue with her?" Cassia said.

"For fucks sake," Tiberius said, "Just get me one of those things John has, I fancy a change to get over that!"

Taking his electrified drink from John he stated, "Right, so in the last hour I have learnt the rules of this place, found a new drink and have been sexually abused by an elderly seamstress. Anything else you need to tell me!"

"What do you want to know?" replied John.

"Everything, how did this place come about? How long has it been here? How did someone afford to build it and do it in complete secrecy? Who comes here? Who was the person in the black clothing? What is the meaning of life? How do I forget about what happened back there?" Tiberius stated sniggering at the last question. "Wow, quite a list," John chuckled, "but you really do need to open your mind more. How long has this been here? No idea, no one has, it just is. It has always been here, no one knows how it was founded, put together or came to be, only that it was some sort of bunker in times past. Its mystery is part of its charm and we all love it more than life itself."

"Lots of people come here, but not too many members so as to create an opportunity to be discovered. You will see over time and learn about the members, their names, lives etc. Let that take time and develop as you become one of us. You cannot rush that one I am afraid."

One of us? That sounded a bit ominous to Tiberius.

"The person in the black that will be one of the hackers," John continued.

"Who are they? What do they do?" said Tiberius.

"Slow down and have a drink," Came the immediate reply. "The hackers are the ones that keep this place invisible. They have gained access to all the security systems that we know of in the New Government and ensure that we exist only in the mist. As you would expect, they are very important people, but as per the rules, equal to any of us. That said not any of us can do what they do and they are very handy when it comes to sorting out your good citizen value. Next time you hand it over ask for a few extra credits but for goodness sake don't ask for a stupid amount. They won't put it on there and it will be too obvious that you have not been to church every day for the last year or helped the authorities catch someone or rescued eight hundred bloody kittens in the last twenty-four hours.

We do not have conversations with them nor them to us, we merely provide for their every need to carry out the things we know about and do not ask questions about anything else they may be up to. They obey the rules of our home and we do not ask any more of a person than that. To be honest I do not know anyone who has seen their faces, so if I bumped into one tomorrow, I would have no idea who they are and I like that as if I ever get caught I would never want to betray them for they have helped me enormously in ways I would never tell anyone, not even Cassia."

Cassia nodded in acceptance that something had been kept from her. "We all have stories to tell about us and the hackers, stories that will stay with us even in a tortuous death," she said.

John continued, "The meaning of life. Wow how long have you got, because that one will take some time to get through, say about the entirety of the rest of our existence. I do however have someone who you might be interested in having a chat to. She is over the other side there," John said pointing to someone alone in a booth. "We call her The Historian. Come I will introduce you."

"See you later if your brain can handle it," Cassia said with a wink.

John led the way to a booth in the far corner. In it sat a woman in a thick, heavy grey cloak with the hood up. "Excuse me Historian, may I introduce you to Tiberius. Tiberius is new and eager to understand the meaning of life."

"That will take a while," came the response. A strangely deep voice for a woman Tiberius thought. "Please sit," she said gesturing to the seat opposite.

"I will leave you two to get acquainted then," John said and left to return to the booth with Cassia, turning mid stride, he said, "and you will never forget what happened back there!" pointing to the curtain behind which he was 'measured up' he turned and walked off laughing.

The two sat in silence, Tiberius nervously drinking and The Historian looking straight down at the table. She held her hands together at fingertips in a diamond shape breathing silently. Tiberius could not see her face behind the hood of the cloak and was starting to wonder whether it was a he or a she, not that he cared particularly. Shaking his head Tiberius thought to himself, wow, within two chaotic visits I am openly thinking about genders...

"Well?" said The Historian.

Tiberius said, "This is only my second venture into freedom and I have too many questions for my brain to contain."
"Well start with one of them then," said The Historian curtly.

"Tell me about life before this?"

"Before what?"

"Before, this?"

"What is this?"

"Exactly what is this?"

"What do you mean, you need to be specific."

'For Fucks Sake!' thought Tiberius, starting to lose his temper before remembering rule five, 'and breathe' he said to himself.
"I have often dreamed of freedom, of a life where the skies are not grey, where I am in a field of some sort of crop and the air is fresh and I am free."

"Congratulations. And?"

Ignoring the praise he continued, "This life, this existence, this experience is not that, why are my dreams so at odds with reality?"

"I don't know."

"Well great, that was really insightful."

"I am a Historian, not a Dream Weaver. If you have a question about the past I can help. Understanding why you think you are losing your mind and turning into some complete fruitcake whose brain is about to melt, well that is for someone else to untangle."

Tiberius took a deep breath and tried to come up with a specific question from the cauldron of insanity in his mind.

"What was it like in this country say a century odd ago?"

"Now there is a specific question that I thank you for," replied The Historian. "It was a time of what some would call normality. People going about their days in relative freedom."

"Relative freedom?" asked Tiberius.

"Relative freedom, yes," came the reply. "Freedom is only what you perceive it to be. Usually it is the fact that someone could go to a bar, such as this and speak freely, perhaps choose their own job, but that was just a ruse to make the people think they were free. All the time they were being manipulated by the secret services, spies, subversive coercion by both the authorities, the church, and the mainstream media as it was known back then.

The authorities made the laws, the church controlled the soul, the 'eternal soul' as they put it, and newspapers and TV outlets reporting the 'news', which was basically covertly pumping the narrative into people's minds every night. The truth is nothing, the narrative is everything.

The authorities hired the mobs to create the problems, the mainstream media told everyone how terrible everything was to keep them scared and want even more laws and the church allowed people to hide from the inconvenient truth of the fact that we are all going to die someday.

You see if you can get people to trust the 'free press' and its independence from the authorities, you create a sense of authenticity, when in fact the 'free press' is just another arm of social control along with the others I mentioned.

The three work hand in hand. A trifecta of control, as it still is today. The things around us change, but the core of society, the control by those in charge, largely stays the same. Now do not interrupt me again."

"Sorry," apologised Tiberius

"It was the days before the woke wars, the pandemics, neutrality. The days before totalitarianism took over and started to rule every aspect of everybody's lives in the name of equality of outcome, where everyone had to have the same result no matter how much effort was put in by them, resulting in the desire to improve things, invent things by people in society slowly dying off to the standstill it is today.

Many believed these to be great times, but again everything is relative. Great versus what? Versus the poverty of 1900? Versus the freedoms perceived of any moment in history?

If you want to use the word freedom you have to qualify what it actually means, the word freedom is utterly meaningless without it.

Other examples, yes you could own a car, but you had to obey rules to use it. Yes, you could go to a party, but there were social rules to obey in doing that. Yes, you could travel to other places on this Earth, but you had to declare who you are, where you were going, how long you would stay there, where you were staying and when you were returning.

All of the times your details were recorded on multiple databases, locations, amount spent, and length of journey, all recorded.

Is THAT freedom? Maybe relatively when balanced, with the threat at the time, of crime or terrorism.

So it was pretty much as it is today, it is only the perception of freedom that has actually changed.

You may speak now."

"Thank you. So, we have always been tracked and followed in some way?" said Tiberius

"Not so in the deep past," said The Historian. "But since the advent of the digital age, yes, your every movement, your every purchase, your every phone call, has been known to someone."

That did not come as a particular surprise to Tiberius. "What is this terrorism you speak of?"

"When people of one group used to use extreme violence against another, the aim to cause as much terror as possible. It was a ruse by the authorities, funded and coordinated by the very same authorities, to ensure that people looked away from them to spend their time and attention against an outside perceived threat. All the time you are looking outward, you are not looking inward, because if you did you would see the corruption and illegality of the very same people who were telling you they were keeping you safe. It was always done in the name of public safety, always."

"Sounds familiar," said Tiberius

"Again it is no different today to what it was back then, only today the outward threat is non-neutrality and the perceived threat comes from within our own borders, within our own minds and words. Quite a clever approach that requires no third country or outside power to be involved. It took some time to implement, but the strategy ran true and here we all are."

"OK so how did they get total control then?" Tiberius asked probing

"No one really knows when the line was crossed and the narrative became the only truth, when even those who started 'cancel culture' for their own narcissistic ends, their vanity, their ego and ultimately addiction to money and status, lost control of the beast they created and it became reality, it became everything. We only know of the rough time period it happened in.

One day they were enjoying voyeuristic hedonism and were ultimately in control, the next they were being cancelled by their peers as their lies and hypocrisy became revealed. Some tried to say that it needs to be stopped, but they were immediately cancelled and usually ended up losing their livelihoods and so often lives.

So they retreated and started to behave and obey the beast they had created. Soon everyone obeyed the beast, which was the only way to survive. No one controlled it, not even the Governments of the day but everyone obeyed it. The narrative had become the most powerful thing in the country and therefore had to be obeyed and followed without exception.

The politicians, of course, simply did what they do, they took advantage of a situation to enable them to achieve even more power.

"I do not understand," said Tiberius

"They are evil and believe so much in their own self-importance that when they speak the world listens, when in fact the world could not care about them for they are only a puppet of a greater power. Everyone is always serving an unseen master of some sort."

"Who?" asked Tiberius

"Whoever has the money has the power, whoever is pulling the strings of a strategy being played out in the background," replied The Historian. "Politicians are lying, spineless creatures suckling on the breast of power. They gain that power by being funded by those with money who hide in the shadows of life, rarely seen, but always in control. A politician is nothing but a puppet."

"So is Premier Xe under the control of someone else?" asked Tiberius

"Yes, almost certainly, it is what history tells us and true history does not lie. We all answer to a master of some sort, you just need to find out who the master is," The Historian replied.

"Who?"

"Like I said they hide in the shadows, I do not know as there are no records on it, but I would extrapolate from history that it would be someone or a group that are extremely wealthy. Even the New Government needs funding to keep the façade of utopia going. If there is no money, then the whole house of cards starts to fall and with it their power and their very reason for existing."

"Who would have that much money to be able to tell Premier Xe what to do?" Tiberius said out loud.

"As I said there are no records, so I cannot answer that question," The Historian stated.

"So freedom is only what I perceive it to be, Premier Xe is in the pocket of some rich person or people and we are being lied to about everything," Tiberius said more as a statement rather than a question.

"That would be a good summary of our conversation, yes."

At this point John returned. "Is you mind blown yet Tiberius?" he enquired. "I could sit here all night," replied Tiberius, "I have so many questions."

"All in good time, now let the Historian be, there will be ample time for future interrogations!"

"Thank you for your time," said Tiberius to the Historian who responded with a nod and said, "I suspect we will be having many more interactions in the future and I look forward to it."

"That we definitely will!" Tiberius said as he left with John.

Moving back over to the previous booth Tiberius sat down next to Cassia lost in thought.

"What's on your mind?" said Cassia.

"Just about everything, but mostly how we are all prisoners of something we created but are too fearful to stop, even though almost everyone wants to stop it. Something that is not even real, just a made-up way of life, to be obeyed at all times and at all costs and nobody knows where it fucking came from! So much misery, so much waste of life for what?"

"Welcome to the club my friend, welcome to the club!" said John as he raised his glass and said, "To living a fucking miserable existence that everyone is too scared to argue against!"

"Cheers!" they all stated as they clinked the glasses together.

"Maybe that is why I keep having these dreams, maybe I am supposed to do something to change this."

"Perhaps," said Cassia, looking at Tiberius over the rim of her glass, "perhaps."

"So what is behind that curtain then?" said Tiberius.

"Do you not remember? It was where you came round after your first visit!" said John smiling

After taking a sip Cassia said, "Come with me," and got up. Tiberius followed as the two went through the curtain. There appeared to be five booths with curtain pulled across the front for additional privacy. Two were occupied. "This is somewhere you may wish to come for a little more, how shall I put it, intimacy for a little more carnal fun," said Cassia. "Here hold this for me and wait in that booth over there, I need to go to the loo." Tiberius sat in the first booth as instructed trying not to listen to the giggling and strange noises coming from the booth next to him.

By the sound of it there appeared to be at least one man and three women in there, doing something that appeared to be very 'entertaining', judging by the noises and laugher drifting out, noises Tiberius was unfamiliar with. They all seemed to have some sort of affliction that slurred their speech, yet seemed to make them giggle, very odd he thought.

Tiberius just sat looking around and half listening to the group when suddenly the curtain pulled back with a swift tug and out came a man with three women, still laughing and joking. Tiberius was quite pleased with himself getting the number of people correct, so much so he did not realise he was staring. "Good evening," said the man, "Would you care to borrow a couple of my friends here?"

The question flustered Tiberius and he immediately blushed, which was a signal for the women to burst out laughing again.

"Errr, no, no thank you, very kind but I erm am just waiting for someone to come back," Tiberius finally managed to stutter out.

"I bet you are, you naughty thing!" the man replied. "You have yourself some fun now won't you!"

Just as they were about to leave, Cassia walked back in and exchanged glances with the man. Cassia nodded as in she knew him or there was some mutual respect for being in the same place. One of the women whispered loudly enough for Tiberius to hear, "I think you have your work cut out with this one. Feel free to use some of the Neeja from our booth if you need it" and burst out laughing again. Tiberius really could not work out what was so funny and was feeling desperately introverted and nervous.

Cassia smiled politely whilst clearly unimpressed with their choice of words and attitude but obeyed the rules of the sanctuary perfectly and sat down opposite Tiberius as the women from the group walked back into the main room and the man went behind the curtain in the corner. Tiberius thought they were going to come back with another man and carry on and was not sure if he could take one of the women's cackling laugh any more without having to leave.

"What was that about? What were they doing in there?" Tiberius asked almost childlike.

Cassia just looked at him, like a sympathetic big sister would to a toddler sibling and said, "You really are that innocent, aren't you?" Tiberius looked down.

"Look," said Cassia, "People come in here to take drugs, drink and have sex, or to do dodgy deals of some kind, or both, or a combination of all of the above perhaps. Who knows it is up to them, no one is judged in here.

This area is deliberately set to one side so that the main hall can be free of some of humanities more carnal desires that are encouraged by freedom and allow the rest of us to just have some fun and a good drink. This is not a rule as such but more an act of respect for each other. This place is not called a sanctuary for nothing."

At this point the cleaners arrived at the recently vacated booth. Consisting of two people and a trolley of various cleaning equipment, soaps, rags, and the like, they set about cleaning it up ready for the next 'party' to use it. Tiberius continued to wonder where all these people came from around this place. It was like a well-oiled machine but had no obvious working parts, it just… worked.

Snapping back into reality Tiberius asked, "So what is this Neeja he mentioned then?"

"Neeja is a narcotic, a drug that changes your brain chemistry and makes you believe that you are the most important person in the world and that the world only has happiness and freedom in it whilst you are high. The outside world simply does not exist for that moment; it is a kind of fluffy world that only exists in your immediate environment and company and exists only for your total pleasure.

It is particularly favoured when taken with others and drink and sex are almost always involved. It creates a kind of hedonism that is so juxtaposed to our existence, it is quite…liberating really."

"Have you taken it?"

"Of course I have, everyone has and if you want some come and see me, but all in good time, you have the same look on your face as you had the first time, so I think you have had enough excitement for one evening! Let's get back to the booth and you can drink up and get yourself off home to take in the night's insights. You are learning so much, so fast, but we have only scratched the surface. Give yourself a break for a week or two to calm down and take what you have learnt so far into your brain and we will see you soon. Come on."

Cassia led Tiberius back over to the booth they were in with John still sat there but with someone he introduced as Veefar. She was short woman but quite stocky with very short brown hair and a large scar on her left cheek. Tiberius, head swirling and looking pale, said various pleasantries and finished with a "Goodnight" before heading off.

Just as he turned, John called out, "Tiberius, you have destroyed my number you shoved up your arse haven't you?"

Tiberius smirked with a tired smile and said, "Yes John. Don't worry, but I might have to come and see you about the paper cuts I now have!" John roared with laughter, "Goodnight my friend!"

Tiberius headed back up the stairs, reclaimed his Personal Citizen Device and left the building with a respectful nod to the Monster on the door, whom returned the farewell whilst looking down at least twenty inches to Tiberius's eye line.

The journey home was uneventful and Tiberius walked into his apartment, sat down on the sofa, stripped off and climbed into bed. Staring at the ceiling about all that he learnt and how the reality of life was slowly being exposed to him and at the same time learning just how naive he was.

As he drifted off to sleep, he found himself standing in his field of crops, staring at the horizon.

Outside the apartment block his observer, wearing a brown cloak with a black cord belt, made a call and stated that he had made contact with Speech Sanctuary 22 and had returned home.

"Good," came the reply on the phone. "See to it that he is kept in sight and above all see that he is kept safe."

# Chapter 6:
# A Case of the Sniffles

"It has been released," came the voice of the Chief Manufacturer on the end of the phone to Premier Xe. "In the usual manner. Anyone touching the Good Citizen publication will become infected and will pass it on to those they come in contact with. All the necessary parties have been informed."

"Good," Premier Xe stated, putting the phone down.

***

The following week or so was largely uneventful as Tiberius took Cassia's advice and spent some time at home, walking about town, sometimes to the park when it was not raining. He was trying to sort out the mess in his head but was not sure whether he wanted to go any deeper or quit now and pretend it never happened. He was scared that he would find something that could never be forgotten and that blissful ignorance of it would have been the better option. His mind needed to be cleared and he needed to work out what his next step would be, but instead he just kept going around in circles in his head.

Saturday came around and it was cold with a mix of rain and showers. Tiberius felt it apt given the current mess of his mind, and the fact he was not making things better there by staying in this apartment. Drinking and thinking was a mix that was never going to resolve the turmoil, so he decided to take in an evening of Brutus. Strangely, for some reason his copy of Good Citizen had not arrived, but he did not care today. You would not have my company, nor be blinding me with your teeth tonight JJ! He said to himself after the decision was made.

He headed out of the door and took the magtrain straight to the stadium, determined to watch people bash each other and basically try to inflict as much pain and suffering as possible. Yes, he thought, that will definitely help me clear my mind, in a certain self-righteous and hopeful way. Others on the magtrain quietly moved away from him as he continued to talk to himself in his own little world, which resulted in head movements that made him look like he was completely insane.

It would not have been a surprise to him if he was.

Leaving the stadium station, still holding the conversation in his head and looking like a human made of oil within a crowd of water, he walked up the long path leading to the entrance.

The path between the station and the stadium entrance gently sloped up and had huge 30-foot stone statues of past fighters all along it, thus was the glory achieved for the simple task of staying alive. Known as the path of champions, each statue saw the fighter in their favourite kit and had a plaque at the bottom, with their fighting name and Xe designation, detailing who they were and their fight record. There were places available for future fighters to be remembered for all time and Tiberius often wished he was brave enough to be stood there, but he was too scared to fight his little apartment friends let alone take part in these games.

As he approached the entrance, he stopped to look at the enormous banners hanging on the outside walls. One was of his favourite fighters, Crixus. The fighters were allowed to go by a name as part of the fight but when out in public they were still called Xe with the obligatory number attached.

Crixus was big, very big. A mountain of a muscle, controlled aggression and sheer power. Not many that went up against the past champion stood a chance. 'Crixus loves the fight because Crixus lives for the fight!' was his strapline, yelled at the top of his voice whenever he won, which was just about every time and which the crowd returned with a loud roar of delight!

Tonight was going to be a good night, Tiberius felt it in his bones as he entered, scanning his Personal Citizen Device. Entrance was free as it was seen as a good distraction for the people, a way for them to let off steam without actually becoming violent towards the New Government to do so and as such Premier Xe declared it was his 'gift to the people' when he took the charge away after he ascended to the Premiership. It got him off to a good start and managed to temper the disquiet starting to rise in the country.

Tiberius picked up his programme and the first of five free alcoholic drinks allowed per person. Walking through into the main auditorium, he stopped to take in the scale and magnificence of the place, it always took your breath away entering this huge space, full of thousands upon thousands of people. It was simply cavernous and he often wondered how on Earth the thing actually remained standing.

Walking up the steps to his row, he shuffled along before finding his seat and sat down. Each seat had a holder for his drink, not much choice on the menu, in fact the only choice was beer and there was only one choice of that but it was beer and it was strong and most of all it was free. No one ever left the stadium less than three quarters intoxicated, if they took their fill of the free drinks.

Next to him were the heat sensing goggles and voting pad that could be used for the interaction of the audience in some matches. Flipping the lower half of the seat down, he sat. The seats themselves were not particularly comfortable but were functional and did the job.

Looking at the people around him the usual insane "Xe", "Xe", "Xe", "Xe", "Xe", "Xe", "Xe", "Xe", "Xe", "Xe" greeting went on as every Xe nodded politely to the one around them using the shorter greeting. The night would have been over by the time they finished using the more formal one with a number, especially with the amount of sneezing everyone appeared to be doing. "The 'one jab' needs to get updated," he said whilst nodding like a maniac in greeting to all of the attentive people around him."

"Yeah, came on yesterday, seems to be spreading like wildfire this one. The 'one jab' will sort it out, no worries," came a reply.

There was no age restriction at the games so plenty of children were here to watch and occasionally steal a sip of a beer left unattended. When children were permitted to attend the audiences grew massively as people no longer needed someone to look after them whilst they went to the games. Their inclusion did not limit the language or violence involved and you could see the influence in playground play as they played out their favourite fights as their favourite fighters.

Looking down at the programme, which was basically a leaflet with space for five tear off strips at the bottom, one for each beer claimed, Tiberius said in his head, so as not to cause anyone the micro-chance of being offended, 'You have got to be kidding me! JJ is the celebrity for tonight's matches? I thought that dickhead was doing his show, I cannot get away from this freak!'

Above JJ on the programme was a huge image of Crixus, surrounded by smoke. Good he will be here tonight. I wonder how many they will set against him to try to make it fair this time he thought.

In the bottom right corner was an image showing the four teams that were in matches. He noticed one was a military and another a police team. I hope they are matched together, that will be a brutal one!

Top right was the order of games. Tonight's matches would start with a one-on-one match between a fighter called Mevia and Flamma. This was unusual in that Mevia was a woman. In the world of neutrality, there was no distinction between the genders of the fighters, and they would be matched by how the league fell fight to fight. In some cases it was a ridiculous pairing which had the result of a very short match with a much larger male fighter winning within a few strikes. A few would result in a much larger woman beating a smaller man, but quite often it made no difference and the pairing would be quite evenly matched. Mevia was known for being small but particularly nimble and very fit. She would often wear a larger opponent down then strike, other times her speed of thought and body would be more than enough to take down many much larger fighters.

The Exhibition match was next. As usual there were no details, but it stated this would be a 'special one'

The Destroyer vs Crixus was the second of two one on one fights. Crixus would have a serious match on his hands tonight. The Destroyer was just as large and powerful. This would be a real battle of the beasts! He thought, hopefully a real slugfest!

The first of the team matches was between team called 'Gladiatori vs The Olypamaniacs. Tiberius had not heard of either of them, so was open to seeing how this one turned out.

Which meant the second and final team match and the final match of the evening was between 'Military Mayhem and The Peditata Pummelers'. Oh yes! that was going to be one to remember!
The crowd roared and Tiberius looked up to see JJ entering the fight zone via a lift in the centre. It seemed that his hair was going to take four times longer to appear than the rest of his body, but sure enough given enough time, those search light like teeth appeared and up he popped, holding a shield, a club and a rose.

He should take part in a fight he thought. Between his teeth blinding the opposition and his hair spearing an entire team in one run, no one would stand a chance against him he chuckled to himself, slowly leaning to his right as to his left the sneezing continued, only to be met by more sneezing from the right.

"Welcome to Brutus! Welcome to the Games!" JJ stated over the PA system, the crowd cheered as the excitement started to rise.

No escape from JJ on a Saturday night Tiberius said to himself, might as well start drinking now!

"Tonight we have games that are going to blow you away. We have the mighty Crixus, the Destroyer, Mevia and Flamma!" The crowd cheered after each name as they started to wind up for the fight.

"We have a Military vs Police match up which we all like to see, I don't think there will be much hugging during that one!" The crowd laughed at the truly dreadful joke that JJ was so renowned for.

"Two new teams, who have never fought before, we all love to see the innocence of a first fight and of course we have an exhibition match that you are not going to want to miss!"

"Are you ready for a fight?" he called out.

"Yeah!" the crowd responded.

"NO, NO, NO! I SAID ARE YOU READY FOR A FIGHT TONIGHT PEOPLLLLLLLLLEEEEEEEEE!"

"YEAH!" came back a louder response

"DO YOU WANT BLOOD?"

"YEAH!"

"DO YOU WANT BROKEN BONES?"

"YEAH!"

"DO YOU WANT BRUTALITY?"

"YEAH!"

JJ threw down the shield and club and gently placed the rose on top.

"THEN LET THE GAMES BEGIN!" he said as he stood with him arms above his head. They still did not match the height of this hair.

The crowd went nuts shouting, screaming, waving their programmes and above all sneezing.

JJ started to descend back into the bowels of the stadium as Mevia came running into the fight zone from the far right, with Flamma coming out walking from the felt. The Rules Commanders came from the two entrances on the shorter sides of the oval. Mevia was carrying a small shield about ½ meter square and a club. She was not wearing any armour, instead just a tight material fighting suit with a medium sized dagger tucked into her waist. The fighting suits were light allowing for much more manoeuvrability but offered absolutely no protection to the fighter. Mevia was clearly going for agility rather than power. Flamma himself was of average build and height but had chosen a full armour suit, massive shield and long sword type weapon that had lots of blunt stubs coming off each side. You would not want to be on the receiving end of that landing Tiberius thought to himself, that would smash all of your ribs in one hit. He was trading speed and manoeuvrability for sheer power and protection.

Mevia was taking a big risk with her choice, but as the two opposing fighters or teams chose their tools for the fight in isolation, no one knows what the others are going to wear or arm themselves with until they face each other in the fight zone. This added a requirement for intelligence and quick thinking into the fighters as they sometimes had to adapt their pre-planned strategy to what was presented in front of them.

Mevia charged at Flamma as he started to rotate his weapon above his head as he hid behind the shield. With almost a blur of movement and perfect timing Mevia leapt over the shield between rotations and brought the club down hard onto Flamma's thick metal helmet with a loud 'dong!' that was audible even with the cheering and sneezing going on. Landing behind him, she twirled ready to launch another attack.

As Flamma turned she leapt again but this time mistimed it and was caught by his sword that sent her flying at least 10 meters away. Screaming in agony knowing that a lot of ribs were gone she lied crumpled on the floor, desperately trying to recover. The Rules Commander came over to check and stated that the fight was to continue. Flamma walked towards her still behind his shield but with the sword raised above his head ready to deal the winning blow.

Mevia was in total agony, every breath hurt like she was being stabbed each time she took a breathe. She had to think and think fast. He was simply too well armoured and she no longer had a shield or club, what did remain on her was her dagger.

Flamma started to play the crowd by turning around in a slow circle, knowing his prey was incapacitated. As he lifted the shield and the sword the crowd cheered and he milked it for all that it was worth.

This was a big mistake, in Brutus you don't show off, you finish the job, but this showboating had allowed Mevia to start to control her breathing and thus her pain and crucially had given her time to think.

Flamma moved over to an apparently critically injured Mevia. Stood before her the crowd were ecstatic, with the noise rising as he lifted his sword and shield screaming "aaaarrrgggghhhhhh!" to finish the job.

Mevia saw her chance. As Flamma brought down his weapons Mevia rolled under them and around the back of his legs. Screaming in pain and holding her damaged ribs as she moved, she grabbed the dagger and cut deeply across the back of his unarmoured ankle. Flamma screamed and went down on one knee, clipping Mevia's head as he did so with a solid thump and dropping both his shield and his weapon. Mevia now in agony and dizzy due to the blow on her head sliced across the back of his other ankle, which had the effect of Flamma falling backwards and grabbing both of his ankles with his hands.

The Rules Commander rushed in a declared that as Flamma was incapacitated and could no longer fight, was out of the match. Mevia was declared the winner just before she passed out.

The crowd was going nuts at this point.

"What a fight!" Xe to Tiberius' right said wiping his nose of snot, now that is how these games should start!

JJ came back onto the PA, "Hey Hey! How did you like that peoplllllleeeeee!" The way he said that really grated Tiberius, in fact everything JJ said and did grated him. You really need to chill out about JJ, Tiberius noted to himself in his head.

"Take a break and grab a beer people while we set up the exhibition match that you are going to love!"

Xe stood up, he had necked his first beer and was ready for another, leaving sneeze city, he went back to the foyer. It had a very simple layout of two rings with the walkway in the middle that went around the entire building. On the inner side were the beer stalls, with the occasional food stand. Opposite, on the outer walls were the toilets with various doors leading off to who knows where in between.

They were designed for two things, getting people in and out and getting people their beer as quickly as possible.

About ten minutes later and with a fresh beer, Tiberius sat down again. When he came back into the stadium arena, he noted that the netting had been pulled up. "Ooo! Looks like a flying animal one!" he said out loud.

Snotty Xe as Tiberius had now called him in his head said, "Absolutely, not feeling great but got to stay for this one!" without noticing again that the child sat next to him took another gulp of the beer in his holder as he had been doing all night so far. Tiberius winked at the kid, who smiled back, not realising the pain he would wake up to tomorrow. Tiberius was in no way going to warn him and prevent this rite of passage from his life experience.

JJ came back on. "Grab your heat sensing goggles because the lights are going out in 5, 4, 3, 2, and lights out." The whole place went jet black, you literally could not see your hands in front of your face, then a gentle green light glowed as the stadium was lit in a strange deep dark green glow. It allowed the forty fighters stood in the centre back-to-back forming a circle, to just about make each other and the various obstacles, out. They looked like shrubs and bushes in the gloom but the level of light made it hard to see clearly.

"Here we go peoplllllllleeeeee!" JJ said, Tiberius clinched his jaw, oh just give me two minutes in there with him, please. "5, 4, 3, 2, FIGHT!"

The fighters mostly sprinted away to find cover and take stock of where they were. Some started fighting immediately with three falling quickly and being judged out of the game, the rest were scattered. For the next ten minutes they were stumbling and moving around trying to find each other in the pitch darkness, before starting to fight. One group of five had decided to create a group and ambush individual fighters to improve their chances and end their opposition's.

Suddenly, as the fighters looked for each other, with the crowd screaming out everyone's locations to try to guide in the fighters, a whole host of smaller heat sources appeared in the fight. They looked like some sort of flying creature about the size of someone's hand through the heat sensing goggles. Tiberius had never seen this before and started to shout out warnings to the fighters. Being about fifty odd rows back, there was no way they would hear him but he was emotionally involved now.

The new entrants were just flying around to start with but then a fighter would trigger something that looked like a puff of smoke in the goggles, by stepping on a trap. Almost immediately after doing this the new entrants would swarm onto the fighter who would start waving their arms around and appear to be screaming. Eventually they would collapse ending up in the foetal position as they appeared to be stung by something, well by many somethings. When one of the group of five triggered a trap and the swarm moved onto them, all five dropped almost instantly, screaming so loud you could hear them over the crowd, many fighters froze, not knowing what was going on, what the animals were or why they were attacking certain fighters.

One fighter seemed less bothered and walked over to each grounded fighter and started to beat the defenceless person with a club. The Rule Commander followed him around calling the fighters out of the match one by one. It was at this point Tiberius noticed them wearing some sort of additional netting around them.

Eventually the combination of traps sprung, stings and one on one fights, it rolled down to two fighters left. One looked big and the other one, who was walking around as if they did not care looked scrawny and much smaller.

The big one approached the other from behind and dropped them in one swipe. In doing so he tripped a trap and the swarm descended. Eventually he fell as the scrawny one got up, stumbling. One quite brutal hit to the head, finished the match and he was announced the winner.

The crowd loved it; it was really different and were cheering for the winner as the lights went up and they took off the goggles. A Rules Commander walked towards a large box puffing something into the air and the flying creatures followed him in.

The winner was seen on the central TV cluster standing with his hands aloft and the biggest smile Tiberius had ever seen on someone's face. As the Fight Zone was being cleared JJ appeared and announced the winner as a prisoner from Detention Centre One who had won their freedom by winning the match.

The prisoner was bouncing around like a child and was wiping tears away from their face, ignoring the blood trickling down the back of their head, as they took the applause from the massive crowd. Eventually the winner went to the centre trap door that JJ had appeared in at the beginning and descended with him. Once out of sight of the crowd JJ screamed, "Get your fucking filthy little hands off me!" The prisoner's smile cracked a little, but he was still a free man now so who cared if this idiot liked him or not.

At the bottom JJ walked off with a mass of people dusting him down and fussing all over him. The prisoner, now free man, was taken down one of the underground corridors and asked to enter a room, where his citizen clothing would be waiting for him. He was told that a New Government official would be in soon to give him his new Personal Citizen Device and assign him an apartment. "Well done," they said to him, "you are the first prisoner to actually win!"

Excitedly cleaning himself up and putting on the new clothing, he waited as instructed. About five minutes later another official walked into the room to find him virtually bouncing off the walls. "Hello Xe," they stated. "Hi, oh my goodness I am so excited! I am going to be able to see my partner and child for the first time in as long as I can remember. My child is going to be around 5 years old now I think, I have not seen them in so long but I cannot wait to cuddle them!" The newly restored and free citizen stated, hardly able to contain their excitement nor the enormous smile on their face.

"Indeed and you should be happy, we are all happy for you! One in the eye for the New Government eh!" They replied as they shut the door.

***

JJ walked back in the opposite direction, with his entourage fussing over him as usual and telling him repeatedly how great a person he was.

As they turned a corner, a single shot rang out. Prisoners never won, even if they won.

Back in the fight zone, next up was Crixus vs the Destroyer. It was an open Fight Zone, with no obstacles, just a straight one on one fight which ended up being a bit of a boring fight. Both were about the same size and similar in equipment choice and strategy. The only difference seemed to be one being left-handed and the other right-handed. It eventually became the slugfest, between the two mountains, that Tiberius had wanted, but lasting fifteen minutes or so was becoming boring. Eventually, with booing from the audience heard all around, an identical manoeuvre was released by both. Due to the difference in hand preference they both swung their clubs at head height without shield coverage.

With a dual "Clang!" that went around the whole building and made even the Rules Commander wince, they both dropped to their knees and fell unconscious. Due to The Destroyer hitting the deck a split second after Crixus he was declared the winner, and they were carted off as per the first fight, only this time it took significantly more people to do it.

Tiberius got up to get another beer, the child continued to steal sips and glugs from Snotty Xe's beer.

More drinks flowed, more sneezes were let fly over the course of the first team fight, which due to the virginity of the teams was very cautious and boring. Eventually The Gladiatori won through, but they were going to have to up their game for the next fight if they wanted the crowd on their side in future. Now the people started to get fired up by the prospect of a Military vs Police fight.

By now Tiberius was really noticing just how many people were sneezing. He started to feel dirty and wanted to just get out, but after four beers and the prospect of the next fight, he decided to stay.

Tiberius got up again to claim his fifth and final beer and wash his face in the sink in the toilet, before re-joining the games for the final match.

"OK PEOPLLLLEEEEEE!" JJ announced. "HERE IT IS! HERE IS THE MATCH OF THE NIGHT THE MILITA RRR YYYYYYYYYYYYYYYY VERSUS THE POOOOOOOOOOOOOOOO LICE!"

The two teams marched in from their respective sides to stand facing each other approximately 20 meters apart.

"NOW BEFORE WE SEE THESE TWO PARTAKE IN A LITTLE SPORT I JUST WANT TO TELL YOU BOTH SOMETHING. EALIER IN THE NIGHT WHEN I WAS SPEAKING TO THE MILITARY TEAM, THEY STATED THAT THE POLICE WERE JUST MILITARY WANNABEES AND THE POLICE STATED THAT THE MILITARY WERE JUST A BUNCH OF FAT, REDUNDANT NOBODIES WHO SAT AROUND IN THEIR BARRACKS PLAYING WITH ONE ANOTHER! I THOUGHT THAT'S A BIT RUDE BUT HEY PLAY NICELY NOW CHILDREN!" he finished off as he slowly descended into the floor of the arena.

The two teams did not need to be fired up any more than they were already, but to be fair to JJ he had managed to do it. It was again an open fight zone but these two teams were very well drilled and very aggressive. They were similarly armed with clubs and small shields of varying types as their preferred styles were up close and personal

The fight started with the two of them prodding and jabbing, trying to find a chink in the defences of the other, if one of them fell the rest were quick to move in as a unit to get them back up and in the fight again. As this went on the crowd started to boo; this was not what they expected and soon empty beer containers were being thrown onto the pitch. "LOSERS! LOSERS! LOSERS!" the crowd started to chant which had the desired effect of humiliating them in front of the very people that they were supposed to be in control of.

Eventually someone on the front row yelled at the police, "You police are all a bunch of losers, we know how to fight you now!" Another voice yelled "The old people in my apartment block can fight better than you!" then disappeared back into the mass of people just in case their face was noted for a later 'conversation' with the authorities.

This was a red rag to the police's pride and they all instinctively charged at the Military, smashing aside shields before it turned into a massive brawl. This sent the crowd wild as the two teams slugged it out in the middle, dropping to the floor could be the end of a fighter, such was the hatred between the two old foes, so they stood firm whilst taking almost inhumane levels of punishment.

Tiberius was well into this fight screaming out instructions that were never heard and waving his arms around like he was in there himself. He did take a second or two to think about how someone could possibly train to be that resistant to physical pain, but that soon went as another police officer fell and the crowd cheered loudly.

Eventually there was one police officer left standing, holding aloft a club with a blackened nob the size of a fist and swirling in style about her head. The pictures that went around of the fight showed her in this position with one foot on the head of an unconscious and bloodied member of the Military team.

JJ, now up in the VIP box overviewing the fight zone, turned to the Brutus games CEO stating that, "That image is going to make the rematch between these two groups no holds barred."

"Oh yes, in fact I am going to give each team up to one hundred fighters with the same kit and remove the negative points for fatalities. It's going to be explosive! In fact, I might put a few of those in there as well!" Said the CEO laughing with JJ.

Speaking over the PA from the CEO's office JJ announced the end of the games for this night in his usual fashion stating, "There we have it people! Speed, strength, action and PAIIIIIN! Just how we like it! Until next time good citizens, BRUTUUUUUUUUUUUUUSSSSSSSSS!" The crowd that was left in the stadium roared with the familiar sign off for the games by JJ.

Tiberius heard it from the stairwell as he made his way out as quickly as possible to get away from all the sneezing people. It was a great night and had cleared his mind enough to get back to the Speech Sanctuary for a couple of Rhapsody Blues to finish the night off.

Walking down the steps and thinking about the great clothing he was about to put on, he walked through the velvet curtain to be faced by John is some sort of panic.

"I am so glad you are here," he said.

"Why? What's up?" Tiberius said.

"People are dropping like flies Tiberius, something has got out and it's lethal," John said looking around. The place was near empty. As soon as anyone came in John was grabbing them to tell them what is happening. "I know someone who works in the manufacture of the jabs I give. He said that we need to get inoculated as soon as possible as this thing is lethal Tiberius, it is lethal! It seems to take a few days to kick in but once it takes hold it seems to be killing people in a matter of hours, especially the weak and the elderly as usual."

"OK calm down John or you are going to give yourself a heart attack," said Tiberius. "I am not elderly and as far as I know, do not have any reason to be worried ok."

"That is not the scary bit Tiberius, this one is also taking out a lot of healthy people and children as well as weirdly a lot of Lay workers!" he continued

"Wait, wait, wait," Tiberius interrupted. "How can a disease target someone by their job type. I'm not falling for this one," suspecting a joke was in play.

"WILL YOU FUCKING LISTEN TO ME!" John snapped.

Tiberius stood to attention. "Sorry, I am just really stressed at the moment because I am part of the group that will be letting people die, and I cannot bear the thought of it."

"Right, slow down and sit down and start again," Tiberius demanded.
John took a deep breath. "I was told that the New Government has released some sort of bioweapon that has spread across the country like wildfire. If anyone has any sort of co-morbidity or are elderly, they are not standing a chance. Remember I told you that I just jab people with whatever they tell me to?" Tiberius nodded. "Well, this month's 'one jab' started just over a week ago and has two variants. I did not think twice at first, but then I noticed anyone

who was a lay worker was given the B variant, those who had a job or some purpose of some sort had the A variant. I suspect that a low citizen score is also a precursor to getting the B variant. Don't you see, the B variant does not protect the person against this disease, whatever it is they dreamt up. If I did not know better they were deliberately targeting people that they deem as 'non-productive' or a 'cost to society' to get their costs down, that is all we are, revenue raisers or costs. Like sheep that are chosen to live for breeding or die for meat, nothing but a line on the Chief Treasurer's books.

Look I have told the hackers to give every Lay worker who comes in here a job, a low level one that nobody will notice has been changed. They will also make sure your citizen rating is high enough to get the right vaccine. I have to give the right one to the right person. If I swap them for anyone, I am just condemning someone else to death. Hopefully you have not been exposed yet but please go home and lie low until you get called for your jab."

Tiberius just sat and looked at him, surely the New Government, even in their most evil throws, would deliberately kill people simply to save money.

"What is a symptom of this new disease John?" Tiberius asked.

"The main one is uncontrolled sneezing. It mimics itself like a cold so people do not seek help, they just try to ride it out. But while they sleep and take pills to deal with the headache, the disease is destroying their internal organs. By the time they feel too ill and try to get to the hospital, it is too late, they are good as dead. It is really quite ingenious in the most horrific of ways," John said shaking his head.

"Then it is too late, I have just come from the Brutus stadium. Everyone was sneezing," Tiberius stated.

"Shit! Go home, stay indoors until you come down to see me for your next jab, it should be due in a couple of days or so and we will take it from there. Now go, the hackers should have done what they needed with your Personal Citizen Device by now, I just hope it is not too late. Be safe my friend."

"You too," Tiberius said and left with a concerned, yet disbelieving look on his face. "Surely not even the Government would slaughter their own people, surely," he muttered to himself as he walked home.

He stayed indoors for the three days before he was due his jab, his nose slowly starting to run more each day as the cough started to set in. Nothing was mentioned on the disease on the TV, in the press or on Global Life. It was as if nothing was happening as it ripped through the nation. He simply could not get the rage out of his mind and it was adding to the turmoil within. How, just how can the New Government get away with this? It is inhumane, even for them and for what, to save some cash perhaps! What price a life? Someone has got to stop this insanity. Someone has got to stand up against Premier Xe and not die in the process, why will his team not stop it?

The time had come and he left to get his jab, please let it be variant A he thought as he sat in the waiting room. Xe 805491997 to room three the receptionist said. He felt sick as he walked in but felt better when he saw John. Closing the door behind him he said, "What's up?"

"Nothing," John replied.

"I have the B variant, don't I?"

"No, you have the A variant, roll your sleeve up."

"So, what's up then?"

"Nothing, I just hate injecting people knowing it will probably do nothing and they may die, even though in that fridge there I have plenty that would save them, I wish I did not know the difference, but I cannot unlearn what I know now. Sometimes knowledge, whilst being power, makes you far from powerful," said John avoiding eye contact
"Show me the vial John," demanded Tiberius, it stated on the label 'variant A'. "Look you have no control over this, just like the rest of us, but I am going to do something, I do not know how I am going to win, I just know that I am not going to lose."

"If you consider being killed as a win, then you really are a winner my friend," said John dejectedly.

John gave Tiberius the jab and he dutifully stated the words of indemnity that he had to. "Stay safe my friend, I will see you soon." John nodded.

As Tiberius left the reception area, John turned and put the empty vial in the allotted bin. Taking a B variant out of the fridge that Tiberius should have had, he knew the next person to walk through the door, who was due the A variant now used, was good as dead, thanks to his decision. He felt dirty but if the New Government were prepared to kill their own people, then he would have to do what he could to save his friends.

There was a knock at the door, "Come in," he said. In walked a mother and a baby. "Say hello to the lovely Xe," she said waving her baby's arm.

John spun round and his heart dropped through the floor. 'Oh no what have I done' he thought as all life drained out of him, 'what have I done?'

After two months the disease was declared beaten. There were 'limited affects' due to the one jab and it was lauded as proof of how the New Government was looking after their people and just how effective the one jab was. The news was triumphant, but people noticed significantly more people being carted off to hospital or simply collapsing in the street. After it was all over there seemed to be less people around. The clean-up crews were efficient but even they were being pushed to the limit with the sheer volume of bodies they were having to deal with.

Eight million were dead, one tenth of the population had perished and the sites used to destroy the bodies and the evidence we working 24/7 to hide the truth, as all bodies that had been affected had to be cremated, immediately, by New Government decree; for everyone's safety of course.

Someone by the designation of Xe 55566342, who worked at one of the body cremation sites, decided he could not allow it to go unnoticed. He could no longer be part of the machine that was hiding the truth, there had to be something wrong, else why would the official line be so different to the truth? His soul broken, he stated 'I may be one Xe but I can make a difference' to himself and tried to post images on Global Life. He felt the truth had to be revealed; something had to change.

Seeing as those involved in the delivery of the virus and the aftereffects were being watched very closely, his posts never made it past the community standards policy. Turning up for work the next day, he had new co-workers that did not seem to talk much, in fact most of the usual team were not around. It was too late to react when he finally realised what was going on. Knowing there was no way out, he offered no resistance when he was placed next to the entrance to the incinerator.

***

"THIS WAS NOT SUPPOSE TO KILL EIGHT FUCKING MILLION PEOPLE, YOU UTTER MORON! WHAT THE FUCK WENT WRONG!" Premier Xe screamed at his chief scientist.

"It appears that in real world environments it was 84% more infectious than in the labs. We did warn you that there was a possibility it could get out of control due to only having been lab tested."

"GET THE FUCK OUT OF MY OFFICE. THIS IS NOT MY MISTAKE THIS IS YOURS. YOU PROMISED ME TWO MILLION DEAD, NOW I HAVE TO CLEAR UP YOUR FUCKING MESS… AGAIN!"

"NO I AM NOT TAKING THAT. I TOLD YOU… XE 1… THAT THIS WAS UNTESTED. DO YOU THINK FOR ONE FUCKING MOMENT THAT I WOULD WANT TO SEE EIGHT MILLION DEAD PEOPLE BY MY HANDS? ALL THOSE INNOCENT PEOPLE, THOSE INNOCENT FUCKING CHILDREN! I AM NOT A FUCKING MONSTER LIKE YOU, JUST, JUST FUCK YOU!" She screamed as she stormed out of the room.

"FUCK YOU!" Premier Xe responded before his phone rang. Composing himself and getting his heart rate and rage down to a more suitable level for the call, he answered. "Good job, that will have reduced our investment needs significantly. We will leave you to manage the fallout," said the voice.

"How come I get all the shit and you get away with it all the fucking time, eh?" Premier Xe stated in a frustrated voice.
"Because we have the money and without us you are nothing. Never speak to us like that again, is that clear Xe?" came back the sharp retort with heavy emphasis on the last word that lacked 'Premier' in front of it. It was a clear warning that should he question them again, things would change and he would not come out the winner.

"Yes, yes whatever, it will take a lot to hide this mess," Premier Xe added

"That is your problem not ours, now get on with your job." The phone went dead.

"FUCK! FUCK! FUCK!" he shouted as he smashed the phone on the desk with each expletive.

Picking up a second device he dialled a number. When answered he merely stated, "The Chief Scientist has lost my trust, deal with it."

"Yes Xe 1," came the reply.

***

The Global life CEO was not happy and was pacing around his spacious living room in the East side housing. Eight million dead was going to cost him a lot of money and a lot of grief trying to sort out the mess. He was just about to call the Communications Chief to agree the next stage of the strategy and inform of the cremation workers attempts at releasing the truth when his phone rang. "Yes," he stated in a slightly irritated voice.

"We know this will hit your revenues, you will be compensated. Premier Xe has failed us again. This is becoming too often an occurrence and his ego and temper is now out of control. We suggest initiating project New Dawn."

"Agreed," he responded and put down the phone.

# Chapter 7:

# Passion Should be Avoided at All Costs

Tiberius sat in a booth on his own in Speech Sanctuary staring at the seat on the other side. There were only three people in there including himself. The other two were chatting and laughing at the other end and besides he wanted to be on his own so was glad for the emptiness of the place.

It had been almost four months since the start of the pandemic and two since its end. It was a crazy time, but life was returning back to normal as the disease, whatever it was, was brought under complete control. He thought to himself that the speed of the recovery could only have happened if they had the 'one jab' ready before the disease hit.

He just stared ahead trying to find some way, anyway, in which all of what he had learnt could make any sense at all, annoyed with himself that he was so damn naïve. He needed to start to learn more about how things are run. He needed to spend some time with the Historian. She always has the answers he said to himself, she will be able to help me catch up with the world.

Finishing the drink, he got up and left, having not put on his suit for this short visit. Deciding a good walk would help clear his head, besides he needed to eat something. Picking up the Personal Citizen Device and hoping that the hackers had put the money on it, as he asked for, he headed out to one of the coffee shops.

It was a cold overcast day, but the chill on his skin helped him relax and think. 'If we are just a financial value to the New Government then my value is going down every day. They have already killed off millions of unproductive people just to save some cash and it would have included me, had I not had John and the hackers creating me a job. This is my wake-up call, I need to do something or just accept that my end is going to be dictated by someone who does not know me sitting in an office somewhere, making a financial phone call. I am worth more than that, I will prove it' his mind clearing a little every day.

Entering the coffee shop he ordered a coffee and a cake, paying with his Personal Citizen Device as always, he was pleasantly surprised to note that there was more than enough to keep him going for a couple of weeks. He silently thanked the hackers and wondered what they were like but agreed with himself in his own little conversation that Cassia was right, better not to know that secret.

Taking the coffee and cake over to the park that surrounded the Brutus stadium, he sat and just watched the world pass by. Watching people going about their lives, probably not knowing anywhere near as much as he did, yet they seemed happy and he most certainly was not. 'Sometimes knowledge, whilst being power, makes you far from powerful' he recalled from his conversation with John, but he was determined to be different, to gain knowledge and use it powerfully, he just needed to find the road he was looking for.

The park was huge and had lots of space but was always dwarfed by the monumental stadium stood in the middle of it. He fancied another Brutus games, but since the short pandemic that managed to kill so many he had linked the place to the New Government in his head and did not feel the love for it so much anymore.

Meandering through the park was a walkway with benches on either side as well as wide open grass fields with trees and little areas of bushes seemingly randomly located throughout, now all covered in a light dusting of snow.

It was lunchtime and all those lucky to have jobs, which was now a much larger proportion of the population than had been not so long ago, had started to resume their daily lives again. Some were wrapped up sitting around talking, some were jogging, some exercising on the outside exercise equipment even though it was warm for the time of year, it was still cold. Good incentive to not stop working out he thought.

Eating his cake and drinking the coffee, he wondered what job he should have been at right at this moment. In the chaos of the time he never thought to ask,

I wonder how I find that out he thought with a huff. 'I hope some boss does not realise that I have not turned up for work, ever, and fires me' he thought, this time laughing out loud. The people on the bench opposite got up at this point and walked off without Tiberius even noticing, so wrapped up in his life and oblivious of what was going on around him.

On the other side of the path and a couple of benches along sat a Sage, hood up, seemingly doing nothing but looking forward, 'what do they do, how do you become a Sage?' He thought. That must be a real easy job, just saying a few words every Sunday. I wonder how much they get paid and by who? This thought reminded him that he had not been to church for some time and he needed to go again, maybe now he did not need to get citizen credits the legal way, he no longer needed the place but although mists in his mind did seem to be clearing a little at times, his dreams were all still the same and he had not managed to make any more sense of them.

He remembered the Sage's last words to him all that time ago, that he could help with that and made a mental note to go this Sunday.

Finishing up he made sure that he put the rubbish in the bin as always, although feeling a little less worried about the fine he would get, he was still worried about the attention it would cause so did his civic duty.

Entering back into the Speech Sanctuary he decided to put on his suit this time. He was feeling in the mood for a good time. Entering the clothing stores he heard the familiar rattle of Flo's sowing machine, making or fixing some sort of clothing. Changing into his suit he headed out to a booth. Ordering a Rhapsody Blue and taking the first sip, he noticed that the place was completely empty but for him. It was a Thursday afternoon 'I suppose and the membership had seemed to have dropped after the last few months, probably victims of the New Government but at least they knew a little of what life was supposed to be like before their ends came' he thought.

"Hello stranger I have only seen you on and off these last couple of months. We seem to be missing each other, which is a shame as you make me laugh," came a voice from the end of the booth. Tiberius looked up to see Cassia stood there. "Well, are you going to get me a drink then?"

"Yes, of course, sorry please sit. What would you like?" He said.

"I will have a Passion Powerhouse please. You cannot say that after too many of them!" She laughed.

Tiberius dutifully got the bright orange drink from the bar assistant and handed it over. "Thank you, I feel in the mood for getting absolutely hammered today," smiling whilst declaring her intentions.

"You know what, so do I!" Said Tiberius. "It has been a while since I have, even watching that dingbat JJ on TV has not appealed to me lately, I feel like I have outgrown him and outgrown that life now. I feel I have awoken."

"Ooo I like the sound of that!" Cassia said looking over her glass with a naughty look in her eyes and promptly necked the whole drink before ordering another. Taking it out of the bar assistant she challenged Tiberius with a wink she said, "Am I going to be two drinks against one all night then?"

Tiberius took the challenge and necked his drink. It was going to be a long session and they were determined to get it going in proper fashion.

"So why do you think you have grown up then?" Asked Cassia

"The mists of the illusion that the New Government are here to look after us and look out for our best interests have been blown away. I always knew they were lying, but I never expected the propaganda to be so far away from reality.

I have found this place, which has offered so much knowledge, both general life and few, specific parts of history from the Historian. The pandemic, that was the final straw, the murdering of so many and for what? I feel an anger but I also feel helpless in that anger," he said

"Yeah, there is lots of talk around the place at the moment that this time they went too far, that Premier Xe finally lost his cool one too many times and is losing grip of the country. If anyone wants to overturn the New Government then this is the time to strike, before he gets a grip again. I have heard that the people are just looking for the leader to lead them," Cassia replied.

"Maybe I should stand against him eh! Then maybe I would have my statue at the Brutus stadium!" he half laughed as he said it knowing full well he would love to have a statue there.

"You would like a statue at the Brutus stadium eh?" Cassia asked as she finished her drink and started another.

"Yes, stupid childish dream, but wish I was brave enough to do something like fight in the arena and become this great hero of the people, rather than this nobody that no one notices as they walk past." Tiberius finished his and started another making sure he kept up.

"Well, I think you are a lot braver than you think Tiberius, you just do not know it in yourself."

And so they drank and chatted for another hour or so before the conversation came back round to naivety. Now somewhat drunk and still in the place on their own Cassia said with a wink, "Come with me" and led Tiberius to a booth in the private area. "What you doing?" he said in a slightly drunken and giggling voice.

"Shhhh," she replied as she put some Neeja on the table and took off her top. "Now we remove the last of that naivety," taking off her bra and throwing it onto his head, she giggled as he sat there staring at her ample breasts.

"Not seen these before then?" She said half laughing, half mocking

"No, but now that I have, I want to see more. I want to touch you," He replied.

Cassia moved closer to him and grabbed his hands, placing them on her chest. "They are yours to do whatever you wish with. I am here for your complete pleasure, my gift, my body, my flesh, I am yours Tiberius, and you are mine, now time to get your fun!"

After a minute or so, Cassia handed some Neeja to Tiberius. "Here rub this on your gums." He did so and the world around him became a little smaller. Cassia did the same and then a second time, handing it back to Tiberius, who applied a second helping.

All inhibitions were now leaving him and he removed his clothes, leaving him sitting there in his pants and socks. "They need to come off, seriously," said Cassia in a voice that sounded soft and almost whirling in nature as she pointed at the socks.

Removing the offending items, he took off her remaining clothing. She stood there at the end of the booth completely naked. "You like what you see?"

Tiberius just nodded with a smile on his face and a bulge in his pants. "Well, you better get them off before they burst! I don't know how you would explain that at the Gov. Stores when you were picking up your replacement ones!" Cassia said.

Tiberius had them off before she had even finished her sentence and she knelt on the seat of the booth, moving towards him on her knees.

Embracing him, she grabbed his hands and placed one on a buttock and thrust the other between her legs. Tiberius was completely out of his depth but just let her take the lead, which she did with great delight.

Another shot of Neeja and they were both in a world of their own. The whole of existence was in that booth at that time and the only time was now, the moment. Cassia pushed Tiberius into a sitting position and wrapped her legs around him, slowly sitting down. "Move with me," she said as Tiberius let out a groan of newly discovered ecstasy. As the pair writhed around, moaning with pleasure Tiberius thought of how much of an idiot he had been for not trying to do this before.

After a few minutes it was proving all too much for him. Cassia looked into his eyes and said, "Let it go," at which point he let out a groan as he climaxed. Cassia started to slow down, eventually just sitting on him, with the both of them panting and sweaty. She kissed him on the lips and he went to say something but she put her finger on his lips.

"Shhh just enjoy the moment," she said and they sat there for another couple of minutes.

Finally, the effects of the Neeja started to wear off and reality started to come back into play again. Tiberius looked happy but awkward.

"How about we take this back to your apartment and have some more fun?" Cassia suggested.

It took Tiberius about half a millisecond to agree and they both ran naked to the clothing stores to grab their normal clothes. Luckily they remained the only two in the place and they ran giggling through the curtain. The whirring of a sewing machine stopped at the other end and they both looked at each other like naughty school children.

Cassia called out, "Night Flo, we are just off now" as they both put their clothes on as soon as possible.

Without looking, Flo replied, "Yeah and to the same destination by the sound it, you naughty little buggers. Have fun, LOTS of fun!"

"I love you Flo," said Cassia

"Yeah, yeah, give him one for me!" She replied

Cassia just looked over open mouthed and said, "we are the naughty buggers eh!"

Flo giggled as she shook her head and carried on sewing without ever turning around.

The two of them went back to Tiberius' apartment without incident although there were a few strange looks as to why they were walking so fast.

Getting into the apartment, they ripped each other's clothes off and headed straight to the bedroom, then the living room, then the bathroom, then back to the living room spending the rest of the night fuelled by Vodinaski, which tasted revolting compared to the drinks in their 'home', Neeja which had almost run out, and sheer lust.

\*\*\*

Daylight came through the crack in the curtains in the bedroom and Tiberius was the first to wake up, with only one eye open his head felt like it had had an argument with one of Crixus' clubs. As he went to move there was something on his arm. He looked across and looked at Cassia still asleep and smiled the biggest smile since his discovery of the Speech Sanctuary all those months before.

He felt that life just could not stop getting better, he also noted that last night he did not have his dream for the first time that he could remember. Maybe that was it, maybe his freedom was meeting someone?

'Slow down T' he said to himself as he gently removed his arm trying not to wake her up. 'There is a long way to go yet'.
He walked into the kitchen area and made himself a coffee. Sitting down on the sofa and reading Good Citizen, which suddenly seemed almost readable in his happy state, he sipped coffee and smiled at the memories from last night.

"Ahem!" came a voice from the bedroom doorway. "Do your guests not get a coffee as well?" said Cassia wrapped in a sheet.

"Morning, sorry I hoped not to wake you," he replied as he walked over to make another coffee.

"Not at all," Cassia said as she let the sheet drop to the floor, beckoning him with her finger to come back to bed. "Fancy some more fooling around?"

Tiberius now had a decision-making process in his brain that was taking significantly less than a second to arrive with a result as he went straight back into the bedroom. Half an hour later the two emerged and grabbed a couple of new coffees.

Sitting on the sofa in their underwear, they sat and chatted like two naughty children planning trouble.

"What is that picture on your bedroom wall then? Is it from your dream?" Cassia asked

"Yeah, it is the small house that appears in it sometimes. I have no idea what it is or means but it is always the same and has been for as long as I can remember."

"It looks nice, perhaps one day we could have a little house in the country like that!"

"Would be nice wouldn't it? Perhaps one day I might actually find out the meaning of the dream."

"You know we should do this more often," Cassia said.

"This or that?" Tiberius laughed nodding towards the bedroom door. "How about now?"

Cassia laughed. "Now don't burn yourself out in one day Big T"—as she decided she was going to call him.

Tiberius laughed his most genuine and stress free laugh he had managed in his entire lifetime; it felt like all of his worries had left him as he sat there talking to her.

"So, what are we going to do now then?" he said

"Well, we are going to have a shower and then I must go. I have catch up with an old friend that I promised to."

With that they shared a shower, first part warm, second not so as the hot water ran out, as well as each other one last time, before she dressed and left, carefully watching out in case people saw her leave.

Tiberius went back into the apartment and sat zombie like looking at the wall. "Well that was unexpected, I hope you all closed your eyes!" he said out loud to his bug friends.

"She has left," the Sage in the shadows reported back.

***

Premier Xe sat in his office staring at the CEO of Global Life saying nothing. The CEO simply stared back.

"Well?" he finally said.

"Well, what?" the CEO replied.

"I have heard things, things that imply that you may not be part of the team anymore."

"I have absolutely no idea what you are talking about. Are we not still blocking anything that can harm you? Are we not still supporting you and keeping you in power?" The CEO responded with self-confidence.

"Yes."

"Well, what is the problem then?" came the CEOs very short reply. Most would not have got away with that and the Communications Chief was looking decidedly nervous, after all he was supposed to be in control of this person.

"My problem is not what you are doing now, it is what you are planning to do, or not to do in the future."

"And what would that be?"

"As of yet I do not know, what I do know is that you are meeting with people who are meeting with others."

The CEO had lost patience with the game. "Oh for fuck's sake, either say what you are trying to, or I am leaving!"

"You are meeting with people that my people believe may be trying to undermine me. I take that threat very seriously. People who do that sort of thing tend to have 'accidents'."

"Are you threatening me Xe?" The lack of official title again, did not go unnoticed.

"Yes and it is Premier Xe to you. Let this be your one and only warning. You live a life of luxury, it would be foolish to risk all that for a silly promise made by someone else with no ability to carry the threat through."

"Do you remember the last time a Government threatened Global Life? You should do, because it was your father that last tried to fuck with us. Remember what happened Xe, huh? Yes, that's right loss of the support of Global Life during the AI troubles and within a couple of months was begging for us to come back on board, begging Xe, begging. Should have been on his knees to make the visual and the verbal match.

I have never seen a Xe cry so much, but there was crying Xe, crying and begging for us to come on side again."

Dismissing the attempt to hit a nerve using his father, easily brushed aside due to his hatred of who he was, Premier Xe fired back immediately "And you made a lot of money out of my weak father, you disrespectful son of a bitch. I could have you killed before you even leave this building…"

"And you would be out of power in less than a month. You know full well if I die you are fucking toast." Moving up close to Premier Xe and pointing in his face he said, "You ever threaten me again and you are over, have we made ourselves very clear Xe?"

"I believe you have declared your position. I reserve my response accordingly," he said and followed through a snarl, "Now get the fuck out of my office, I don't like the stench of death in here."

"The only death around here will be your leadership. You need to get back in with the team Xe, before it is too late!" growled the CEO

"Is that a threat?"

"Yes," Came the simple reply before he walked out slamming the door behind him.

Turning to the Communications Chief Premier Xe said, "You had better get him back in line and on the same page as us before it is too late. Remember if any of us goes down we all go down and the Commander Generals are not going to be appreciative that one of your reports has gone rouge and is threatening their positions and lifestyles."

"Yes, Premier Xe," said the Communications Chief nervously and hurried out of the office screaming for his direct reports to meet him in his office.

Premier Xe simply sat in his chair, hands forming a fist and resting his chin on them. The wheels were starting to come off and he needed a strategy or something to get them back on again. He needed the Global Life CEO dead and his company under the control of the New Government. He needed his spies to give him some good news.

*** 

And so the love affair ran on, Tiberius and Cassia together as often as possible but keeping everything secret, she wanted it that way, not even John had a clue about them. The days slowly started to lengthen and Tiberius was looking forward to spending more time with her, but his dreams had come back and the burning desire within him to change things was raging again.

He now had something to lose, but it did not stop it. Often they would talk about his dream, and how someone had to end all of this, but who would do it. Cassia offering her support and building Tiberius up to make the move, supporting her partner in any way she could and more.

"I do not want to lose you T, but I cannot see you like this, watching the worlds collide in your mind with this internal fight going on. If you want to do this then I will be with you every step of the way that I can."

Leaving the Speech Sanctuary and heading back to his apartment, they wrapped up warm but walked separately so as not to give the game away.

As they rounded a corner there was a police patrol that had stopped a youth.

"Uh oh," said Tiberius.

"Just keep walking," said Cassia catching him up. "It is not our problem."

The voices became raised and the whole thing became very confrontational.

Tiberius said, "What is his problem, does he not know what is about to happen?"

"It is the police who do not know T, like I told you things are changing around here."

The youth yelled out, "Now!" Suddenly there were about twenty kids in their late teens. Tiberius had a flashback to the magtrain station and started to look around for other police officers or worse a whole Troop.

"Shit!" said Cassia. "This is starting to get out of hand now."

"What is?"

"These attacks on the police, a hit and run tactic. No one is talking openly about them but apparently they are happening all over the country. The kids are ambushing the police. The people are smelling that Premier Xe is losing control and as usual it is the kids leading the charge. Everyone is on edge, both on our side and on the New Government side. It is a dangerous mix and one that I do not want to be involved in right now."

Taking a convoluted route around two corners, the couple were back onto a parallel road to the one they were on, but there was no escaping the police, they were everywhere now and sure enough a patrol vehicle pulled up next to them and two officers got out. One commanded them to stop, which they did immediately, whist the other looked around in nervous anticipation of an attack but with a furious anger when their radio said that officers were dead.

"Who are you?" the officer demanded.

"Just two friends walking home officer," said Cassia.

"And you?" the officer said to Tiberius.

"The same as…Xe said," he stumbled just about managing to stop himself saying she.

"Why did you stumble, what are you hiding?" the officer said directly into Tiberius' face, red faced, neck strained and spit flying around due to the intense anger from the recent news about the fate of their colleagues.

"Nothing officer, we are just walking back to our apartments when all of a sudden sirens started and you pulled up."

"Personal Citizen Device NOW!"

Tiberius gave her it, which she duly scanned. It came up with his Xe number, citizen status and police interest level of 'insignificant'. "Your apartment is over the other side, why are you over here?" the officer demanded.

"Xe was walking me home officer. The streets are becoming more dangerous and Xe offered to try to protect me," Cassia interjected noting that Tiberius was flustering.

"Oh is that so? Not exactly a Brutus fighter is it!" the officer said looking Tiberius up and down and gesturing as such with a club with a blackened, fist sized end.

Tiberius had a flash back to the fight, she was the one that won that match. He recognised the club and became increasingly nervous.

"No but it was still a nice offer in these troubled times."

"Personal Citizen Device NOW!"

Cassia handed over hers and the officer scanned it. It did not display any information but instead simply came up with a police interest level of 'protected'. She looked up and across to the other officer on lookout, then looked back.

Stating in a calmer, more respectful voice, "OK go straight home is that clear? We are cleaning up these streets and you do not want to become collateral damage."

"Yes officer," said Cassia. They were both home within five minutes and when they got in Cassia seemed flustered.

"Wow that was a close call!" said Tiberius.

"Was it?" snapped Cassia. "Why do you say that?"

"Erm, well they let us go without attacking us or going into one with us verbally. You usually get an earful at the very least with a stop like that!"

"Well maybe we were lucky eh!" snapped Cassia again.

"Are you ok?" Tiberius said caringly.

"Yes, yes sorry. It has been a long day and a stressful couple of weeks. I just need to go to bed." With that she said goodnight and went to bed.

OK maybe I said something I shouldn't have he thought to himself. Pouring a drink, he decided to give it half an hour before going to bed himself. In the end he just laid down on the sofa and slept there.

When Cassia came out of the bedroom in the morning Tiberius was already up. "Feeling better now?" he said cheerfully.

"Not really. Listen I need to ask something of you. I cannot believe I am going to do this but I need you to run an errand for me," Cassia said calmly but assertively.

"Sure, coffee?" said Tiberius.

Ignoring the offer she stated, "I need you to go to 2-3 city to meet with someone and pass a letter to him."
"Err ok, but I have never left the capital, will it not flag up that I am making an unusual journey?"

"No, we will go via home first and get the hackers to make something up to hide your journey."

"OK sure. May I ask why I am doing this? I mean it is a bit out of character and you have been acting weird since the police stopped us last night? Are you on some sort of watch list?"

"I wish I could tell you T, I really do, but if I tell you then it puts you in danger and I do not want that, ever, I care for you T and I wish I could get someone else to do this?"

"Why can't you, why not John or anyone else at home?"

"The only person I trust is you. Spending these last few months together has told me that and it is critical that this message gets through and it needs to be sent by someone I can trust totally."

"Ok well if I end up dead in Detention Centre One, on your head be it," he said laughing.

"That is not even funny."

"Yes it is, now where is that letter?" he asked.

"I have not written it yet but will at home. We must go; it is urgent."
The pair picked up their Personal Citizen Devices and phones and headed off

to home. Whilst Tiberius waited for his device to be set up and for the letter to be written he had a cheeky Rhapsody Blue. Why not he thought, if I am going to die running an errand I may as well go down with that taste in my mouth.

About twenty minutes later, Cassia appeared with the letter and said, "This needs to be given to a man called Thomas. He will be sat on the seat outside of the main station with his legs and arms crossed in 2-3 city. Sit down next to him and he will introduce himself. You will accept the greeting and reply 'Fine thank you Xe, may I ask a question?'

"Upon agreement you will ask him, 'Where do the birds fly in winter?' to which he will answer, 'I suspect to free lands.' Once you have verified who each other is, give him the letter but keep discreet.

"Do you understand? You must remember these words Tiberius, otherwise he will make an excuse and leave."

"Why don't you just send him a text, they are 100% encrypted so the New Government cannot read them."

"Oh T, you are so sweet when you are naïve," she said touching his face gently. "Now go, you need to get the next magtrain from station T1, hand over the letter and get back here tonight."

"I know this person is from another Speech Sanctuary and you are breaking a sacred rule but I am doing this in complete trust with you Cassia. You have me running around and breaking rules for you, don't let me down, don't make me some sort of pawn in some dodgy game. I never ask about those people you go off to meet or have to catch up with and I never ask for anything in return. We are better than that are we not?"

"We are Tiberius, you know that and I love you, but now you really do have to go," she said giving him a kiss on his cheek.

"Why are you sending me there, at least tell me what is in the letter?"

"I cannot and you know that," she snapped. "Look it will put you in too much danger, the more you do not know the better. I do not want to see you get hurt. I love you."

Tiberius looked at Cassia and with a sigh said, "I love you too, but please do not lie to me, do not make everything we have be for nothing." Before heading off to station T1.

***

"The target is meeting with people we do not know, people who we have not seen target Xe with before Commander," said Commander General Police.

"What are they talking about?" replied Premier Xe without turning his chair around.

"Something called project 'New Dawn'. We do not know what it is yet or who is involved."

"Describe those present."

"Both average looking Xe's in the standard clothing. Nothing of note, both were wearing coats with the hoods up so was difficult to see their faces. One unusual word used was Veefar, although we do not know what that actually meant. It could be a code word or, as we suspect, that it is a name and they are a member of a Speech Sanctuary somewhere in the capital," he reported.

"Extremely dangerous to be using a name in the open isn't it?" Challenged Premier Xe.

"If it was not a code word but a name then yes and it would suggest that they are becoming emboldened now."

"Where did they meet?"

"On two back-to-back park benches by the Brutus stadium."

"I want this thing dead Commander, but I need to be careful, this one comes with teeth and definitely knows how to bite."

"An accident?"

"No, Global Life have back up plans that will end us all, we need to be more subtle than that. Keep a look out on the security of the house, I want to know every single breech in the security that can be exploited."

"It will be done."

Turning his chair around Premier Xe stated, "If I go down we all do Commander. It is in all of our best interests to eradicate this threat, these so-called Speech Sanctuaries have to be annihilated and annihilated now."

"Yes Xe 1," came the reply.

# Chapter 8:
# Danger and Discovery

Walking out of the train station Tiberius looked at the benches. There were a long row of them all facing the station itself on the other side of a road. Looking for a man with crossed legs and arms, he saw one on the bench furthest left.

And another one two benches to his left.

And another one on the far-right hand side.

'You have got to be kidding me' he screamed in his head and started to look obvious as he stood there staring at the men on the benches.

The police officer stood just inside the entrance to the station prompted him to make a decision and he went for the one on the right.

Sitting down he crossed his legs and waited. After what seemed about an hour to Tiberius but was probably more like a minute, he eventually said, "nice day today."

The man sat next to him turned and replied, "Yes, it is."

Tiberius was shifting nervously and starting to sweat, so much so that the man next to him shifted to the far end of the bench.

"Anyway, nice meeting you," Tiberius said taking the lack of an interested response as him not being the right one, he stood and moved to the man in the middle of the three and sat down. Fortunately, he did not seem to have seen the awkward conversation further along, nor his previous conversation partner looking at him like he was some sort of madman.

Clearing his throat and in an increasingly more panicky voice again completely forgot that the person was to introduce themselves to him. Turning to look at the man, who had turned himself to look at this person shifting around next to him, Tiberius was just about to introduce himself when he saw the man on the far left looking directly at him with scorn all over his face.

Tiberius apologised to the confused person he was sat next to, stating that he thought he was someone else before moving along to the man on the left admonishing himself for being such an unlucky idiot who was completely out of his depth right now. If Cassia was here she would deservedly put a rocket up his backside and he would land somewhere just past some distant star.

Finally, he sat down and the man introduced himself, "Good afternoon, I am Xe123456789. How are you?" he stated. Tiberius initially forgot the reply due to nerves but eventually gathering himself replied, "Fine thank you Xe, may I ask a question?" to which the man stated that it would be fine and to calm down before he got them both killed.

Doing as he was told he asked his question and received the correct answer, or so he thought. His mind was in full panic mode and he would have accepted just about any response right now almost starting to cry.

The man shifted nervously and said, "Sure", to which Tiberius desperately clinging onto sanity blurted the question, "Where do birds fly in winter?" at a speed not natural to a normal conversation.

Tiberius mind blacked out. The police officer had now left the station and was casually walking around outside of the station and was menacingly tapping a large club like baton into his hand. Whilst the man sat next to him was talking Tiberius heard no words. Eventually a sharp but indiscreet dig to the ribs snapped Tiberius out of a world of silence and back into reality with a sudden return to the noise around him.

"I suspect to free lands, now just give me the letter and fuck off before you get me killed you bloody idiot!" was the less than expected response, hissed through gritted teeth.

When the police officer was not looking Tiberius stood up leaving the letter on the seat behind him and walked straight back into the train station. 'I am never going to do this again, I do not care what she asks or what she offers to do to me, fucking shitpots!' he screamed in his mind as he walked to the platform for the return home.

The Commander General Military stood looking out of his office window at some troops running a drill in the parade square of the barracks. Behind him stood to attention was one of his spies.

"At ease," he stated. "Tell me what you know."

The spy stood at ease. "Commander, we have intercepted communications with Global Life, they are not happy with Premier Xe."

"Continue."

"They were talking about 'options' for the future, but no detail, just high-level strategic thinking."

"We also have reason to believe that someone called 'Slickback' was talking to someone called 'Umbra'. We are looking into these two further, but they have some sort of link over something called the 'New Dawn Project'."

"Anything else?"

"Not specifically no."

"Anything else that is not specific then?"

"Well, they did talk of a Speech Sanctuary in the capital, but there was no evidence of where it could be so I was going to investigate further before reporting back to you."

The Commander General Military turned on his heels to look at the spy.

"Carry on."

"As reported, we do not know where it is but we are investigating further. We believe the police are close to finding one as well. It could be the same one, it could be a different one, we do not know at the moment."
"How many others know of this place?"

"Currently, only myself Commander."

"From now on, you report directly to me with any further details, that is a direct order. If your immediate officer asks why, send him to me. I want us to find it not the police, clear?"

"Yes Commander!" the spy stated standing to attention and saluting.

The Commander General Military returned the salute. "Well done, I see a great career for you here if you keep this up."

"Thank you, Commander!" the spy stated with a smile before turning and leaving.

The Commander General stroked his chin with a smile. 'If I get to it first it will really piss off Xe 3. The look on her face will be priceless' he said to himself before turning again to look back out across the parade square.

*** 

Tiberius went straight to the Speech Sanctuary upon his return. It was getting late now and he sat there lost in his inner mind as he looked at the drink sat in front of him but not drinking from it. His awesome outfit that Flo had made for him did not seem to be having the effect intended.

With only eight or so people, including him, in the Speech Sanctuary, there was not any distraction and so he went deeper into his thoughts. Why had Cassia sent me to meet up with someone else? He was certain that he was from another Speech Sanctuary, especially as the way Cassia just ignored the comment when he made it, she may as well have just said yes. If he was why had she broken one of the rules to get in contact? He felt he was being played or was he just being naïve as usual and completely missing the point of what was going on?

And those damned dreams that had come back with a vengeance. Why can I never see the person behind me, calling me?

So much had happened this year and the more he found out, the more complicated life was becoming, well life in his head at least, not to mention now Cassia was part of his life. He thought about her and how he was increasingly getting nervous about her. She was always meeting someone but had no job, it just did not feel right and the sex aspect was no longer managing to gloss over these thoughts anymore. He really wanted to raise it with her, but he did not want to upset her, or the whole situation or have to give up the drugs and sex to be frankly honest with himself. She was clouding his thoughts and judgements and he wanted to get back on track with finding out who he was, not who she was.

"Hello," came a voice that made him jump and almost throw his drink in the air. Sat in front of him was The Historian. "Wha…How did you get there?" said Tiberius.

"You were so far away in your thoughts I could have parked a Troop vehicle here and you would not have noticed," came the response.

"Well, whatever, please leave me alone," said Tiberius.

"OK," said The Historian and stood up to walk away.

"No stay."

"Please make up your mind. Would you like me to stay or to leave you in your self-induced mental quagmire?"

"Stay, I have more questions."

"OK," said The Historian and ordered a Flaming Flamingo. An odd drink, pink in colour that actually came out of the bar assistant on fire. She skilfully used a bar mat to put out the flame stating, "Best to leave that to cool for a minute. I deserve a treat, I am in a good mood tonight," she said.

"Why is that?" Tiberius replied.

"I just finished another batch of Brutus matches," she said.

"Sorry, you fight in the arena?" The Historian fell about in hysterics. "No you idiot, I am part of a team of Historians that do the research for them, I investigate what weapons etc. they use, even what names to give to some of the new fighters. I absolutely love ancient Rome and the gladiators so use that for a lot of my research. They are really fascinating, so ancient and yet so relevant and similar to today's society."

"I have absolutely no idea what you are talking about but am glad for you as it seems to make you happy," Tiberius replied.

Tiberius sat and watched as The Historian lowered her hood to reveal long blonde flowing hair. Looking up to see Tiberius staring straight at her she asked, "What?"

"You're so, so beautiful," he said out loud without realising, so lost was he in her beauty. He did not know where this thought came from, it just ambushed him from nowhere and he completely lost control of the part of the brain that stops you from saying stupid things before you actually say them.

"Well thank you," came the reply. "What? Oh sorry, I meant, well I…" Tiberius flustered. "It is fine, I will take it as a compliment. I presume you meant it as one?"

"Yes…yes absolutely!"

"Now what is your question?" She stated taking a sip of her drink and recoiling. "Still too hot."

"You are called The Historian right?" He asked.

"Yes, I hope the questions are going to be a little more challenging than that."

"And we have had many conversations about many things over the last few months."

"Yeeeeeeees," The Historian was in a slow drawl.

"Well, where do you get your information from? If you do not mind me asking of course."

"I like that question, not many people ask it. History is whatever the current owners of the narrative want it to be. If you own the media, if you own all passages and routes of knowledge into people's minds, well then you 'own' history.

Currently Premier Xe would be that owner seeing as he owns the media through the New Government, but they are not completely stupid. All aspect of the past are not simply destroyed, they are stored should the need arise to bring them back into life to further a particular political need or change in narrative, hidden away for later use you could say."

"So where are they stored?"

"In a number of warehouses spread across the country, with some smaller satellite ones where necessary. They are all in secret locations and guarded by the military. You can only get in if you are one of the historians or if you have the right political clearance."

"Who runs them?"

"The Government oversees them, the military guards them and the Historians look after the contents."

"Tell me about the Historians."

"Well, there are two types, those who speak and those who do not. Those who do not speak have been specially bred and raised to be a Historian, as were their parents before them. They have their tongues removed as a baby so as never to be able to talk about what they know. They are born, raised, live, work and die in the warehouse complex that work in. It is seen as an almost religious vocation serving the protection of history."

Tiberius recoiled at the thought of babies' tongues being cut out.

"Do not concern yourself with this, it is merely something that happens and the tutoring and life guidance they go through at childhood, added to the lack of outside exposure, removes any thoughts that they should be doing anything but that which they do. They are happy, of sorts, and know nothing else. I suspect that if you took them away from what they do, they probably would not be able to handle it and would want to return and have their tongue removed a second time."

"So, what about the ones who do talk?"

"I was coming onto that but seeing as you have prompted me so bluntly. Those of us who do talk, were raised in a similar way. Our parents raised us to do what we do."

"And what is that?"

"Remember when we first met and told you to not interrupt me?"

"Yes."

"Well you are doing it again, stop it, it's annoying."

"Sorry."

"Anyway, we were raised in the particular warehouse we were born in. Our parents showed us the ways and knowledge of history and we are as such part of the building and of history itself. We like to consider ourselves the Guardians of History.

Those of us who can talk are allowed out into the wider world to investigate history, remove it and replace it, whatever is required by the New Government. Everything is catalogued and so we can communicate across warehouses to ensure that true history is maintained, even if hidden. If there is a need we can travel between warehouses to meet others like us to discuss and learn, but that is rare."

"But you do not have a Personal Citizen Device."

"No, we have no need for Citizen Credits, money or any of that nonsense as we live, work and die in the same place. If we need to travel, we get one of these," retrieving a small silver disc from her cloak.

"It allows us to use anything that requires a Personal Citizen Device as well as unlimited money and travel."

"So, the past, history still exists."

"To the victor go the spoils. Prime Minster Hendricks, remember him?" Tiberius nodded. "Well, he was the first to gain total control, his son had to handle the AI 'issue' but was not such a good politician as his father, so it took his death, at the hands of the current Premier Xe to regain total control. From then on in this country became a complete dictatorship and the people actually asked for it." She said with a smirk, "It always amazes me how so many in history basically raped their countries for their own gains and the people did nothing to stop it, often asked for it, and never tried to get it back, even though they had far superior numbers.

The fear of dying is a very powerful persuader that politicians use so effectively, in some ways you have to admire them."

Sipping on the drink that had at last cooled down she stopped and looked at Tiberius.

"Say that again, Premier Xe killed his own father?" he asked.

"Yes," she said flatly. "He injected him with a lethal drug between his toes. The coroner reported it as he was instructed to, as a heart attack on the official death certificate, but on our records the true history was recorded."

"That…idiot," Tiberius was trying to be polite in front of a woman "killed his own father to keep control in his line and…and…"

"Yes. Why do you sound surprised? He is a politician and politicians since the dawn of humankind have lied, tortured, conquered, and murdered their way through life, simply for the prized joy of power. Which if you look at it is a bit of an oxymoron as with power come great pain, distress and lack of any joy in life. They do this believing that it will bring them great wealth and happiness, only to give them the wealth and a soul that is dead and completely hooked on the dark desire of power," She stated again without emotion.

"So how did you come to be here?" Tiberius said.

"Easy question. Knowledge of the Speech Sanctuaries are held in our vaults, we know of a lot about them, however this is always after they have been destroyed and everyone killed, which is a bit of a pain as I have been interested in researching them in my own time, for a long time.
After extensive investigations I managed to locate one called Oscar, which was over on the other side of the capital. I was about to go there, when the police drove past in great numbers and destroyed the place. That really annoyed me… almost as much as people interrupting me.

So I continued my investigations by understanding how they were being found in the records and basically it was through piecing together late-night movements and use of Personal Citizen Devices. New Government analysts piece together the dynamics, neutrality spies keep out a keen ear, Global Life monitor their platform and eventually, they work it out."

When I found this place through that research and a bit of luck, I observed both entrances from the shadows, watching who went in and who went out. Eventually I picked someone at random and challenged them about it under the threat that if they did not invite me in, I would tell all. They immediately turned round and took me in.

Sure at first people were suspicious of me, due to the unusual method of invitation, but I wear a grey cloak of the historians, not the cloaks of the Sages, but after telling people of the past, I was slowly welcomed in as people realised I offered something different to the group and they gathered a certain desire to learn of the past and of what the New Government was hiding. The more I speak to people here and see the lives of people that could be so different, the more I get angry. I know what it was like before all this and how people have been tricked into not only living this way but wanting to live this way because history has been hidden from them. A history I cannot tell the outside world about.

The colour in Tiberius' face drained as she explained how easy it was for her to find this place. "If it was that easy for you to find it, the authorities must know this is here!"

"Do not worry, why do you think this place has been running for so long and not found?"

"I have no idea."

"Well firstly the hackers. They are unusual in that I do not know how they came to be here. Hidden history is like a magnet to me, I like to know all of the details of everything and record it, but the hackers are something I, in fact no one in history, knows about. Where they came from, how they have access to what they do, how they manage to stay hidden from literally everyone in existence. I want to find out but respect the rules as we all do. Being so close to them but not being able to talk to them is frustrating, but you never know, one day."

"Secondly?"

"We have a powerful member here. Premier Xe is fed the information that is required in order to keep him in a certain place physically and mentally. This Speech Sanctuary is not required to be found right now, so remains hidden from him."

"Right now, but perhaps later? That is something I would like to ask you about in more detail another time, but right now I would like to ask if I can go to this warehouse?"

"What for?"

"I need to see something."

"What?"

"I need to see if I can find something or at least something about an object. A staff of some sort."

"Why?"

"Because it has been burning in my mind since the day I was born. I do not know why but sometimes I just want to scratch it out of my head, but I cannot. I hope that sleep will save me from it, but it doesn't. I see it in my dreams as well. I sometimes stand there holding it just before I try to turn around to see who is calling my name. I do not know why, but maybe, just maybe there will be something in there that could help me answer some questions about my dreams."

"That would be an incredibly stupid thing to do, I mean I would have to smuggle you into a military guarded facility, where discovery would mean my death along with all those I work with and everything I know. You need to have a very good reason for it."

"You will probably think I am some sort of mental institution applicant but I think someone or something is trying to tell me something through my dreams. I think it is something very important and I think if I find out what that staff is, it will help. Other than that, I cannot offer any other reason other than my honesty."

"You know, I like you. There is something different about you, I cannot quite place it, but you have a character trait of people from the past that achieved great things. You know you are not as rare as you might think. Many of the great leaders and warriors in history thought that someone was trying to tell them to do what they were doing, whether it be Gods, dead relatives or just simple voices in their heads. They were like you."

"Gods?"

"Great beings that ruled their version of reality on the planet. Never seen by the masses but believed to be in existence by the masses. Those that represented these gods would command the masses by word of the God they believed in, usually whilst living in luxury completely contrary to the teachings of the original God, but that is another story. Anyway, they were outlawed decades ago when neutrality came along, but they are still worshipped in other countries other than our own."

"You have contact with other countries?"

"Sure, part of the job, but are we not getting a little distracted here?"

"Yes. You know every time I talk to you, you leave me with a million more questions and I love it."

"I know isn't history just the most magical thing in the world?"

"So can we go there?"

"Where? Another country? Not a chance, even I cannot make that happen!"

"No, the warehouse, you doughnut."

Evie thought for a few seconds partly about the request and partly about being called a doughnut, which she should have found offensive but actually found quite cute coming from Tiberius. "OK, but we cannot go right now. Meet here tomorrow, I will bring a historian cloak to wear and you will have to pretend to be one of the mute members.

"Sure."

"Before you go, you said two entrances. Where is the other one?"

"Well listened, I like that about you, you actually pay attention and want to listen to me, sometimes I feel like a bit of a joke and that people ask me things for entertainment, but this is my life, history is my life, my very reason for existence as it is the same for all those I live around, as it was for my parents. I live and I will die for history. You know even in these Speech Sanctuaries people can still be close minded within their self-proclaimed freedom."

"Freedom is only what you perceive it to be," stated Tiberius.

"You see again, you listen," she said smiling. "There is another secret entrance on the other side of the building that is used by the politician."

"Politician?"

"Well yes, you do not believe that anyone actually agrees with the narrative do you? Even those in the highest echelons of power do not believe in it. They know the past, they know how it has come to this, but they are politicians and they see what power it grants them, so they carry on. People who do not think for themselves are condemned to follow the same failures as their predecessors and that is exactly what they encourage the mass population to do.

"Look Tiberius, no one believes in the narrative but we all belong to it. The narrative is everything, it has become the reason for life itself in this country and now so much time has passed and laws voted in, no one can get away from it, it is the new way of life and there is nothing you can do about it without completely overthrowing the New Government and all of its parts and no one is in a position to do that right now.

"Look, chill out and I will see you here tomorrow."

"You know, I could talk to you for eternity. I like you, be careful," said Tiberius.

"I like you too," Said the Historian as she nodded and left.

Tiberius did not want to miss this chance and stated to the cleaners that he would be staying that night and could he have a breakfast in the morning. They dutifully agreed. As the last of the members left for the night, he thought he might just have a little further look around and headed straight for the private area behind the curtain.

Pulling the curtain to one side, he walked into the dimly lit room. There were five curtains pulled across. Starting from the left he looked into the first booth, he did not know why as he had been in there twice already and he smiled about his last visit there and the loss of another aspect of his naivety. Moving to the next, it was identical as was the third. The booth in the corner had a little narrower curtain but made of the same sublime material, pulling it to one side he noticed that there was no booth behind it.

Ah so that is where that man went, who was with the women, that means he must have been a politician then? I may have to start watching the news to see if he pops up anywhere. Walking through the small area he went through the door. This led to a staircase which he went up, to find a foyer the same as the other side of the Sanctuary with its own monster standing guard and what looked like a room to pass your Personal Citizen Device through to the hackers, again as per the other side.

Making a smile at the monster, who simply stared back at him unflinching, he turned round and headed back down and back into the private area. Just for completeness he decided to have a look into the last booth. It looked the same as the others but the cleaners had not got to it yet. It had a few glasses laying around as well as some other artefacts he did not recognise and in the middle of the table was a bag of white powder.

Just as he thought I wonder if that is, a cleaner said, "Excuse me I need to clean up here." Moving past Tiberius they pointed to the bag and asked, "Is that your bag of Neeja?"

He replied, "Yes." Why he did not know, it was either instinct, or impulse, but whatever it was he picked it up, gave a thanking nod and walked off to the first booth. Pulling the curtain across he ordered a Rhapsody Blue and sat looking at the fine white powder, knowing exactly where it would take him.

Tiberius peered around the curtain as the cleaner walked off. He guessed that he still had some sort of innocent or naïve look about him and must have come across as it not actually being his, but he wanted it anyway.

He was not in a great frame of mind, back to being confused, but back on the long path led by his dreams. He necked his drink in one and took some of the powder onto his finger. Rubbing it on his gums, he started to feel lighter as he started to hallucinate, becoming less stressed about things. Knowing it felt better the more he took he did it again and the world started to mean less and less to him, he only wanted to be in this moment.

The Neeja took him away from his troubles and he was beginning to like it.

Putting a third round of Neeja on his gums, he became lost in that almost dream like state. This time there was no Cassia but instead the imagery replaced reality and he was back in the damn field, but it felt good and he simply did not care. Images started to play in his mind, they felt so real, like he could reach out and grab them, touch them, interact with them, perhaps even turn around and see the others in his dream.

Suddenly the booth seemed like it was in a cloud and he was free as a bird floating around. He looked down and saw a field, his field, so decided to float down, which seemed such a sensible concept at this moment in time. The mist around the edges started to clear so a fourth, then fifth application soon brought them back and he found himself standing in his field. There was the usual crop growing and the feeling of the wind was so real he thought he felt his hair moving.

A small, wooded area was to his right and the sky was a beautiful pure blue colour, with hardly a cloud in it. Animals ran around him as he walked over to the wooded area that had a little house in the middle. The house he had painted on his bedroom wall. He walked up to the house and knocked. There was no response, so he peered in. There was a single room, a fireplace to one side was lit. Opposite it was a bed and in the middle some chairs and some sort of seating area. In the corner by the fireplace was a big metallic bath. It looked inviting but as the fireplace was in full flame did not want to appear to be prying so walked back towards the field.

He needed to stay here, to be here and find out more and Neeja was the portal to do that, or so he thought in the moment so applied two more applications of Neeja and was floating through the growing crop, as were the animals as well. He stopped and looked in his right hand, for just as in some of his dreams he was holding a staff of some sort with a beautiful red stone set in the top. He had no idea what it was but it was there and he always looked at it just before he heard his name being called. "Tiberius"; there it was like clockwork and coming from behind him as always, he started to turn but a blinding headache took over, he grimaced in pain, then doubled over groaning. The pain was intensifying and he knew something was up.

Hearing the noise a cleaner walked into the booth and stated, "They never listen, there is an art to taking this stuff and you ain't got it!" Rushing off he returned with some pills. "Here, take these with water," handing two of the pills to Tiberius as he was grabbing his head in pain. It felt like the aftereffects of all of his late Saturday night 'events' watching JJ rolled into one. His brain felt it was twice the size of his skull and it was getting worse.

"Water," the cleaner ordered and sure enough 15 seconds later out one came. "Here," he said sitting Tiberius up. "Take these and drink all of this." Tiberius dutifully did so his head pounding like his brain was using a hammer to get out.

"I never felt like this when I took it with Cassia," he said out loud not realising.

"Because she knows how to use it properly, now lie down there, the pills will knock you out and allow you to sleep it off. Go on pass out. If you are still alive in the morning I will have your breakfast sorted for you," he said in a manner showing a high level of annoyance.

Tiberius laid down and promptly passed out, or passed out and laid down, either way he could not remember in the morning when he came around. It felt like a thousand Sunday mornings after 'Show Me Showtime!' but there was no bathroom to crawl and his head was still pounding He no longer felt sick though and his eyes felt like they had relocated back to where they were supposed to be. Getting up, he stumbled into the main hall.
"Now that is a Neeja hangover if I have ever seen one. You survived the night then?" said the cleaner, this time in a slightly better mood. He had big, thick eyebrows, with a scar over his right eye and was not one of the monsters, being of slim build, but as they all seemed to appear out of nowhere, he did not seem out of place to Tiberius, especially with his head pounding like it was.

The cleaner continued, "Hello? Hello? Are you there, have you lost your hearing? Take these then go sit over there and I will bring out some grub to get you going again," gesturing to a booth.

Tiberius slumped into it and ordered a water, necked it along with the pills that he had no idea about or what they were supposed to do, nor did he care, he trusted the cleaner to clear up the mess he had created for himself. Ordering another water, then another and another, gulping them all down each time. With a deep sigh he started to feel human again, just as a huge plate of food was put in front of him. He took one look and started to feel sick.

"You will need that in you if you want to feel better."

Tiberius dry retched again.

"Make sure you eat that, they get very grumpy around here with wasted food and I would not want to upset a Keeper, if you know what I mean," the cleaner said in a slightly more intimidating but sympathetic voice. Sticking with the sympathetic tone he continued, "You need to be more careful Tiberius, you need to know what you are doing before you decide to play around with that stuff or with anything and especially women who are stronger than you. Too much and you will burn yourself out and tear your mind to shreds. It doesn't matter who you think you are, Neeja takes no prisoners!"

Tiberius just sat and took the lecture like a child being chastised by their parents for a reason they could not understand or comprehend.

Sitting down next to Tiberius the cleaner stated in a more hushed tone, "Cassia, she's too strong for you, you will always be three steps behind her. If you want the truth, you will eventually work it out, but right now you are a child playing in an adult's world. Be careful you do not promise what you cannot deliver ok? Don't believe me? So be it, but that love you think you feel for someone you do not really know, it can be dangerous if you do not look before you jump.
Relationships can be a bitch if they go sour and it can be painful. We cleaners see it every day in here, day after day, when we clear up the mess in the morning. Freedom sometimes comes with risk, to the body, the soul, the mind but most of all the heart.

The Neeja, the sex, sometimes you just can't keep away from the flame, it lures you in with its apparent warmth and beauty, but the flame burns every time it is touched."

Tiberius was not entirely sure of what he was being told but listened intently none the less.

Standing to walk away, the cleaner left with a last comment. "Only the good die young Tiberius, remember that. Now eat before you brain melts again!"

Forcing the food down, he completed the plate and the water and promptly started to feel sick and dizzy again.

Deciding to try to hide from the pain again, he laid down, swiftly falling back to sleep.

# Chapter 9:
# History Hidden

"OI! OI! Wake up," Tiberius opened one eye and felt a kick on the bottom of his shoe. "What are you doing there?" came the voice again. Tiberius sat up to see the Historian stood there with an additional cloak as she promised.

Shaking his head and sitting up he looked at her feeling a touch better. "Were you on the Neeja last night?" Tiberius nodded with a grimace. "Ha ha you naughty thing you, now come on we have not got all day. Oh, and sober up or you are not going at all, too risky."

After another several glasses of water and changing into the grey cloak in the clothing stores, he dutifully hung up his suit as instructed and turned to the Historian. "How do I look?" he asked.

"Like a Historian actually, put the hood up so I can be sure that your face is completely covered, I don't want to scare the little historian children!" she said giggling. Tiberius did as instructed.

"Good it looks perfect and remember you are a mute!"

"What is your name? I mean everyone in here is given a name are they not, so what is yours?"

"I am The Historian," she replied.

"I cannot go around calling you that, it takes too long and I have a headache, give me a name that I can call you," said Tiberius.

The Historian looked vulnerable for the first time, Tiberius looked at her, head tilted and said in a softer voice, "Come, let me call you by a name, please."

"My...my parents called me...Evie," she said nervously and for the first time. Tiberius had seemed to get through the strong confident exterior she always presented to the world. "It was a name I have not used nor heard used for me since the day they died," she said, "Now come we have to move otherwise I won't be able to get you in."

"Sure ok Evie. I like that name, it's pretty just like you," he said as they both walked off to the entrance.

"We will pick up the Personal Citizen Device later," she said to the Keeper who nodded an acknowledgement and they left to the street. It was mid-morning and there were a few people around, but it was surprisingly quiet.

Evie led the way across town until they came to a large building with no windows. Tiberius knew of the place from one of his boredom reducing walks around the capital, but had never given it a second thought, so 'normal' it looked even without windows. It was here all that time hidden in plain sight he thought.

Opening the door Evie led with Tiberius following closely behind into a small room with two doors and no windows. The only light was a single light bulb lit the middle of the room. Evie acknowledged the two soldiers confidently, Tiberius just kept looking down trying to avoid any form of contact, either conscious or unconsciously. Closing the door behind her Evie moved across the room to the one on the opposite side and placed the silver disc against the handle. A click sounded and the door opened.

"Come," she said gesturing to Tiberius to follow, which he did dutifully and silently. Through the door was a long corridor with rooms leading off on both sides, no windows just doors. Walking down, they arrived at the end where two big silver doors were located. Using the disc again Evie opened the doors and on the other side was a small box room which they both went into.

Evie selected a button from the rack of options and the doors closed. Tiberius looked nervous and when the whole room started to move he yelped. "SHHH! You are a mute!" Evie growled, "you give us away, we both die!"

After about a minute the whole room shuddered to a halt and the doors opened again, this time opening up to an enormous warehouse that had rows upon rows of shelving. Upon each of the shelves were boxes, artefacts, art works, statues, just about anything and everything you could imagine and as far as you could see with platform ladders to be able to reach the upper levels. "Come," Evie stated and started to walk off.

After walking for what seemed an eternity, they reached the other side of the warehouse, or so Tiberius thought. Turning left and right he could see that it was as wide in both directions as it was long in the first. Wow, he thought, there is a seriously large amount of history in here and this is only one of them.

Evie walked off to the right until they reached a door on the left. Opening it using her disc, Tiberius could see it opened up to another corridor, again with rooms to either side, this time they had windows so you could see inside. There were five rooms on either side and they looked empty as they walked along until they reached the last two doors opposite each other.

Looking into the room on the right, Tiberius saw the back of someone with short, straight ginger hair, it reminded him of Cassia and how he wanted to speak to her about what she had asked him to do the day before. The person was talking to a politician as he now knew him to be, from the Sanctuary. With them was a tall Historian that towered over both of them. The politician looked across to Tiberius who almost jumped across the hall and immediately looked down. 'DAMN!' He thought, 'you fucking idiot you may as well be announcing your arrival with a full on Historian street parade!'

Evie opened the door to the room on the left and walked in, Tiberius followed as the politician looked back and continued his conversation with the others in the room. "If you could relax and not get us discovered it would be appreciated!" Evie hissed in a whisper.

Tiberius went to apologise but stopped himself as Evie closed the blinds at the window.

"OK you can talk in here but whisper," she said, "Sorry, I am not very good at sneaking around," said Tiberius. Evie replied, "Well that is blatantly obvious, you could have told me this yesterday! Anyway, we are here now so let's just get on with what we are here to do and get back out.

This room has access to all of the historical records around religion. You mentioned a staff and I thought that would be a good starting point. There are 86,754 references in our records here to such an item so you will need to help me narrow it down a little."

"Who were those people in the other room Evie?" Tiberius whispered

"The Historian is the Chief Historian who raised me after my parents died when I was a child. The man is the Chief Treasurer and I do not know who the woman is. I presume it is a woman anyway."

"Chief Treasurer, as in Premier Xe's Chief Treasurer?"

"Is there another one that you have kept hidden from me and history?"

Tiberius shrugged off the sarcasm understanding that Evie was stressed with the situation she had created for herself and he was not doing anything to ease due to his inability to be inconspicuous. "He was in the…I saw him at home," he said.

"Yes, I know, like I said home, as you put it, has some powerful members. It is one of the reasons why it has been around for so long. Remember the rules of the place Tiberius, everyone is equal, everyone keeps their mouths shut."

"I know but he is part of the New Government, is he not part therefore of the problem?"

"Not everyone believes in the narrative," Evie started.

"But we all belong to it," they finished together.

"It's wooden," Tiberius said.

"What? Oh, the staff yes." Evie moved her hands in front of a giant screen inputting the information, which reduced the potential results in number. This was technology that Tiberius could not have dreamed existed. Clearly if you were in the 'right job' you got the 'right toys' to play with.

"It has a beautiful red stone of some sort set in the top." Again, Evie moved her arms in graceful arcs and the number reduced further to 5,642. "What else?" she asked.

Tiberius closed his eyes. "The stone, it had straight sides as if it was sculpted in some way rather than being natural from the earth. It was set inside a teardrop kind of shape at the top, again wooden and was part of the main section as one piece of wood."

"Good keep going."

Around the top, the wood is arced and twisted as if to continue the shape of flame yet somehow speaks of peace; of how that peace is born of anger and hate. It looks like the wood is in some sort of pain, desperately reaching to the stars for release, for salvation from its pain, but requires the stone for some sort of soul, some sort of anchor for its existence.

I am not 100% sure I am talking sense now."

Ignoring his passion for the description, Evie stated "We are down to 2,654. What else?"

Somewhat disappointed at Evie's response, Tiberius continued "Well, that is about it, I cannot think of any other features worthy of mentioning," Tiberius stated.

"You are going to have to I am afraid; it will take days to view all of those images and cross check them. Think," came the immediate response.

"Well, there was one other thing I guess, that I remember from my dream, but it sounds really odd."

"Continue."

"It seemed to sing."

"Sing? What do you mean sing?"

"Well, when the wind blew through the top of the staff it seemed to sing, with a beautiful calming note and sounds that made you feel relaxed and uplifted, I know it sounds odd but it was almost magical, almost mesmerising and forced you to stop and listen, like an entrancement spell of some kind."

"A singing staff. Good we are down to 58 possible matches. Put your hand here and swipe to the left to move onto the next image. Let me know if you see one that matches," Evie instructed. As Tiberius was swiping, he asked in a whisper, "How does he get away with it? I mean how can he be both the oppressor and the oppressed?"

"Complicated I guess. Apparently he is not a very nice person, but is always polite to us, I guess we have something he wants so he is nice to us. He is always here asking about stuff, plotting, enquiring. Funny as most of the stuff he asks about is all non-connected as far as we can make out, it is like he is looking for something specific but does not know what it is. Still, I let the others worry about that, he seems to only talk to the Chief Historian who does not let us know the content of their conversations, saying that 'it is New Government business and not for us to worry about'."

"At least I now know how the place got financed anyway," Tiberius said before asking the question he really wanted to ask, "The woman with the ginger hair, really looks like Cassia."

"Cassia has long hair, she has short hair, it isn't her. I suggest you address it directly and you could ask her if she has the same mole on the inside of her thigh to check."

"Cassia does not have a mole on the inside of her thigh," Tiberius said without thinking, before realising he had been led straight into that statement.

Evie just looked at him and smiled. "Now can you keep your attention on the task at hand please, like I said she has short hair and Cassia has long hair. Pay attention."

Noticing that he had stopped looking at the staffs, he continued to swipe. "This one is pretty close but not identical."

"Keep going then."

As Tiberius swiped onto number 44 on the list he stopped dead in his tracks, like he had seen a ghost. "Tha…tha…that is it, that is exactly it, the one from my dreams, that is exactly it!" he said stumbling backwards pointing at the screen. "How…how can it be there, I have only seen it in my dreams, I…"

"OK calm down and stay quiet before you have a meltdown and bring half the capital's military into the room," interjected Evie as she pulled up the records relating to the image. "OK sit yourself down and I will tell you all you need to know about it."

Tiberius grabbed the nearest chair and sat down, his eyes almost as wide open as his mouth.

Evie continued, "That is the staff of Shu according to our records. It was one of two staffs created by ancient people called the Egy…Egypt-i-ans, at least that is how I think you say it and the Hit-tit-ies. There was a great battle called Kaa-desh. Apparently, they had both fought themselves fiercely but there did not seem to be any winner. They eventually decided many years after the battle that they had had enough fighting and wanted peace between their two kingdoms.

My limited research into war has found it has a habit of starting off as a great quest full of promises and bravado to banish your enemy and soon descends into a quagmire and a battle of attrition. They are usually started for the most ridiculous of reasons as well, did you know one was fought over an old wooden bucket, people actually fought and died in their thousands over an old wooden bucket."

Evie looked up to see Tiberius staring at her under his hood. "Ah yes sorry I do get carried away sometimes and thank you for not interrupting. Anyway, so the two rulers decided that they would gift a staff of peace to each other. The Egyptians gave the Hittites the one you identified and they gave one of the same design back but with a blue stone within. They were both said to sing the sound of peace or 'Desert Song' and should war ever erupt between their nations again for the rest of time they would hold aloft the staff which would immediately stop all confrontation.

Ah it says here Shu was the Egyptian God of peace and the blue staff is named after Ellel, the Hittite god of keeping oaths, makes sense about ending war and sticking to your word. Nice story, shall we go and have a look at them?"

"What? They are here?" Tiberius said leaping off the chair.

"Yep, the red staff is in warehouse 33. That is us here, section 33, row 8, shelf 2, so should be nice and accessible. The blue one is in section 32, row 24, shelf 3, might need the ladder for that one. After the way you were looking yesterday, I would say that this is turning into a good week for you. Come."

Tiberius followed Evie out and back into the main warehouse. After walking for what seemed an age she stopped and said, "Here we are, first stop the staff of Shu," opening the crate and moving the various stuffing around she pulled out the staff. It was magnificent and exactly as he had seen it in his dream but with the red stone.

This was surreal for Tiberius, to have something that he did not know existed but appeared in his dreams in his hand right now just blew him away. What did it mean? How did he dream of such a thing? Was it a total coincidence? His mind raced without friction as he stood there, staring, completely mesmerised by the jewel, such was its beauty, its meaning to him.

"Ok, ok go easy, don't start waving it around like some sort of weapon. We need to put it back now before we trigger attention," Tiberius handed it back and almost wanted to cry as he shook his head as it was placed back in the crate and resealed.

"OK now for the staff of Ellel. You know that was kind of pretty, where did you say you read about it again?" asked Evie.

"I didn't, it only existed in my dreams, I did not know about the blue one until now."

"Definitely odd that, will have to talk about that at a later time with a Dream Weaver. Right follow me." They went to the location of the staff of Ellel. Tiberius was visibly shaking at this point. "Hey, hey! Chill!" Evie commanded.

"I am sorry, but this is blowing my mind."

"Well, let it blow in your apartment and not in here ok!"

"Sorry."

"And don't forget you are mute!" she growled climbing the ladder. Upon opening the crate and moving the packing around as before she stated, "oh, that's odd."

"What?" said Tiberius forgetting immediately that he had just been reminded that he was supposed to be mute.

"It isn't in here. That's not right, there were no extraction notes on the record. It should be here. Nothing leaves this place without the official paperwork. I will have to follow up on that. We need to go now, it feels like we are looking somewhere we should not be and are starting to push our luck."

"Bu…" Tiberius started then stopped. Evie could hear his voice trembling. He had come so close but was now almost as far away again.

"Let's get back to you know where and we can talk, but not here. It isn't here and I do not know why, you will have to leave that with me."

Closing the crate and resealing it, Evie climbed down the ladder and they both walked straight back to the Speech Sanctuary. Going down to the main area Tiberius changed into his authorised clothing in preparation for going home.

"So where was it?" he asked.

"I have no idea. This is not right and I will need to try to find out."

"Please be careful Evie, I am sensing that something is going on here and we are not meant to be part of it. If you make it too obvious they might kill you to keep the secret."

"I am aware of this," Evie snapped. "Sorry, you did not deserve that. My mind is not as clear as usual. Things are not under their usual complete control."

"No problem, things are starting to happen and come into focus. There is something big coming, I feel it but just do not know what."

"I agree, I need to talk to my fellow Historians. I will see you back here in one week ok? One week from today at this time. Here."

"Agreed. Please take care Evie, and thanks for taking the risk, it meant the world to me that someone trusted me and helped me, even if nothing else happens, when my life is at its end, I will die knowing what the staff in my dreams was at least. I can only thank you from my soul for that."
Evie turned and left, leaving Tiberius slumped in a booth completely lost in thought. Eventually standing and returning home, a mind in turmoil, a mind confused and lost once more.

"Talk," said Premier Xe

"We have further news on 'New Dawn' Xe 1."
"Yes, and?" he snapped back.

"Our spy overheard two people talking.

"Where?"

"At a table in a coffee shop in 3-6."

"Who?"

"The one we believed to be called Slickback and the other, who we do not know of but are following currently."

"What did they say?"

"They were talking about the damage you have done and how you are blind to it. How your anger and hatred appears to have been handed down through your family to you. How they are waiting for an opportunity to get rid of you once and for all."

"Tell me something I do not know please."

"Something about the fact that they believe you to have no soul."

"Boo hoo, anything else?"

"The last thing they said was that 'You cannot hide from their anger forever, everyone and everything is now in place. It is coming.' Before the one called Slickback got back on the magtrain to the capital."

"Very well," Premier Xe stated then put down the phone.

\*\*\*

Tiberius stood at the window in his apartment. For the next two days no one would see him, staring at the rain.

# Chapter 10:

# The Power of the Narrative

The Primary Function were sitting looking at each other in silence.

"Well?" said Chief Treasurer. "What are we going to do with Premier Xe?"

"Kill the dick," said Commander General Military.

"And what instil yourself as the new Premier Xe? Not a fucking chance, you will have to fight the Chief Treasurer for that one."

"Would not be hard," Commander General Military said with a smirk at the Chief Treasurer.

"Reckon you would have a hard time though. Xe 5 spends so much time in the bloody warehouses, prick must have a million ways to kill us all by now!" said Commander General Police laughing.

"Hard to run an army with no money prick. How long will your bitches put up with your shit if they are not being paid? I give it two weeks," the Chief Treasurer growled. "And yes, history does provide me with…information," he finished staring directly at the Commander General Military in a threatening way.

"For Fucks sake will you lot grow up. The reason we are here is because of Premier Xe and yet within twenty seconds we are at each other's throats!" interrupted the Chief Scientist. "What we, yes all of us did, was mass murder, you know it, I know it."

"And what? You suddenly have a fucking conscience now do you? You devised the virus, engineered it and even came up with how to infuse it into the pages of a magazine to ensure it got to every single person, including children, so save me the fucking sob story will you. Even that idiot could not make you look innocent or even caring on this one." Stated the Commander General Police pointing towards the Communications Chief.

"Premier Xe is losing control and we know it." The Chief Scientist stated, ignoring the jibe.

"So, what are we going to do with the dickhead then?" repeated the Chief Treasurer.

"Kill the dick," said Commander General Military.

"Oh, for crying out loud!" stated the Chief Manufacturer. "What do you think?" he said to the Communications Chief.

"What I think is irrelevant. Whatever you lot choose to do I will make it look like it was the right thing to do," he stated in his usual non-committal and irritatingly neutral way.

"Yeah, and you would make it look like we were at fault and needed removing from power," said Commander General Police.

"If that is what is required, then so be it," he replied.

"And what if it was not what was required," said the Chief Scientist.

"Then it would not be required," he replied.

"For fucks sake! We are not getting anywhere," said the Chief Scientist throwing her hands into the air.

"Maybe you should just accept that you are all nothing without Premier Xe, that in fact that is the glue that is holding all of you useless leader wannabes together and actually sitting here having this conversation is actually making the case for not killing but in fact perhaps, supporting Premier Xe. If Premier Xe goes down then we all do," stated the Supreme Sage finally joining in the conversation.

"You all sound like you want to be the leader but none of you have the balls to actually do what is required to be the leader. I only see a bunch of whiners in this room wanting to take the glory but not have any of the responsibility that goes with it."

"So, you think Xe 1 should stay then?" challenged the Commander General Police.

"Would you give up beating up defenceless people in the street and fighting in the Brutus arena in exchange for leadership and never-ending paperwork? I somehow doubt it, you get too much of a thrill in your groin hearing the cracking of skulls, to try to replace it with a click of a pen.

How about you Commander General Military? Kill Xe 1 sure, easily done, but what if the incoming leader desires to kill you. It would be easily done and a pre-requisite of the new order to be introduced. Do you want to give everything up for Xe 1's worthless existence?

Chief Manufacturer, nice easy job, loads of money and all the sex, with all the people, you want, whenever you want. Fancy replacing that with meetings and phone calls?

Perhaps you Chief Scientist would like those for yourself in place of your endlessly funded research into anything you want, including torturing those prisoners with poisons 'just to see'. Who covers your arse on that one then? Oh yeah that would be the one you seek to kill.

Communications Chief, I do not doubt your slippery words would weasel your way into anything, but you do not like the focus on you, you like the shadows where your words can hide you. Leadership would be purgatory for you.

Now Chief Treasurer, I have no doubt you would have a shot at it, after all you have been planning for this day for years. All that time spent in the Speech Sanctuary (there was an audible gasp from the group at this statement) plotting, taking drugs and as much sex as you could get your hands on. All that time in the warehouses of history, researching new ploys from the distant past, new ways to generate a coup, new ways to kill and most importantly new information on each and every one of us in here, that when tactically presented to Premier Xe would result in our untimely death.

Yes, I could totally believe you would step into his shoes, but no one likes you, not even the financers. You are a weasel of the highest quality and whilst none of us can be trusted with anything other than wanting to maintain our own luxurious lifestyles, whilst denying it to everyone else, you cannot be trusted on anything. We know it, Premier Xe knows it and the financers know it, so you would never get the opportunity.

I can see by your face you do not like the truth. To be honest I do not care what you think, what any of you think. You see all of you here giving it large and banging on about how great you are, are in fact nothing, not a speck on the bottom of my wine glass, because you are all ultimately cowards hiding behind your ranks and status.

Admit it you are nothing without Xe 1 and as I say none of you have the balls to do anything about it, so if you do not mind, I am going to leave this pointless meeting. In fact, I am no longer going to be the Supreme Sage, I am leaving the role with immediate effect as I simply cannot believe what it is that I have become, mixing with you imbeciles, you have all poisoned my soul and I am going to reclaim it back.

I have lost touch with reality, as I believe you have too, hidden away in your offices and rooms and labs pretending to be important when actually you are utterly irrelevant and have become nothing but mass murderers of children. You have become the very thing that you claim is a monster and needs to be removed.

I bid you farewell and hope that I never have the misfortune of ever seeing any of you ever again on this plane of existence or the next."

As he stood and left the building, the rest looked at each other, accepting that every word he had just spoken was the cold hard truth.

As the Chief Treasurer got up to leave, the Commander General Military stated one simply word, "SIT!"

\*\*\*

It was exactly one week after they last met as Tiberius walked over to Evie, who was sat staring ahead in deep thought.
"Hey," he said softly so as not to make her jump.

"Hey," she replied without moving.

Tiberius sat down next to Evie. "Are you ok?" he asked.

"Been better," she replied.

"What's up?"

"That staff, it was removed but no documentation was recorded for it."

"I remember you saying that was unusual."

"It has never happened before."

"OK so what does that mean?"

"I do not know, but with its significance and the rumours of change coming, it may mean something bad. Why would you need to smuggle a staff of peace out of the warehouse just at the time when Premier Xe is looking like being overthrown?"

"No idea, but surely this is a good thing for the Historians? I mean change needs to be recorded for all of prosperity like you say, if it is coming then you will be busy doing what you love best?"

"This change involves the total removal of all history, the destruction of the warehouses, of us."

"What is this change?"

"Historians from a working group in political history, have picked up a lot of indications that Premier Xe is increasingly losing his grip on power. His funding sources are rumoured to not be happy with his 'performance' lately and are looking at alternatives, members of his team are not blindly following his orders anymore. These are dangerous times."

"Why, is it not good that he would be thrown from power, surely we should be celebrating and helping it happen?"

Evie looked up and stared into Tiberius' eyes. "There has never been an example in the whole of known human history where a tyrant has just gone 'OK I give up then, I hand everything over to you'," she said with a sarcastic voice.

"They always go down in flames. You have to understand that these people's minds do not work like most of us. They are narcissists, in their mind they are everything, they are the greatest thing and absolutely nobody could possibly be as good as them at anything, let alone being the top dog, the leader. They are not normal people like you or I and actually believe they are Gods of some sort."

"Suffice to say that they believe they have achieved perfection and those who do not agree with them are lesser mortals, less adept, less intelligent, less brave, less everything. A lot of these leaders have literally walked over the dead to get to their positions. All have sold their souls to anyone or anything that will give them what they seek. It has been said in the past that those who seek power should be barred from having it, because once they have it they never let it go, it is their drug and they are hopelessly hooked on it."

"Sorry I am a little lost, are you saying that Premier Xe will kill everyone in the country rather than resign?"

"I am sure if he has to, yes."

"I know he is a maniac but even he would not do that!"

"Why? Did he not recently kill eight million of his own people?"

"Yes, but because how can he be a leader of people, if there are no people left to lead, he would just be a person on his own!"

"Then so be it, but he would still be the leader. Like I said most people's minds do not work like theirs."

"So why are you so worried, why would he destroy history?"

"Because it gives him even more power, it would enable him to create a new narrative and that means that history is bad for the country. The only way to save neutrality will be to destroy it."

"But the people do not know about the warehouses."

"He will just announce some sort of underground movement that is conspiring to destroy the peace of the nation, to bring back the arguing, the wars, and the hatred. The PR machine will kick in and we will go from keepers of history to dead historians without any of us ever being shown to the people."

"How can he do that?"

"It is the power of the narrative Tiberius, not to mention the military and the police are completely under his control."

"Please explain."

"In order to get into power you have to have a message, a point to make people want to believe in what you say and what you are going to do. Just saying I will do X to fix Y is not enough as the message will get lost in all of the discussions and muddying of the water. How often have you had a conversation where you said you were going to do something and within five minutes you do not know what it was that you said in the first place?"

"Err never."

"True, you are a loner."

"Thanks."

"You are welcome. Basically, your message gets lost and soon people forget what you were even standing for. So, what you need to do is create a narrative, a story. It is irrelevant if it is true or not, you need to create something that gets into the people's minds so that they perceive that there is something major that needs to be resolved, then you create the impression that you are the only person who can do that.

Then you have to pump it up to extreme levels by getting the major outlets of information on your side either through encouraging revenue for them through online clicks and/or advertising or just good old-fashioned threats and bribery and the majority of people will follow suit. When the celebrities see it could get them influence and followers they, like the politicians who do not care about the people, nor have the moral compass to stand up for what is right, jump on board in the hope that it will make them celebrity number one, just like the politician wants to be politician number one, they are both narcissists, exactly the same, although of course they would never admit anything as such."

"Example."

Evie paused, thinking. "Ok so the narrative is that road names are an example of the patriarchal nature of society and that is because 99% of roads do not have a woman's name on them. I, Premier Xe will stand up for women and change the road names to numbers.

Also note there would a good chance that he had already spent a lot of time quietly changing roads named after women to those named after men to create the whole thing in the first place. Keeping people's eyes away from what is actually happening.

Now the fact that there is only 0.5% of roads with men's names on them, because 98.5% are names after plants is not released in the building of the narrative, men have less roads named after them than women, that is the fact, but it is also a fact is that only 1% of roads are named after women, 99% of them are not.

The narrative is that road names are an example of how women are oppressed by men.

If anyone tries to state the fact I just mentioned, they are immediately dismissed as being part of the problem, they are representing the patriarchy and shouted down, the facts are also skewed or basically ignored by the information outlets that you have on side and so they never hit the mainstream knowledge of society. Those that state the facts are labelled as wanting roads to not be named after women because they want to oppress them, they are an example of the problem and then they are initially dismissed, better still labelled 'conspiracy theorists' and ridiculed.

The facts become irrelevant and are buried, never to be seen, it is the narrative that is important. If it is not going fast enough for you then add a sufficient level of violence against anyone who wishes to state or defend the facts. That does not even have to be a physical threat, cancelling the person publicly is a far more effective way of taking someone's life away from them without touching them. The harm is still inflicted but from behind a screen rather than face to face, which is the preferred method because those doing the cancelling are often cowards physically.

Eventually good people will keep their heads down to avoid an argument, even if they are in the vast majority, after all who cares what name a road has? Replace it with a number I do not care, but in doing so you have fed the narrative, it has won in its argument and it has become more powerful, because it has become more legitimate to the masses.

Repeat these enough times for small minor things and no one will notice the pieces of the puzzle building up before it is too late.

The silence of the majority becomes a fuel for the minority.

You can see how this has happened all around us can't you? The Personal Citizen Device, the numbers on everything, the 'one jab' to save us all. We have been played by the Premier Xe's dynasty for decades.

The smaller changes are quick to implement but the larger one are not a fast process. The strategy can take decades to implement. Go too fast and you give the game away, you have to take it very slowly, so people remind blind. You may ultimately not be the end recipient of the reward even. That may be your children, or your children's children, but you have achieved your goal. After all Prime Minister Hendricks raped this country, lived in absolute luxury and murdered thousands of innocent people and yet was rewarded with the finest funeral possible."

Tiberius looked confused again.

"Add that to all the other future conversations," Evie said.

"Racking these up at the moment," he replied.

"Coming out from the darkness is not a short process. If you spent the rest of your life in my warehouse you would not be able to catch me up with the knowledge of the past. No offence intended," Evie stated.

"None taken, I think," Tiberius winked and Evie smiled. "Anyway, I am interrupting."

She continued, "For you I no longer mind. So, what you have to do is not look out for what politicians or in fact any narcissist is doing, more look out for what they are not doing, or doing without any fanfare, remember the changing of road names from women to men I mentioned earlier? Loud proclamations are always a smoke screen to hide something else that is going on and whilst attention is diverted elsewhere small steps go by unnoticed. Whilst they have aimed your attention and concentration on A, which always makes them look good, they are doing something with Z, which you would not want them to do, or perhaps seemed odd, had you known they were doing it.

Like a fighter in the Brutus arena, they may take swing or make a movement with one arm but actually land the blow with the other.

Societies are easy to manipulate, it has happened all through history, the entire planet entered two world wars, yes the entire planet was at war with itself all because of a few narcissists. Less than around a couple of hundred 'leaders' ended up creating a narrative that would kill hundreds of millions of people.

When you own the narrative and the media outlets, your voice and opinion is heard, your opposition's is not and so eventually the people will fall into line and start to back your narrative to make them seem to 'fit in' and avoid being cancelled.

Drip, drip, drip, drip, it takes time but eventually your sink fills up to where you wanted it to be and suddenly everyone is going for a 'one jab' every month.

You do not have to like the narrative for it to win, you just have to not try to stop it."

"Wow, people really are dumb!" Tiberius said.

"No, even extremely clever people can fall for it. You have to look at the character of the person who is leading the discussion and ask why are they doing this? When they reply remind yourself to not listen to what they are saying but what they are avoiding saying, because that is where their goal usually lies."

"So, to get rid of Premier Xe, I need to create a narrative and get people to follow me," Tiberius asked.

"Yes, but you will not be the one to create it. He has total control over everything, except the current narrative. It has grown beyond him, even he has to follow it. To overthrow him would take him screwing something up and it looks like he has started doing just that. If I were you, I would keep low and wait for a moment to pounce on whatever starts to fall out, on what the new narrative is and then do exactly as he did, stand up and claim to be the one who will deliver it," advised Evie.

"But if I do not create the narrative, then I would expect the person who did to be the one to say that they will resolve it."

"Great point, you really are cleverer than most in here, you know that. In another life you would have made a great Historian," she said looking deep into his eyes and soul, smiling in both. "Yes, they may, but there is a chance that the new narrative would betray who wants to run the country after Premier Xe and that would not be good for them, whilst he holds the power with the police and military. They would become a huge target for him to remove and reset the narrative back to what he wants it to be."

"I am completely confused at what I have just learnt," Tiberius said scratching his head.

"Politics is a very complicated process Tiberius. It takes time and a lot of energy to think up and implement a strategy. Even more to then create the problem, announce the solution and to keep the truth under your absolute control."

"I think I may just have to have you stick by me forever," laughed Tiberius.

Evie smiled. "I would very much like that Tiberius, or is that Premier Tiberius," winking.

Tiberius laughed. "As long as I get my statue at the Brutus stadium I do not mind. You know I really like you, Evie."

Evie went coy. Tiberius held her hands and looked her in the eyes. "I want to be with you Evie."

"But what about Cassia?" she replied.

"She is playing me. I know she is; it is like I am her assistant, doing the dangerous work. I do not know why but I do not like it and I do not want to be part of it anymore. With her it was pure carnal lust, but with you, I feel a real connection, something that is more than just sex and drugs, something that is meaningful and worthwhile. I am going to end it when we see each other next."

"Do you really care about me Tiberius?" asked Evie.

"Absolutely. My life has been turned upside down and back to front in these last months, but you, you are my constant, you are the one I think about when I think about my future. You are the one I want to be with for the rest of my life Evie."

Evie smiled as she looked him in the eyes, moving from one to another "I want to be with you as well Tiberius but I am a Historian and our lives are history. There is no us, no me, just history. In another life I would throw it all to the wind and be with you forever, but in this life it is not possible."

Taking her hands away and getting up, she stopped and turned around. "I have only loved one other than my parents Tiberius and that person is you." Then turned and walked off to the exit.

Tiberius ordered another drink. He was having difficulty managing the emotional turmoil along with the mental turmoil. Things were coming to a head and he knew it.

# Chapter 11:
# Dream Weaver

"So, a member of a Speech Sanctuary eh? Wait till Premier Xe hears about this!" Said the Commander General Military.

"We have to sit here and take bollocking after bollocking about them being around still and you are a fucking member of one! Are you taking the piss?" Said the Commander General Police.

The Chief Treasurer just sat looking around the room, and internal rage increasing with each breath.

"Look at you, just look at you, all sat there in your self-righteous perfection. Mass murders, liars, scum. Don't sit there and all pretend you are fucking perfect!

A Communications Chief that has a particular desire for kinky sex. Tell us all now Xe what is it like to tie someone up in that dungeon under your house, abuse them and then kill them by whatever sick method you feel like at the time. Tell us all how you get a kick out of this."

"Oh Xe, bless you. Is that the best you have bitch? I am going to destroy you for even suggesting that. You do know that don't you. You are going to be dead before sunrise tomorrow for this lie!"

"What dead in this dungeon?" Stated the Chief Treasurer as he projected a still image from a security device in the room, clearly showing the Communications chief and a dead woman, prostate in a collection of ropes and leather straps.

"Fake news everybody, manufactured images with no proof."

"Oh, I have plenty of proof, you see when you put the cameras in your little 'play room' for you to play back your little sick games, you did not realise that

Premier Xe had them send all images to the Historians, for…prosperity. You see they have hours and hours of this on film. To be fair to you some of it is so disgusting, even I had to turn it off. You really are one sick puppy, aren't you?"

The room looked at him in utter astonishment as well as complete disgust and contempt, not to mention that for the first time he had actually been beaten in an argument.

Now how about you two? A scientist that developed and released, with the help of you Chief Manufacturer, such a sexy title that, isn't it?" He said with a wiggle and supreme sarcasm, "a killer virus. Two people that are directly responsible for the death, slow and painful death of children and others. Two people who sit judging me for going somewhere to have a drink and relax.

You!" He said pointing directly at the Chief Scientist. "You took science, something so pure and clean of this world's traits and you poisoned it with politics. Now not even the politically virgin scientific process can escape you, now politics uses science and science has become politics.

And you Commander General Police who loves to look into people's eyes as they are tortured before killing them and for what? Your own sick pleasure. Oh, and tell me, how is that underground church thing you go to doing for you? What was the religion again? Oh yes Christianity that was it. How unusual to find someone who enforces the law with such vicious passion, so openly breaking it. Maybe I should be having a chat to Premier Xe about that perhaps?"

The Commander General Police looked apoplectic with rage but remained seated during her complete character annihilation. "Naughty, naughty, police officer!" The Commander General Military said with a smile on his face and wagging his finger at her.

"I do not know what you are so happy about tin soldier. You do not think that history has a lot to say about you eh? Remind me, how was the 5-1 city back in the day? They had a little trouble up there didn't they, back when you were just a wee little Lieutenant General? Now I do believe there are many historical videos of that time, but one in particular took my notice. It is a video of someone of the rank of Lieutenant General being brought a child by its parent amongst the chaos and devastation, desperate for it to get medical assistance from the medical troop stood right behind him."

The Commander General Military's smirk was now gone from his face as he shifted nervously in his chair recalling the event and looking around, knowing that his utter brutality was about to be exposed.

"Shut the fuck up before I come over there and fucking smash your skull in!" He screamed.

"Ooo a loss of composure, how unlike you, a little worried are we?"

"You stay right there! Stand up and I will drop you before you take your first step," said the Commander General Police placing her firearm on the table. "I want to hear this. Continue prick."

The Chief Treasurer nodded in acceptance and dismissiveness at the same time before continuing, "And what exactly did this Lieutenant General do eh?… hmmm? Cat got your tongue, tin soldier? Well, for the benefit of the others in the room, a little video."

The Chief Treasurer played a video on the big screen in the room. It showed the now Commander General Military not only refusing to treat the child, maybe three years old, perhaps four, but actively pushing away the medics that rushed across to help, not once but three times before issuing a direct order for them to return to the rendezvous point, at gunpoint.

The child said to its mother, "I am cold Mumma, can I go to sleep now?" to which she replied with tears streaming down her face, "yes my angel, sleep now, be free and I will see you when you wake up."

"I love you Mumma," the child responded before dying in her arms. The Lieutenant General could be seen just standing and watching with a cocked head, as if to be analysing the death that he had just guaranteed." The Chief Treasurer stopped the video.

Apparently, those in the Military are not all psychopathic arseholes like this one here." He stated to his gathered audience, "Some did try to save the child."

"FUCK YOU!"

"Not tonight Josephine."

"Who? What?"

"Ha ha you really are an ignorant prick aren't you tin soldier! So, what happened then I hear you all ask," He said addressing his now captivated audience. "I will tell you seeing as that mouth seems to be incapable of saying it for itself. Funny how someone who yells a subordinates for kicks has suddenly gone mute isn't it. Someone so cock sure suddenly wants the world to end around it so that its deep, dark soul does not have to be publicly shown."

"SIT!" Commanded the Commander General Police pointing her weapon at the Military Commander as he started to stand. "I will fucking drop you, go on please, take a step, just one. Give me the pleasure of fucking ending you right here, right now."

The Chief Treasurer continued, "Looking up the parent shouted bastard, at which point it raised a gun and shot the parent in the head. Adding a second round to make sure as the body lay on the ground still holding the child. Then Xe 2 simply turned and walked away."

"You are one sick son of a bitch!" screamed the Chief Scientist.

"It was one kid, you killed thousands! So, you can fuck off as well!" screamed the Commander back at her.

The Chief Treasurer openly stated, "So you are all going to judge me based on the words of a former Supreme Sage of the Stoics. That twat was exactly right when stating that none of you has the balls to stand up to Premier Xe, only I do. He was exactly right when stating how you are all cowards, milking the good life on the bodies of the poor and the innocent. Yes, I am part of this group and guilty by association but by fuck, I will not be judged by it!"

The Chief Treasurer stood up and walked towards the door. Before opening it he turned and said, "Everyone in this room is scum, every one of us has been part of the death of millions and for what, so I can have another shot of Neeja, so you can order around kids in uniforms, so you can beat up innocent people in the street for no reason, so you can play with your bugs and experiments, so you can sleep with anyone and then murder them in your dungeon, and so you, well you can continue to make TVs," He stated patronisingly to the Chief Manufacturer.

"Every one of us is going to your Hell for it Commander, and fuck we so deserve to!" he said pointing at the Commander General Police before turning and leaving.

The room sat in silence, looking at each other. Everyone's worst secrets were out in the open now and it only led to more hatred between them, hidden no longer and the secrets, the glue that held the group together, was now failing as the pressure built.

*\*\**

In the park by the Stadium an ordinary citizen was walking along and sat down on one of the benches. On the bench opposite sat the person that had been following her for the last thirty minutes.

She stood and walked over to sit down next to him. Talking quietly she stated, "We know who you and your friends are. We know why you are spying on us and we have a message for you to take back to your superiors. Why do you not think we hold our meetings in secret? The people are no longer scared that you know about us and your Commander Generals, yes we know you serve both, had better be on the right side of history this time around. This time the incident in the 5-1 will seem like a mere scuffle. There are millions and millions of us and we are not scared of dying anymore."

With that Veefar stood up and walked away, this time unfollowed.

The man on the bench made a call, "I need to meet with the Commander General Military immediately."

*\*\**

Several days past and Tiberius sat in the Speech Sanctuary exhausted. All this was becoming too much for him to bear. He felt if he found out one more secret or piece of information, his brain and sanity would simply melt on the spot. In many ways he hoped it would happen, at least it would end the turmoil once and for all, but then, there it was, that spark, that reason to keep going. If only he could understand that dream.

John came over. "Hey Big T!" he stated.

Tiberius just looked at him, why did he just say that? How did he know that phrase? Only Cassia called him that, in that moment he realised that had not seen Cassia for a while now. He must call her to catch up and so he could ask that question that he had decided not to hide in his head anymore.

"Hello John," he decided to ignore it for now, more secrets to keep, it was getting too complicated for him to bear. "How are you, not seen you for a while."

"I am good actually now that the pandemic has passed, I am a lot calmer. It was horrible Tiberius, so horrible. All those people that got the variant B jab. I just hope they were strong enough to fight it off although it is certainly a lot quieter in the clinic now."

"What have you been up to?"

"Not a lot, coming here, jabbing there! Ha ha," the laugh was half hearted.

He did not sound like the John of old, he sounded like his spirit had been broken. Whatever was going to happen needed to happen soon, people were ready for a fight but fatigue was setting into some that were going to be relied upon.

"What's up John?"

"Nothing," he replied looking around.

"John for fucks sake, just tell me."

"Cassia."

"What about her?"

"Well, you know what."

"No, I don't, stop playing games."

"I like her Tiberius and I find out that you are…with her."

"Oh shit, I did not know John, I mean were you 'with' her when we… well you know got together?"

"No, nothing like that. We had had a fling in the past and broke up, I don't know why, maybe she found out I was spying on her, but I wanted to try again."

"WHAT? Why?"

"Because as you know she is forever going off to meet people and run errands. She always has enough cash for everything without having a job and I guess I got jealous."

"She gets her cash from the hackers John."

"I know."

"But I do agree with you on the rest of it. To be honest I am waiting to meet up with her again as I want to ask her why she sent me…Well why she asked me to do something."

"Would it be to go to another city with a message?"

"Yes, how do you know that?"

"I did it all the time. She would promise me it was the last time each time until I flatly said no. Was not long after that we split up, I guess I had served my purpose for her."

"Where did you go with the messages?"

"Always to the 2-3 city."

"Same here although only once."
"So how did you track her then?"

"I had the hackers do it and let me know on paper."

"And?"

"And what?"

"Where did she go?"

"All over the capital mainly. Oddly into a Government building a couple of times, but mostly around town, one of the churches and in the park by the stadium."

"I felt awful about it as there was nothing to say she had done anything other than what she said. I guess she must have met up with friends as she said she did and there was me tracking her. I feel so guilty, she was totally innocent and I did that to her."

"And this is the thing you said a while ago that you could not tell her about?"

"Yep."

"I don't know what to say John, other than this world can screw around with your head. I would not read too much into it. Yes it was odd running to the 2-3 city, but there are questions that I do not want to know the answer to quite frankly. I am finished with her, so she is all yours."

"Thanks, you make her sound like a piece of meat."

"You know I do not mean that John. Look I am out of the game now, so feel free to try to start again but whatever you do, do not tell her you had her tracked, she will go ballistic and I have seen her angry side, it is not pretty."

"Yeah, we had a couple of arguments, I know that side of her too well."

"Look on the bright side, if you get stopped by the police with her, they just wave you on."

"What?"

"Well, we got stopped a while back, but they scanned her Personal Citizen Device and just waved us on, no idea why, but was thankful we did not receive a kicking!"

"There is something odd Tiberius, I don't know what it is, but I can feel it. Something big is about to happen."

"I know what you mean and I have a horrible feeling that I am going to be involved."

"Hey," came a familiar voice.

"Hi Evie," Tiberius said as a big smile came to his face. "Good, you are in normal clothes, I need you for a while, have you got a couple of hours?"

"Well now that I am not a Lay worker anymore I have responsibilities you know. If only I knew who my boss was I would ask them for some time off!"

"You are funny Tiberius," Evie giggled.

"Oh well, seeing as it is you, I will take a risk and bunk off work!"

"Good, now come she is going to blow your mind."

"This is sounding dodgier by the second!"

"See you later John, take care of yourself ok?" said Tiberius.

"Yeah sure."

"Oh and if you see Cassia, tell her to return my calls would you please?"

"Yep," said John without looking up from his drink.

"Are you two back on again then?" Said Evie. "No, not at all, I am trying to get in contact with her to call it all off, but she is not returning my calls. Hidden history annoys you; hidden present annoys me. So where are we going then?"

"Ah you will see, follow me."

The pair left the Speech Sanctuary. It was late evening and dark, with completely clear skies showing off the stars in all of their twinkling beauty.

"A little adventure, I like it, unless you are taking me to the police."

"Stop it," Evie said, "I am taking you to find some answers."

"So, tell me did you find out about the Staff of Ellel?" asked Tiberius.

"Yes," came the short reply.
"Aaaaaannnnnnd?"

"Aaaannnddd I do not want to talk about it."

Tiberius stopped walking. "Tough, I do and I won't go to this place with you, whatever it is unless you tell me."

Evie looked around nervously, it was odd enough that a Historian was walking with a citizen, to be seen stopping and talking would attract unwanted attention.

"OK but keep walking," she said through gritted teeth.

"Aaaaaannnnnnd?" repeated Tiberius.

"I could slap you at times, you know that."

"I know, it is why you cannot stand to be apart from me."

"Yep, that'll be it, I'm certain of it," she said with deep sarcasm.

"Aaaaaannnnnnd?" repeated Tiberius.

"Ok! OK! So first I checked the records. There was none for the removal of the item, but the box was left there I guess to make it seem that whatever was in it was actually still there.

So, then I reviewed the monitoring tools for that area and found it had been switched off or erased and a certain time, which I suspect was when it was taken. When I checked the monitoring tools for the entrance and all areas leading to that one for the same time period, they had also been wiped. This went against everything the Historians stand for, the accurate recording of history, not the removal of it, which is what the New Government does. Not us!

So, I checked one from further down the corridor and around the warehouse and eventually found one that had caught the person with it in the reflection of a window."

"Wow you are good."

"I know but I am worried I may have alerted someone to it as it took a lot of digging in a specific area. These types of investigations tend to not go unnoticed."

"So, who had it? Did you see them in enough detail to know?"

"Yes."

"And who was it?"

"The Supreme Sage of the Stoics."

"What? He just walked in and took it?"

"No."

"So how did he get it then?"

"He was given it."

"By who?" Evie hesitated before saying, "By the Chief Historian. I do not know why, but for some reason the Chief Historian, the person who took me under his wing when my parents died and raised me as one of his own, the person who drilled into me the importance of history and its accurate recording, removed an item and deleted all record of doing so. He gave it to someone else and tried to delete all evidence of him doing so."

"That's odd."

"Odd? It is more than odd."

"Why the Supreme Sage? Hang on, he is part of the New Government as is that politician? I wonder if that has anything to do with it?"

"I do not know, but I need to keep my nose out of it for a while in case I go too far too quickly."

"Well I certainly did not see that one coming."

"No nor did I. There is something happening and I am not aware of it, nor know its details and that worries me. I have never experienced anything like this before and, well quite frankly it scares me."

After walking for a further twenty minutes towards the centre of town, Evie ducked down an alleyway. Following, Tiberius asked, "Ok I am getting a little nervous now. Where are you taking me?"

They stopped by a door and Evie knocked in a strange way, but it had the desired effect and the door opened. Inside stood an older woman, dressed in the allowed fashion. She had crazy white hair and looked around outside to check no one had followed them there. "Come in, quickly now!" she said.

The two moved inside into a backroom/warehouse type of room. "Stay there," the woman said as she disappeared into another room.

"What are we doing here Evie?" Tiberius asked.

"Her name is asabikeshiinh and she is a Dream Weaver."

"Ah yes you mentioned that when we first met."

"Always remembering, if only you were a historian. Anyway they are people who can try to unravel what is going on in your head, so I thought as a treat I would bring you here. Clearly the New Government does not like this sort of activity so keep it quiet."

"Sure, I mean I have been running around telling everyone where the Speech Sanctuary is, so you can trust me."

Evie giggled and looked caringly into Tiberius' eyes.

"You are the most precious creature I have ever known, you know that don't you?" Tiberius asked.

"Tiberius, I do not know what to say. My life has been so linear so planned up to when I met you and now it is like I have been missing something all the time. I know history, I can predict the future in many ways, but you have completely changed my outlook on life and my reason for being. Up until now it was just about recording history and following the rules, but now it is so much more, it is about building the future not just recording the past.

It is something so alien to me, yet so exciting. Like a caterpillar becoming a beautiful butterfly."

Tiberius looked confused "Another one for the list. Look there are things afoot. The past has examples of this all over, but I cannot quite put my finger on it, but what I do know is you are the key, you are the future, you are...well you are the centre of the storm of the coming change and of my heart," Evie said, slightly embarrassed and looking down.

Tiberius gently lifted her chin with his hand and gazed into her eyes "and you...you...I don't know the words; you are everything to me. It seems that everything that has happened in my life has led me to meet you. The Speech Sanctuary is no longer relevant, no longer my passion but simply a vessel to that which is and that is you. All I want in my life is you."

"You, here," the Dream Weaver said snapping them out of the trance and lighting some sort of wood that stank to Tiberius. It made him feel sick and her wafting it around the room was not helping.

She was now dressed in some heavily patterned material that was a single garment from neck to feet. It looked like the dresses from the Speech Sanctuary but was made of a lighter fabric and had flowers and animals all over it. Her hair was now braided and had feathers in it and looked much neater. Around her waist was a thick brown belt. She looked like nothing he had ever seen in his life.
Tiberius, smiling at Evie, walked over and sat at the seat as instructed as Evie sat and listened.

"I am told you are having dreams."

"Correct."

"And these dreams are recurring, the same one time and again"?

"Correct."

"Tell me about them, do not miss out any detail, however inconsequential you think it might be."

"OK, well I always start by standing in a field."

"Describe the field."

"It is huge, in the countryside. There are crops of some sort, brown in colour with wispy tops to them about waist height. There are hedgerows and trees but they are far off in the distance."

"Are you alone?"

"No, there are animals all around, but they are friendly and do not run off if I approach them."

"What animals?"

"Erm, I think deer, rabbits, colourful bug type creatures, little birds oh and a big bird high in the sky, but I do not know what it is."

"Continue."

"There are also people I think behind me."

"You think?"

"Yes, because they call my name and whenever I try to turn around to see them, I wake up."
"And that is it?"

"No, sometimes I go to a small group of trees with a small house and a small, gentle river running through it. I go into the house and there is a single room with a bed, a bath and something that looks like a kitchen area with a black metal thing burning wood I think. A table and chairs are there but no people."

"How many chairs?"

"Erm, I do not know."

"Think! It is important!"

Tiberius closed his eyes searching his mind. "Three, there are three chairs."

"Continue."

"That is about it, I cannot think of anything else, just that, night after night after night."

The Dream Weaver sat with her eyes closed and appeared to be asleep or in some sort of trance. Tiberius noticed that she was chewing something now and mumbling or chanting very quietly.

When she opened her eyes, they were plain white, which made Tiberius jump back and look at Evie, who smiled and mouthed 'relax' to him. 'If it was not for you Evie I would have been out of here in a flash' he thought and looked back at the strange woman.

Without a change to her eyes she said in a strange voice, "The house is a symbol of home, of a safe space, the table with three chairs indicate place settings for you and two others, perhaps those behind you, perhaps not."

The fire is on, not for warmth as you indicated the crops were ready so it must be warm, in the summer, correct?"

"Yes."

"So it must be indicating something is being cooked or prepared, possibly for you, waiting for you to return to sit and eat, perhaps with the others, perhaps not.

The running river, indicates flow of your soul which is always continuing whether in life or in death, never stopping and being gentle in nature, indicates love, not anger.

The animals tell me that you are at peace with the world in this place wherever it may be. You make no attempt to kill them or eat them as they are not scared of you, instead you are as they are, past death.

The bird in the sky represents someone or something looking over you, looking for dangers that they can swoop down upon to protect you."

She reached out and grabbed his head roughly with her fingertips. Tiberius recoiled a little before recovering as she said in the same strange voice, "Sit still, I need to see your dream in case you missed something."

'See my dream? This woman is nuts' he thought to himself as she dug her fingers into his scalp ever deeper, which hurt. 'Just stick with it and get out of there before she starts something else,' he thought internally.

Suddenly the women jerked and let out a long sigh as her eyes returned to normal. Talking back in her original voice she said, "You already possess everything necessary to become great."

"What, you know this from my dream?" Tiberius asked in a somewhat patronising voice.

"Everyone who is successful must have dreamed of something," she replied.

"I admit I am a little lost Dream Weaver. I do not understand that you can know this from my dream that you have never seen."

"I have seen not only your dream but your future. You still fear death, yet there is no death only a change of worlds, from this adventure to the next one."

"So, you saw me die then?"

"No, but do not fear death for a brave man dies once, a coward many times, and you know this in your heart. That is all I can tell you, I hope it was of some use to you, my child. Rest assured that it was a scene of peace and happiness, a good place and a place filled with love. Now you must go.

She stood up and asked Evie to help her with her clothes and told Tiberius to stay where he was.

The two women went into a back room and the Dream Weaver closed the door. "How can I help you with your clothing?" asked Evie.

"You cannot."

"Then why do you need me Dream Weaver?"

"Evie, my darling child, he has not seen his whole dream, but I cannot tell him what part he is missing, only you can do that."

"Why, what has he not seen? Why have I got to tell him?"

"Because he won't believe me, I can tell he thinks that I am some sort of cheat, making things up, but as you know my child, this gift I have, is never wrong."

"I'm sorry I don't get it, what have I got to tell him?"

"You need to tell him who I saw in his dream."

"What the people behind him?"

"No, he has never seen them so nor could I, but there was someone in front of him, but at the moment his soul is blind to them, he cannot see them. He has not made the connection in this life that will allow him to see this aspect of his dream, so it remains invisible to him."

"So, who is it then? Let me know and I will tell him."

"You Evie, you are in his dream"

Evie face dropped as she stood in stunned silence looking at the Dream Weaver.

"He is powerful this one, he holds the key to the future and you are part of it." The Dream Weaver said.

"How?"

"I do not know, that remains hidden from me, but his dream is about the next journey not this one. Evie my dear child, I have known you for years, you are so special to me but seeing you in his dream tells me that you must have died as well."

"I know Dream Weaver. I made the connection when you told me. Do not worry about me, I do not fear death as long as it is recorded properly! Shall I bring him back at another time?"

"No, the path is now set, be brave my child, I feel it is a righteous path one that the spirit Gods approve of. To know more, I would need to invoke a full Ghost or Prophet Dance perhaps a Medicine Wheel to understand what the Gods wanted further, but I feel that time has run out."

"As always Dream Weaver I follow your advice, but this news is somewhat unsettling," Evie said.

"I know my child but go knowing that the ancient Spirits are pleased with you and are confident in your life choice. Remember what I said to you all those years ago that a people without a history is like the wind over buffalo grass, and you my child, know both the history, but also, in your heart, the future."

Evie turned to leave back through the door before stopping and saying "You once said to me no river can return to its source, yet all rivers must have a beginning. Is this the beginning?"

"No, I have no vision of when the beginning was but everything is in place now. When you were born the world rejoiced. Live your life so that when you die, the world cries and you rejoice."

Evie nodded and left.

"Ah there you are," Tiberius said, "What's up?" seeing Evie's pained expression.

"Nothing," Evie replied, "Just got some things to think about that's all, let's go."

# Chapter 12:

# Betrayal

Tiberius was standing in a field of brown crop. There was a gentle breeze and it was warm and sunny. He looked at his right hand and in it held the Staff of Shu, as he now knew it was called, with the red stone. He just stood there looking, listening to the sweet sound of peace, the desert song played as the wind blew through the head of the staff.

Turning his head to one side as if to examine it from a different angle, he studied the stone mounted inside. As he did so he saw a reflection behind him, two people were approaching him from behind.

Just as he swivelled around to see he sat bolt upright in his bed. Damn it! He thought to himself, who are those people!

Wiping his hands down his sweating face, he took a deep breath and wandered out to make a coffee. Looking outside the window, it was raining again, but he liked that, it settled his mind. Taking his coffee, he decided to turn on the news for the first time in forever, to see if he could see his favourite politician. He did not find him but he did learn that the water quality was now the purest it had ever been, the roads were in perfect condition, probably because hardly anyone actually has a car these days and Premier Xe was planning a big announcement soon that would benefit every citizen. It looks like he is starting the fight back thought Tiberius. Time is running out.

"How lucky we all are for having Premier Xe, Whoop Whoop," Tiberius said to his bug friends sarcastically as he lifted his arms in mock salutation and almost spilling his coffee all over himself.

'Who are those people behind me?' He thought, 'grrrrrr, why can I never see them!' He felt he was getting angry again and decided that the best course of action was to go to church and calm down this inner turmoil that was starting to get scarily out of control. He had not been there for an age and would have to apologise to the Sage who promised to help him understand his dreams whilst not letting on that someone had beaten him to it, although, he thought, maybe the Sage's interpretation would make more sense to him or at least not go all weird on him with the eyes!

It was Sunday and finishing up his coffee, he looked into his 'dynamic' but never changing wardrobe. Selecting what was wearable (washing day was… well not recent) he headed off to church. Everything seemed to be eerily quiet about town. There seemed to be a large amount of police and he was starting to feel that something was up, like when animals run away just before an earthquake, people had appeared to stay indoors.

He was not worried about the police presence, the hackers always did a thorough job of making him invisible to them, but he did still feel a little unnerved as to why there so many around.

As he approached the bottom of the steps of the church he looked up at is magnificent entrance. The stone steps led up to three huge pieces of carved perfection. On the left and right were huge towers with rounded tops with beautiful and ornate carvings. There were some sort of figures inlaid but most had seen better days and the wind, rain and most of all time had taken their toll. In between was the entrance. Those two huge wooden doors, so heavy, yet so easy to open, never ceased to impress him and the sheer size of the tower in the middle was always awe inspiring.

Just as he was about to put his foot on the first step a large club like object was placed on his chest stopping him from going any further forward.

"What are you doing here?" Came a threatening voice from his right. He must have been so lost looking at the church that he not only took too long going in but also attracted the attention of the police.

SHIT! He thought to himself, CALM DOWN as he felt his mind rushing and his heart pounding.

"Are you mute or something? W H A T A R E Y O U D O I N G H E R E D I C K H E A D?" The officer stated with the maximum amount of derision that she could muster.

"I am just going to church officer," Tiberius stated with a shaky voice.

"You sound nervous," came the reply. "What are you nervous about?"

"Nothing," Tiberius said with a more confident tone. "I am just trying to go to church as I have not been feeling well lately and was hoping that the Sages would give me some good advice."

"Why not go to the hospital?" The Peditata enquired.

"I have not been feeling well in my mind officer. I am sorry if I have upset you in any way."

"You some sort of nut? Here you lot we have ourselves some sort of nut over here!" she said to the laughing officers behind her. Maybe if I hit you really hard over your head, it might fix the problem. Shall I have a go?" She said raising the club.

Tiberius recoiled and put up his arms waiting for the blow to come. "No, please don't!" he blurted out.

With a deft twist of her wrist she dropped the club and hit him in the stomach, enough to make him double over but not drop to the floor. She was clearly well versed in dishing out enough, but not too much, pain to keep the pleasure going…for her. The officer burst out laughing along with the others. "Well, you may be mental, but you seem to be able to take a hit, I will give you that dickhead," and promptly swung around and swiped him across the backs of his knees. This time he went down with a thud hitting his head on the pavement with enough force to draw blood and make him dizzy.

The officers around her gave out a big cheer. "There you go, I fixed your head for you!" she said still laughing and raised the club for another hit.

Tiberius crawled into the foetal position waiting for the beating.

"Please, officer, let me take this one in so you can go about your duties," said the Sage coming down the steps so fast he almost tumbled. "You don't want to go about wasting your effort on someone like him, look at him, crying like a baby, there is no sport in that is there? How about I take this one and leave you to find one, how should I put it, more deserving or perhaps a little more a challenge?"

"Yeah, I guess so, this pathetic excuse isn't worth the time it would take to clean my clava," she said longingly looking over the handmade tool of her trade. "Do you know it took me four weeks and twelve beatings to get this balanced just right? I have used it three times in Brutus matches and it is quite the tool for breaking bones."

"And worthy of being in your possession officer. I bid you good day and thank you for being out here keeping us safe."

"Yeah, well just do as you're told and tell this dickhead the same," she said as she casually walked off high fiving her colleagues. The Sage, lifting up Tiberius said, "Come Xe, let us get a bandage on that head," and walked him up the steps and into the church.

As they walked in with the Sage basically carrying Tiberius on his feet, two other Sages rushed over. "My Sage, can you get the bandages please?"

"Certainly my Sage," as the small and very young man dressed in a white cloak with a blue cord around their waist hastened off.

"I will help you carry Xe," stated the second, a man, older and slightly stockier, average looking except for the thick eyebrows and a scar over his right eye, but this time dressed in the brown robes of the Sages.

"Thank you," the Sage said as they took Tiberius over to a pew and sat him down. Shortly afterwards the other Sage returned with the medical kit. "Thank you, please return to your duties, I can take it from here," stated the Sage and started to clean and bandage Tiberius' head.

"OW!" said Tiberius.

"Good you are still alive in there then," came the reply.

"Yes, why did they do that, why are they such arseholes?" Tiberius asked.

"Who knows and quite frankly who cares, they are what they are."
"How come they did not beat you for trying to help me, I have seen many a person get beaten half to death for trying to save someone from the police."

"Whilst we are treated as filth like everyone else, we do have a seat on the Primary Function with our head of the order known as the Supreme Sage of the Stoics. We never see the Supreme Sage just get the occasional demand of what we are and are not allowed to do, which we interpret in our own ways. Dressed in the finest red velvet cloak of the position, he likes what he has in life, but at least due to his presence he keeps us from being beaten by the police. It is a frosty and tense standoff really, but it works, especially in occasions like this. If the officer had beaten you to death against my wishes or hit me, then the officer would have had retribution. They know it, we know it, but no one speaks it out loud."

"Why are there so many around anyway?" asked Tiberius.

"We do not know. It has been like this for a couple of days, they seem to be systematically searching for something, but we do not know what though. There has been a heavily military presence as well with military vehicles as well as police troop vehicles all over the place. Added to that the strange people walking around hiding in the shadows, people are sensing something and wisely staying indoors for the most part. Virtually everyone has gone to ground.

The authorities definitely have something in mind; you were very brave or indeed foolish to try to get here today. As you can see there is only one other person here apart from the Sages.

So why did you come to seek us today my occupati, after all this time?"

"You remember me?" Tiberius said.

"Yes, of course I do, although, as I say, it has been some time."

"Yes, I know and for that I apologise, a lot has happened in my life recently but my mind is in turmoil again, although I guess I am lucky my mind is not on the pavement outside and for that I thank you."

"You are welcome."

"I have learnt a lot these past times and I have trouble putting the pieces together without creating another 500 questions."

"What have you found out?"

"I cannot say, but I need some advice on how to quell a mind that is akin to a sea in a force ten gale. Even when I sleep the turmoil continues."

"Sleep does not offer a hiding place to our worries; it brings them forward to a place where we cannot hide from them. During the day you can change your thoughts via a distraction, at night, we and our dreams were locked within, intertwined and as one until they are completed or we wake screaming, or both." The Sage stated.

"I just do not know, I feel like a slave, yet I also feel that I should not be. These dreams keep teasing me, seemingly keep telling me that I should be doing something else but exist, but even if that is the case how do you go about dismantling the entire New Government?" Tiberius stated without realising what he has said.

"Show me a man that is not a slave to something, a slave to Neeja, a slave to their master, the boss if they are lucky enough to have a job, a slave to misfortune, even those at the top are slaves to something and ultimately we are all a slave to the narrative. The art to life is accepting what you want to be a slave to and then treat those inferior to you how you want to be treated yourself. If you ever want to display that power in a negative way, remember that your master has that power over you and allow the thought or feeling to bring Stoicism into your life.

Who do you feel you are a slave to?"

Tiberius looked at the floor. "I do not know, it feels like everything, it feels like my life is not my own and I am just a bit part in something bigger; I just want to know the truth."

"Whose truth? No one has a monopoly of the truth. Truth is only events as you see them, bolstered by your own personal experience and position. Is a six not a six to one person but a nine to the person stood opposite you? Is it really truth that you seek?"

"I do not know, maybe because life is so unequal, those at the top have it all, those at the bottom nothing."

"Ah yes indeed, this is certainly true. We may be born unequal but we all die equal, we all end up a pile of ashes. Money and power cannot change that, it cannot make you escape that, but those in power and with wealth have their own issues. Some prefer to have a child and spend their time loving that child at the expense of having the time or money to seek power, others spend their time and money seeking power but do not have the time for children. You need to identify what is it that you want from your life first, then clarity will start to follow."

"I guess that is the tricky bit," Tiberius said.

"Try to look for the whole to start with, not the parts. Start with what you want to achieve and then break it down into smaller pieces that are manageable and achievable, then pick them off one at a time. Each one will be a step forward, no matter how small that step is, it will still be a step forward."

"I want to change the world, I want to be free myself but to bring back freedom to all. I have no idea why, I just feel it in every part of my being, both physically and mentally, that is the only thing I know I want," Tiberius stated raising his voice slightly.

"Then go change the world, but do it one little bit at a time, very rarely does the opportunity to do the whole, but you never know. What are you going to start with?"

Tiberius sat shaking his head side to side as is fighting the demons inside. "The whole, I will change the whole."

"That is a brave statement and an enormous task. You will not be able to do that alone, so look around you for friends to assist you, both those you can see and those you cannot."

"How can I ask for help from a friend I do not know about?"

"A friend will always help, even if they can see you but you not them."

"So, you do not think that I am insane for stating to you that I want to overthrow the New Government and restore freedom to all."

"I am not here to judge what you want to do with your life; I am here to protect your soul. If you want to change the world, go ahead, but if your soul needs to talk, then we are here for you, always."

"Thank you, my Sage, I will return soon to discuss my dream with you in detail, hopefully you will make more sense than the Dream Weaver I saw the other day, I think she was nuts!" Tiberius immediately cursed himself for mentioning the Dream Weaver. He needed to get a grip of himself before he betrayed everyone he knew.

"The Dream Weavers are masters at their role, do not dismiss what they say."

"You know of them?"

"Of course, we both look after the mind and the soul, just in different ways."

"I feel like the world is moving along and I am simply not part of it," Tiberius said shaking his head. "I must leave now, thank you."

The two rose slowly to ensure Tiberius was physically fit enough to leave. As they walked back towards the doors the Sage stated, "Whatever you chose to do remember the four virtues, wisdom, courage, temperance and justice. Wisdom to take advice and think about your life choices, courage to follow them through, even when faced with adversity or even death. Have a temperance to not take things to extremes and manage your passion and always have justice at the centre of your plan. If you follow these virtues, then your decision and life choice will be wise and worthy.

Stay safe and try not to argue with any more police officers," the Sage said as he opened the front door to the church and looked around to make sure the coast was clear. "I would advise that you go home. The bandage on your head will attract attention."

At the front of the church a lone woman with short flaming red hair turned back her head to the front facing the glass window.

\*\*\*

Tiberius decided he needed to chill and headed off to the Speech Sanctuary when it got dark, he needed a drink. Looking carefully and taking all back roads, alleyways and hidden paths, he was so well aware of now, he got there without being seen.

Entering in the usual manner, he asked for an extra forty credits to go on his Personal Citizen Device as he was planning to need some extra help in the next few days, he had finally decided that he was going to change the world… he just needed to work out how on Earth he was going to do it. Luck had taken him this far, he hoped it would carry him further forward still.

Going down the stairs he got changed and sat in a booth. It was quite busy for a Wednesday night, especially recently, but that only added to the atmosphere. Ordering a Flaming Flamingo to see what the Historian saw in it; he put out the flame and sat looking around waiting for it to cool down. "Tiberius you old sod!" came the shout across the room, to a little irritation to the gather guests. It could only be John and he was certainly a few drinks down, "How are you feeling tonight, today, yesterday oh whatever time it is!" he said as he plonked himself down opposite Tiberius with a thud, spilling his drink everywhere. "Whoa there!" he said to himself before squinting at Tiberius' head. "Is that some sort of new hat from Flo or did your head have an argument with something and lost?"

"Oh that, yeah banged my head at home, I'm fine and to be honest I just felt like I needed a drink, so I popped by, looks like you have been here a bit longer than me though."

"Yes I have and it was a good choice! You never know when it will be your last do you!"

"What do you mean?" asked Tiberius.

"Your last drink, you never know when it will be your last drink. At any moment the bastards could come storming in, take us all to jail and finish us off, so I thought sod it! If they do I may as well be drunk and off my nut on Neeja when it happens. Nobody can live forever so you may as well go out with a bang eh!" John promptly rubbed more Neeja into his gums; this went against etiquette and people were noticing how obnoxious John was being.
"John, what is going on you are scaring me, do you know something we don't?"

"Nope, shhhhhhhhh!" he said holding his finger to his lips, with his eyes wide, swaying and giggling like a small child. "Why would I know anything that you don't hee hee."

"I do not like this, it is not funny John. Where is Cassia?"

"Gone, poof like a genie popping out of a bottle, like a puff of smoke from a fire, like a fart in the wind ha ha ha ha. She was here as usual earlier, but then left, did not even say goodbye, but at least she left me the Neeja and wow this stuff is potent, she said to enjoy it. I have no idea where she got it from, it lasts for ages, do you want some?"

Tiberius shook his head.

"I want to be with her Tiberius," he said still swaying and now looking sad. "Have you ever needed someone or something that you do not seem to be able or allowed to have?"

"Is that why you are like this John? Look she is not worth it; you have to let her go. She will never be around for you. She is like some sort of crap TV actress, always promising a great performance but never actually delivering one."

At this point a Keeper came over to deal with the issue. Tiberius said not to worry he would take him out to the private booth and sort him out in there. The Keeper nodded, but Tiberius knew he would be back if this was not sorted now.

Carrying John over to the private booth, everyone in the room looked across annoyed but in lines with the rules, not interfering. Putting John down on one of the benches he said, "John, this doesn't feel right, you have not been yourself since we last met, what is going on?"

"Well Cassia said to me that she would never get together with me again and was really not nice when she said it, although she did look harassed for some reason. I think she was looking for someone, but they were not here, I wonder if it was you eh? No matter, have a drink. Did I ask you if you wanted some Neeja? Come on Big T let's get out of our minds and not feel guilty about it anymore. Ohhhhhh T, T, T, freedom, that's all I want," he said rubbing an enormous amount of Neeja onto his gums.

Tiberius grabbed the Neeja. "John you are going to kill yourself if you do not stop, now pack it in!"

John stared into Tiberius' eyes, still swaying and simply continued, "You need to get out of your mind my friend, they are coming, is it too late for another drink or are they here? Is it too late for my heart to feel love? Well it is with Cassia! Oh I miss you my Cassia. I only wanted you, to kiss your lips and your heart." John was now fully into a full-on hallucination. "Cassia," he said as if reaching out to her, "I want to be yours, to take you home with me, to hold you, caress you. Let me be yours."

Tiberius finally snapped, pushed John back down onto the bench and whilst pointing a finger at him, stated firmly, "Stay here and do not move!" Leaving he went to find a Keeper to see if there was any way he could keep John safe and give him some of the pills he got for his hangover. John needs help and when I find out what Cassia said to him I am going to be using more than some strong words to let her know she is bang out of order.

Walking back into the main hall, people looked at Tiberius as he walked over to the steps leading up to the front door to grab a Keeper to get help. What the hell did she say to him, he has completely lost the plot, this just doesn't feel right, he thought to himself.

As he approached the velvet curtain, there was an enormous BOOM! The whole building rocked. The two door keepers at the main entrance were instantly killed. 'What the fuck was that?' Tiberius said to himself. There were about fifty people inside and every single one froze, looking terrified.

BOOM! A second huge explosion from the other side of the room, this was bad, very, very bad.

Within seconds the police stormed in, pumped to the max and a manic desire to kill. The Peditata started as they meant go on one, smashing heads, punching, striking but strangely none delivered a fatal blow, perhaps they were trying out a new more painful technique before the fatal blow was dealt, perhaps just having some sort of sick fun, whatever it was their victims did not care, in their minds they were dead already.

People simply gave up, there was no escape, their Speech Sanctuary had been found and their lives were now forfeit. Some necked their last drink, some rubbed as much Neeja into their gums as they could hoping that the fatal blow would not be felt.

Tiberius ran towards the curtain to the clothing stores when there was a thud as a club hit him on the back of the head, he fell straight down. Dazed and confused he half sat up and promptly threw up all over the officer's legs and boots. This displeased the officer to put it mildly and with both hands on her club she raised it above her head about to deliver the fatal blow.

"KEEP THEM ALIVE!" commanded the Praefecti as he strolled in. Looking very pleased with himself, the discovery of this Speech Sanctuary was going to come with a great reward, promotion at a minimum and he was going to milk the occasion for every point and benefit he could get from it.

"Take them up to the wagons and load them up, if any die you will have me to deal with." He stated loud enough to be heard over the screaming. "And make sure none are wearing those ridiculous outfits by the time they get there."

One by one every member was stripped naked and marched up the stairs. The wagons were approximately twenty meters from the entrance, so each had ample time to feel humiliated as they were paraded naked and over to the police vehicles. A few were in fact stopped on the way and displayed to the gathered crowd. Some of which responded without reaction but with tears in their eyes, some jeered, all knew that each of these people being paraded were going to their deaths, as did those naked and looking back crying, screaming for help that they knew would never be forthcoming.

One managed to break free and started to run, within five meters he was promptly dropped by club to the stomach than had him doubled up and vomiting. Coughing up blood, the officer looked nervous and threw him back to the one that let him get away. "If this one dies, it is your fault!" he stated and turned away. The man was promptly picked up and thrown into the wagon.

Once a wagon was filled with its load of terrified and huddled people, it drove off to Detention Centre One. One by one they were all led out, the cleaners included. The keepers were all killed on the spot, too big to tackle they were simply removed from the equation with ruthless efficiency.

The whole thing was over in less than fifteen minutes. The Praefecti was the last to leave, looking around one last time before an investigation team came in. He looked at the tattered remains of the stunning establishment, he smiled and walked out kicking a dead keeper in the head on the way for good measure.

Walking back out into the early evening air, he stretched a relaxing stretch, knowing the fun he was about to have with his prey. This is why he joined the police and he was going to damn well enjoy it while it lasts.

In the back of the wagon Tiberius was crushed in with others, all naked, all crying except one. One just sat there, not trying to cover her modesty, she just stared at Tiberius, staring with dead eyes. "I cannot help you now," he said, "I'm sorry." She did not hear him; she had died in her mind so terrified of what was to come. He just thought that it would help the end come quick and less noticeably for her.

The journey became more uncomfortable as it went on. More people were either being sick, defecating, or sobbing seemingly without end. A couple were crying out for others by name but no one could hear. The wagon was becoming increasing filthy, smelt disgusting and the sharp metal edges were taking their strips of flesh whenever the thing rolled around. The woman at the end did not flinch once during the journey.

Then the wagon stopped, there were some muffled voices outside, then it started again, eventually stopping about twenty seconds later. The whole journey had been a terrifying, uncomfortable nightmare lasting about half an hour. Tiberius had a feeling that this was going to be the nice part of his journey to his death, he was not wrong.

The door swung open and the officers retched and withdrew at the stench that hit them. "Fuck Me, it is my turn to clean the fucking wagon as well!" one bemoaned. "OUT! NOW! MOVE!" he commanded.

One by one they were pulled out and marched over to an open area. One by one they were hosed down as they went. The water was cold, they were naked and it was not particularly warm, they were soon shivering to add another layer of discomfort on top.

The woman did not get out, she simply sat and stared as she had done since she was loaded into the truck. Being non-compliant she was thrown out of the back and dragged by her feet to the open area with the rest, still staring that dead stare, but now it was up to the stars.

Tiberius looked around. There was a big wooden sign sarcastically stating 'Welcome to Detention Centre One, we hope you have a lovely stay and please do ask if there is anything we can do for you' The wording was accompanied by a picture of a woman in swimwear on a beach with a drink of some kind in her hand.

All around the perimeter there were double layers of wire fencing with razor wire on the tops, he thought it was particularly cruel as you could see and taste freedom on the other side but you could not get there. Large towers with armed guards on the top and a search light gave oversight all around, including the terrified group, naked and huddled together.

Looking to one side there were long wooden huts, wincing in the gloom he thought he counted four deep by four wide. Right at the far end appeared to be a building made of metal or brick, not like the huts. To his right the wagons were parked and being cleaned out, passed them was a gate and a high solid wall.

The ground was basically dirt with the occasional weed trying desperately to bring life to somewhere that stank of death.
This place is medieval he thought to himself, strangely chuffed, given his predicament, that one of his conversations with the Historian had sunk into his battered brain.

"LISTEN AND LISTEN GOOD BECAUSE IF YOU FUCK IT UP I WILL HURT YOU!" shouted the guard dressed in a police uniform the same as out in the town. He however, had a red sash from his left shoulder to his right waist. Whilst pacing back and forth he yelled, "I AM THE DETENTION FACILITY COMMANDER AND HERE YOU HAVE NO LIFE, YOU HAVE NOTHING, YOU DO NOT EVEN OWN THE BODY YOU ARE STANDING THERE IN, I OWN IT! IF I SAY SOMETHING YOU DO IT, IF YOU HESITATE YOU WILL BE BEATEN, IF YOU ARGUE BACK I WILL MOST LIKELY CUT OFF PART OF YOUR BODY AND DISPLAY IT IN THE CABINET IN MY OFFICE.

"MY GUARDS DO NOT LIKE YOU, I DO NOT LIKE YOU, HELL I DON'T EVEN LIKE MY KID SO I SURE AS DO NOT GIVE A SHIT ABOUT YOU OR YOUR LIFE. YOUR LIFE IS MEANINGLESS TO ME AND TO THE ENTIRITY OF TIME. YOU ARE NOTHING AND YOU WILL BE TREATED ACCORDINGLY. ON YOUR WAY HERE THE COURTS FOUND YOU ALL GUILTY AND JUSTIFIABLY SENTENCED YOU ALL TO LIFE IMPRISONMENT, AND I AGREE WHOLEHEARTEDLY WITH THAT FINDING. THE BEAUTY OF LIFE IMPRISONMENT IS THAT IT DOES NOT STATE HOW LONG A LIFE YOU GET TO HAVE HERE, ONLY I HAVE THAT RIGHT.

SO YOU DO AS YOU ARE TOLD, YOU ANSWER THE QUESTIONS MY NICE GUARDS ASK YOU AND WE WILL ALL GET ALONG LIKE GOOD FRIENDS."

At this moment he noticed the woman lying on the ground and staring at the sky. "WHAT THE FUCK IS SHE DOING? DRAG HER OUT HERE NOW!" The Commander demanded. She was promptly dragged out to the front. "WHAT IS THE MATTER WITH YOU, ARE YOU TALKING THE PISS OUT OF ME?" He nodded his head to one side as a guard dressed in the usual police uniform but wearing a white medical overcoat ran over and examined the woman.

Looking up at the Commander she stated, "This one is gone, her brain has shut down completely," got up and walked back to the edge of the open area.

The commander promptly pulled out his side arm and shot the woman in the leg, she did not flinch. He shot her other thigh, again not even a blink. 'Wow well gone this one is' he thought to himself and shot her in the head. Lucky cow Tiberius said to himself, at least she is not suffering like we are going to. He thought it a strange feeling wanting to cling onto life no matter what, whilst willingly welcoming death as a saviour.

"SO AS YOU CAN SEE IF YOU BECOME USELESS TO ME, TO THIS CAMP, YOU WILL DIE"

With this he turned and walked off in the direction of the gate. The guards stood on the edge moved into the open area and using electric sticks moved everyone into one of the huts. It was basically one long hut. It had a heating stove in the middle and along both sides were racks four layers high. Everything was made of wood. It appeared to already be full of people lying on the racks.

The group worked their way down and were invited to lie down in any available gap they could find. They did not have any clothing. Someone said, "Welcome to Detention Centre One, if you find someone dead you can have their clothing, else tough sorry." There was whimpering all around as Tiberius squeezed himself into a narrow slot. He had not seen John all evening and hoped he would find him before anything happened so he could kill the bastard himself, how could he betray us all, how?

With that thought he collapsed into a deep emotionally and exhaustion driven sleep.

***

The feeling of the wind on his body felt beautiful, he stretched his arms out wide and embraced the fresh, warm air and the freedom. This time he knew he was in his dream and he was terrified of waking up, how do I stay here forever, how do I stop myself from waking?"

At that point he felt a sharp sting to the top of his head, a guard had come in and randomly zapped someone with his electric stick, and it was just his luck it was him.

"YOU! OUT! NOW!"

Tiberius did as instructed, heeding the very clear instructions he was advised of upon his arrival.

"MOVE!" barked the guard giving him a jab with the electric stick and they walked out of the hut. Using the stick to guide him along, they made their way to the large building at the far end. Now he was closer to it, he could see it was made of brick and well maintained. It almost looked like an apartment block. Whilst nervous he was naively thinking maybe he had been chosen to go in to stay there, he could not have been more wrong.

As soon as they walked through the door he could see that there was a long corridor with what he assumed to be cells on each side, the corridor was too long and dark to be able to count how many but there were a lot. It had white tiled walls and floors, with a white painted ceiling, it looked almost like a hospital, but the sound of the whimpering, screaming of pain and screaming of insanity as it gripped the poor souls in here, told him it was anything but. This is it he thought, might as well make it quick.

He was shoved into a dark room and the door slammed behind him, putting him into total darkness. Before the door shut he managed to see that the room had the same walls and floor as the corridor. In the middle appeared to be a small hole in the floor which he crawled over to, it stank and made him retch, so he moved to the far side corner, sat himself up and tried to go back to sleep. He was exhausted but the terror would not let him do so as would the pitiful and constant cries torment him and force him to keep his eyes open.

He sat and shook uncontrollably before eventually exhaustion took over and he passed out.

Awaking to the sound of the door being unlocked, his heart started pounding. As the door swung open strong daylight swept into the cell and blinded him. All he could see was the dark outline of a human who stated "What is your name?"

He promptly said "Xe 805491997" through parched lips and a stone dry throat whilst trying to shield his eyes. As he started to focus he could see it was a woman dressed like the other in a medical gown. "DO NOT LOOK AT ME!" demanded the voice, Tiberius immediately looked down at the ground.

"Sorry," he said voice trembling.

"SHUT THE FUCK UP! YOU SPEAK WHEN I TELL YOU TO SPEAK!" with that statement came a jolt from an electric stick direct into his ribs. It hurt like hell but he did not yelp.

"This one seems to have some strength left," she said, "Best deal with that whilst I write up the paperwork." With that she left and another guard walked in.

The next forty minutes were the most painful of his life. Beaten on every part of his body, with teeth smashed and receiving an inhumane amount of electric shocks, he thought this must be what death feels like, yet the guards were skilled enough to do just enough damage whilst inflicting enormous pain yet not go so far as to kill him. As one took their turn with the beating the other stood and watched whilst having a cigarette, then they would swap until the cigarette was almost done. At that point it was put out on various parts of his body, starting in his groin, one on each nipple and the final one in between the eyes at the top of his nose.

It had got to the point where the guards realised there was no resistance left at which point one spat on his face as the other urinated on him before leaving.

He was left lying in a pool of his own blood until he passed out. Please take me in my sleep he said to himself.

He was awoken by the door opening again. He was too hurt to move so just laid there as someone pointed in a hose and hosed the whole room down. After thirty seconds or so the hose stopped and the door slammed shut again. Tiberius immediately passed out again.

The door opened again. It was a guard with the medical woman again; well he thought so as his eyes were still almost swollen shut. "Are you alive still?" came the question.

"Uuuuurrrgggg," was all he could muster as a reply, the pain of the broken teeth still stabbing him in the gums and brain.

"Another two days," they left and slammed the door.

The door opened again. Tiberius had no idea what day it was, what time it was or barely who he was. This time someone threw a bottle of water at him, hitting him in his damaged ribs. It hurt but he grabbed it and drank it immediately, it felt like he had not drunk anything in a year and the water, whilst quenching the thirst, did not help with the dehydration.

After getting every last drop out of the bottle he promptly fainted again through the pain.

The door opened again, another hosing down.

The door opened again, the guards came in and nudged and prodded to cause pain but no further injury, laughing they left slamming the door shut again.

And so this cycle was repeated for the next, who knows many days, time no longer had any relevance and never getting any real sleep he was becoming delirious but had managed to work out that with every hosing down, if he held the water bottle right, he could get some water in there from the hose. It only helped a little, but the smallest piece of help right now felt like a massive win.

Eventually he felt strong enough to sit up, albeit propped up by the corner of two walls.

After getting over the dizziness he realised the all over pain had reduced to all over aching, it looked like he had survived his first beating.

Eventually the door opened and in walked the medical person again "Give him some food, he is ready," she said and walked out, as she did so he heard a woman screaming and sobbing, "no, no please I have a child", followed by a shot. The noise stopped. He was not ready for that but could understand why people in here were and knew one day he would suffer that fate gladly.

A bowl of fowl smelling gruel was slide into his room, which promptly hit the edge of a tile and fell over spilling its contents all over the floor. This did not stop Tiberius from eating every last bit he could pick up with his fingers. His stomach ached as it had to work for the first time in days, but it was a good ache.

Not long after in came a guard, he looked familiar but Tiberius could not quite place him.

He brought with him a chair and promptly put in down and sat astride. "Who told you about the Speech Sanctuary?" he asked in a cool calm manner.

"I am sorry I do not remember," he replied.

"Oh, that's ok, I will ask someone else, you rest up," at which point the guard stood up and picked up the chair which was them wrapped around Tiberius' head so hard he almost left the floor. The guard got up and walked out; after all Tiberius was out cold and would not be saying anything for a few hours.

The door opened and it was pitch black outside. "Look if you kill him he is not going to be able to tell you anything is he?" a woman said.

"You do your job and I do mine, that is how it works around here, so shut the fuck up," came a man's voice.

"Let him go now, he is not to be killed. You can beat him or do whatever but if he dies so will you," the woman said clearly in a confident, yet smooth and controlled voice.

The door shut. Tiberius opened his eyes, it was light again and the walls were not white, but wooden.

"Welcome back," said the person stood in the middle of the hut. "We did not think you were going to make it; you were pretty roughed up when they dumped you outside."

Tiberius tried to get up. "No, no, no, no, no getting up just yet. You are staying there until you are strong enough. Don't worry we will share the gruel and water with you, soon be big and strong again, ready for another beating ha ha," at which point they left some gruel and water and walked off.

Tiberius immediately ate every last morsel and drank the water. Lying back down he blacked out again.

Coming around in the darkness he found himself lying packed in as most people had gone to sleep. The hut door opened and a guard walked in. He pretended to be asleep, desperate to not go back to the cell for another 'chat' with a guard.

The guard walked through and grabbed a woman by the hair. "You out now," he said surprisingly quietly. Taking the woman outside and closing the door, Tiberius laid back down. About five minutes later she came back in sobbing quietly. Tiberius made space for her next to him and held her gently. This place really was the stuff of nightmares, he thought as he listened to her gentle sobbing.

Several days passed and as Tiberius got his strength back he managed to have a few conversations with some of the other prisoners. A few were left from the Speech Sanctuary who he recognised but did not know personally, a few were just unfortunate enough to have fallen foul of the police and ended up here for no reason at all, but one was interesting. He was an old soldier that had fallen foul of the police for no real reason, like so many and received a beating for it.

He said he awoke in the back of a wagon and had been at the camp for a while but like most, no one really knew how long they had actually been here. Having had three more beatings, he said he had had enough and decided that he was going to try to escape whilst he had strength left in him to do it.

Everyone laughed when he said so as no one escaped this place. It is best to keep your head down and hope you get out alive somehow.
'We are all innocent in here' was the going joke.

A day or so later ten people from each hut were pulled out and taken to the open area. They were ordered to split into two groups from each hut comprising of five people in each hut. One group would go to one side and the other group to the opposite side.

When complete the camp Commander walked out and stood in the middle. The ex-soldier was marched out stood five meters opposite from him.

"APPARENTLY THIS CHAP WANTS TO ESCAPE. YOU SEE THESE TOWERS, THEY HAVE GUARDS, GUNS AND SEARCHLIGHTS. IF YOU ARE CAUGHT BETWEEN THE WIRES YOU DIE. THE AREA AROUND THIS FACILITY IS OPEN LAND, IF YOU ARE IN THERE, YOU DIE. THAT AREA ALSO HAS MOTION SENSORS, IF THEY GO OFF BECAUSE OF A TUNNEL BEING DUG, YOU DIE." At this point he raised his gun and shot the soldier in his right kneecap, going down on one knee he was ordered to stand or die, so he struggled up hopping on one leg, at which point he was shot in the other knee cap. Again, ordered to stand up, he could not. Looking up at the commander and said, "I look forward to the day that we meet again, one on one, when I will…" Before being shot dead mid-sentence.

"NOW, SEEING AS HE COULD NOT HAVE BEEN THE ONLY ONE INVOLVED IN THIS TALK, HALF OF YOU WILL DIE AND

Walking off he did not even turn to see the group on the far side being gunned
down.

Tiberius walked with the rest back into the hut, thankful he was in the 'right'
group that were still alive. Someone had given away what the soldier was up to
and now everyone was suspicious of each other. Tiberius made a mental note
to keep tabs on who was not receiving the same treatment as the others, who
was being treated with a little less brutality.

Many more days passed and he had started to settle into a routine when his
luck ran out. "YOU! OUT! NOW!" came the command. He was marched back
into the same cell as before and the door was slammed shut in its usual manner.

Some time passed and another beating was administered to soften him up.
When Tiberius came round he felt like he was not alone, fumbling around he
felt a warm arm and a body. What? Why have they put someone in here with
me he thought to himself. Nudging them a couple of times he thought they
must be out cold and left them alone but chatted quietly telling whoever they
were all about his life to pass the time.

Mid-sentence, the door swung open in the usual manner and in strode the
guard with the chair and sat in the same way as before. "Oh, have you met
your new roommate?" he said gesturing for Tiberius to look. Looking across
Tiberius yelped, and scampered away on his backside, scrabbling with his
hands and feet as the person he had been talking to was missing their head.

"Who told you about the Speech Sanctuary?" he asked in a cool calm manner
again.

Tiberius was knocked off guard, but tried to strike a convincing tale, or so he
thought, that he had spent some time coming up with of how he met someone
whilst sitting on a park bench who said it to him. He did not see the person
but only knew that it was a man. He said that at first he thought it was a joke
but curiosity got the better of him so he went.

"Why did you not tell the police of this place?"

"They threatened to kill me if I did, as I would be dead anyway I decided that I would at least have some fun before I died," he said.

"Would you recognise this man if you saw him again?"

"No, I did not see his face." He could see the guard getting annoyed, he needed to up his game.

"OK follow me," he said standing. Tiberius did as instructed.

They walked out into the small courtyard in front of the building. Kneel. Again Tiberius did as instructed. Someone was forced to kneel next to him and Tiberius turned to look. The weapon was hit across the back of his head and he fell. Promptly pulled back up he was ordered to look down. As this happened a third person was added to the end.

The guard walked around the back of him and a click of a weapon was heard. "I love these ancient weapons," he said lovingly caressing the old gun. "It was called a six shooter, six chambers for bullets. I have put two bullets in here at random, now let's see who the lucky one today is shall we?
He rolled the cylinder and clicked the weapon shut at a particular cylinder. This is it Tiberius thought. The gun was put to the back of his head and the trigger pulled. 'Click' went the weapon.

Tiberius twitched then realised it had not gone off.

"Lucky Xe," pointing the weapon at the person next to him, click the weapon went. Moving along again and a shot rang out. "Oh dear not your day was it?" the guard said mockingly. Walking back towards Xe, he said, "three more shots and one more bullet." Pointing again at Xe, he pulled the trigger. Click. He felt like he needed to get up and run but knew it would be the end. If the person next to him, who was sobbing, did not die, it would be him. He felt ashamed hoping it would be them.

"Fifty-fifty chance now," the guard said pulling the trigger which immediately ended the person's life. At least it was quick for the poor bastard he thought.

Tiberius, utterly broken again, started to cry uncontrollably. He was kicked to the floor and instructed to go back to his hut. Sobbing, he got up and sneaked a quick look to those who were next to him. The one on the end he did not recognise, the one next to him made his heart sink. Through the bruising, the dried-up blood, the damage the bullet had inflicted and the swelling, it was still clear that the person he had just wished take his place on the trip to the next world, was John.

He had clearly taken a hell of a beating; such was the mess of his face and that his luck had finally run out. At least it was over for him now, although the urge to hate him for revealing home to the authorities was still there, it was now softened with sympathy, after all I would have expected the person who grassed up the place to be treated better or even released, but here he was, Tiberius thought.

When he got back to the hut he laid down still sobbing. He could not stay here any longer he had to find a way out.

Several weeks passed and the beatings and torture continued, sometimes not so bad, sometimes savage. He could almost take the beatings if the mock executions would stop. He had been shot, hung and shown an open gate and told to run through it. He simply stood still knowing one step forward would be the end.

Finally he had had enough and could take it no more. Screw it he thought, the only way out of here is if we escape. He had had a couple of conversations with people who had been successful in the past at beating the police. They simply said you have to accept that you are already dead and charge them in numbers, you have to overwhelm them as their main tool of control is fear of death. If you do not fear death, then they have no control over you.

After a few more days in the huts or sitting in the white room as he called it waiting to be beaten, Tiberius had worked out a plan in his head, but first he needed to get rid of the one that betrayed the soldier. He had noticed recently that a wiry man seemed to have not had a beating for some time and managed to spend a lot of time in the torture house without coming back with any major injuries, Tiberius made the decision that he needed to get rid of him whilst desperately hoping that he had the right man and was not condemning someone innocent to death.

That evening Tiberius approached two guards. "Get the fuck away from me" was his greeting from them."

I need to tell you something Guard," he said making sure he kept his eyes on the ground.

"I need to tell you something Guard," one guard said to the other mockingly. "Well go on then, entertain me."

"I just wanted to tell you that a man in my hut said that if it was not for you lot of morons."

At his point he was beaten to the ground. "MORONS!"

"Please, please it was not me that said it," Tiberius said thinking that actually this was a really bad idea, but he had started it so he would have to finish it.

"Well?" stated the guard, your worthless voice has our attention.

"He said that if it was not for the strong and handsome guards"

"Better, continue"

"He would kick the Commander in the nuts and give him the beating of his life, whilst fucking his wife in front of him."

"Really now, what filth said this?" asked the guard, this time more humanely.

"The thin, wiry one with the v shaped hair and scar on his cheek."

"Get the fuck out of my sight," was the command and Tiberius did it immediately, scrabbling and scrambling to his feet.

About thirty minutes later it looked like his strategy had worked as he saw the person he thought to be the grass dragged off to the torture block, followed by the camp Commander. This time he never came back.

Now that he thought the coast was clear he spread the word around the camp, on a certain night at a certain time, the whole camp, or at least those not in the torture house or those too scared to go for it would make their move.

This torture would come to an end either through escape or death, he no longer cared as to which.

# Chapter 13:
# Escape

In Detention Centre One the time had come. It was a night timed to be without a moon to limit the visibility of the guards. In between beatings Tiberius had been watching the guard towers and noticed a regular slot in their routine where they seemed less vigilant, usually about an hour before they changed personnel.

The plan was actually remarkably simple. Based on the advice that sheer numbers trump aggression and bullets, they would simply storm the fence with an initial subtlety of using the tower guard's hubris and regular routine against them. The newest arrivals who had more strength and any that had any experience with a weapon of any kind, were to go over first.

There would be three on each group and their target would be the guard towers, with their ladders unprotected, they would climb up in silence and take out the two guards that were in each tower. If successful they could provide covering fire for the rest of the group. If not anyone who was successful would put down fire on one that was still in police hands, before others would climb up and take it at a second or third attempt.

Whilst they were doing this, the rest would be climbing over the fences. There was no plan to this just that you had to get over and run, run anywhere away from the entrance to the camp. Get out and run for your life. You could go for it on your own or team up, whatever worked for you, but just get as far away from this place as you could as fast as you could.

This is the time, he thought, now or never. The word was silently spread around all of the huts and each one's content of wretched humanity started to creep out towards the section of the fence and guard tower each was assigned. Using two bed boards from the hut they got a leg up and pulled some of the razor wire flat, creating a gap.

The guards were in their usual switched off state and everything was going according to the plan.

This initial move was silent and successful. The fence had not been maintained as much as it should have been, the guards and Commander had obviously thought that no one would try to escape given the frequent demonstrations of what happened if they tried. Another mistake that Tiberius would hope to go in their favour.

Tiberius' biggest fear was that the fence was electrified. A couple of times he and others had gently touched it whilst walking around and did not seem to get a shock, even though it was designed to be electrified. He hoped that this was not just because someone had switched off the power to save electricity and thus it would be switched back on again when the attempt started but was as a result of arrogance and that it was not properly maintained. If they switch it on and it worked, this was going to be the shortest escape attempt in history. History, huh he thought as the memory of the Historian came into his mind. Shaking his head to get Evie's image out of it so he could focus on the task at hand and thus actually stand a chance of seeing her again for real, he started to move.

By sheer luck the weather had turned really bad in the last hour or so. Pouring rain and cold weather would keep the guards heads down and in their barracks so their numbers around the camp were at a minimum. The clear sound of some sort of party going on as well was a good sign he thought, if they are in a noisy place, they won't hear what is going on until the alarm goes off. For once in his life he was actually thankful to hear the repetitive crap of Dracona Doob. Things were as good as they were ever going to be, now was the time, they had to go.

There were only four guards on duty, moaning and muttering as they walked around about missing the party and not paying attention. They were easily dispatched by some recent arrivals who were arrested for various crimes but of course claimed full innocence.

As per the plan, the strongest went over and started to climb. Tiberius was thankful that so many ex-military people seemed to still end up in here just like everyone else, as it gave him exactly what he needed, strength, training, discipline and understanding how to use a weapon. When the guards were paying little or no attention to the camp itself, instead many sitting down and not looking out at all, some were dancing around to the beat of the music, in one tower could be heard an officer admonishing their colleague stating, "Stop snoring, you will get us shot in the Commander hears you!"

The planets were aligning and Tiberius thanked his guardian bird for looking out for him but irritatingly wondered where it was when he got caught in the first place! Mumbo Jumbo crap from the Dream Weaver he thought.

So far all was well, he could see that all of the towers in his field of view, had people climbing. Some guards were being taken out, without noise, "Good, good," he said nervously under his breath. Then all of a sudden all hell broke loose as the prisoners started fighting with the tower guards that had noticed what was happening. Shots rang out and everyone was shouting.

Without an order of any kind, a mass of human bodies started to clamber over the first fence in any way they could. They saw that their chance of escape evaporating and they needed no encouragement to start their escape.

The tower that Tiberius was next to had successfully taken out their guards by disarming them and then throwing them off the side. The thud as they hit the ground was enough to confirm they would not be getting back up again. So had the one to the left but the corner one was successful in taking out the escapees.

Tiberius yelled out to them to cover the corner tower, as soon as those guards exposed themselves they were dealt with by a short burst of fire. In some cases where the shooter was not so experienced, they probably took out more birds than guards, but no matter how many rounds you fire, it only takes one to do the job and they were landing, thankfully. Precision was not a requirement right now and the minimal blind training by the ex-military prisoners for citizen prisoners had done their job. With the tower guards neutralised they had cover and everyone started to climb over the second fence in the same manner.

There was now a mass of humanity pouring out of the Detention Centre, like ants crawling over some piece of discarded fruit on the ground, or a storm wave crashing over poorly build sea defences. Thousands of people desperate for life but not fearing death going it alone, or helping others, it was a total free for all and that was the plan. With no specific target or plan the heavily outnumbered guards had no defence plan, they simply could not take everyone out, certainly not now the tower guards had been removed from the equation.

Standing still and watching the mass escape attempt Tiberius was almost frozen to the spot. He realised that he had created a narrative, but this time it was one of hope, he had managed to convince thousands of people not to fear death but instead chase life and they were doing it. Evie was right, 'I can make a difference!' The gravity of what he had created and the risk he was taking on so many lives did not leave him though and he felt sick that if this failed, thousands would suffer horrifically. The guards were piling out of their barracks now the alarm was wailing. Grabbing their uniforms and weapons in a very disorderly and in some cases drunk manner they tried to formulate a plan. The prisoners in the towers closest to the gates managed to take out as many as they could as they came out of the building. Eventually running out of ammunition and in some cases not remembering how to change the magazine in the heat of battle, the hurried down the ladder and started their own escape over the second fence. They had done their part for the others, now it was their turn to chase life.

Hundreds of prisoners were now escaping on Tiberius' side. The constant firing of weapons on the other side indicated that they were not fairing so well, it sounded like a tower was still up and firing but everyone did this knowing the chances and Tiberius hoped that eventually the tower would be overwhelmed and the escape would happen on all fronts.

Without the barracks covered guards started to come through the gates. Anyone within range were cut down, some saw the writing on the wall and instead of going over the fence turned and attacked the guards. Tiberius was still frozen to the spot, organising everyone and ensuring they were going in the right direction in his head, but actually saying no words. The whole world has slowed down as he looked around, like it was moving at half speed, or his brain was working twice as fast as everyone else.

If he did bark out an instruction, no one would hear, his plan was playing out in front of him, some dead, many already over the second fence, which thankfully was not electrified either. The Commander had really screwed this up and had become totally dependent on threats to keep order. 'It is amazing how powerful a lack of fear of death makes you' Tiberius thought as he saw one person climbing the fence with someone clinging on around their neck. Tiberius' heart filled with the joy of true humanity but his brain was filled with chaos and it snapped him back into the now.

He looked over and saw a soldier that had been in the tower had come back over the fence back into the camp. Running over to the guards by the gate, in a flash of some pre-practiced moves had them disarmed and dead. She was now giving covering fire for the whole left side of the camp. If any officer came through that gate, they were dead.

Tiberius could not believe what he was seeing, standing there staring at this soldier, her hair flowing free, who had already done more than enough to deserve to escape, actually came back to help. He felt that she would be the last one to climb over the fence if she could. She turned and screamed at Tiberius, "GO! I WILL COVER YOU ALL FOR AS LONG AS I CAN!"

Tiberius turned and ran; there was nothing more he could do for anyone. As he started to climb the first fence he heard the screams, the panic, the gunfire, the shouting. It was a cacophony of chaos, hate, fear, hope, humanity and murder all rolled up into one.

He was over the first and now charged the second. Looking back, he saw the solider get hit, she fell but managed to keep firing until a bullet ended her life. The police swarmed around her emptying their whole magazines into her now dead body. She had given her life willingly and without any hope of reward for people she did not even know.

Tiberius' mind simply could not process this act of love and hope.

Bullets were landing all around his feet but he did not look back again. Whilst climbing over the second fence he was nicked by a bullet on his right thigh. It hurt, burnt his leg and he temporarily lost his grip. Regaining it out of sheer determination he got to the top and jumped down the other side. "Arrrggghhhh!" he screamed as his leg buckled, but he got up, to stop and moan meant death. "Escape first, fix yourself up later!" he screamed out loud.

He was now half sprinting, half hobbling for his life along with hundreds of other escapees, with no direction or plan other than to get away and hide as fast as possible. There were people literally everywhere, running in every possible direction.

The whole thing was probably hopeless but better to die doing this than crying in a cell being beaten. After approximately 200 yards he ran into a forest, his feet were being cut to pieces but he just had to ignore it for now. His feet would heal, so would his leg but a bullet in the head would not.

As the sound of the alarm faded into the night, he came through the other side of the wooded area to find himself standing in front of another wire fence, this time with no razor wire on top. Climbing over he looked back at the sign on the other side which read "Nature Reserve No Trespassing."

Spinning around he saw that he was on the hill overlooking his town. He had been to the park at the bottom on this hill so many times and had no idea what was at the top and through the wood. He was glad that was the case for if he knew of those horrors he would not have survived the place. He was lucky that his ignorance gave him hope, no matter how small a hope that was.

He looked around watching people running all over the place. 'Good luck my friends, I hope you make it', he thought as he started to descend down the hill. 'You never were any good at this' he said to himself and he started stumbling, tripping, sometimes rolling but ultimately arrived at the children's play area at the bottom in a heap.

"SHIT!" he said out loud. He had not thought about getting this far. Where the hell is he going to go now? I am dressed in rags, no shoes, with bleeding feet and a knackered leg. If I run into someone they are going to report me.

Panicking he had to tell himself to calm down and think. There were no sirens so word had not got out yet, it must still be chaos up there he thought. The first thing he needed to do was hide, then get some clothes and lie low somewhere. Then he needed to get out of town. What he would do for food and water he did not think about, this was his plan and it had to do for now, time was not on his side.

Running across the play area and the fields, the grass wiped his feet clean of blood. Again, luck being on this side as the trackers and their dogs would lose his scent and sight of bloodied footprints. He fled down an alleyway down the back of some shops. He hoped that he would find some old clothes in the bins out the back. Come on, he thought, give me a break big bird thing in the sky now, please!

After rummaging through the fifth bin, bingo! He managed to find a shirt that was too small and a pair of trousers that were too big. He promptly put them on and stuffed his rags into the bottom of the stinking bin.

Sirens were now blaring everywhere, the alarm had been sounded and shots started to ring out as people were being discovered. There was no escape from this place. He only had one option and so Tiberius climbed into the bin and hid in silence.

***

The doors flew open in the Premier Planning Office. Premier Xe stormed in screaming in an apoplectic rage! It was an intimate gathering of the Commander Generals of the Military and Police along with the Communications Chief.

The Supreme Sage's less than subtle reminder that none of them actually had the nerve or the desire to do the job of the one they wanted to get rid of and the Chief Treasurer's reminder of their own indiscretions had hit home and they decided to continue to support him, for now, albeit with less fervour than before. So here they sat taking another bollocking.

Waving his arms around he screamed, "FOR THE LAST THREE MONTHS I HAVE BEEN SPENDING 24 HOURS A FUCKING DAY TRYING TO KEEP THIS THING TOGETHER AND YOU LOT IN YOUR NICE COMFORTBALE LIVES. ALL YOU HAD TO DO WAS JUST DO YOUR OWN FUCKING JOB AND NOT ADD TO THE PROBLEMS, BUT NO, NO YOU CANNOT EVEN DO THAT! NOT THREE FUCKING MONTHS GO BY AFTER WE SHUT DOWN ONE OF THOSE CESS PITS BEFORE YOU MANAGE TO FUCK SOMETHING ELSE UP! HOW ON THE FUCKING EARTH DID YOU MANAGE TO LET 3,000 ODD ARSEHOLES ESCAPE FROM THE CAPITAL'S PREMIER DETENTION FACILITY AND A BODY COUNT UP THERE THAT IS GOING TO KEEP THE CLEAN UP CREWS BUSY FOR DAYS!" he demanded of Commander General Police.

"Xe 1," Commander General Police started. "It was an unexpected mass escape. I know the commander well and they are impeccable in their 'methods' to keep the prisoners under full control and within the facility."
"WELL, IT DID NOT FUCKING WORK THIS TIME DID IT!"

"Indeed not and I have launched a full investigation as to what happened. I am meeting the Commander tomorrow to discuss matters at the site, to improve matters," Commander General Police replied.

"No you won't," Said Premier Xe.

"Why is that Xe 1?" Commander General Police asked.

"Because I just had them executed."

"Xe 1—" She started to reply.

"DON'T FUCKING XE 1 ME YOU FUCKING UTTERLY, FUCKING USELESS…FUCKING FUCK! I HAVE HAD ENOUGH OF YOU AND YOUR INCOMPETENCE, YOU DID NOT EVEN FIND THE SPEECH SANCTUARY, A PRAEFECTI DID! YOU ARE A FUCKING LAZY INCOMPETENT WASTE OF FUCKING SPACE."

"But…" Commander General Police started to say.

"SHUT THE FUCK UP WHILE I AM TALKING! YOU DID NOT FIND IT. YOUR PRAEFECTI DID!" Premier Xe pointed to the Praefecti stood to attention at the door.

The Praefecti stood there with his number one outfit on with medals pinned and plume in the top of his helmet, which he held under his arm. "Premier Xe it was a pleasure to rid the country of another den of debauchery. Allow me please to continue this work and close them all down!"

Commander General Military smirked, hiding his irritation that the police had piped him to the post on this one, especially when he was so close to finding the place himself and within it the Chief Treasurer as the icing on the cake, but neither were to be his this time around.

He looked across at Commander General Police in total delight with eyebrows raised and a smile so broad it would almost touch the walls on either side of the room. The Commander General Police did not miss the gesture.
The Commander General Police turned to ask how the Praefecti had managed to locate such a place and why he had not told the chain of command of it.

"I commanded my force to patrol an area that had seen a lot of unusual yet regular citizen activity but was lacking in places to meet. We observed the comings and goings of the local populace and noticed a pattern. When my spy network told me about the place, they said they had contact from someone telling me we were in the right place. As head of the police intelligence unit I have many spies, even those in different uniforms." He stated still staring forward, but with a shift of his eyes betrayed that the uniform was not only of the police, as he caught the stone-cold stare of the Commander General Military.

The Commander General Military's face dropped at the statement, was his spy a double agent with the police? A mental note was made to 'have a word' with him at a later date.

The Praefecti continued, "I had to take the chance there and then to maximise the potential catch. It worked to perfection Commander, and we captured over fifty people."

"Why did you not inform me of this plan?" demanded Commander General Police.

"With respect, there was not time to manage the bureaucracy Commander. By the time the forms were completed, filed and the levels of command instructed, they would have realised that we were close. We would have had the location but no people within. We had to take a decisive decision and act immediately."

"SEE, THAT IS WHAT YOU HAVE BROUGHT TO THIS TEAM. BUREAUCRACY, DELAY AND FAILURE. YOU ARE FIRED, GET OUT OF MY FUCKING SIGHT AND REPORT TO COMMANDER GENERAL MILITARY FOR FURTHER INSTRUCTION! I CANNOT TOLERATE YOU FOR ANOTHER MINUTE!" Premier Xe interjected.

"But…" Commander General Police tried to respond.

"OUT OR I WILL HAVE YOU SHOT RIGHT HERE, RIGHT NOW!"

Commander General Military pulled out his side arm and played with it invitingly with a smile on his face, it was now his turn to put a weapon on the table.

Commander General Police got up, glaring at Commander General Military who was having real trouble hiding his delight and the events unfolding, but tried non-the-less by gritting his teeth so hard that the muscles on the side of his totally square jaw were bulging. This was definitely worth the trip here he thought, I could do this every day.

"Sit Commander General Police," Premier Xe said to the Praefecti.

The previous Commander General Police turned to look and sit back down, thinking this was just another rant that never actually went anywhere.

"I THOUGHT I TOLD YOU TO LEAVE XE, FUCK OFF!" Premier Xe stated.

As Xe, as she was now known, left the room, she knew she had become nothing. She would be thrown out of her home only for it to be given to the new Commander General Police. It was over and so soon would her life be over. She knew what she had to do and she would not give the Commander General Military the pleasure of pulling the trigger.

Travelling home she said to her partner that was going to meet someone. Driving to the far South of the city, she pulled up to a barn that looked derelict from the outside. Entering she worked her way to the corner and climbed down a ladder, hidden behind some old broken furniture. Under the barn was a large open area in the shape of a cross.

She walked up to the front end that faced East, that had a table with a sacred cloth over it and was covered in candles, above it was a man nailed to a cross. She dropped to her knees sobbing. A man walked over dressed in the finest robes and carrying a golden staff of some sort with a cross and the same person seemingly attached to the top in the same position. It was made of the finest gold and was a sight to behold.

The man asked her what the matter was. Replying she stated, "My life has come to an end Father. It is now forfeit and I come here to seek one last blessing before it finally ends."
Placing his hand on her head he stated, "By being a parishioner here you have accepted Christ into your heart and your soul my child and should this life come to an end then you will join him in the Kingdom of God, in peace. Do not fear death as he will welcome you into his bosom of love.

Your body may die and decay but remember your soul is eternal and you knew this day would come; we have spoken of it often in our gatherings. Heaven, a place more glorious than anything you can ever imagine. It is a place of joy, free of pain, free of sorrow, free of any Earthly responsibility."

The person she called Father finished by saying, "I remind you of Matthew 27:45-46 From noon until three in the afternoon darkness came over all the land. About three in the afternoon Jesus cried out in a loud voice, 'My God, My God why have you forsaken me?"

He continued, "He had been forsaken but only for this moment as at this moment he had become sin for us. He died for our sins after which he was became exalted.

Anyone who humbles themselves will also become exalted. You kneel here humble in the presence of God, with him in your heart, you too will be exalted."

"But I have done so many terrible, evil things," she started sobbing, "and I cannot end things myself as I will never be admitted to his Kingdom!"

"All that matters is you have God's love in your heart my child." He replied, "I ask God through Jesus for you to be forgiven for your sins. The Good Book is clear that whether you go to Heaven or Hell is dependent on your relationship with Jesus. Again, I say you have him in your heart, you will be with him however you end up starting that journey to his presence."

Taking a deep breath to control the sobbing, she finally stood, "Thank you Father, I will see you one day in the Kingdom of our Lord and Saviour."

"Walk tall my child," He stated as she stood and turned towards the ladder out from the secret and sacred place.

Finding a small, secluded copse some miles further to the South, she knelt and said, "I kneel before you my Lord hoping that you will allow me to enter your Kingdom. Now at the end I see my sins, the wickedness of this life and of my hand. I pray that you allow me entry and cleanse my soul of this evil that I have done. I am forever your servant."

With that she placed her weapon in her mouth, trembling and sobbing. A single shot rang out.

"Now that we actually have someone who knows how to find a Speech Sanctuary, I will be putting Commander General Police in charge of all operations going forward. It will be your job to end the bureaucracy and close down the pits of filth," Premier Xe said in a more calming voice.

"Commander General Military you will report into Commander General Police on this matter." Commander General Military went from total amusement to sheer anger in the space of that short statement.

"My soldiers do not hunt down Speech Sanctuaries!" he stated.

"They do now," came the reply. "Do you have a problem with that Commander General Military?"

After a long pause staring at Premier Xe, he replied, "No, we will work together and end these wretched places once and for all," he really was weak, just as they had said. He had just confirmed his subjugation to Premier Xe for the rest of his life.

"Good, now get on with it, go on, fuck off!"

Standing in the hallway listening to the ranting, the CEO of Global Life took a call, "Yes, ok…yes…yes… I understand"

\*\*\*

Tiberius stayed in the bin burying himself under the stinking rubbish. He decided that he would stay here until the sirens ended. Eventually they tailed off and the shooting and shouting could no longer be heard; give it another day he thought.
Eventually hunger and thirst got the better of him and he had to move; he did not go through the last day only to die of starvation in a bin. As he moved to the top of the rubbish the lid opened. Tiberius froze as he stared at a woman who was staring straight back at him. Staring intently, he thought he recognised her, yes he did. It was the woman in the black dress from his first visit to the Speech Sanctuary!

He looked at her with begging puppy dog eyes, she looked around. "You do know that the entire New Government and half the citizenry is looking for you, don't you?" She said.

Tiberius breathed a sigh of relief knowing that she recognised him and had not shouted out to anyone. "Yes," he replied, "I had to hide somewhere and this seemed the best place at the time, but I cannot stay here forever, I need food and water and somewhere to stay but will attract attention dressed like this."

The woman looked around thinking. "You will have to stay here until nightfall, I will bring out a bag later with some food and water in it for you, but you have to stay hidden, bury yourself back under the rubbish until I come back. Only after it gets dark can you risk moving around," At this point she promptly dumped the rubbish on his head and walked off. The lid slammed shut and Tiberius buried himself once again.

Over the course of the day the lid was opened and a bag thrown in. Opening each bag, he found stinking rubbish within. Eventually a bag came in with a comment "food." The lid shut. He opened the bag and ate every last piece of the out-of-date sandwiches within, initial painful swallows made way for easier eating when washed down with water. The heartburn and indigestion felt like he was having a heart attack but again, to Tiberius it felt great.

Eventually the lid opened, "clothes" and a bag came into the bin, which was promptly shut again. Changing clothes quietly in a bin was not the easiest thing to do but eventually he managed it. The clothes fitted but the shoes were too small. He squeezed in his toes; it was painful but potentially it was freedom. He laughed inside when he remembered the conversation with the Historian again 'Freedom is only what you perceive it to be' he thought as he realised freedom right now was simply shoes that were too small and not being shot in the street.

Laying on top of the rubbish he waited nervously, hoping that she was the only person to use this bin. The lid opened and he froze. "Move," came the command and the lid shut again.

Opening the lid only a fraction he peeked out into the dark alleyway. "Come on," the woman said, my apartment is not far away. We will take the back streets to avoid the police and as many cameras as we can. The coat has a hood, put it up."

Doing as instructed they worked their way around a convoluted route to her apartment. Once inside she told him to go into the bathroom and wash. He stank and he knew it. After washing both himself and the clothes, he walked back into the apartment with a towel around his waist. The woman was sat on the sofa.

"I do not know how to thank you," he said.

"You do not need to; I would have done it for anyone from our sanctuary. I cannot believe it is gone. All those lives lost, all that fun to be had been taken away and we are back to square one, but this time it is worse as we have to wait for another invitation knowing they exist and knowing their members are going to be extra careful going forward. The invite will probably never come." She took a sip from her cup.

"Tiberius," he stated offering his hand.

"Alexis," She replied shaking it.

"Nice name."

"It's ironic as when they gave me that name, they said it stood for "Saving men." Apparently, it was a bit of fun from the Historian and we all laughed, joking about how it is always a woman that is the real support for the man who changes the world, usually in the background, usually without fanfare, but probably the most vital cog in the machine. Little did we know it would be more than just a causal reference to a past age!"

"Yeah, ironic I guess. Have they caught many of the escapees?" he enquired.

"Yes, they hunted many of them down with the help of scum citizens reporting them. I have to be fair the bounty you all have on your heads had everyone out looking for you. I do not know how you got away."

"Neither do I, but I am so glad that it was you that opened that bin. How many escaped in the end?" he replied.

"According to the news there are only 300 odd left to get. All escapees were either executed on the spot or thrown into the back of a police wagon,"

Tiberius shuddered.

"I guess Detention Centre One was not a holiday camp then. Not a 'pleasant' experience for you?"

"I would not like to explain what happened in that place. I knew everyone was terrified of it due to all the rumours, but I have to tell you the rumours were not even halfway to how bad that place is. I do not want to tell you more as it will give you nightmares."

"No please do she said, I have not got anything to do tonight and it takes a lot to frighten me"

Tiberius sat down and spent the next couple of hours explaining what had happened, with some content left out, whilst a steady stream of water and coffee was brought to him. By the time he had finished Alexis had had tears streaming down her face.

"That is utterly inhumane," she said, wiping a tear away. "Why did they not just shoot you?"

"No idea, I guess that would not be enough fun for them, perhaps the woman who said to not kill me was in charge or something, perhaps pure luck, who knows? Did you know John from the Sanctuary?"

"Yes," everyone did. He was the life and soul of the place!"

"He didn't make it either," he said without explaining the way in which he departed this adventure for the next. "The Keepers were killed everything just destroyed and for what, because people want have a good time, without being instructed as to what the 'good time' defined as by New Government dictate. They just stormed in and snatched us all, I just hope that enough people managed to get away and will be able to have a taste of freedom before they get cut down."

Alexis put on the news. "Here watch this as I get some food sorted out. You can rest up for a while and I will try to get some clothes that fit better, then you have a chance. Could do with the hackers still being around, I could have even got you a Personal Citizen Device. I assume they got taken as well?"

"Don't know, I would not know what they looked like if they walked in here now. I hope they did, but something must have gone wrong, I thought they made the place invisible according to Cassia. She was lucky not to be there as well considering how often she visited the place."

"I guess there is only so much luck to go round, and she had yours that night by the sounds of it."

Tiberius sat watching the news. The first article was all about the escape. There were only 232 left to get, well if you believed the news anyway. Tiberius just hoped that it would be more and they were just not admitting it. The faces were scrolled across the bottom of the picture with a huge bounty attached to each one, anyone would take their chance and hand them in if they did not know about what was going on behind the façade that the New Government creates. Who could blame them, not knowing what he did now.

After that article, came one about a new car, which nobody could afford, then they started talking about how great Premier Xe was regarding his control of the economy. At this point he had seen enough and switched off the TV.

Alexis came back with some food. Here get this in you, I suspect you could do with a few calories, so I did you two. She offered him alcohol but he declined.

"Water please, but thanks," he said. The temptation was great given how long ago it was that he had any alcohol, but he wanted a clear head for a while at least.

They chatted about the good times at 'home' and how Flo made him strip naked to be fitted out. Alexis laughed out loud, she had not laughed this much since the place was raided and it felt good.
As she took away the plastic trays and put them in the sink, it occurred to Tiberius that he had no idea what day it was or what time it was, perhaps even what year it was, such had the passage of time, so intrinsically part of life, so important to the majority of people, become so pointless to his existence. "What day is it Alexis?" he asked.

"Wednesday," she replied not thinking to give him a date or year even, such was it taken for granted by some, yet denied to so many others.

"Huh, time, why do we really need it?" he said mockingly.

The two of them chatted well into the night about Detention Centre One and the Speech Sanctuary and by the end he was lying down on the sofa. Eventually he drifted off to sleep and Alexis put a spare blanket over him before going to bed.

In the morning Tiberius awoke from the deepest sleep he had had in ages, yet still in there, like clockwork was his dream, his field, his escape. As he shook his head and sat up a note fell to the floor. It read 'Tiberius, I am sure I do not have to tell you this but do not leave the apartment! I will be back after work. Help yourself to food and water but again do not put on the TV, have a shower or flush the loo. If the neighbours hear it, they will get suspicious. PS I left the curtains drawn, please leave them that way,'

Tiberius smiled as he read it. She was such a trusting soul, he could not betray that, so did exactly as he was told and spent the day lounging around and reading the latest copy of 'Good Citizen' from front cover to back cover. It was still the pile of drivel it had always been; somethings never change he thought.

He heard the lock on the front door go and went and hid in the bathroom. Alexis walked in and closed the door. "Tiberius?" She said quietly.

"Here. I did as I was told!" he said with a smile on this face.

The two spent the evening talking and laughing again, it was exactly what they both needed to help hide the pain and sadness of recent times and gave them a little reminder of what the Speech Sanctuary stood for, friendship and freedom.

And so it went on for a couple of weeks as his strength returned. Tiberius enjoyed the conversations and he really felt for Alexis, but the dreams returned to their intensity and his mind started to think of other things. He felt fully recovered, strong and ready for whatever was to come next. Only this time he knew what was coming next. His mind was made, his course plotted, he just needed to put in place one more thing. Saying to himself I will give it till tomorrow, then I must go, I cannot risk her life anymore and I need my Sage.

Tiberius's woke with his sleeping mind immediately handing over his turmoil to his waking one. He did not know what to think or what to do.

Recognising that he had now healed and recovered, he knew he needed to move on, move forward. The momentum was taking him along now as his life journey was pulling him rather than him pushing against some invisible force.

He knew could not stay in Alexis' apartment any longer. It was putting her at risk and he could not forgive himself should anything happen. He could only go to one place, that place that had become his true home, before in spirit but now physically, seeing that his own had been taken from him, that one probably had the next person in there already. 'I wonder what they thought of my picture?' he thought for a second.

He needed somewhere he could finally switch off the crashing thoughts and emotions, like interplanetary collisions, smashing together to destroy the massive creations into dust in an instant and so this is how he felt, like his mind was colliding with itself and he was starting to descend into total madness.

He needed his darkness, his safe space but with the support of the Sages and he needed them now.

Having planned this for a few days now and the moonless night arriving; he got off the sofa, his bed for these past couple weeks. Already dressed and waiting for the right time, he calmly folded the blanket and left the note he had written in preparation the day before.

*** 

My dear, dear, beautiful Alexis,
You have saved me, not only physically but emotionally and mentally.

Once a person said to me that I have guardians in my dreams looking out for me in my life. I used to think it was a joke, but now I know it was true. Now I know there are good people out there like you, people true of heart and of soul, beautiful inside and out.

Your name is one of hope, of love, of protection and is probably the most apt name I have heard anyone be given. Now I must go and give hope to others, to everyone.

You have saved one man now but perhaps have saved all men and all peoples of this country.

We will meet again someday and I promise when we do the whole country will be a Speech Sanctuary!

Yours thankfully for eternity
Tiberius

***

Leaving as quietly as he could, he opened the door to the apartment. Peering round the corners all was quiet and he slipped out in silence. Taking the emergency escape stairs and quietly slipped out of the side of the building.

All was quiet as he disappeared out into the night except for a Sage stood in the shadows on the other side of the road who went unnoticed.

"He has left the apartment," the Sage said, "Without a coat in the rain. I will follow."

# Chapter 14:

# Pursuit

Tiberius was heading straight for the Church, to his Sage, who had often spoke to him in a way that no other could and seemed to be able to help him contain his mind and his urges and had become the drug of choice for him now. No more Neeja, just peace, even if it had to be delivered via his death.

Within twenty yards of the apartment block however, Tiberius was cursing himself as he became soaked. He was so eager to leave the apartment he left his coat behind. With no way of going back to retrieve it he had no choice but to ignore the rain and push on. The fact that it was pouring with rain did not bother him, it was like a shower for his soul and rain was his friend after all, however, to been seen out at night, in the rain with no coat, well that will attract attention of the sort he did not want right now.

Knowing he could not use public transport as he no longer had a Personal Citizen Device, he half walked, half ran across the sub district towards the church. Rounding the corner of road 55 and 54 he walked straight past a police vehicle travelling towards him. "FUCK! SHIT, FUCK!" he muttered loudly as he continued, picking up his pace to an almost jog.

As he feared and dressed as he was, he did not go unnoticed and the Police vehicle turned around immediately. Panicking, he started running, lights and sirens now started. He knew that other units would be called in immediately, so he started to sprint for his life.

Immediately cutting down an alleyway where the vehicle could not follow, Tiberius ran for his life. If he got caught, he would surely end up dead; he was a wanted murderer after all. Glancing over his shoulder he saw that the police vehicle had stopped and the multiple officers poured out, armed with their hand to hand 'tools of the trade' and started a foot pursuit. FUCK! FUCK! FUCK! Tiberius thought as he took another sharp turn down another alleyway.

He could hear more sirens in the distance and knew he was on very limited time, unless he can find a way of hiding somewhere. Deciding all alleyway exits will soon be blocked, something inside told him to bolt for the large park area about a hundred meters away, there was no other choice, so upped his pace again and bolted for it.

He started to run out of steam as he charged through the open gates to the park, in some strange way he thought he would be able to hide in a bush somewhere from the police with their searchlights and dogs. It was hopeless and he knew it, but without any other option he charged into a small, wooded area in the direction of the church on the other side of the field, stumbling and tripping as he went, swiping branches and shrubs out of the way. 'Please big bird in the sky, look down on me again, make the police miss the other side of the wood', he screamed in his head as he ran.

The police were now getting close; he could see their torches and multiple sirens could be heard from his hiding place. They were not far away. The police did not bother to shout stop, they were on the hunt now, eyes wide, and adrenaline pumping as they hunted down their human prey. The murderous beating would commence soon and each officer wanted to be the one to administer it.

Barking. The dogs had been released, time was running out, death was near. Tiberius ran again smashing through tree branches as he hurtled deep in the wooded area. He had no energy, no breath and every part of his body felt battered, bruised and broken…again. Soon he would be out the other side and straight into the brutality awaiting him. Where was that bloody bird, fucking useless crap as usual from the Dream Weaver!

The centre of the wooded area arrived, a strangely familiar area where he had a real sense of Déjà vu. He started to slow as he felt his inevitable demise coming closer by the second and simply stopped awaiting his fate. He was doubled over, he hurt, he had no breath, and he knew what was coming. 'Death would be welcome right now' he thought, just make the first hit final, then they can do whatever they wanted with his body. The spark that had been so bright had now faded to almost nothing again, such was one minute he was high and determined, but thirty seconds later he would feel lost and aimless. This roller-coaster was more extreme by the day now and he just wanted to get off it. He knew the swift end he yearned for would not happen, so skilled were the Peditata in keeping their victims alive for the longest possible time for the longest amount of pain and suffering and mainly for the maximum amount of their pleasure.

Just as the lights reached the edge of the wood, Tiberius stood, soaked, sweating and still breathing hard with his hands on his hips. He was not going to go down cowering like a crying coward and he would look into their eyes before the first blow put him on the floor.

Suddenly something grabbed his foot, Tiberius looked down panicking. He had not prepared for this in his mind and he was in sudden abject terror.

There was a hand grabbing his ankle. "Quickly!" demanded a voice. "Jump down or die!" He did not know how deep it was or what was in there, but there was a human voice and taking more than three seconds to decide would mean his death. Jumping in he fell about ten feet before hitting the ground, hard.

"Argghh!" he stated through gritted teeth.

"SHHH!" came the voice as it repositioned something that filled the hole and cut out all light. They were now in total darkness and Tiberius could not even see his hand let alone who he was in this place with. His ankle was badly damaged, not broken but he could feel the warmth and swelling starting already. It was absolute agony, but he could not even whisper a sound, so crushed his teeth together ever harder. "You must stay absolutely silent!" whispered the voice.

Above ground they could hear the faint barking of the dogs and the shouts and arguments of the Peditata. They were clearly furious that their prey had got away and started blaming each other for losing their sport in these woods. For about ten minutes the searching, bellowing and what appeared to be sporadic fights breaking out between the officers continued until it eventually went silent.

The voice whispered, "ok we can move now." There was no response. "Come we must go!" again no response. A small torch flickered into life to search for the one they had just saved from certain death. The beam found its target. Tiberius lay unconscious on the ground. You look like you have just been on the receiving end of the Peditata, let alone just escaped them, the owner of the voice thought, chuckling to itself, as he moved over and threw Tiberius over his shoulder. Looks like I may have some company for a few days he thought as he walked off down the stone arched underground tunnel.

Tiberius woke hours later. Slowly opening his eyes at first before the first shot of pain raced up his leg made them open wide and fast. "nnnngggggg!" he said with maximum intensity but minimal sound, thinking he was still in the hole in the ground and remembering what his memory was telling him had just happened.

Opening his eyes, he noticed that things had moved on since he passed out and now, he could see. He was lying on cushions on what appeared to be a large slab. Looking at the ceiling he could see fine stone arches with carvings and shapes that looked familiar but with the pain coursing through his body, focussing on anything at all was impossible. Closing his eyes, mostly to control the pain, he opened them again when a voice stated "Ah! You are back with us again Tiberius. Whilst you are in no immediate danger, please do try to keep your voice down as loud noises will be heard above us and may attract unwanted attention."

Tiberius sat up like a shot, then promptly screamed a muffled "nnnngggggg!" again. His haste to move was greater than the speed of his brain telling him that he had a badly damaged ankle.

"Shhh calm down, I will come round to you, just stay there before you do yourself some mortal damage!" the voice stated as a figure entered Tiberius's peripheral vision to the right.

It was a Sage, in a heavy brown cloak. "You!" said Tiberius, "How did…when… where," stumbling over his words.

"Slow down," came the reply as the Sage pulled back his hood to reveal himself. Yes I am a Sage, one of the brethren who belong to this church"

"Am I in church C2?"

"Yes," came the reply, "You are in the crypt, deep underground. Which is where you will need to stay until you are well again."

Tiberius could not believe his luck, he had ended up in the very church he was desperate to get to, and if only he had put a damn coat on he would have made it in a much more comfortable fashion.

He laid back down with a muffled, manic laugh, putting his hands over his face, half through pain and half through sheer relief.

"I am glad you are in such good spirits, if in more pain than you had realised. It will take some time for you to heal, perhaps two weeks, but we will look after you until you are better," said the Sage.

"Then what?" replied Tiberius composing himself.

"One step at a time, if you will pardon the intentional joke. First you get healthy, then we work out what happens next."

This sounded rather ominous to Tiberius. Am I a prisoner here? Why can I not just get up and leave? Screw you, he thought, as a fire swelled in his belly and he started to move. "nnnngggggg!" came the next noise out of his mouth. 'OK fine! But when I get better, I am out of here', he stated angrily to himself.

"If you really do want to leave go up those steps there but given that Xe 805491997 is at present one of the most wanted people in the country, I would suggest that this would be rather foolish. A two-year-old could outrun you right now and three troops of police would move more quietly, but there is no law or rule of the Sages that states you must remain. That is your choice and your choice only."

Lying back down Tiberius simply stated, "Fine, you do make a couple of good points there."

Smiling the Sage turned and left.

Over the next few days, various Sages came to treat Tiberius's ankle as a well as bring him food, water and a bowl of water with a towel in order to keep himself clean and replace the bucket for the resultant output of the food and water.

Tiberius did not like the latter requirement but he had no choice in the matter right now. Practicality had to be the primary concern here, not modesty.

They also brought him books on Stoicism to keep his mind occupied whilst his body healed. Tiberius could not remember the last time he had actually held a real book in his hands, they were rare as all information these days was conveyed electronically, after censorship by the New Government of course.

He was dressed in a cloak similar to that of the Sages but the white one he had seen in the main church. It had the blue sash around the waist. It was surprisingly warm and comfortable yet light and easy to move around in.

Hobbling around the crypt with the help of a makeshift crutch, Tiberius looked but could not find his original clothing. 'Looks like I will have to escape naked I guess' he half joked to himself.

The crypt itself was entirely made of stone yet was not as cold as he thought such a room would be, especially as it had no windows and was entirely lit by torches of flame, regularly changed by the Sages when they came down to tend for him.

The outer walls were all covered in pods where a coffin or ashes could be placed. Fourteen sections for coffins and ten for ashes. All were made of stone as was just about everything in there.

The coffin sections each could fit a coffin head to foot. Each section was eight pods high, each separated by a shelf, so as to create a space for each coffin. At the front of each section was a small iron grill, upon which was a plaque describing who was laid to rest there.

The ashes sections were open shelves upon which there were multiple urns containing the ashes. Again, each section was eight pods high in line with the shelves for the coffins to the left.

Within each pod were the urns of those cremated. Each urn was unique in size, shape and material they were made out of, from what Tiberius could see, and each urn had writing on the side detailing who the person was. Only two of these pods were full and had the same iron grill on the front, so you could not see all of the urns within.

Again, Tiberius was taken aback by how most appeared to be empty, given the apparent age of the building.

Moving to the left Tiberius started to read the plaques on the coffins.

'Here is a Sage of the order. Dedicated to enlightenment and to the people'

The plaque on the coffin above read 'Here is a Sage of the order. Dedicated to enlightenment and to the people'
Huh thought Tiberius, this could be a little more boring than I thought. Moving up to the next coffin, this one at eye level, the plaque read 'Here is a Sage of the order. Dedicated to enlightenment and to the people'

"OK this better get more interesting soon," Tiberius mumbled as he moved to the next column of coffins, but he knew there was nothing else to do right now, so even if they are all the same, I may as well just read them so I can say I achieved something.

On the bottom plaque, as indeed on all the coffin plaques that Tiberius could read it stated 'Here is a Sage of the order. Dedicated to enlightenment and to the people'

"Ok, well that killed about 15 minutes," Tiberius said openly. "I wonder what other really interesting things I can read in here whilst I wait for the book to be changed."

"Perhaps, a conversation may be more to your requirements to break your boredom Tiberius," came a voice from behind. It was the Sage that Tiberius met on his first visit to the church.

"Ah! It's you, my Sage, I came here looking for you!" Tiberius said as he turned round on the spot, grimacing as again he forgot the slightly better, yet still damaged ankle.

"Indeed it is me," came the reply from a smirking mouth.

"How are you feeling now after a week of our care? You certainly seem able to stumble around now."

"Yes, yes. Erm much better thank you and I would like to thank the Sages for looking after me, through the few days, I feel much better now," Tiberius replied feeling a little rude in the abruptness of his initial response.
"And how is your soul?" said the Sage.

"My Soul?"

"Yes, your soul," The Sage said as he poured himself a glass of water. Tiberius looked at the Sage with a confused expression on his face.

The Sage looked up and clarified, "You are made to three parts, your physical form, your exterior person, the one you project to the world and the real you, the one inside. That is the one that is your soul, the person who you really are. The person that speaks to you without saying words, that guides you through life, without telling you the plan. It is your soul that is so vital to you, yet is always the one that is suppressed, ignored, even killed off in those lost to believing that the world makes them and not they who make the world around them, so common to today.

So I ask again, how is the soul of my occupati?"

"Scared," replied Tiberius. "Lost and scared. I do not know how I will be able to go back out there," he said pointing up the stairs which the Sages came to him down. "The Police are after me, I have no Personal Citizen Device, I no doubt have lost my apartment, I have no job, no bank account, no money, and no future and to top all of that off my beautiful sanctuary is gone. What am I supposed to do now? I have absolutely nothing."

"Your beautiful sanctuary?" enquired the Sage

"SHIT! Oh well it does not matter anymore. I used to go to the speech sanctuary on the corner of 3rd and 45th street. It was my escape, where I could be free if only for a few hours, but the bastards even took that from me. If I knew who had betrayed us, I will kill them with my own bare hands!"

"I am familiar with it," interjected the Sage.

"How?" demanded Tiberius slowly losing control of himself.

"Tiberius, there are many things that you will find out very soon, but I can assure you that I had no part in its discovery nor destruction. For that you will need to look elsewhere.

"How do you know about it?"

"We may be based in this church but we do go out once in a while you know to do wild and outrageous things like talk to people," the Sage said smiling and raising his eyebrows.

Tiberius turned back around, more carefully this time.

"The plaques on the coffins, they seemed to bore you. Why?"

Tiberius shook his head to clear his mind, he replied, "They all say the same thing 'Here is a Sage of the order. Dedicated to enlightenment and to the people'. It was just not very entertaining, I did not mean to offend."

"So, if you were in one of those coffins, what would you like it to say? What would you like to project into this world after your death, to people you will never meet?" Asked the Sage inquisitively.

"I don't know, I don't care really but it would be nice to be different, to have made a change, a difference to this miserable existence that at its heart really just wants you to die to save a bit of cash. Like I said I am going to change the whole, but I still have no idea how I am going to do it, I am just more determined to."

The Sage pushed Tiberius further, "Give me some words. Here lies Tiberius, he did…"

Tiberius thought for a few seconds and stated, "Here lies Tiberius. He changed the world by giving freedom back to the enslaved!" in a sarcastic voice.

"And why would it not say that?" came the swift response.

"Because it will never happen, will it! I will show my face outside and be beaten to death less than thirty minutes later. I do not know why you bothered to save me and put me back together!"

"Maybe it is because we believe in you even if you do not believe in yourself. Perhaps we can see that which you cannot, know things about you that you do not. Perhaps we can see past the exterior person and see into your soul. Perhaps we can see a fire in there that needs to be released but is being held back. Maybe," said the Sage.

"OK so I will go out now and tell everyone to be free then, shall I?" Tiberius retorted.

"Oh, I would not do that Tiberius, according to the news you are a terrorist and a child murderer. Your face is on the list of most wanted around these parts for some reason. If you show your face outside you will most certainly be beaten to death less than thirty minutes later." The Sage said with a big smile on his face, seemingly enjoying his teasing in this conversation.

"Then what am I to do? I cannot spend the rest of my existence in this room!" Tiberius said, clearly losing his cool again.

"And to be honest we would not want you here doing that Tiberius. We are happy to patch you up but we cannot hide you forever. Perhaps let us think for a day or so and come up with a plan. Oh, and you can use the ladder there to read the plaques further up if you want to carry on," said the Sage as he turned and started to walk up the steps.

With that he disappeared around the corner of the stairs leaving Tiberius alone again but at least with some fresh food, water and thankfully new books to read.

*** 

Cassia sat in her apartment staring ahead, lost in thought.

In her hand was a letter given to her from an unknown yet expected person just outside the main capital magtrain station.

She had read it at least five times, which was a lot considering its content. '2-3 stands ready as do the others. We await the signal as described.'

*** 

Tiberius had read the two new books cover to cover and was contemplating reading one again such was the boredom now getting to him, when he remembered what the Sage had said to him about the ladder.
Taking it from the side by the steps, it looked a rickety old thing and when Tiberius placed it against the wall of pods, was concerned he would fall off and damage his ankle again. Going back to square one in this place was not an

option but nor was putting up with this boredom anymore.

Climbing the ladder, he read the first plaque above head height 'Here is a Sage of the order. Dedicated to enlightenment and to the people'. Here we go again

And so it went for all of the plaques above head height on the first two columns of coffins. Turning to the last column he was almost at his challenge of simply reading the whole 'collection' rather than what was actually written on them, so up he went. There were three to read. The first of course stated 'Here is a Sage of the order. Dedicated to enlightenment and to the people'. Yup Tiberius thought, how would I have guessed that?

Moving up to the next he read 'Here is a Sage of the order. James was a proud advocate of freedom and of love for our flock. Strong, proud and firm he stood tall against our enemies. A leader of the leaders.'

Whoa! Thought Tiberius, a name.

Moving up to the last he brushed the dust off the plaque to read better in the half-light. 'Here is Sarah. A Proud mother who defied the authorities and lost her life fighting for the freedom of her child, her partner James and all peoples of this land. She leaves behind Tiberius and hope of a new dawn'

"Tiberius, huh same name as me," he muttered as he went back down just as the Sage walked into the room. "Have you read them all now?" he asked inquisitively.

"Yes, do you know who James and Sarah were?" Tiberius replied. "And why do they have different plaques to the rest?"

"Indeed I do. Why are you so interested in them? They are just another couple of bodies in these racks are they not?" asked the Sage.

"Because they have names, it means they were somebody, not just another Xe or just another Sage. Sorry I did not mean that to sound disrespectful, but it feels more personal with them, like there is a story to tell, not just another existence of no real importance," Tiberius said quite forcefully.

"They were my parents," said the Sage.

Tiberius just stood there and looked at the Sage in total shock and silence. "Erm, wow ok. I am sorry for you."

"No need. They led full lives, loved me, nurtured me and kept me safe. I could not have asked for better parents. They went to a demonstration when I was little. I remember it clearly. They brought me here and as I played, I saw them speaking to the Sages who looked sad, but nodded. I remember my dad telling me to "Be brave as a lion and change the world my boy!" I had no idea what he meant at the time, I was too young, but I remember the words as if they were said yesterday. My last memories of my mother were her crying as she held me so tight I thought I would burst. She looked me straight in the eye and said how much she loved me and how she was going to make the world a better place for me, then gently kissed my forehead, and they both left without turning around.

I just sat there staring at the great big pretty picture on the wall that is the coloured glass window you see in the church today. I just sat there and played as the innocent child does with whatever they can find around them, staring at the big picture and giggling not knowing that I would never see them again.

I guess they knew that there was a good chance of them dying at the protest, which they did. My Uncle brought their bodies back, which was a huge risk for him but he felt that they should have a proper burial and not be removed by some sort of clean-up crew, burnt and dumped.

They had asked the Sages to look after me should they not return and the Sages stood true to their word. And here I am today before you and before my parents."

"But do you not wish them here with you now?" Asked Tiberius in a more respectful and caring tone of voice.

"Sometimes perhaps, but you see they stood and died for something they believed in. They were strong and brave and showed how sometimes you need to leave behind what is most precious to you, to be selfless and to go and try to improve the world, one soul at a time if necessary. You can spend your life scared to death of everything, not willing to take that chance and you will still die, but without actually living at all. What is the point of getting to 100 years old if you have been a coward, hiding in the shadows, jumping at every pin drop? That is not life that is merely existence.

Every journey has to have an end, a final destination, but it is the journey to that destination that matters not the destination itself. It does not matter at what age you die and a good death is something to be proud of, to be noted and for those left behind to be proud of, for it is only when you die that you are truly free, free of the pain, the suffering, the angst, the duty that life puts upon you.

So live that life like a lion, not a mouse, leave this land and life with your head held high. They gave their child something precious that money cannot buy, they gave him life, they gave him hope and above all they gave him love."

"I do not remember my parents," said Tiberius. "I do not remember anything of my earlier life after waking in the hospital when I was a teenager. Apparently according to the nurse I had a beating from the Police. My two friends and I had been showing our bottoms to them and running off. For this my two friends were beaten to death and I barely survived. I have hated the Peditata every single second of my existence since." Tiberius started to cry at the memory suppressed for so long. "It was just a joke and it cost them their lives."

The Sage took a huge intake of breath followed by an extended sigh and gestured for Tiberius to sit on the large stone in the middle of the crypt which he had been using as a bed and covered in pillows. "Tiberius, please sit. What I am about to tell you may blow your mind completely, but I think the time has finally come for you to hear it, the planets are aligning, time is running out and you need to know the truth."

Tiberius sat as requested, wiping the tears from his eyes and looking confused.

The Sage continued, "Have you not wondered how you came to be at that exact place when I saved you. Have you not thought how I know your name, when you have never told me it?"

Tiberius looked at the Sage in total shock, he had not told him his name for sure and he had not actually wondered what a total stroke of luck it was that he happened to be at that exact place when he was saved. He had never been there but for some reason had to get there when being chased.

"That is a good point. How come you were there at that moment? That seems like one crazy piece of luck, maybe that bird was looking down on me…"

"Bird?"

"Another conversation."

"Tiberius." Looking down, the Sage paused as if to triple check his own given permission to say what he was about to say. Looking back up he stared so deep into Tiberius' eyes he was talking to his soul within "Tiberius, James and Sarah were your parents, not mine. You were that little boy left in the church that day and I was with the Sages as we spoke to your parents."

"NO!" screamed Tiberius looking up at the coffins then back to the Sage repeatedly and sobbing like a lost child. Panic took over him, this was it, this was the final piece of the puzzle that would destroy his mind once and for all, he was sure of it.

"Yes Tiberius, and you were right about the beating you received causing you the brain damage. It was a small act of defiance but one that we could imagine your father doing when he was young. When you left the hospital you went to the borstal run by the Sages. I know I was there; we were always there. We let you go mostly to allow you to lead a normal life. Sure, we kept an eye on you and helped grease the wheels of how you got to this day, but we watched from afar. Why do you think that John was so open in offering up the location of the Speech Sanctuary? He had no authority to do that but we instructed him to."

"Why?" Tiberius asked confused as his mind raced.

"Because we could see how much turmoil you were in, remember we promised your parents we would do what was best for you. You have your parent's blood flowing through you Tiberius, their strength, their desire to make a difference, but you are living the life of a mouse just staring out of your apartment window or walking over to the park, wandering around aimlessly. We needed to see if you had the heart of a lion, of your parents, or were happy to live out an existence rather than a life."

"Tell me what happened, I mean to them, what happened to them?" demanded Tiberius.

"They went to an uprising in 5-1. They were the leaders of a group called The Freedom Phalanx that had managed to get word out and gathered enough people, or so they thought, to start an uprising across the country and get rid of Premier Xe and all that was rotten in our society, to create a new dawn and they very nearly succeeded.

They and their supporters had taken the main New Government buildings and the centre square. They were starting to move out trying to gather more people to join them, and all was going well. There is a seething hatred running through the underbelly of this country and it just needed a leader to release it, but they made one crucial error.

Everything was organised and managed on Global Life who managed to shut down communication as soon as their code words were deciphered and what was happening became apparent. It took them a few hours to do so, but they did it and soon the whole thing started to fizzle out as the police started to regain control.

With the threat of the military being on the borders of the town and ready to move in, most people blended back into the background, who could blame them, to stay there meant certain death.

Only the core group, or what was left of them, stood defiant to the end. When a child died and its mother was executed by a soldier, they decided it had to end and the only way to end it was with their own lives being forfeit. They walked out of the last Government building under their control, heads held high. They strode confident and true straight towards the police and military line without missing a step.

Holding hands until the very end, their love for each other and for freedom overwhelming till the end, your parents were, well, let us just say they died in each other's arms, proud, strong, brave and true until their last breath. They were all cut down by the police and the military, but at least it was through their guns and not at the hands of the Peditata and their clubs, so scared were they of your parents and what they represented. It was an immediate death in the arms of each other.

The whole thing was brutal, from start to finish, but it created a movement, that the Sages have felt ever since all over the country when we visit each other.

Something has been awoken by your parents, something powerful, but in these times it is very difficult to get information out of people, even in these places, but the feeling is still there bubbling away under the surface.

You see Tiberius when society has become tinder dry with disquiet, it only takes one spark, be it a person or event, to ignite a firestorm. Most leaders dampen the tinder with small platitudes but Premier Xe has chosen a different and more antagonistic approach, perhaps believing he is invincible.

No one trusts anyone, not even us Sages but there is a need for a leader out there, we just need to find whoever it is."

Tiberius just sat in disbelief staring at the coffins and trying to understand what he had just been told, to take in the fact he had spent the last week or so not fifteen feet from his parents' bodies, not knowing. He felt like he had just received another beating but this one was to his soul not his body.

"Tiberius…Tiberius!" barked the Sage. "Are you ok, shall I leave you to take this in?"

"Yes, I need time to think," replied Tiberius staring down at the floor.

"OK I will come back tomorrow morning. Rest up. They really did love you Tiberius, even when they knew they may never see you again, they wanted what was best for you. They fought to give you a better life than they could ever have imagined and it cost them their lives. There is no greater love than that of someone who is willing to give up their life to make someone else's life better. Add that to a parent's love and you have something exceptional. You were not just another Xe, you had a name and they told us it. It may not feel it now, but you are a lucky man Tiberius. Take rest and I will see you tomorrow."

Tiberius did not even acknowledge the Sage, nor really hear what he had just said, he just sat there sobbing. Eventually he curled up in the foetal position on the cushions on the stone slab, sobbing like a baby and crying out for Muma and Papa, until he finally fell asleep.

# Chapter 15:
# Repository of Secrets

The Sage came down the stone steps in the crypt at the rise of the sun to find Tiberius up and awake already. Sitting on the floor cross-legged and staring up at his parent's coffins.

"Good morning, Tiberius. How are you feeling this morning?"

"Lost, confused. I have a renewed energy for life, a desire to kill everything around me and a willingness to die for it. I have lost everything, yet I sit here looking at my parent's coffins and feel that I have gained the world," said Tiberius.

The Sage came and sat next to Tiberius on the floor. "It is only when you have lost everything do you realise what you have gained, for only those with nothing left to lose can see with the clarity of their mind and the love in their heart, what freedom, was life is actually about. It brings a certain clarity that enables the coward to stand against his foes, like a child standing up to a bully after they have finally had enough torment and become the leader that his peers so desperately need."

"I dreamt of freedom again last night. The same dream that I have so often. Walking free in the fields in the sunshine. There is no anger, no hatred, only peace and love. I hear my name being called but I never saw who was saying it up to last night as I would awake before I could turn around, now I know. Last night I turned around without waking from my dream and saw my parents calling me. I was an adult as I sit here now, yet my parents were as I remember them as a child.

It was as if they were telling me to come to them to play again as that child, without fear, worry or understanding of the brutal world we live in right now. It was freedom, it was love, pure love.

They have been telling me for so long that I need to continue their work, to give freedom back to the people but I just could not put two and two together to realise it." A tear streaked down Tiberius's cheek.

"Do you remember when we first met and I asked what my purpose was?"

"Yes," replied the Sage.

"I now know for sure, no doubts, no mists are left to cloud my vision. I have to end this, even if the end is of me. I believe I am the leader we spoke of ready to ignite the firestorm." There was a stillness in his voice, a calm determination. Gone had his fears of dying, of embarrassment of being scared of anything. It was replaced with an almost adult attitude. Tiberius no longer cared, he was going to try to wrestle back freedom, to finish the work his parents had started.

"The path to enlightenment is now clear for you. No longer do you have the material things of life holding you back. The clarity is there, I see it and it is strong," said the Sage standing up.

"Come, follow me and put up your hood," said the Sage.

Tiberius did as instructed and with his ankle now fully healed, followed the Sage up the steps to a large room and instantly felt like two pokers had been driven through his eyes, such was the effect of seeing sunlight for the first time in weeks. "Take your time to adjust," said the Sage.

Shielding his eyes, Tiberius looked around the room. It was semi-circular in shape. In the middle of the curved wall sat a large wooden writing desk that was starting to look a bit shabby but once would have been a magnificent thing to behold. The leather on the top had long gone and the drawers looked out of alignment, but it still had a sense of solidity and quality about it.

On either side of the desk lining all the walls were books cases. Covered in cobwebs, all were empty of any books, and just had what Tiberius could only assume was junk on them. They had gone from being a place to seek learning to a place to dump things that did not have a proper home.

In the far corner was another room, peering through the open door it appeared to be some sort of dressing room, but Tiberius could not see deeper than the wardrobes.

"Come," said the Sage standing at the door in the middle of the straight wall. "I want to show you something."

Tiberius, still blinking as his eyes adjusted followed through the door into the main section of the church. He was starting to get a sense of the layout now and was glad to have put up his hood as there were more people in here than he was expecting, whatever that was as he realised just because his world had stopped, it did not mean that everyone's had and that the world continued whether he decided to be part of it or not.

The hood also helped shield his eyes that still hurt. The people in the church were talking to various Sages or just sitting, lost in their own little worlds, probably trying to escape life rather than have to face it.

One older woman sat sobbing whilst clutching a toy of some sort, another just stared ahead as if she were dead, so lost was she in her mind, Tiberius felt for her as a kindred spirit.

There was a group of three men over to the far side in a robust conversation with a Sage and a larger group towards the front who were just sitting and looking at the enormous, coloured glass window. The sun shone through it in astonishing magnificence. It had such a beauty about it that anyone looking at it was simply mesmerised, especially as like today the sunlight shone through warming the church physically as well as bathing the whole interior in beautiful colours.

Tiberius and the Sage moved to the very front in the middle and sat on the front pew away from all the others.

The window was huge. Circular in design. It was broken into nine parts by two vertical and two horizontal sections of stone to which the window was inlaid. A main section in the middle showed two naked people, they were stood next to a tree and appeared to be using leaves as clothing.

Above them was some sort of Godlike figure, Tiberius thought I bet that was how Premier Xe saw himself, sat at the top with all the finest clothing and objects, lording it over everyone and telling everyone what to do like they were some kind of slave for him alone and for his personal pleasure and passing whims.

To the left was a child with wings flying through a blue sky with some clouds. The top left section which had an image of the sun seem to blend into this one as it if was one image.

Top right was an image of the moon and below that was a scene of a battle with a knight of old standing over a fallen creature of some kind. The image was familiar after his conversations with Evie about the Medieval period of history which he found fascinating and she enjoyed teaching him about.

Underpinning the whole image were the lower three parts which when combined made up an image in three parts of wide-open fields, with trees and animals seemingly free.

"Beautiful, isn't it?" the Sage said, asking the rhetorical question in hushed tones so as not to allow anyone else to hear the conversation. The church was cavernous and sound travelled easily.

"Yes. What are the images of?" Tiberius replied.

"We know after working with the Historians, but that is not important right now, what we like to do is to ask people what their interpretation of it is. It helps calm and unlock the mind. What do you think it means?"

Tiberius looked at the bottom where the fields and trees were, with the animals running free. "This is what I dream freedom to be, in fact it exactly like the fields in my dream, full of open land and rolling hills in the sunshine. Animals run free and are not afraid of us, they see us as another soul to enjoy peaceful existence with, not as a mortal and hungry predator that would eat them if they could catch them. The land at the bottom says there is peace there, wherever there is and it almost seems to underpin all other images above it. I guess now I know where I got that image from in my dream."

"Go on," prompted the Sage.

"There in the middle, I see those two humans as my parents, looking down and smiling upon me, as if they are in some way proud of me, even as the total mess that I have become. I am not sure why they are naked with a leaf positioned where they are, but that is who I see there. They seem so happy, so peaceful, I like to think that is how they are now, wherever that is.

"To the left there," Tiberius said discretely motioning with his head, "I see that flying baby as me, free although I have no idea why I have a bow and arrow in my hands, nor why I seem to be pointing it at my parents, but I feel it is me, under the sun, which is ever present, warming the land, bringing life.

"And on the right?" asked the Sage.

"I am not sure, but I would like to imagine that as me standing above this way of life, this nonsense, saving the world like some sort of hero after killing a beast, perhaps Premier Xe or this narrative we live under after a mighty struggle perhaps.

The moon is there to balance the sun, I cannot think of a reason or purpose for that at the moment, except perhaps that light and dark are both required in life and have a never-ending struggle to find balance. During the day the light wins, at night the moon. A battle that has been going for all time, especially in my head of late, and will never cease until whatever end comes in the future. Symbols that we have to have both in order to remain in some sort of balance."

"And the person at the top?"

"No idea. I guess being at the top he is some sort of king or God that Evie told me about. What do you think?" Tiberius asked of the Sage.

"The Historians tell me what all these images are, but I care not for them, I only care for what they mean to my occupati. I am like you Tiberius, I spend a lot of my time just sitting and looking at it lost in thought. Flying babies do seem a little weird, but I like your interpretation. Yes, in fact for now in my mind Tiberius is the flying baby on the left!

So, who is this Evie then?" he asked inquisitively.

"She is a friend from…that place, a Historian. Wait, this is the point where you tell me you know her right?" Tiberius said.

"Indeed, we do know each other. The Sages and the Historians are pretty much one and the same. They look after the history; we look after the soul. The soul is built by the memories, the life experiences and the history of the person. History in reverse is created by those very people's souls. They are both intertwined forever and always will be. Evie says she likes you very much because you listen and I second that observation. Sometimes you have you father's rashness and desire to change the world instantly, but you use your mother's love to do that in such a fashion, it is, well beautiful to hear about. Come, the time has come."

"For what?" asked Tiberius.

"You will see, follow me and keep that hood up."

Tiberius followed the Sage back into the previous room and back down the stairs to the crypt. He was annoyed that he had finally got some sort of daylight vision back and now he was back to square one and sat back down looking at the coffins."

"I will return soon, remain here."

Acknowledging the statement without words or action, he sat there staring at his parents. It was if all of the mists had been cleared by a sudden storm and he now, could see with perfect clarity.

He climbed the ladder to his parents. "I will not fail you; I will finish what you started." He said to them in a whispered voice. "If it kills me, then so be it, I will simply be closer to you, but I will try to deliver your dream, I will be brave as a lion and change the world father.

"Mum, I wish I could have a cuddle right now, I so need to be in your loving arms, feeling them wrapped around me and knowing as long as you are there then I have nothing to fear, that your love is like an impenetrable shield against everything that may try to hurt me physically and mentally and that I can do anything, achieve anything with my life."

Tiberius returned to his seated position and just stared with watery eyes, he had made peace with his past, his present and now his future.

"Are you ready?" the Sage asked.

"Yes," stated Tiberius without knowing why he was there or turning to look at him. He did not really understand the question but simply responded to it. This new confidence he had inside him, this grown-up attitude almost scared himself half to death in itself. "Tell me first, how did you know I would be there when you saved me?"

"As a child you were a complete nightmare to keep control of, always running around, exploring, and getting into mischief. One day you found the secret tunnel that leads to that part of the forest. We did not find out that you knew about it before you had been using it to sneak out for months. I heard the sirens, and our Sages that watch you twenty-four hours a day, told us you were running in that direction. I just hoped you remembered it and took myself there, I hoped you were running back to us, hoped you were running home."

"Thank you," said Tiberius.

"You can thank me when all this is over. Now put on these clothes." The Sage passed Tiberius a different cloak. This one was purple in colour with a black cord belt to it, the same type of cord belt that they wore. Tiberius did so dutifully, again feeling very comfortable in something that on the outside would make you want to scratch the skin off your bones. The belt was tightened by the Sage who stepped back to admire the perfection in the dress standards.

"Now we begin," stated the Sage.

All but one of the flames in the room were extinguished, essences were lit and the Sage started to recite chants in a language Tiberius did not understand. The occasional word made sense, such as occupati but the rest was a mystery to him. During these rites creams and marking were placed upon him.

On his face was placed a white cross of some sort of cream or paint running down the middle of his forehead and over his nose and across just underneath his eyes. His Eye lids were covered in a purple powdered dye.

The Sage then placed strange rune like markings on the backs of his hands that seemed familiar to him without him ever seeing before.

The Sage continued to chant, now joined by the others in the room and Tiberius continued to obey, feeling that he was now part of something, he now had a reason for existing. Cutting his own left palm with a ceremonial knife, he then proceeded to do the same to Tiberius. He did not flinch as the knife drew blood, holding their hands together their blood was shared as if they had become one.

"Drink," instructed the Sage, who sounded as if he was in a trance like state. Tiberius did as instructed. Whilst tasting like water, whatever it was that he drank it had removed all sense of taste from his mouth.

"Now the blindfold," instructed the Sage.

"What? Why?" replied Tiberius.

The Sage continued, "It is only when we are truly removed of our senses that we can communicate with our soul. To do so requires the removal of as much noise or worldly input as possible, to allow the focus to be pure. This clip goes on your nose. You will be bereft of visual, taste or smell-based input."

Tiberius again did as instructed and was now totally in the hands of the Sage. 'Was this a trick?' he thought. 'It cannot be', he replied to himself, 'they could have given me up weeks ago'. Tiberius started to feel anxious but a new inner voice told him to steel himself, this was his purpose in life, his duty and he was damn well going to do it. He imagined the strong voice to be that of his father and the softer voice telling him to trust them as his mother, still protecting him even after their death, always, until they met again.

After all of the preparation was complete, there was a sound of stone moving. Tiberius felt a hand on each shoulder guiding him down some steps, but where were they? He had spent weeks in the same room and there was no sign of any steps at all, he knew every square inch of that place! Apparently not he thought.

FOCUS! He demanded of himself as he took each step downwards into the depths of the church.

As he walked down the steps the Sage whispered into his ear, "Just say what your soul tells you to say. Do not think about it, just say it." As they got to the bottom of the steps, there was utter silence, he could almost hear himself think. Leading him forward, shuffling one small step by one small step, the Sage stopped him.

Tiberius felt a sharp point on his left breast.

"Do you feel this?" said a voice.

"Yes," replied Tiberius.

"If I drove this knife straight through your heart, would you accept your fate as thus?"

Slightly confused by the question Tiberius replied, "Yes" mostly because he did not really care about life anymore. Life/Death, they were both completely interchangeable, one and the same.

"Then you are ready," came a different voice from his right.

"Sit," stated the commanding voice. Tiberius once more did as instructed and sat in something other than a chair. It took him off his feet into what he thought was some sort of bucket seat, but it did not feel of anything. It was almost like he was floating, without the ability to feel anything. Another sense was taken away.

At this point some chanting started. Many voices were now present in the room and they were talking the same strange language that the Sage was in the preparation.

Tiberius heard a whoosh as a flame lit to his right.

"Do you love, or do you hate? What thus describes your Desire!" demanded the male voice.

Tiberius was immediately confused and scared, had he bitten off more than he could handle? Had his bravado earlier now crumbled at the first sound of a voice containing authority? What was the right answer and what was the wrong one?

"I love," he stated in a mumbling voice.

"You love!" boomed the voice. "You love what? What is it that you come here and declare love for?"

"For freedom!" Tiberius blurted out without thinking.

"Anyone can state that, this is no reason to love! How can we be sure that this love comes from the heart, the soul and not be some politicians answer to please a crowd?

"Because before I came here, I had no parents, I had no idea of freedom other than what I saw in my dreams. Being here has given me the inner strength to chase those dreams, those, those, desires! To feel them for the first time without shame or fear, to accept that what we experience today is not right!"

"What do you hate?" demanded the voice.

"I hate... I hate... I hate life! I hate this pathetic existence of slavery and cruelty and nothingness!" This time said with more confidence. "I hate being nothing, being without meaning, being without purpose, being without... without... without LOVE!"

"And what makes you think you will find love here?"

"Because I have finally felt love, love for my parents, love for freedom, I need love!"

"Desire accepts," came the voice.

At this point Tiberius was becoming increasingly terrified as to what he had let himself into. I am going to die here he thought and I won't even see it coming. Again, the inner voices calmed him as the group around him continued.

As his mind rushed, a second whoosh sounded as another flame lit. This time it was directly behind him.

"Do you seek war, or do you seek peace? What thus describes your strength?" Demanded a new voice, this time a woman.

"I do not understand," Tiberius blurted out.

"I do not care what you understand or not! Answer the question," came the less than sympathetic reply.

"War! War describes strength."

"Why?" said the voice.

"Because you have to be strong to win a war, the weak do not win wars only the strong!"

"What makes you think that those who chose peace over war are not strong?"

"Because the victor gets the spoils!"

"What spoils?"

"The spoils of war, the land, the treasures!"

"And these constitute strength to you?" Do you not think that those who gain through war and violence ultimately have no strength? They may own the world but they have no inner strength. Tell me now!"

"I...I..." Tiberius had to clear his mind and clear it fast, he was losing this argument and he knew it. "I suppose that to win a war through peace takes greater strength as it involves dialog and compromise rather than mindless violence. To want to own the world is to never be satisfied, to never be happy because greed can never be satisfied. There is never enough, there is only the need for more and more and more, and even when you have everything it is still never enough, so you are never truly happy, no matter how much gold, how many slaves, how much land you own, you can never be happy.

Strength comes from peace not from war. War is weak, war is failure, war is an admission that you do not have the ability to see past death and destruction. It only sucks in more pain and suffering, continues to kill and to drive up hatred. War only leads to more war; war only leads ultimately to the loss of your soul.

Peace allows people to rise above death as the ultimate threat, it allows those who chose that road to put life and love above material wealth. PEACE IS STRENGTH!"

"Strength accepts," came the voice.

Tiberius was becoming exhausted and started to breathe heavily.

Immediately, whoosh went a flame to his rear and left.

"Are you a coward or do you have bravery? What thus describes your fortitude?" demanded the new male voice!

"I am brave," Tiberius commanded back.

"Brave?" said the voice insultingly. "You are breathing like someone who is about to have a heart attack! You are not brave, you are a minnow in the ocean, completely out of your depth! You are a coward!"

"HOW DARE YOU!" shouted Tiberius in response, clearly not happy at that reply. "I have spent the last two weeks in a crypt with the dead. I have found my parents there, I have discovered my life, who I am, what I was and I have not run away. I have faced every test, challenge and question asked of me. I sit here now, without any sense but my hearing, not knowing what is going on around me, what this is about, what is going to happen, yet I do not take off this mask, nor do I stand or rip off this clip on my nose, I sit here in compete darkness and confusion answering your demands and you have the nerve to call me a coward?

I do not have a clue what is going on at this moment in time, what the future holds or even if I will be alive in the next ten minutes, yet here I am. I am not afraid of death, I see it as a release, as freedom. I challenge you! I challenge you who can see, smell and direct what happens next, to sit here and to do what I am doing. I DARE YOU AND I DARE YOU NOW!"

"Fortitude accepts," came the voice.

Tiberius, hands made into tight fists, was now riled up and wanted to fight someone. He was angry that he was being questioned like this.

Whoosh went the next flame, this time to his left.

"Do you fear or do you hope? What thus describes your attitude?" demanded another male voice, the pace and questions were relentless, demanding not only an answer but a real answer from his very soul.

"I hope," Tiberius stated firmly. "I hope for freedom, I hope that all people can be free of the tyranny we are oppressed with, I hope that I can be the catalyst that restarted the work that my parents started, for I will finish it!"

"And you fear nothing?"

"No!"

Cold steel was immediately pressed hard against his skin, pushing through his flesh. Tiberius squealed.

"I think you are a liar! A point of a blade makes you jump."

"I have survived Detention Centre One. I was tortured, beaten to within an inch of my life. I have lost everything, what have I got left to fear?" Tiberius stated.

"Indeed, yet here you are squealing at a mere prick of a blade. You still feel fear and that still drives an emotional response."

"Attitude declines," came the voice.

"Wait!" demanded Tiberius. "Why do you condemn me for feeling fear, why do you not realise that is part of hope? Without fear there is no hope. We hope for things but we allow fear to prevent us from seeking that hope even when there is nothing to worry about. Sometimes fear is good, it can help define the hope that we desire. Without fear, hope becomes merely a formality!"

"Continue," demanded the voice.

"Whenever we hope for something, we fear it may not happen, sometimes we fear that we may be hurt in the pursuit of that hope, but the brave still push forward, through the fear, even if the fear is the fear of fear itself!

"Where there is hope, there is always fear."

"Attitude declines!" came the voice.

"Fine, fail me then, for I do not care, I have nothing, I am nothing, press that blade through my chest and pierce my heart for it is now devoid of anything, I no longer care, finish me off but make it swift."

The blade was pushed into Tiberius's chest. Its cold steel drew blood as it slowly drove deeper. Tiberius did not flinch; in fact he grabbed the hand of the person who was holding it and pulled it further towards him against the will of the person holding it who was trying to pull it away.

This was the end, he was tired, and he had endured too much. If he lived then the road ahead was going to be full of uncertainty, probably leading to his death anyway so may as well do it now. He felt this without fear.

His grip on the blade was released by force, by a second set of hands and the blade withdrawn.

"DAMN IT!" Tiberius shouted. "Just get on with it! I do not fear death, JUST DO IT!"

"Attitude accepts," came the voice.

Before Tiberius had a chance to recover from his imminent death there was another whoosh from in front of him. Breathing heavily, he was still trying to gather his thoughts and feelings, trying to communicate with his soul that was awash with turmoil, with his inner thoughts and advice when it stated in the same calm yet authoritative manner.

"Are you calm or are you full of angst? What thus describes your mindfulness?" demanded another male voice.

"Oh, I do not know," Tiberius wailed. This experience was starting to become unbearable, the quick-fire questions drilling his mind and his soul, both of which were laid bare for anyone in the room to see. He was emotionally exhausted and was starting to wish he simply was not here anymore.

There was complete silence.

Tiberius spent the two silent minutes calming his breathing and searching his mind for some sort of answer that he thought might be the 'right' one, one that would result in the words Mindfulness accepts. 'What shall I say?' He thought to himself, 'a minute ago I was begging to be finished off and here I am now trying to answer another question.'

Tiberius took a deep breath and said, "Calm" in a surprisingly calm voice.

It was met with silence. What is going on thought Tiberius, starting to feel nervous. Aha! I got you on this one he thought and stated, "You are trying to scare me with silence and to fair it almost worked! As before when I was prepared to die, I was calm in my soul, at peace and happy to move on to whatever adventure comes next.

As I sit here now with a clear and calm mind, I do not care what you do to me anymore, I am at peace with existence and the turmoil that was once within me has gone. So yes, I may have at times had angst but I have cleared that and replaced it with calm as I replace fear with hope and hate with love."

As he said that he felt all the turmoil leave his soul. For the first time he felt at one with himself. His mind and his soul had finally connected on the same wavelength. He felt...free.

"Mindfulness accepts!" Came the voice.

Whoosh another flame lit and Tiberius was starting to think this is going to go on for ever. This time it was to his right and front and the various voices appeared to have come full circle. I must be in a circle he thought and this feel like the last one, I wonder...

His thoughts were interrupted by the next voice. This time female, "Are you Lazy or Resolute? What thus describes your conscientiousness?"

Tiberius actually felt stumped with this one, before all this started, the speech sanctuary, the journey he has been on he would have said lazy, but now he had a purpose of some sort, he felt a new energy about him a new reason for existing.

He knew the right answer had to be resolute as it was when he stated a reason as to why he was the positive option, the voice would accept it. Tiberius was now feeling mischievous and wanted to get one back on whoever was in here with him, thus was the level of his uncaring about what was going on around him added to the new inner confidence he had.

Not quite fully supressing a small smile he confidently stated, "LAZY! I am really lazy, cannot be bothered to do anything!"

"Why?" came back an immediate response.

"Because I do not care anymore, so why keep fighting, I may as well go open another bottle of Vodinaski and drink myself to death. Why should I care what you think, I think or anyone thinks? Just be me, and drink and a new adventure."

"Conscientiousness accepts," Came the voice.

"Wait! What?" stuttered Tiberius. "How did I pass that one!" Tiberius burst out laughing at the fact that he had absolutely no idea what was going on and felt that he actually could have said anything in the six conversations and ended up at this same place.

At this point he felt someone pick him up out of the chair. "Come," said a new, previously unheard voice. Tiberius, shaking his head in confusion, humour and disbelief, shuffled along obligingly until the stopped a short distance on his left had he been in the chair still.

"In this place, in this order as in life we acknowledge that with knowledge comes peace, hope, love. Only the resolute stay calm of mind and fill their soul with hope. Knowledge is power and that ignorance is for the lazy, the fearful, the coward, those with angst and those who hate or have a lust for war." Stated this new voice.

"Knowledge over ignorance, always," the room stated in a low tone making Tiberius jump just slightly as he realised that there must be at least forty people in the room.

They shuffled a little to the left and stopped again.

"In this place, in this order as in life we hold high honour. Honour comes within the heart of the brave, a resolute calmness that values love, hope and peace above all else. The treacherous are cowards, they use their angst to drive hate and fear ultimately leading to war. Their laziness of goodness only driven by their cowardice."

"Honour over treachery, always," the room affirmed.

They shuffled a little to the left and stopped again.

"In this place, in this order as in life we worship truth. Only the brave will state the truth when faced with the baying mob, hoping that their message may just get through to one person and if it does then that is one person closer to peace and with peace comes love, hope and a calm resolve knowing that they know the truth, no matter how bad it may be it is the truth. Deceit is a bedfellow of the coward, the fearful. They do not want to invest the effort to discover the truth so they are lazy, often full of angst and hate and that combination always leads to war. The deceitful are the lowest kind."

"Truth over deceit, always," the voices stated almost melodically.

Another shuffle to the left and the voice stated.

"In this place, in this order as in life we trust. Trust requires bravery and hope that those we trust are not out to harm us. Fulfilled trust leads to love and a calmness that supports peace. The resolute use trust over suspicion, which is owned by the lazy, the selfish. Suspicion fuels their hatred of others, their fear that they are being manipulated by others. This leads to angst and ultimately war which the suspicious use to hide cowardice."

"Trust over suspicion, always," came the anticipated affirmation.

Continuing to shuffle around the voice stated.

"In this place, in this order as in life we seek serenity over turmoil. Serenity is the peace that we all ultimately seek for a soul filled with love and hope. The Brave and the resolute have a calm about them that can take on any challenge they may face. There is no peace in turmoil only war. The lazy let turmoil toss them around like a ship in a storm. With no peace they feel angst which leads to fear and to hatred and to war. Turmoil allows the coward to hide using that which is causing the turmoil to hide their own failings."

"Serenity over turmoil, always," the room stated.

Further shuffling around what Tiberius was now convinced was a circle the voice stated.

"In this place, in this order as in life we seek loyalty over betrayal. Only the resolute and the brave will put loyalty before all else. Loyalty is born of love, filling the soul with hope knowing that you do not stand alone, ever. When in the presence of true loyalty, you feel the inner peace and calm of the soul. It does not take much to take advantage of fear and angst of the coward whose escape is always betrayal. A lazy way avoids observation of their own actions. Betrayal always leads to hate and to war.

"Loyalty over betrayal, always," Came the final statement.

Tiberius started to feel a strange inner sense of belonging and of confidence, to go with the linking of his mind and soul. A clarity starting to wash over him, the removal of everything that had been holding him back all these years. As he thought this, he was shuffled forward again, this time back to the centre where whatever he had been sat on had been removed.

"Tiberius," came the same voice that had just been speaking to him. "Do you understand what you have just experienced?"

"Yes," replied Tiberius, lying but just wanting to go with the flow to end this ceremony of some sort.

"Tiberius, do you understand that what you have been told here tonight is to remain between us, do you accept this knowledge into a mind that wants to discover truth only and a soul full of honour and loyalty?"

"I do," replied Tiberius.

"Tiberius, do we have your trust?"

"Yes," replied Tiberius.

"Lastly Tiberius, do you let serenity fall upon you with a clarity to forthwith remove pain and suffering of your soul and bring about a life of helping others?"

"I do," replied Tiberius.

"Then we will allow your senses to be returned."
As this was stated the blindfold and the nose clip were removed.

Tiberius blinked several times to try to get his eyes to focus to his surroundings.

"Take your time Tiberius," said the voice coming from the Sage stood next to him. This Sage was dressed in all black with a black cord belt, with his hood up Tiberius could not see his face, but his eyes appeared to be the most brilliant and shining blue colour, that pierced straight into your mind.

As Tiberius's eyes adjusted, he could see that he was stood in a huge chamber that resembled one end of the church. He stood in the centre of a circle that lay within a larger circle in the centre of the chamber. The ground was stone but had some sort of dusting of sand or something similar upon it. Tiberius noticed the dagger used to pierce his skin at his feet. Seeing it reminded him that his chest hurt right where he was stabbed with it.

Between the two circles there were six points each leading outward to a torch flame and at each flame stood a Sage in the brown cloak, hood up.

Within each pointer lay one of the challenges in words with the two options written at the end. The positive word outside the outer circle and the negative trait inside.

Between the outer points were the final six sets of traits that the Sage spoke to him about.

All of the writing was in some sort of white dust sprinkled onto the floor, so as to be able to be swept away at short notice if required.

Against all of the stone walls were rows and rows of bookcases made of the most beautiful polished dark wood, with every shelf packed with books. It was a beautiful sight that made Tiberius audibly gasp. There must be thousands of books here and it was a sight that struck his soul.

'I could spend the rest of eternity reading in here and never finish all of the books', he thought to himself, 'but I should still like to try.'

As he looked around, he saw all of the other Sages stood in silence observing; he was not far off as there must have been around forty in the room. All were wearing the brown cloak, again with the hoods up, none with the white cloak with blue cord belt. I guess that must signify someone who has not gone through this ceremony he thought.

Only one had the black cloak with the black belt and he was stood right next to him. Tiberius thought that this Sage must be their leader of some kind, but it was not important right now, he could ask that question, along with all the others he had, later.

The Sage stated, "This is our most sacred place, that only those of the order know. You stand in the circle of the soul. The six flames of enlightenment surround you as you stand here in the centre. Outside of this circle you will find freedom, within it lies only slavery.
You are now a member of our order and as such have reached the level of enlightenment that you require to complete your life reason, whatever that may be. No matter what happens you will always be a member of The Order of the Sages of Stoicism, except in the event of betrayal where you will be cast out from the order. In the last 3,400 years, in all of our recorded history you see on the shelves around you, no one has ever betrayed the order, not even in a tortuous death.

With this you are now free to do whatever you wish to do next, if you need safe haven seek the order and we will be there for you, if you need support seek the order and we will be there for you, for the order is everything and all in your life, you are it and it is you, as one until death takes you to another place.

Freedom, strength, knowledge my fellows"

"Freedom! Strength! Knowledge!" the audience acclaimed before filing out through the stairs that Tiberius guessed he must have come down as there was no other obvious exit to the room.

Soon Tiberius was stood alone amongst the burning flames with only his thoughts and thousands of books and manuscripts to keep him company. '3,400 years' he thought, 'wow now that is history, Evie would absolutely love this place!'

After looking around he turned to leave and almost tripped over a pile of clothes on the floor. It was a brown cloak with a black cord belt. His heart swelled as he smiled and changed into it, put up the hood and proceeded up the stairs back into the crypt, through the very place he had spent the last two weeks recovering.

"This place is a repository of secrets," he said to his Sage waiting for him as he reached the top of the stairs.

"We are all a repository of secrets in our own way," replied the Sage he knew so well and now considered a friend.

"Welcome Sage."

# Chapter 16:
# What is it to be Free?

Tiberius and his Sage, as he liked to call him now, walked through the park by the Brutus stadium. Even though it was a warm, sunny day, their hoods were up to avoid the inevitable attention his identification would case. Tiberius had needed some fresh air and with their Sage cloaks they knew they would be left alone and unrecognised by the police.

"How are you feeling my Sage after yesterday's events?"

"Like I belong, like I have a reason. I am no longer lost; I have found myself and I have found my purpose. I must admit it would have been nice to find it through dialog rather than what I have been through, but as you say, sometimes you have to lose everything, almost even your life itself for the pathway to become clear to you."

"You are correct my Sage. I cannot tell you how proud I am of you. It would normally take many years of wearing the white cloak of learning before you even attempt the ceremony of enlightenment, but you have this inner power that simply cannot be ignored or buried. Your fire has to be released; it cannot be tamed."

"I have a question my Sage. How did I pass the conscientiousness question? I was deliberately answering the question with what I thought was the wrong answer."

"Ahh yes, the Sages were impressed with your answer. You see there is no right or wrong answer as such in the ceremony. It is designed to question who you are in your core, your soul and not some words in a book that have to be recited. Anyone can memorise a book or a set of answers, but the order is not looking for academics, they are looking for keepers of the soul.

Your answer in all its contemptuous glory was actually a perfect one. To be resolute you have to be supremely confident and determined, most of all bold.

To be where you were with all your senses removed, with all grip of reality removed, with all perceived safety removed and to give an answer that was deliberately wrong and bordering on the insultingly sarcastic proved the character trait we were seeking, the way in which you said it was just the icing on the top.

I have to admit I did not try to pull that one off, nor have I seen any others try it. You really are unique, something special."

Tiberius paused smiling and gestured to sit on a bench. Both Sages sat looking at the stadium.

"I used to think this stadium was my ultimate goal. To stand in the middle, the winner of an epic fight, a champion, the people's champion! To have my statue on the path of champions for all to see for eternity. Here is 'muffled name' undefeated champion of the world!" he said laughing. "And now it seems so insignificant, the dream so pointless. I often wonder if my current path is equally as pointless. I have to say that I am still in a little turmoil."

"How so my Sage?"

"Should I step back and help the individual as a Sage or carry on the path I have chosen?"

"Was it not you that said they were going to change the whole? You cannot do that sitting in a church waiting for people to walk in through the door. You have your destiny my Sage. There will always be doubt, a need for more clarity but at some point you have to take the first step, then the next and then go down the path you have created for yourself, without self-doubt but with that resolution you have shown."

"In many ways I feel sorry for Premier Xe. He has not lived a life. He has been a slave all along to the narrative but more so to his dynasty. He could have walked away from that and lived a very comfortable life, yet his path was to remain shackled to something that nobody else cared about. He is lost in his own world, generated in his head."

"Classic narcissist. In this world we are all desperate to find a meaning for our existence, exactly what you said when we first met, well when we first met in the church, well when we first me in the church as an adult"

"Ha ha I know what you mean," Tiberius laughed.

"Yes anyway, you said 'I know not of my purpose'. You are not alone in asking that question. So many do. Some find it, some never do and go to the next adventure still wondering what the point of life was. To Premier Xe his purpose is to carry on the Hendricks Dynasty. As strange and bizarre that is to us, it is the absolute truth to him. A simple and comfortable life seems great to us; it would be a waste of his existence to him."

Tiberius looked around nervously at the outward use of gender types. Seeing that they were alone he said, "Freedom would help in finding that path."

"I agree but what is it to be free? Is it to sit here and say what I said without you looking like a thousand police officers were about to descend on us?"

"Evie told me that freedom is only what you perceive it to be."

"And she was right for it is born of the mind and of someone's life experience. Someone who has been held in a single room all their life would consider freedom as to be able to walk into the next room. Someone who has had everything given to them from birth would perhaps consider it to be allowed to be above the law.

The mark of a person's character is not what they do when the rules are in place, but what they do when they are no rules, for only then is the person manging their life or behaving in a manner that would be considered acceptable through their own inner reasoning.

If you removed the fear of any retribution for any of your actions, what do you think you would do?"

"You know what, but I cannot say here," Tiberius said.

His Sage continued, "Indeed and for you that would bring you freedom? But what about the police officers, those in power that have kept this façade running for so long. They would lose their perception of freedom. Like most things in life, these things are what you perceive them to be, as our friend so often says.

If we gave everyone freedom to say whatever they wanted, it would bring a great responsibility on the individual for free speech and it would be the responsibility of every person. It is absolutely necessary in a normal society to be able to say whatever you want, even that which is overtly offensive for as soon as you bring in rules about what you can say, you have to then have oversight on the ones who are making those rules. Who gives them or indeed anyone the right to say what you can and cannot say?"

"I agree but you could say something deeply offensive to another to cause them mental pain," Tiberius challenged.

"And you should be allowed to do so, not because I agree that it is ok to cause mental pain that goes against our teachings but if you allow it to be said then the person can be identified and managed in the way in which you have created your society to be.

Let the ridiculous say ridiculous things and be ridiculed for it. Let the offensive say offensive things and for society to shun them. If you ban people from being able to say things, it does not stop them from saying them or believing in them, you merely force the thinking and behaviour underground. You will never change someone's inner being by rules and laws, only society can enlighten the offensive person by making them reflect on their actions by the rejection of those around them."

"But is that not desirable? After all, at least you have saved people from mental pain."

"In some circumstances, perhaps; but at what cost? And how do you balance what someone says claiming it not to be offensive with the views of someone hearing and saying it was. You should not have a right not to be offended, what may be seen as offensive to one person may well be seen as funny to another, even his very brother.

No two people are the same, a person may say something to a group in a joke, whereby ninety-nine people think it was funny but one thought it was offensive. Do you stop the words for the sake of saving one-person mental pain, but to the detriment of causing ninety-nine other people mental pain by ruining their fun?

Who should police what words can and cannot be used? Who needs to overlook those who are making those decisions? Should you have people overlooking those overlooking those making the decisions? Where does it end and who ultimately has the right?

Add to this that offence can be taken when not offered, can be taken on behalf of someone, even be taken on the perception that it could harm someone whom the person that is claiming offence does not even know, and perhaps does not even exist. This is not to mention sometimes taken in order to further…a narrative. How do you police all of those connotations without creating a legal system so bloated and full of cases belonging to those whining, those seeking fame etc. The message is completely lost in the quagmire of the argument."

"Somebody once told me that you lose the argument like that, and that it is better, for control, to have the narrative rather than a specific point," Tiberius said thinking about Evie again. "I wish Evie was here. Her knowledge and logic would be of great input."

The Sage nodded, "So do I, but we are all on our own paths now till the end, who knows those paths may cross again. Back to your question though on what is it to be free? In my experience it is self-managed responsibility, discipline and respect for others but also that respect to be given back by others. Life is a mirror, what you give out is what you receive in return. There is no rule book, no right or wrong, mostly; but you cannot 'create' freedom like it is something that come off a manufacturing line. It has to be nurtured through love, truth and trust, which takes time by a group of people seeking the same or similar path."

"I agree but perhaps some allow their freedom to be removed in order to make it easier to understand and to save them the effort of having to think, to be not bothered or lazy as I so declared myself to be," Tiberius said with a hidden smile.

"I believe you may well be right my Sage," said the Sage laughing gently.

The two sat on a bench, virtually alone in the park, looking over at the few people wandering around. Taking in what has happened and the short pause before the inevitable had to happen. It was a moment of rare peace and contentment with life and was to be relished.

Eventually Tiberius stated in hushed tones, "You know I thought I heard a familiar voice in Detention Centre One."

"Who would that be?" enquired the Sage.

"I am not sure; it was when I was in the cells being beaten. My eyes were swollen shut but I could still see the light when the door opened if not the people. I can remember what they said by word, it was 'Let him go now, he is not to be killed. You can beat him or do whatever but if he dies so will you' although it felt like I had already been ended."

"What made you think you knew the person? And why do you think you were spared? Someone must had thought you were of value to their cause." The Sage questioned further.

"On the first question, I do not know, just the way they spoke, such a…well familiar voice. Why was I spared? Again, I cannot tell you. Sometimes I feel like a pawn in a game that I do not know I am playing, yet I appear to be the main piece in it. It is a weird sense rather than what anyone has said to me.

It has been bothering me, but I try not to let it interfere with my journey now. Maybe in the next adventure I will find out, even if I still care about this adventure when I get there," stated Tiberius

"That is wise my Sage. Keep your mind clear now, you are going to need as much of it as possible in the upcoming days. Keep in mind the price of inaction can be greater than the cost of action."

"Let it begin then, let us send out the word and start the change. May you be safe my Sage." Stated Tiberius, consigned to his fate and the path laid out before him.

"As you my Sage," he said as they looked ahead lost in their own thoughts of what the very near future would hold form them all.

*** 

The Commander General Police was walking around what was left of Detention Centre One. He had ordered it to be rebuilt but with everything working again. There was not a lot of actual physical damage, compared to the political damage the mass escape had caused.

Speaking to the new Commandant of the Camp as they were now to be called, he stated that the treatment of the prisoners was not to change, however the routines and procedures were to be sorted out to prevent it ever happening again.

"And take down that fucking billboard," he stated point to the image of the beach.

At that point a military vehicle pulled into the courtyard at an unnecessary speed for effect and skidded to a halt, which had the effect of damaging the ground and pissing off the Commander General Police and Commandant of the Camp.

"Fucking idiots running around trying to look like a fucking bush, cannot do anything right, not even park a car," said the Commandant of the Camp.

"In that you are not wrong. Carry on, I will be back in a week to check the final results."

"Commander!" The Commandant said standing to attention and saluting and walking off barking orders at the builders.

The Commander walked over to the military vehicle where the Commander General Military still sat, playing power games as usual.

"Tell the bush wannabe sat next to you to fuck off, I want to talk in private."

The soldier at the wheel of the vehicle, looked furious. The Commander General Military simply stated, "Dismissed soldier, go and stand over by that plain white wall, they will still not be able to see you even then. While you are there see if you can find one of their escapees still running around. They seem to be having a little difficulty in finding 3,000 people dressed in rags."

The solider smiled as he stated, "Commander!" and walked off grinning at the Commander General Police who replaced him in his seat.

When the soldier was out of earshot he stated, "Look I know we do not like each other but we are both in deep shit right now. It is all falling apart, the dickhead has lost control and we will be the ones who have to sort it out." "And receive the bollocking for doing so, don't forget," replied The Commander

General Military.

"Exactly! Anyway, all I need to know from you is that you will be there if this shit gets too real. I have full confidence in my officers and they will dispatch anyone causing trouble, but as you know a good Commander has back up plans, and, unfortunately, my only one at the moment is you."

The Commander General Military just stared at him, "You know I hated your predecessor, an arrogant loser, but even the person you stabbed in the back had more guts and front than you. They would never have come to be begging me to dig them out of a hole."

"Fuck you!"

"Yes, my forces will be on the outskirts of the towns and cities as they were the last time this shit happened and we will stand ready, but I can promise you one thing. I will not lose one of my officers trying to save the pathetic arses of yours when they cannot keep a bunch of unarmed citizens under control despite having whatever weaponry they desire at their disposal. Your officers will lose control because they do not have the guts, not because they do not have the equipment."

"My officers are the ones on the front line doing this day in day out, not like your 'mighty military'!" the Commander General Police stated with maximum sarcasm, "that have not done a fucking thing in years. The military have done sweet fuck all but suck up cash that would have been better spent on the police, then spent it running around chasing each other playing with their guns and shouting 'bang! bang!' to each other!

So before you fucking dare tell me mine are not capable you should take a good look in the fucking mirror prick. Just make sure you are there and have not become fat, lazy, useless police officer wannabes."

"No one wants go backwards in their career so I would not worry about that ever happening. Anyway, my turn for a question, seeing as you got me to come all the way over here. I do not believe that you told the whole truth as to how you found the Speech Sanctuary."

"And?"

"Did you ever find out anything else before you raided the place? It seems your spy was actually my spy."

"Or vice versa."

"Irrelevant now, I had him executed, cannot have that in the ranks as I am sure you would appreciate. Well?"

Looking around the Commander General Police simply stated, "Yes, I had inside intel. Slickback was someone who frequented the place, I will not say who, but they approached me. I could have simply reported it, but where would that have got me? A fucking medal and a pat on the back, no, I was going to use this to the maximum personal gain. The previous Commander General Police would not have known my name and yet here I am now with their job."

"I don't like you, but I do like your style. So, what was the New Dawn project and why were Global Life talking about you then?"

"That I will not tell you. I am sure you will appreciate that."

The Commander General Military took a deep breath and let out a sigh. "You know this is all going to turn to shit very soon, everyone can sense it and with the small pockets of fighting starting to appear around the country it will only grow."

"Agreed, the word only needs to be released by whoever is organising this and we are going to be in a proper fight. We are ready for it but sense this time it will be a numbers game, these pockets of resistance, the hit and runs on my officers, they are probing us to test the weaknesses. That is why you are going to be the deciding factor again, just be ready."

"Times are indeed changing, we have to look out not only to what is about to happen but to the future, post the end of the dickhead."

"Yes and IF that happens, I fully intend to be sitting in that seat."

"Will have to beat me to it!"

The two Commanders looked at each other with a sense of mutual respect, so rarely displayed.

"Good luck, you are going to need it, but if required we will be there to hold your hands and wipe away your tears!" Said the Commander General Military reverting back to the insulting digs.

"Just fucking be there, and this time get your fat bushes to use real guns, if they can drag themselves away from the burgers for long enough," the Commander General Police replied and stormed out of the vehicle, leaving the Commander General Military seething. The truth hurt, the military had had nothing to do in years and he was getting itchy for a fight.

# Chapter 17:
# Fight to the Last Breath

The Chief Manufacturer called the Communications Chief. "It's kicking off, there are uprisings everywhere. It's all over, I have got people disappearing left right and centre. I cannot guarantee the manufacture of anything right now. I have diverted all of my remaining resources onto public control items such as ammunition but just be aware the house of cards is falling."

"Get a fucking grip of yourself!" came the reply. "So, you have lost a couple of people, boo fucking hoo! The current message to all is that we are under full control and the reasons for this uprising is frustration which will be listened to and understood. Things will be better going forward we just need time to arrange things. Got it!"

"Yes," he replied submissively.

"Good now go and make some stuff that will help us deal with this!"

"Of course."

"By the way have you seen the Chief Scientist?"

"No, not seen Xe 6 in a couple of days. I reckon it has done a runner."

"OK," came the calm response.

The Communications Chief called the Commander General Police. "The Chief Scientist is out of comms. Find it and bring it in."

"Nope, not a chance, way too busy keeping your arse in its seat to do missing people calls. If you need someone to go running around looking for missing children, call the useless prick in the shiny tank and get those idiots to do it," he replied putting the phone down. "For fucks sake, can nobody get a grip around here!" He shouted out before calling the Commander General Military.

"The Chief Scientist is out of comms. Find it and bring it in!"

"Please, please, remember your manners now," he replied.

"Just fucking do it!"

"Remember the rank system," He stated firmly. "Especially if you want me to do something for you because the police won't or more likely can't, thus I have guessed why you are asking me to do it for you."

"If this goes down badly, there will be no rank system, there will be no us, so I suggest that you extract your head from your arse up there on your pedestal and get on with it, unless of course your lack of use in the past decades has actually made for an incompetent military in finding a missing person let alone fight a war," he said and ended the call.

Again, the Commander General Military was left seething. He was 2nd in command and they were all talking to him like he was some sort of Premier Xe loser. "Fuck it, I'll find the bitch then," he said and ordered every single available officer available to go and find her.

***

Evie gathered the Historians into the warehouse.

"Historians, every single day history is created. Small little things here and there that often go unnoticed by the people, but never by us.

Soon there will be great events and we must all be at the ready to record it in the most intimate detail for future prosperity.

Should events take a certain turn then there could be a reason for us to work extensively to look into our history to create a new world, we can only hope so, but should things go in favour or Premier Xe, then we will still need to record with as much detail and desire as we do for any occasion.

We are neutral of politics; we are neutral of sides. We simply do our duty and record what happens.

I have asked two of you to help me with something very important. I would never normally ask anyone to become part of history or to influence it in any way, but this time I must. I know in doing this, I break our solemn oath of neutrality, therefore, I must relinquish my role as Senior Historian for the Capital Warehouse which I do with immediate effect. I give this role to my deputy, I only ask for this one thing to be allowed of me, with the support of the Chief Historian, which I have."

The gathered Historians nodded in agreement.

"I thank you all. History is about to be created and I want to take this opportunity to thank you all for simply being who you are and doing what you do.

"Things may change out there," she said pointing towards the door, "but in here things will always remain constant. I love you all."

The gathered Historians taken aback slightly by the gesture of love, solemnly nod and left to go about their duties as instructed.

Turning to the two remaining historians she said, "I have given you my instruction. Meet me at the mentioned place as instructed. I thank you with all of my heart for what you are about to do and I assure you that for once something that someone does will not be recorded for history, your role will never be mentioned as per your wishes."

The two Historians nodded and turned to do their duty.

Evie turned to her deputy, "I know you will continue the tradition of the Historians, I have every confidence in you, my sister. Our parents would be proud of you, as I am."

"I know I am a Historian, I know we are allowed more than one child due to our duties and hidden nature and I know we are a pair, but I want to say one thing. Instead of stating my usual 'Yes Senior Historian' I will say 'Yes my sister and I love you. I have always loved you and always will. Be safe, you will live forever in these archives, I will see to it."

The two sisters hugged for the first time since being children, Evie simply stating, "I love you," with tears running down her cheeks before she walked away without turning.

***

A conference call was rapidly put together by the Communications Chief.

"Ok we are all here. Commander General Military report."

"I have the Chief Scientist, found trying to hide in its house in the country. Was not that fucking hard to find, even the police could have managed this one, so panic over and you can all say thank you now, fucking losers," said the Commander General Military with utter contempt to the conference call of the Primary Function.

"Good," said the Communications Chief ignoring the insult and call for a thank you. "Did Xe 6 have anything to say as to why they were out of communication?"

"They only thing said was the hate of us and what we have made Xe 6 become. When pressed for what it has been up to or if it has any nasty 'surprises' for us Xe 6 stopped talking, despite some 'gentle' questioning. I would not read a copy of Good Citizen for a couple of months though if I were you.

Had to stop the poor thing from killing itself once already, so is currently tied up, literally, next to me. Say hi to our friends now," he said showing the gathered group the dishevelled and roughed up former colleague.

"OK keep Xe 6 there, I will tell Premier Xe, hopefully it will get the blood pressure under eight thousand," he said wiping his mouth with his hand as he tried to coordinate some sort of response to the collapsing world around him.

"Hopefully not," came the Commanders' reply.

Ignoring the comment again he said, "Finances, do we have them in place?"

"Just do what you have to do," came in the Chief Treasurer. "I will balance the books as usual at a later date but…"

"But what?"

"Our usual supply of cash has stopped; it looks like Premier Xe's backers have cut us off."

"Fuck, what is that dickhead doing to us all?"

The Commander General Military continued, "End game suckers, it's been fun. I am going back to my units to polish up my number one uniform. No need to go down looking like a scruff bag like you eh bitch?" presumably said towards the Chief Scientist currently in his 'care'. "Looks like the dickhead was right, those Speech Sanctuaries have been the end of us all. If only we had someone on the inside who could have helped us find them."

"Fuck you tin soldier," stated the Chief Treasurer.

"That is Commander to you. Maybe the old Sage was right, maybe we deserve it for not having the balls to do the job, but undermined the poor psycho when we all thought we were better. Still, I do not give a toss anymore. Prepare for the fight ahead losers," and put his phone down.

"End game, huh for once I agree with the idiot," said the Commander General police and put down their phone.

"Where is the Sage?" Said the communications chief.

"Not been seen since the lecture. The red robes were delivered to the Premier Xe's office with a message saying 'he' had gone back to 'his' teachings and could no longer serve the Primary Function."

"For fuck's sake, does anyone around here actually want to live?" Stated the Communications Chief and ended the call ignoring the use of a gender in the sentence, such was the world falling apart around them, this major indiscretion was no longer relevant to the situation they faced.

The escape from Detention Centre One had sparked a renewed hatred of the New Government. As much as they stated they had all caught the escaped murderers and rapists, it had actually backfired and given people hope. Hope that actually you could do something to stand up to them, you could beat them and so a small but crucial chink in the New Government's armour had been exposed. Fear was no longer a weapon to use to control to people.

The citizens that wanted change had been testing and prodding the authorities' defences for some time now. The hit and runs on the police by the kids had shown the organisers hidden in the shadows, that numbers was a viable option, but this would only work on small scale. It needed to be tested in large quantities.

The escape provided them with the trigger that they had been longing for and they took full advantage of it.

Small scale trials were initially run all over the country by the organisers but were now ramping up and the numbers were steadily increased and the pressure raised on the police. The hit and run tactics were working and grinding them down.

This all took the New Government by surprise as there was no communication or organisation it on Global Life. They were blind to it because the word was being spread by another means unknown to the police, who continued with an increasing full and heavy presence but were still considerably outnumbered.

2-3 was the flashpoint, the police verging on exhaustion due to barely having a break let alone day off for a week. The hit and runs were being maintained twenty-four hours a day, every day.

Eventually a huge crowd flooded out onto the streets. The police stood firm using their usual tactics, but these required physical effort and rest to recover, they were being given neither. The seemingly endless mass of people just kept coming. The injured taken away simply to be replaced by what seemed to be another ten.

They just wanted the old days back; they wanted things as they were. Who could blame them, they had a job, they had a car and whilst in no way did they have the luxury of the rich, they did not have the poverty of the poor and most were prepared to do anything to keep what they did have.

Not to mention the fact that they loved their job and so with every 'encounter with the non-compliant public' came the opportunity to partake in some 'sport' whilst carrying out their duties, if they lost this fight, well the thought of that was terrifying, but before long the sport of the hunter became the sport of the prey as the fatigue started to draw in and the realisation that the population was no longer afraid of them hit home.

The police were being overwhelmed and injured at every city as it spread through the country that numbers and a preparation for death combined could win, because that is how they won at Detention Centre One.

It took bravery but the people just kept coming and the police just kept beating them back. A battle of attrition had started and the loser would forfeit their lives. For the first time the fear of death had moved from the people to the police.

Some citizens were standing with the police as they had 'interests' to maintain, but their number was not close to those who stood against. The politicians continued to call for calm, the celebrities simply hid, such was their 'depth' of honour and morals. They were playing a waiting game, ready to come out on the side of whoever the victors turned out to be, with their lame excuses as to why they supported the New Government in the first place, or the people now, already lined up via their PR people.

Churches all over the country were now full to bursting as people tried to escape the violence or where injured were being taken. The hospitals had been ordered to not treat any injured person unless they were from the authorities. Eventually they chose to ignore the order by treating some in back buildings and storerooms to escape the gaze of the officers standing guard on the front entrance.

When the police realised what the hospitals were doing, the staff there simple stated that if they stopped citizens being treated, they would stop treating police officers as well. This was not taken well and the doctor giving the statement to the officer at the door was felled. The entire staff walked out leaving two officers to die where they laid. This event had spread around all hospitals immediately and medical staff refused to treat the police in every hospital.

The police immediately relented and issued an order to all hospitals to treat whoever came in after hearing that dozens of officers were being taken in all over the country. The Auxilium cohorts simply were not set up to treat so many injuries and required the hospitals to deal with the major traumas, the medical staff were simply not going to allow the police to dictate who lived and who died.

When word got around that the police were trying to storm the churches to close them down. A mass of humanity immediately went to them and forced the police back, through sheer weight of numbers, the strategy was working. Once saved from the police they stood guard, no quarter was given nor taken when an attempt to move them was enacted by the police.

For the first time their brutality failed, they had lost the edge of fear. One hundred people can keep ten thousand under control if they have fear on their side. Without it, it simply becomes a numbers game. The police did not have the numbers and they were losing the fight, especially with every image now being shared on Global Life.

Premier Xe called the Global Life CEO screaming at him down the phone. "WHY ARE YOU ALLOWING THIS TO BE SHOWN?" he demanded. "GET THESE IMAGES SHUT DOWN AND SHUT DOWN NOW!"

"Premier Xe," came the calm, statement like reply, "There has been a policy change at Global Life. These images no longer contravene our community standards and as thus I am unable to censor them."

"WHAT! Who authorised that?"

"I did."

"WELL UNAUTHORISE IT!" Premier Xe demanded.

"That will not be possible," came the reply. The phone line when dead.

Premier Xe called back, there was no answer. He called the Communications Chief who answered.

"Where are you?" he said.

"In the TV station," He replied.

"Good, Global Life have just reneged on us. Can you shut them down?" By now he was pacing around the Premier Planning Office his mind in full overdrive. "I can see and no, they are a private company with their own infrastructure. We have been trying to infiltrate them for years to be able to do just that should we need to, but every time we get close, they manage to find a way of moving their sensitive code to another place. Only yesterday we found that it is currently housed outside of our shores. They are not in this country."

"What do you mean not in this country?" Premier Xe replied.

"Their operations do not run from somewhere in this country, they are offshore and we do not know how they are managing it. To be able to carry out that sort of operation as well as evade us for so long would take someone who knew what we were doing and an enormous amount of money, way more than their revenues could generate. We now believe they may be being funded by an alternative means and we have a mole somewhere."

"Who is the mole and who is funding them?"

"We do not know but are working with the police spy network to find out. Apparently, they are called 'Umbra', but is always one step ahead of us. We have spies in the company, in the military and in the police but again they always seem to be able to find them before we get anywhere sensitive infrastructure or data. Apparently, it was called the 'New Dawn Project' but that is all I know at the moment. We will continue until we get to the answers."

"Make it fast Xe 4 I am not sure we are going to survive this one if we cannot shut them down."

Premier Xe hung up and called his Commander General Military, who answered immediately. "Commander, you need to position your troops on the outskirts of all the cities, we need to have your presence there to back up the police who are being overwhelmed."

"Understood."

"I have instructed Commander General Police that they are to contact you directly and should there be a call you are ordered to enter the towns and end this nonsense once and for all. You have authority to use any means necessary to achieve this task…any."

"Understood."

"Good, at least someone is still standing with me around here."

"Till the end Premier Xe, till the end."

"OK, oh and Commander, thank you."

The Commander hung up, wow a thank you from him, this must mean something very serious is up, Premier Xe is never polite, never not shouting yet here he is saying at least someone is still with him and being polite. This is not good, this is really not good at all, he thought as he ordered his troops as instructed, to every town and city and to wait, very visibly, on the outskirts. Drones were flying overhead, but none dropped anything on the demonstrators…yet.

The police continued their open warfare approach to civil disobedience. It was brutality on a mass scale and some even put down their weapons and defected to the 'other side' realising what they were doing was wrong and something had to change, but most did not, most were enjoying it too much as the fight coursed through their veins.

Finally, the flashpoint arrived at a demonstration on the 5-1 main high street. An industrial flare was thrown. It landed between the officer's visor and his shield. They say that you could hear the screams from a mile away as his face melted to the bone, collapsing in agony he eventually died there on the spot.

For a moment the two sides just stood and looked at each other, not sure what they next play was to be made. The police at the scene made the decision, enough was enough, this had to end and end now.

Shots were heard; demonstrators started to drop. At first there was complete panic as no one knew who was firing or from where and people started running in all directions. Soon the single shots were replaced by automatic fire. People were being slaughtered. Penned in with nowhere to run, they were sitting ducks. The slaughter only stopped after the police had run out of bullets, some continued into the crowds with electric sticks deliberately forced into groins and eyes, riot shields and batons used with deadly force, some were even filmed using their riot helmets on people already on the floor dying.

Global Life screened it all without filter or censorship. This no longer contravened their community standards after all, and was gold dust to the viewing figures, sign up rates and revenue now needed to plug the financial hole created by Premier Xe's use of the virus. Everybody in the country had signed up to Global Life, this had to be seen and the terms of service were ignored. Terms of service that allowed Global Life to harvest every single piece of data belonging to almost every single person in the country. They now had more information than the military and police combined, now they were the most politically powerful entity in the country.

Seeing the events on Global Life, in amongst an occasional truce and standoff, violence continued across the country. Some said it was a civil war, others called it by its real name, civil annihilation.

After four days of almost continuous fighting, finally Premier Xe went on TV demanding that both sides step back.

It did not work and people continued to demonstrate, knowing full well that the security forces could not arrest nor kill, every citizen of the country.

Tiberius seized his opportunity, he needed to be the face of the opposition, he needed to get the message out to the people, but Global Life could so easily cut him off if ordered to do so, he needed to use the TV to get the message out there, to raise the cry for freedom and not make the same mistake as his parents.

Arriving at the centre of the capital he made his way through the throngs of people. It looked like every single person was on the streets. As he got closer to the TV station, he could see the police line. SHIT! He thought it is in front of the doors, how am I going to get in there, actually how am I going to do any of this he thought, you have no plan and no one is in your group. Idiot!

Stood there proudly in his Sages robes with his hood down but with no army, he suddenly thought all was lost. Sage! Came a shout from his right, turning to look he saw Evie looking down from a window in the New Government complex that formed a huge building complex in the centre of the city. "Door down there!" She shouted whilst pointing to what looked like some sort of emergency exit door with no handle on the outside. Tiberius made his way over. Waiting he heard a click as the door unlocked and opened slightly, he rushed in, but people around him saw it as an opportunity to get into the New Government building. They tried to shut the door but two people verses that crowd was no match.

"HELP US!" Evie shouted to the guard who stood frozen not knowing what to do. "If you do not help us, they will kill you, now help!" The guard snapped into life and pulled his weapon.

"Shoot over their heads!" Tiberius stated. "Over their heads, do it!"

The guard complied and let a burst of fire out over their heads. With the screaming came relief as the pressure on the other side of the door relinquished and they managed to shut it.

"Get that heavy furniture over there and put it against the door. It won't take long for them to try again and we won't be here the next time," Evie stated to the guard who looked absolutely terrified.

"HEY! HELP ME!" said Tiberius to the guard. The guard helped move three very heavy, and luxurious, pieces of furniture behind the door.

"This will last for a while, but if I was you my friend, I would get a change of clothes ready, if they get through and see you dressed in a police uniform, you are a dead man," said Tiberius.

The guard baulked, not at the threat he faced but that someone had used a term of gender such was the misalignment of priorities in this current world.

"HEY!" Tiberius continued, "Life is about to change, listen to me and be part of that change or stay in the old world, dressed like that and die. I do not have time to stand here having a nice chat with you, but it is your choice. Good luck friend."

With the guard still looking confused Evie and Tiberius ran up the stairs. "How did you get in here?" he asked.

"The Historians are part of the New Government structure remember. I have access to just about anywhere so that I can carry out my duties." Evie replied.

"That's handy," he said.

"Quite! Right what do we do now?" She asked.

"I have not got a clue," he said openly admitting his plan was basically non-existent.

"Well, that sounds like an excellent plan! Let's do it!" Evie stated sarcastically.

"That is not helping!" Tiberius snapped back.

"Why are you here Tiberius? Come on focus."
"I want to give the people freedom again but I have no idea how. The only thing I can think of is to use the TV station to broadcast some sort of message, but I have no idea how to get to it, the police are guarding it with far too many officers. I cannot solely use Global Life, as that is where my parents went wrong."

"Your parents?"

"Yeah, they led an uprising in some Northern town but relied on Global Life to be the comms channels. They got shut down and died."

"Your parents are Sarah and James, I know," Asked Evie.

"Yeah, been talking to my new boss a lot about me, so I found out!"

"Don't take it personally, a lot of people have been looking out for you Tiberius, seeing this day coming. The uprising was in 5-1." Evie seemed a little too excited and a little too knowledgeable about Tiberius' life seeing as she knew more about it than he did.

"What else do you know?" Tiberius said.

"Just how close they came to succeeding. The police had lost, they had won, they had beaten Premier Xe, but the military intervened. If it was not for them, you would have them with you right now."

"Who was running the military back then?" Tiberius demanded.

"Commander General Military, the same one as today," Evie replied.

"Shit!" Tiberius said out loud, whilst thinking this was going to be a case of history repeating itself.

"Hey, we are with you, the people are with you, this is your destiny, this is what your turmoil is all about. Be a lion Tiberius, be a lion."

Tiberius snapped back into the room.

"It's this way, but I suggest we put up our hoods from now on," Evie said. Tiberius agreed without a word by putting his up so his face could not be seen.

*** 

Premier Xe called the Communications Chief for the fourth time in the last thirty minutes.

"Premier Xe, I need to be allowed some time," he said.

"We are out of time, either we end this now or it is all over and I have failed my dynasty. I am coming over to you. Set up the news for an announcement."

"Sure."

Just as Premier Xe was about to leave his office, he received a call. "We are informing you that we can no longer finance your operations Premier Xe. All finances will be cut off immediately," The phone went dead.

Premier Xe just threw the phone onto the desk. He was not going to go down without a fight and ran over the sky bridge to the TV station. As he did so he looked out at the masses of people gathered, this cannot be put down simply by force, 'focus Cornelius, focus' he said to himself.

Entering the studio he said, "Are we ready yet Xe 4?"

"Not yet, you need to go to make up otherwise your forehead is going to blind everyone."

Not one month ago, Premier Xe would have torn him apart for that comment, how things had changed and how the powers were shifting almost hourly. He had never come up against this before and he was losing his fear factor with almost every conversation. He sat down as the makeup artist trembled as he put on the makeup.

"You know when this is all over, I just want you to know I did all this for my family, I did it all to keep my people safe and to stop my people being hurt.

Neutrality was supposed to save us all, why did it not? I just wanted everyone to be happy." He said to Xe 4.

"When all this is over we will both be dead and you know it so save me the fucking sob story Xe. You did this for the power and for nothing else as did your father and his father. You are a fucking snake and I have hated being part of your 'Primary Function'. You have ordered children killed, then ordered me to cover it up, you have ordered pandemics, then ordered me to make it look like it was natural and to broadcast how great you were at resolving it whilst knowing that the Chief Scientist and her obscene organisation had the antidote but did not give it out, on your orders.

You have thought about no one but yourself and your fucking 'dynasty', well your dynasty is over."

Pushing away the makeup up artist he screamed, "WHAT! MY DYNASTY WILL NEVER DIE!" he shouted back.

"Well it has. I was told an hour ago that your wife and kids and all of their security have been murdered by a mob. To be honest I feel most sad for their security. It is over Xe, now do one decent thing with your life and accept it. Go on TV and end this. Tell everyone that you are calling off the police and the military and you will step down to allow a new Premier the chance to finally put some common fucking sense back into our lives."

Premier Xe did not care about his wife but reeled from the finding out about the death of his son, his future, the dynasty's future. "There is nothing left for me now, no future no dynasty to hand over. You are right, it is over, let's do it. Are we on?" He asked.

"It will automatically start ten seconds after you press this button. Just look into that black screen there and end it Xe. End it."

"Ok, so press button then I have ten seconds. Got it. Thanks, I will end it, well end it for you anyway," he said as he pulled the knife from his pocket and plunged it into the stomach of Xe 4. The makeup artist fled. "No one, No... fucking...one, says I have got a shiny head," he said as he dropped him to the floor with the knife still embedded. The last images of his existence were that of Xe pressing the button and shifting to prepare for the speech. His last sounds were hearing him state, "If I am going down then this whole fucking country will go down with me."

Back on the other side of the sky bridge, Evie and Tiberius were stopped by a guard. "Sorry you cannot go over there" said the guard as a makeup artist ran by screaming his head off.

Ignoring the panicking artist still clutching a makeup brush as they ran by, Evie stated, "I am a Historian and this is a momentous occasion, I have to be there to record it for the archives."

The guard stood firm. "I have my orders and they are to prevent anybody, of any order or rank from going over there. If I do not then Premier Xe said I am dead. And I am not letting that happen."

"Just take a look out there," interjected Tiberius. "Look at the crowds, this is happening all over the country, it's over. You have a choice to make now. Stay as you are and die when this whole country tears itself apart or let us through. We can put an end to this, we can bring back peace, freedom for all with none of this death and destruction!" he said waving his arms around. "Think of your family for crying out loud, they will die at the hands of the mob once they discover you were in the police!"

"I do not have children; I only have the police. The police is my home, my life, my people and I will not let them down and I will do my duty," He replied and raised his weapon, "Now back the fuck off!"

"No," said Evie, "We will not, this is history in the making and I will be there to record it and that is my life!"

With one swift movement, the guard hit Evie around the head with the butt of his weapon and dropped her to the floor. "NO!" shouted Tiberius as he held her, she was out cold but still breathing. "What is the matter with people like you?"

"Pick up your friend and fuck off before I pull this trigger," he stated pointing the weapon to Tiberius' temple.

He had been here before and survived, but it still terrified him, flashbacks of Detention Centre One, flashbacks of the pain that ran to the core of his soul. He had come too far and would not lose at the last 100 yards.

BANG! A shot rang out followed by a thud. Tiberius flinched, then looked at Evie. She was starting to come round. Patting himself down, he noticed that he too was alive.

Looking up he saw the guard on the floor, minus most of his head. "I have a child, the other sky bridge guard said and I love, I love." He started to cry. "Is your child a boy or a girl?" Tiberius said as Evie started to shake her head.

"A, well a," he stumbled, "she is a girl," he finally blurted out. "And she is the most precious thing in the world. She is my Angel, my life. Please you can have my life but please see to it that hers is saved."

"No one is going to take your life here, enough has been lost already and so many more will be. But if you are found wearing that uniform you are dead and so is your family. Get out of it fast. Write your designation onto a piece of paper and we will make you an ordinary Xe again," Tiberius instructed him calmingly and firmly.

Taking a pen and paper from the desk next to them, the guard did it immediately and gave it to Tiberius. Tiberius chuckled; this time I won't be sticking it up my arse! "Not this time John! Not this time!" he laughed as he remembered his friend as the cheeky bloke from the Speech Sanctuary not as the man beaten to a pulp and murdered in front of him, irrelevant of what he thought he had done, life had moved on now.

"Sorry?" replied the guard nervously backing off and raising his weapon.

"Whoa there!" I was remembering a friend. Tiberius realised at that moment that words have to be crafted carefully and not just blurted out. "Listen get out of those clothes, lose the weapon and get out of here. Oh and remember us my friend, remember us" he said.

The guard nodded, dropped his weapon, then turned and ran. Evie was back in the land of the conscious and was helped up by Tiberius.

"You ok?" he said.

"Yeah, going to have a headache tomorrow though," she said.

Tiberius helped her to her feet and over to the receptionist's desk.

Evie swiftly entered the New Government systems to change the guards' details. "If I do not do this now, he is a dead man. The revolution will have to wait for five minutes," she stated.

Tiberius just looked at her and his heart melted. She was so loving and caring for everyone, every person. "You could have been a hacker extraordinaire," he stated.

"It's actually frighteningly easy once you know how, that is why fear and deception are so powerful, you soon realise that the whole damn system is built on quicksand," Evie replied rubbing her head. "Done, now let's get over there."

Premier Xe started his address. It was being shown on every TV in every home, on every outside broadcast location, and of course on Global Life. No one could miss this and no one was going to. Every single person in the country stopped, Premier Xe had the attention of the entire country.

"Citizens. It appears that there has been a huge misunderstanding. It appears that our enemies have made it out to be that the people who escaped from Detention Centre One were innocents, were just average Xe's like you and I. This is not true, they were murderers of the worst kind, they killed children, families, they were the worst of society and we were keeping them away from you to keep you safe.

I and my New Government have from day one always wanted to keep you safe and it is our primary purpose, it was at the heart of what we did and continue to do.

Yes there are lots of you out on the streets and we accept that but if we do not deescalate the issue many people are going to die and I do not want that, I value every single life in our country and if so much as one of you dies that would be failure on the parts of both I but also you. We must seek peace, we must find a common ground and we must find a way forward for us all to live in peace, it is our way of life, it is who we are and we must embrace it and I, as your Premier Xe will work night and day to achieve perfection in our society, if you all go home.

If you all go home the police and the military will be called off immediately and not come onto the streets again until we have found that solution.

This I promise you, as your leader, as the Premier and as a family man."

The crowd gasped, did he just say man? They all turned and started talking and looking at the police who had absolutely no idea what was going on. Desperately calling on their commanders to give them instructions. Were they to stand down or start shooting?

"So, what be it my people?" Said Premier Xe.

Following the signs to the TV studio, Tiberius crashed through the door. Premier Xe yelped as he stormed up to him. "YOU!" he shouted "YOU! WILL RESIGN!"

The crowd outside were enthralled, they could see all of the drama but could not see who had just walked in.

"I will do no such thing I am the Premier, and you are just a Sage," The crowd gasped as Tiberius came into view. "You have killed and maimed so many innocents, so many lives snuffed out on your orders!"

"Utter rubbish, you are part of the conspiracy to bring down the New Government for you own lust for power knowing it will kill thousands of my people out there!" He jabbed his finger at the screen suddenly remembering it was still on and playing to the crowd.

"YOU ARE A MURDERER!" Screamed Tiberius.

"And how would you know that unless you were part of it," he said starting to create a new narrative of Tiberius' involvement in whatever crime he claimed Premier Xe had partaken in. He learnt a lot from the, now former, Communications Chief and gas lighting was his favourite. "We have justice in this land not mob rule!"

"I was one of the escapees from Detention Centre One. You and your henchmen beat me, tortured me and I had to stand and watch as person after person were cut down in their prime! All on your orders!"

"As I have just said to the people that is a conspiracy theory made up by our enemies!"

At this point the Historian walked into shot. "No, it is not. As a Historian it is my job to maintain the whole truth. There are warehouses all over this land full of our history. A history hidden, warped and twisted to fit your agenda." Addressing the people, a Historian out of sight started to use Global Life, she stated, "By now you should be able to see images of these places on Global Life. Look for yourself. This man is a liar and a murderer; we speak the truth!"

On every phone Global Life started to show the images, not only of the warehouses full of secrets but also images of Premier Xe living in luxury, his house an enormous complex full of luxury that the ordinary person could only dream of. Evie had also sent images of Detention Centre One, the less gruesome ones anyway.

"That is how your leader lives, that is how he treats those who disagree with his lies and want to deliver freedom to these lands. That is your Premier Xe!"

Looking around him and knowing it was over Premier Xe said, "I could do with a Communications Chief right now, but my last one fell asleep on the job," pointing to the dead body on the floor. As everyone looked at the corpse, Premier Xe ran out of the studio, down the emergency stairs and into the street. Luckily this was just behind the second police line, where the Commander General Police stood. Composing himself as if he meant it to happen, he marched over and stated, "OK what next? How are you going to get us out of here alive?"

"I'm not," he said, "There is no escape, we are surrounded on all sides by more people than we have bullets for. I have created a fall-back position over there in the crossroads where we will hold our last stand."

"For crying out loud, I thought you were supposed to be better than that last idiot. Give me that comms unit!" Premier Xe demanded. The Commander General Police did so casually.

"Commander General Military, Commander General Military can you hear me?"

"Premier Xe."

"Are you on the outskirts of the city?"
"Yes, Premier Xe."

"Are you ready to roll in and end this?"

"Yes, Premier Xe."

"Then do it, now is the time!"

"That would be a negative, as I told Commander General Police not two minutes ago whilst we all watched you whine on TV, I have to decline, disrespectfully. My troops have been ordered to turn and return to base. I have seen enemy soldiers that were only children have more spine and courage than you. You are everything that I stand against. With respect Xe you can go and…"

Premier Xe threw the comms device into the ground smashing it to pieces and stormed over to the crossroads where there were six police vehicles arranged in a circle with officers lined all around within, shaking and pointing their weapons at the crowd. Premier Xe snatched one off an officer demanding, "Give me that!" before taking up his station in the middle. "This is where we all stand, this is where we fight to the last breath!"

Out the front of the TV station the 1ˢᵗ police line fell back in line with the second. The station was now in the hands of the people.

Evie switched off the TV camera. "Historian!" she called. At the command a historian appeared from the shadows of the room. "The staff," she called out for.
"What?" Tiberius said turning to see one Historian pass the staff of Shu to one another. Evie turned and gave it to Tiberius.

"Here," she said, "before you go on you need this, it was made for this purpose, it was made for peace. You now call for peace, you will need it."

Tiberius gasped as he took the red staff of peace. "But it needs the staff of Ellel to fulfil its purpose, it does not have that," Tiberius said.

"Yes, it does," came a voice from the far side of the room. Tiberius looked up. There stood the former Supreme Sage of the Stoics. He was wearing a brown cloak with a black cord, just as Tiberius did, not the red cloak of his previous position.

"I have erred in my ways, I do not deserve the red cloak, nor the position appointed to me. I had become lost in the Primary Function. The power, the money, the debauched lifestyle of alcohol and women and drugs. I have become everything that I pledged not to be in the chambers of the church. I had let my fellow sages down and for that I will be eternally dammed for. I accept that and it was my choice, no one forced me to do it, only my failures did that.

I know you could say that I am only saying this as I have seen the writing on the wall, I have seen that it is all over and I am trying to save my own skin. I would not blame you, nor hold it against you if you cut me down here and now, it is only that which I deserve, but if you give me the chance, I will stand shoulder to shoulder with you out there. I ask, no I beg, that you allow me to aid you in bringing the staffs of peace together and release their power to save this country, these people, our people. Give me this last chance please, I beg," he said as he lowered his head in submission.

Tiberius thought for a few seconds, trying to measure the apology and promises to be that of a Sage or that of a politician. Ultimately, he was a Sage, they both were, and neither worthy to judge the other. "Supreme Sage…" Tiberius started.

"No, just Sage," he was interrupted with.

"My Sage, as a fellow Sage I accept your apology and I trust you to your oath, we will walk together and stand for peace. Come, let us go."

"Your parents would be so proud of you, Tiberius," his Sage said from behind. Tiberius swung around to see him standing there. "I knew we made the right choices, no matter how hard they were at the time and I am pleased that I have fulfilled my oath to Sarah and to James. Now go end this once and for all and if it costs you your life, lose it knowing you were that lion your father said you were, that you left behind a better world and know most of all that you will again return to your mother's arms and warm embrace. Supreme Sage of the Stoics, I give you the red cloak. Wear it now as our leader."

A tear streaked down Tiberius' cheek. "I thank you and I hope that one day I will be back in my mother's arms, but I am a common person no better than any another. I care not for rank, for power, for having a title of power, with the utmost of respect to the position of Supreme Sage of the Stoics." Both Sages nodded their heads indicating no offence was taken. "If I die, it is of a Sage, it is of a Xe, it is of a mortal, it is of a person fulfilling their purpose in life, no matter how short that life has been."

The three historians and three Sages stood tall and proud in their robes. The end game was here and they would all play their own part to see it through.

*** 

In the studio Tiberius nodded at Evie who turned to the screen again. Once again, the people stopped to watch and the drama as it continued to unfold.

"People, my name is Tiberius and as I said I am one of the escapees from Detention Centre One. I would not blame you if you did not believe me, you have heard so many words in these last minutes, words that will decide the future of this nation, but I say to you I am Tiberius and I am a Sage of the Stoics!"

A Historian released an image of Tiberius from a news report about the escapees onto Global Life.

If you look on Global Life you will see my image from a news report as one who escaped. Let me tell you now, I am that man and that place did exist, that place was all that the rumours said it was, all that and a horrifying lot more.

I stand here in front of you as one of you. I was Xe just like all of us, I am still Xe, but I have broken the fear of death to stand here and to exclaim that this is the end of the New Government. Today and from this day on it shall be no more fear, no more oppression and no more Personal Citizen Devices, I ask you now to rip them off and throw them, destroy them and never wear them again!"

The crowd followed the command without any hesitancy, cheering as they did so.

"Now the first step of freedom has been taken, but this freedom has been fought for with blood on all sides and I ask for it to stop. There has been enough killing, enough violence and at some point it has to stop. That point is now. I ask that all police officers lay down their weapons and walk away, equally I ask that all people do not harm them, for they have just become one of us. We must treat them with love and compassion because that is the only way this violence will end, the only way the tit-for-tat killing will stop, I ask knowing that it will be one of the hardest things for us all to do, given the past, but today we draw the line.

Police officers, look to the outskirts, the military is not there, they are returning to their bases, you are alone. The fight is lost, please I beg you to make this the last day of hatred between the people and authority. Please I beg you to lay down your arms and walk away. People LET THEM LIVE!" he stated raising his staff.

All over the country the police looked nervously at the people and the people nervously looked back. Neither wanted to be the first to make a move and pay for it with their lives, but the events of the day were momentous and the military had left. Eventually one or two officers put down their weapons and walked away through the crowds, ripping off their uniform as they did so. They were left to leave without harm and so more and more nervously de-armed and walked away.

In some isolated places, the police were attacked and after so many years of brutality, you could hardly blame the people for doing so, but reconciliation had started.

In the Capital at the crossroads, they started to drop their weapons. Premier Xe stood in the middle stating that if any officer dropped their weapon, he would shoot them himself. They nervously obeyed the command, knowing they now had no chance at all of surviving.

Tiberius continued, "The coming days will be tough as we all start to rebuild, but we must rebuild with love and peace. In peace there is strength, we must love each other with passion, be resolute in our conscientiousness, be calm in our mindfulness, have an attitude filled with hope, steeled with fortitude and bravery.

Knowledge over ignorance. The Historians will help recover our lost history; they are here to serve but I must ask you for patience.

Honour over treachery, we must end the spying on one another and come together as one family.

Truth over deceit, we must never hide the truth again, no matter how hard that truth may be, it must be bared to all for us to manage, discuss, debate and use in a peaceful and loving way.

Trust over suspicion. Learn to trust again, with the ending of the spies and the creation of a new police force we must trust each other knowing that if a trust is betrayed it will never guarantee death.

Serenity over turmoil. We must return to peace in order to live as free people. The lack of peace will only lead to turmoil and we risk starting the cycle of hate again.

Loyalty over betrayal. Be loyal to one another again, gone are the days of being rewarded for betrayal and betrayal only leads to hatred. We have had enough hatred.

If we follow these six simple rules we will find freedom, go against them and we will only see slavery once more.

These are the commands of the Sages, these are the rules for freedom. Take them, cherish them and above all love each other.

My people, us, each as equals, free and peaceful. Let us rebuild together as one in love, compassion and harmony."

Evie switched off the screen and a huge cheer went up all over the country, at last freedom had arrived!

Tiberius stated to the small group, "You know someone once said to me what is the point of getting to 100 years old if you have been a coward, hiding in the shadows, jumping at every pin drop. That is not life that is existence.

Every journey has an end, a final destination, but it is the journey to that destination that matters not the destination itself. It does not matter when you die and a good death is something to be proud in, to be noted and for those left behind to be proud of, for it is only when you die that you are truly free, free of the pain, the suffering, the angst, the duty that life puts upon you."

He continued, "So I chose to live that life like a lion, not a mouse and I leave this land and life with my head held high."

All three Sages all nodded again and put up their hoods, as did the three Historians. "No," said Evie, "My job now is to be part of history and yours to record it. Record it well for all future peoples to see what happened here today, knowing that freedom is sometimes only what you perceive it to be, should now be free of that perception and as clear and pure as it can possibly be."

The other Historians nodded in acceptance.

The Commander General Police ordered the second police line to do whatever they chose to do; you can either drop your weapons and take your chances or join me at the crossroads. To an officer they dropped their weapons and walked away. He acknowledged this and walked back to the circle of officers.

Outside the cheering changed back to anger as those in the police circle showed no sign of standing down. Evie, Tiberius and the former Supreme Sage followed the route that Premier Xe had taken and walked out to see what was happening. Walking in front of the crowd and turning to face the police corralled in the crossroads, "Premier Xe," Tiberius said in frustration. "What has to happen for this man to accept defeat?"

"He will never accept it," said Evie.

"Then I will face him down."

"I stand with you my Sage," said Evie.

"As do I," said the Sage.

All three stood firm in front of the crowd and formed a line. Tiberius on the right with the red staff of peace in his right hand and the Sage on the left with his blue staff of peace in his left hand. Evie stood in the middle.

The crowd hushed.

"It's over Xe!" called out Tiberius. "The time has come for peace, not for war, love not for anger. Lay down your weapon and allow those around you to live!"

"WHAT DO YOU KNOW OF PEACE? YOU ARE A JUMPED-UP LITTLE BASTARD THAT HAPPENED TO BECOME A SAGE! YOU KNOW NOTHING, NOTHING OF WHAT IT IS LIKE TO RUN A

COUNTRY, TO HAVE THE WEIGHT OF YOUR FAMILY DYNASTY ON YOUR SHOULDERS. I WILL NEVER SURRENDER AND I WILL DIE AS PREMIER XE!"

"That title is no longer yours Xe, you are just one of us now." Tiberius said.

"I WILL NEVER BE ONE OF YOU!" said Premier Xe, sweating heavily, his face twisted and contorted, spitting as he said it. His eyes were like fire and his mind no longer under any semblance of control.

"You may kill me Xe but I am free now, we all are free now and nothing you do can put in me in chains again. Death will merely be a new adventure a new freedom for me to explore."

"DEATH IT IS THEN!" replied Premier Xe, with a grin on his horribly twisted face.

Tiberius clasped Evie's right hand in his left. Staring forward he said, "I should have liked to have got to know you better Evie, but alas it was not to be, but I tell you this, you were a light in my life, a star in the darkness of the night sky and I am proud to have called you…my friend."

"You are a breath of fresh air Tiberius, unique, powerful yet filled with love. I should have liked to have got to know you better too, but as a Historian I know that a noble death is written down for future generations to learn from.

Tiberius, I love you."

"I love you too my Historian."

The three of them started to slowly walk forward towards the police. Tiberius could only imagine that it was the same as his parents, filled with love, with hope for the future, even though they knew they would probably die. The two Sages held their staffs aloft and the sweet sound of peace rang out.

The crowd was absolutely silent and this end game played out, some were holding up devices to film and show on Global Life, but most just stood and watched.

"KILL THEM!" Premier Xe commanded. He was ignored, all of the officers including the Commander General Police dropped their weapons.

"I will be honest with you Xe, I had thought that my strategy would play out different to this but I accept that perhaps being the head of intelligence still does not give you all the answers. No, no I will not order my officers to die," he stated as the officers climbed over the vehicles and walked towards the crowd, to be greeted with love and peace.

Tiberius saw this and smiled, his words had worked and finally peace was coming to this land.

Premier Xe looked over his left shoulder at him. "WHAT?" he screamed, face red and spittle flying everywhere, "THEN I ORDER YOU TO DIE!" and pulled the trigger. The Commander General Police dropped as the crowd screamed.

"Xe, stop this, end this!" Tiberius called out again in one last attempt as the continued to walk towards the crossroads. The crowd continued to be rooted to where they stood.

"YOU WILL NOT WIN! I ALWAYS WIN!" he screamed back.

"Even if you kill me, you will not win, even if you kill every person here or every person in the country you still will not have won! You can never win through hate Xe! Put the weapon down and join all of us in peace!"

"AAAARRRGGGGGHHHHHHHHHH!" Premier Xe screamed. His mind completely lost, his emotions in such turmoil that nothing mattered, nothing made sense. It was all over, his life, his future, his dynasty, everything he had worked so hard for, his self-perceived reason for being on this Earth at this time was being taken away from him by this nobody in front of him. Everyone had deserted him, but he was still Premier Xe and would be until his very last breath. This time there would be no end to his fury, his mind was too far gone.

Tiberius' mind, in such turmoil and angst not so long ago was now calm and in control. He gripped Evie's hand more tightly.

Xe opened fire and emptied all of the ammunition in his weapon, some flew past the three as they walked forward and struck the mass of humans behind them, dropping them where they stood. Some did nothing but scare passing birds as he lost control of the weapon, but enough hit their mark.

The former Supreme Sage fell first, holding the blue staff of peace aloft until life finally left his body. Evie was struck only once but directly in her heart. She fell immediately just as Tiberius was hit three times.

Tiberius fell to his knees, staring forward. He had stopped breathing but there was still enough life for him to see the crowds ahead of him surging towards the crossroads. The crowd behind stayed still and silent, aside for the weeping for those who had just fallen amongst them. They stared at the three ahead with tears streaming down their faces, reaching out from meters away in an attempt to somehow change what had just happened and bring the three back to life.

Tiberius could still see Xe trying to reload his weapon as the crowd swarmed over and he could still hear as Xe screamed out before falling silent. He now knew his work was done and Xe was dead. Peace would return to this land; freedom would be restored. He had completed the work of his parents, he had fulfilled his reason for being, the thing that he had been so desperate to find and to do all of his life.

Still holding hands with Evie, he used the red staff to hold him upright as he swayed and his head bobbed as the last ebbs of life left him. He blinked one last time and the world around him disappeared in a beautiful white mist.

When it cleared, he was stood in a field on a beautiful warm day. He walked along and as he did, ran his fingers through the crop being grown. He could see animals that had stopped what they were doing to look at him but were unafraid and did not run away. He could see the birds in the sky, so clear and blue it looked like one of the glass panels in that old church's window.

And in his ears was the sweet sound of the two staffs of peace singing in perfect harmony.

As his body fell to the floor in the physical world, he heard his name being called from behind him. He turned and saw his Mother and Father behind him with the biggest smiles he had ever seen. At last, he could embrace those who were calling him in his dreams for all these years and as he looked at them walking towards him, although an adult, he felt just like that little boy again in the church.

All his worries had left him and all his pain had been replaced with that of the love of an innocent child, pure and unjudging, looking at their parents with happiness and joy.

He walked towards them. As they closed in his dad gave him a big bear hug and said, "Well done my boy, you were the lion that I always knew you would be. You changed their world and now it will be free, I am so proud of you my heart could burst here and now."

His father released him and his mother stood forward and wrapped her arms around him, they were both sobbing with love and joy that they had finally been reunited. "You will always be my little baby boy; you inspired us to start the fight that you have now finished because we wanted you to live a free life. Now you are free in your heart and your soul. I simply could not love you anymore than I do. I love you not only with my heart but with my very soul."

His father joined them in their embrace as their three souls were finally reunited. Words no longer needed, just love and contact with each other was enough to convey all feelings required, they gently wept tears of love and joy. Opening her eyes, his mother said, "Who is that?"

As they all let go of each other, Tiberius turned around. There stood Evie dressed in the cloak of a Historian with her hood down, in the field about twenty yards away.

"Evie?" Tiberius said in a voice that made it clear that this person had Tiberius' soul and held it with love.

"Go my baby boy," his mother said, "Go into your next adventure knowing that if you ever need us we will be here waiting for you for all of eternity. Just reach out to us with your soul with your love and you will find us here waiting. Our love is eternal and nothing can stop it now. I love you my little Tiberius, my angel, I love you"

Tiberius' father nodded as if to give permission for him to leave.

Walking up to Evie, Tiberius looked with a love he had never felt towards anyone other than his parents. Evie told him that she had seen her parents and said her goodbyes to them and that they had said that they were so proud of her and that she should follow her soul now. "I know my soul belongs with you Tiberius, I have no idea why, I just know."

"I feel the same Evie. I do not know why but we were brought together by some higher force, we are one."

He stopped talking then stood upright and took Evie's hands in his. "My Historian, Evie, would you be so kind as to allow me to get to know you better?"

"Absolutely," replied Evie, "I would very much like to do that."

Tiberius turned and nodded at his parents and they replied was a smile that can only be born from pure love.

He turned back and holding Evie's hand walked off over the fields, dressed in a blue shiny silk suit with a green shirt.

# Chapter 18:
# A New Dawn

It was a gloriously sunny day outside as a woman sat in the hairdressers. "There," said the stylist, "how does that look?"

"Perfect," the client purred as she looked at her straight white hair with a wisp of black running through it from the front. "Exactly what I needed. Thank you."

"You are welcome, it was quite a transformation! I like a challenge!"

As she was leaving the stylist called out, "Good luck with the election tonight!"

"Thank you," she replied knowing full well it was a forgone conclusion, she had already won and was to be the next Prime Minister, they just needed to do the formality of counting the votes, whether they were genuine or not. She had to hand it to the former Premier Xe's dynasty; they may have been monsters but making voting electronic was a master stroke that allowed the right people to give 'democratic' victory to whoever they chose.

Nine months to the day had passed since freedom was restored. It had been an expected but peacefully bumpy ride as people started to live life free again. There was a lot to do.

Some members of the previous administration had been captured trying to flee. Such hatred was aimed towards them that nobody shed a tear when they were 'removed from their post, permanently'. The only person who had not been found was the Chief Scientist and the search continued for her.

An interim Government had been announced and mustered with no specific head but more of a group of unsullied high ranking civil service officials from the previous administration which set about the fundamental changes that had to be made. Any symbol of the previous New Government was systematically and methodically removed.

Piece by piece it was dismantled, by the will of the people. With no specific head of Government, committees were formed and held consultations with the people. These would then be discussed and sometimes put to the vote, but mostly just carried out.

One of the first to go was removing all of the monitoring cameras around the country, along with the much-maligned devices that you had to use a Personal Citizen Device with, such as transport.

Other infrastructure to go was the Detention Centres, the murderous camps were wiped from the surface of the Earth, with the exception of one. Detention Centre One would be left as it was, a reminder of the brutality, but also a beacon of the resilience of freedom. Even in its darkest times, it always finds a way to fight back, it just takes one spark to light the fire before it can be extinguished and the flames will rise and act as a beacon for all those who can see it.

As well as the physical infrastructure removal, so were the removal of the laws deemed incompatible with freedom. The demands for neutrality were removed, people now openly used 'he' and 'she', although some still felt uncomfortable with that so remained with 'Xe' but without a number. This was respected and people were allowed time to adjust without judgement from others.

The right to gather was permitted again, the right to protest, to openly criticise the Government as well as one another. If this led to disagreement, people simply agreed to disagree and went on their way. The vitriol of enforced neutrality was no longer desired in society, in fact if someone started to get heated in a conversation or started to get physical, society around them would resolve the issue peacefully.

A new narrative was being created to replace the old. A narrative of tolerance and acceptance towards each other.

Clothing could be whatever you wanted now and the old art of the fashion industry sprouted up all over the country. People wore the brightest clothes and gone were the days of having limited clothing options. Flo's was the most popular clothing emporium in the capital. She was always rushing around and was becoming quite the celebrity dresser. She may have been in a wheelchair due to the beatings at Detention Centre One, but she still had a wicked sense of humour. She did however stop getting men to strip naked when being measured, those times had passed now, much to her annoyed mutterings under her breath paired with a wry smile and a chuckle that often had clients confused and thinking she was quite mad.

It was going to be a long journey, but a journey that everyone was on and the direction was largely one way, with everyone pulling together to try to rebuild in a way that worked for most but heard as well as listened to those who felt a difference.

The police were completely disbanded and rebuilt using something called the 'Peel principle'. The Historians had done their part and looked into the archives for what police force seemed to be the best at what they did. As the new officers were sworn in, they were issued with a small extendable stick and a comms device. No firearms were given, nor were any wanted. From now on the police would serve through public consent, not through a military style force. No previous officers were allowed to re-join; this would be entirely new. The people would respect the police; the police would serve the people.

The military had made the right decision and nothing major was changed within. They provided the police force in the interim, with barely any need to be used. They had come out remarkably unscathed and due to their 'help' in overthrowing Premier Xe, resulting in that they largely avoided scrutiny after the events of that day.

Commander General Military had pulled off a strategic masterstroke but did stand down and retire. The Historians had threatened to release incriminating evidence but the transition was to be peaceful, so as long as he stepped down, then his past would remain hidden as would the fate of the Chief Scientist.

Thanks to the ability to hide the truth, the military's previous support of the New Government went unnoticed and they were seen as heroes. The only thing that mattered now was what was happening currently, not the past, not matter what horrors it held hidden. There was no desire to re-surface those events and risk losing the peace that had been so hard won.

As a result of this compromise there was a real air of freedom and peace across the country.

Some however, decided to make use of the events to serve their own purposes. The sudden change in life gave the perfect cover for the Government to reset the finances. The debt was written off, gone had the need to print money and when she wins, the woman looking into the Flo's clothing store window reflection to see her new perfectly dressed hair, would remove the need for the Statutory Monthly Allowance. With the two gone, the financial woes would be resolved once and for all.

These recent months had served her well, her plan was almost complete, her patience and efforts rewarded.

Elections had been called and initial candidates had been whittled down, all of them promoted peace, prosperity and of course freedom, only one said that she would remove AI and robots and restore pride as she gave everybody back a reason to get up in the morning. It was a step back technologically but was required socially even with the greatly reduced population.

She was the front runner and appeared to be able to advertise herself more and seemed to be the most prominent on Global Life. Due to her increased presence everywhere she was ahead by a mile and the snowball effect helped her gather even more support as the others started to fall away.

Not that it really mattered anyway, she had already won, but it needed to be seen to be a valid victory, it needed to be seen a democracy in action. She smiled as she resumed walking down the street towards the new TV station.

The last act before the election was to rename the road in which freedom was delivered, 'Our Saviours' Way'. The first of the roads to have their numbers replaced by names.

The Historians took what they needed back to the warehouses, no matter how painful the memory, to ensure that what happened was recorded as per the wishes of 'Our Saviours' as the Sage, Evie and Tiberius were now known.

The country was being rebuilt with peace and dignity.

Three days after the day freedom was restored, Our Saviours had received the highest possible honours during their farewell parade. Presided over by the new Supreme Sage of the Stoics, in the velvet robes that came with the position, Tiberius' old friend and Sage, led the tributes.

The funeral took place on the first Sunday after that fateful event. It started at the church that Tiberius was saved within, which the Sage made no mention of, but instead said that it was a place where Tiberius came to settle the turmoil in his mind and in his life. Through working with the Sages, he had managed to calm the storm and start to see clearly his path in life. A path that ultimately led to everyone's freedom.

He spoke of Tiberius' bravery, how, in the end he was resolute and calm and his ultimate hope that he could bring peace through love to the people.

He spoke of how we must all now be loyal to each other, to use knowledge and truth to build trust and honour back into the nation, to bring back serenity to life.

He stated it was Tiberius' wishes that a line is now drawn, that all previous ills were forgotten and forgiven and that people started to look forward; to build a better life and through the Sages, they would help the people come to terms with what had happened and start again with love at the centre of their hearts.

In perfect and beautiful sunshine, the funeral cortege slowly made its way through the centre of the capital over the course of the day, passing as many people as possible that were packed onto the pavements desperate to get one last glimpse of their Saviours before they were finally laid to rest.

Lying in polished oak coffins with gold handles that lay on open backed military vehicles, Tiberius was the first. On his coffin was lying the red staff of Shu, placed to rest in his robes within. Behind his vehicle was Evie's. Again, she was dressed in her robes within a polished oak coffin. Atop hers was a book, bound in the finest leather and had been handwritten by her fellow historians. It was her story; her history and it would be with her for the rest of eternity.

Lastly came the Sages' vehicle. Again, a coffin of the finest polished oak and gold handles. The blue staff of Ellel lay upon his. He was laid within wearing the brown robes of an ordinary Sage as he had once again become.

After several hours the cortege made its way back to the church from whence it started. The coffins were carried into the church with Sages stood on either side, hoods up. As the last coffin passed they turned and followed it in. After the last Sage entered the church the great doors were closed. The last of the ceremony would take place in secret.

Their bodies, positioned in peace in their coffins were taken down to the crypt, where Tiberius had spent so many weeks resting, recuperating, and ultimately identifying his role in this world.

Here, he was placed next his parents. "Together again at least in the physical form," the Sage stated.

Evie and the Sage were laid to rest next to him in their own slot. As they closed the little metal gates to their final resting places the gathered sages who packed the crypt all stated in unison.

"Knowledge over ignorance, always!"

"Honour over treachery, always!"

"Truth over deceit, always!"

"Trust over suspicion, always!"

"Serenity over turmoil, always!"

"Loyalty over betrayal, always!"

"Freedom! Strength! Knowledge!"

On the Sages' plaque it read 'Here is a Sage of the order. Dedicated to enlightenment and to the people'. The former Supreme Sage has achieved his desire to return to his teachings and to become just another Sage. Now he would do that for all of eternity.

On Evie's plaque it stated, 'Here lies Evie, A Historian who used the power of knowledge to defeat ignorance and hate, bringing about peace to the land.'

Finally, Tiberius' little gate was closed. The Supreme Sage read out the words with a tears running down his cheeks and remembering their conversation 'Here lies Tiberius. He changed the world by giving freedom back to the enslaved!"

Whispering under his breath he said as if he was talking to Tiberius right now.

"I promised your parents I would look after you. I treated you like my own child, I just hope I served you well my son, my Sage. Rest in peace, you will live forever."

At the Brutus stadium a statue of both Tiberius and Evie were raised on the two pedestals nearest the stadium itself. His stood in his cloak, hood down, with the staff raised above his head, when the wind blew there was a sweet sound of peace outside the stadium that contained so much violence. The games continued as before, however the level of lethality was reduced.

His statue reached out to hold hands with Evie's statue on the other side, again in her robes, hood down, so that all who entered walked underneath their symbol of love. In her other hand she held aloft a book with History written above truth, written above love.

Tiberius had got his statue on the path of Champions he so desired, with the woman his soul had fallen in love with, for eternity.

Over the following weeks a monument was raised on 'Our Saviours' Way', depicting the three standing up to authority. It would always to stand there looking towards the sun, to act as a reminder of what can be achieved in the fight for freedom.

On one side of the road was the main entrance to the Government's building complex. The entrance had been rebuilt and its centre piece was the blue staff of Ellel in the hands of a huge statue of the Sage pointing it towards the other side of the street. On the plaque at the base of the statue it read 'This statue represents that peace can be achieved, even in power if you overcome your personal desires and that you can come back from the brink and again return to who you really are, not what the world around makes you. Never forgotten Our Sage.'

On the other side of the street stood the old TV station. It had been rebuilt and repurposed to be the building of truth. It would hold history, the truth and always be a counterbalance to the power of the Government, a permanent reminder that the two must exist in peace for freedom and prosperity for all to flourish.

In its entrance was an equally huge statue of Tiberius holding hands with Evie, exactly as they were on that day. Again, a plaque was located on its base, this time it read 'This statue represents that truth when hand in hand with the demand for freedom, is an unstoppable force. This statue here stands facing the Government buildings as a permanent reminder that truth and freedom always prevail. Never forgotten Tiberius and Evie.'

In Evie's hand was held a book with the same inscription as that at the Brutus stadium, a simple inscription History written above truth, written above love'. In Tiberius' hand was the red staff of Shu pointing in the other direction.

The room that Tiberius called out to the people and to the Government to end the suffering and live in peace had been left exactly as it was, with mannequins of the people from that day stood for all to see. This was the beating heart of the new freedom and it will always be.

In between the two buildings, in the middle of the street, stood their monument which was a representation of moment before they were cut down by Premier Xe. This was all designed so that never again would anyone have the power that had been so destructive in the last decades passed. Never again could one person have ultimate control.

The street itself now pedestrianised, allowing the steady stream of people to come and look and pay their respects.

One such person stood placing her hand flat on the statue's base. "You said the next time we meet we would all be free and that is exactly what you have done. I will see you in the next adventure, my friend," said Alexis with tears running down her face.

***

Election night arrived. Everything was shown on TV and over Global Life. Just about every single person in the land watched as the frontrunner with her white hair and black stripe won by a landslide.

"I did her hair!" squealed the hairdresser at home to her partner sat next to her on the couch. "It was a real pig to do as well, I mean it was all ginger and fiery and curly, I mean it looked great as it was but she was determined to change to that and it took ages to do!"

Flo's partner yelled from the living area that she should have made her clothes, "They would have been so much more colourful that the black suit she was wearing. Anyway, why are you hiding in there and not out here watching this?"

"I don't feel well," said Flo as she sat on the side of the bed staring out of the window.

"Oh well, I hope you feel better, she is going to change the country this one!" he replied.

"She has been for some time now, only we did not see it," Flo muttered under her breath.

The people rejoiced that another step had been taken towards a new dawn and a new start with partying and celebrations all over the country. The atmosphere was electric and full of positivity and a desire to change everything for the better.

The following day the new Prime Minister gathered the cabinet in the Premier Planning Office, renamed the Cabinet Office. The Historians were in their element finding things from the past to use going forward, never had there been so much energy in the warehouses, or visitors to it, or research being conducted within it.

Within the Cabinet Office the décor had not changed with the exception of the three previous leaders' portraits being removed for storage and replaced with those of Our Saviours.

The Prime Minster looked at her Cabinet.

The head of the military was now the previous Commanders' immediate subordinate. Rewarded for not bringing down the military forces on the population. He was known a General Brooks and the position remained second in charge.

The head of the police force, now known as Commander Peel sat to his left. General Brooks looked at him and saw a shadow of the woman that originally sat in that seat opposite his former boss. Staying as number two is going to be easy in this new world he thought to himself.

Opposite was the head of Communications. A man that now went by the name of Frederico. He was previously at Global Life and had offered to help immediately after the day of freedom. At the acceptance of the Prime Minister he moved across to take the position permanently.

To his left was the treasurer. It was the same man as before but now had named himself Marcus. No one really knew how he had managed to keep his job, everyone guessed that he knew too much and was too dangerous to cross, so here he was. Able to start again with no debt and a recently deposited massive cash injection into the Government's coffers.

Opposite him was the new chief scientist. A woman by the name of Zwinfall. She had been working with the Military scientists and had been put forward by General Brooks.

To her left was the head of manufacturing, the only other person to hold their place. He knew how to get the country running again and had not done anything directly to kill that was known to the populace, so he stayed and was now called Isambard.

Lastly opposite him sat the new Supreme Sage of the Stoics. He was the only one in the room that did not seem to be too happy to be there and simply stared ahead.

"All, from this day forward we will serve the people in freedom, we will listen to them, we will help them and we will guide them. We need to ensure that whilst they take the lead in some matters, we still maintain control and not allow mob rule to return. Mob rule has saved us but it must not be allowed to remove us from these seats.

We start at our new dawn tomorrow, here, to discuss how we will take this country forward. Now leave and prepare your areas of responsibility."

The gathered ministers stood and left, the Supreme Sage was last to leave and turned to look at the face he had been dealing with these last months. The Prime Minister smiled a smile of smug satisfaction that her plan had been executed with perfection and there was nothing that he could do to change it now the truth was out.

The Supreme Sage turned to leave knowing that he had to keep his silence, it was the way of the Sages, treachery and betrayal always lead to slavery. It must remain with him until the last breath leaves his body no matter what he thought.

Stopping he closed the doors and turned to the Prime Minster, "I told you his name, his past so that we could bring about change. I also promised his parents that I would do what was best for him and I believe that I have honoured that promise. If we return to the old ways it will be a betrayal of him and of hope. I will not let that happen Prime Minister," he said.

"Of course, did I not save his life in Detention Centre One? We are all here to move the country on now and deliver freedom again. It will be a long road, sometimes bumpy, but we will get there and I cannot do it without you in the team," came the politician's reply.

The Sage turned and left, closing the doors behind him. He did not trust her as far as he could throw her. He did not like politics but at this point they were a must and he had played her as well as he could. She may be evil and untrustworthy but she was better than that which went before her and a step had been made in the right direction. Yes, the road would be bumpy and it definitely will be long, well outlasting his lifetime before freedom was fully returned, but they had finally broken the narrative, the first step had been taken.

The Sages swore to bring freedom back to the people and they would make sure that happened, it was just unfortunate that some good people had to die in the process. "I hope you are in a better place Tiberius my occupati, I really do hope I have made the right decisions. Either way you have made your parents proud." He said to himself as he pulled up his hood and walked back down the corridor.

Immediately after the doors were closed and she was alone the new Prime Minister made a call.
"Yes, Prime Minster," came the voice at the other end.

"I trust that your servers and data are now secure in this country," she asked.

"They are," he replied.

"Good then I will ensure sufficient funding comes your way to run the oversight operation we talked about in our private booth at home."

"Then it is complete. Global Life looks forward to working to maintain stability and peace through deep and opaque oversight with your administration," came his response.

She put the phone down; it immediately rang again.

A voice on the other end stated, "Congratulations on being voted in. I trust our presence in the Speech Sanctuaries will be wiped from history."

"It already has," she replied, thinking those Speech Sanctuary hackers she saved from the raid and were now set up in the bowels of the Government building complex with all the latest tech they wanted, but hidden from the rest of her Cabinet, really were damn good at what they do.

"Good, then we look forward to financing your administration and having a strong and, more importantly, profitable relationship with your leadership, under your banner of bringing freedom to the people."

"As do I, as do I," came her reply.

The phone went dead; she stood and looked out of the window across the Capital with a wry smile on her face.

"Freedom is only what you perceive it to be. How right you were, Evie…how right you were," said Cassia.

www.ingramcontent.com/pod-product-compliance
Lightning Source LLC
Chambersburg PA
CBHW071529260626
47170CB00002B/556